Praise for *Miss Julia Hits the Road*

"Ross's latest will bring a chorus of 'Thank you, Lords' from faithful readers."
        —*Publishers Weekly*

"Ann B. Ross and Miss Julia are fast becoming Southern classics. Readers eager for entertainment should tuck in their skirts, strap on a helmet and hit the road with them."
        —*The Winston-Salem Journal*

Miss Julia Throws a Wedding

"Good fun . . . lively entertainment perfectly suited for anyone who can relate to the thoroughgoing effort involved in keeping up appearances in such thoroughly tacky times."
        —*The State* (Columbia, South Carolina)

"The third Miss Julia is just as fun as the first two. . . . You can count on Miss Julia to conquer adversity, one way or another, and you can count on thoroughly enjoying yourself while you read how she does it."
        —*The Winston-Salem Journal*

Miss Julia Takes Over

"Imagine Aunt Bee from the *Andy Griffith Show* with a lot more backbone and confidence and drop her smack in the middle of a humorous, rollicking plot akin to that of the movie *Smokey and the Bandit* and you have the tone and pace of Ross's entertaining second novel."
—*Publishers Weekly*

"Ross allows the reader to laugh gently at feisty, opinionated Miss Julia while thoroughly enjoying the view through her eyes . . . [for] readers who love Jan Karon."
—*Booklist*

Miss Julia Speaks Her Mind

"I absolutely loved this book! What a joy to read! Miss Julia is one of the most delightful characters to come along in years. Ann B. Ross has created what is sure to become a classic Southern comic novel. Hooray for Miss Julia, I could not have liked it more."
—Fannie Flagg

"In the tradition of Clyde Edgerton's Mattie Riggsbee or that quirky passenger Jessica Tandy brought to life in *Driving Miss Daisy*, Ann Ross has created another older Southern heroine in Julia Spring, who is—as Southerners say—outspoken, but by whom? A late-blooming feminist, Miss Julia is no shrinking violet in this comic plot that tweaks stuffy husbands, manipulative small-town neighbors, snoopy preachers, and general human greed, but ends by endorsing the love and vitality that energize Miss Julia's sharp tongue and warm heart."
—Doris Betts, author of *The Sharp Teeth of Love*

PENGUIN BOOKS

MISS JULIA HITS THE ROAD

Ann B. Ross, who taught literature at the University of North Carolina at Asheville, is the author of *Miss Julia Speaks Her Mind*, one of the most popular Southern debut novels in years, *Miss Julia Takes Over*, *Miss Julia Throws a Wedding*, and *Miss Julia Meets Her Match*. Though Ann Ross is certainly *not* Miss Julia, there are some undeniable coincidences: they both live in small Southern towns, they've both been involved in the organizations of their small communities, and they both were brought up with a healthy respect for proper etiquette and polite society. She lives in Hendersonville, North Carolina.

Miss Julia
Hits the Road

Ann B. Ross

Penguin Books

PENGUIN BOOKS
Published by the Penguin Group
Penguin Group (USA) Inc., 375 Hudson Street, New York, New York 10014, U.S.A.
Penguin Books Ltd, 80 Strand, London WC2R 0RL, England
Penguin Books Australia Ltd, 250 Camberwell Road, Camberwell, Victoria 3124, Australia
Penguin Books Canada Ltd, 10 Alcorn Avenue, Toronto, Ontario, Canada M4V 3B2
Penguin Books India (P) Ltd, 11 Community Centre,
    Panchsheel Park, New Delhi – 110 017, India
Penguin Books (N.Z.) Ltd, Cnr Rosedale and Airborne Roads,
    Albany, Auckland, New Zealand
Penguin Books (South Africa) (Pty) Ltd, 24 Sturdee Avenue,
    Rosebank, Johannesburg 2196, South Africa

Penguin Books Ltd, Registered Offices: 80 Strand, London WC2R 0RL, England

First published in the United States of America by Viking Penguin,
a member of Penguin Putnam Inc. 2003
Published in Penguin Books 2004

10 9 8 7 6

Copyright © Ann B. Ross, 2003
All rights reserved

THE LIBRARY OF CONGRESS HAS CATALOGED THE HARDCOVER EDITION AS FOLLOWS:
Ross, Ann B.
Miss Julia hits the road / Ann B. Ross.
p. cm.
ISBN 0-670-03207-7 (hc.)
ISBN 0 14 20.0404 9 (pbk.)
1. Springer, Julia (Fictitious character)—Fiction.   2. Women—North Carolina—Fiction.
3. North Carolina—Fiction.   4. Widows—Fiction.   I. Title.
PS3568.O84198M565 2003
813'.54—dc21   2002044910

Printed in the United States of America
Set in Fairfield with Park Avenue display
Designed by Carla Bolte

Acknowledgments

I am grateful to a number of people who took pity on my ignorance by answering my questions with both patience and enthusiasm. Some answered a specific question; others instructed me in long, but highly entertaining, monologues. A motorcycle enthusiast is truly that. Here they are, with my thanks: Greg Rummans, Cathy and Steve Gospodinoff, Tim Sitton, Diane Ludden, and Dennis Dunlap.

I occasionally needed help in other areas of expertise so, for being willing and available, I thank Delin Cormeny, Jon Blatt, and John Ross.

My thanks, also, to Pamela Dorman for her dandy idea, and to Susan Hans O'Connor for always calling back with the answers.

Finally, I want to thank the woman, whose name I can't recall, from whom I first heard about Poker Runs. That mention during a casual conversation gave me the idea for this book.

For Pamela Dorman
and
Susan Hans O'Connor

They don't come any better.

Miss Julia Hits the Road

~Chapter 1

Pushing through the swinging door from the dining room, I started talking before I got into the kitchen good. "Lillian, I need to ask you something, and I want a serious answer. What in the world is wrong with Sam Murdoch?"

She turned away from the sink and squinched her eyes at me. "They's not one thing wrong with Mr. Sam. An' what I think, Miss Julia, is you ought not be pickin' on him."

"Well, he's acting strange, if you ask me."

She turned back to the sink, mumbling about not having heard anybody ask anybody. Lillian was bad to mumble under her breath whenever she disagreed with somebody, namely me. I didn't mind, though, since I'd been known to do a little mumbling myself on occasion. She'd been taking care of my house, my meals, and me for so long now that we pretty much knew what the other was thinking, whether we spoke up or not. And I knew she never liked hearing anything against Sam, which was why I hadn't brought up my concern about him before now.

"Lillian, please," I said, "Would you just come sit down and help me with this?"

"If you want these green beans for supper, you better let me finish stringin' 'em."

"For goodness sakes, you can do it easier sitting down. Bring them over here and let me help you.

"Maybe the first thing I ought to do," I went on, as she brought the plastic bag of beans and the bowl of snapped ones to the table, "is ask what's wrong with you. I declare, Lillian, neither you nor Sam have been yourselves lately."

"I don't know nothin' 'bout Mr. Sam," she said, busying herself with spreading the morning's newspaper on the table. "He actin' like he always do, far's I can tell."

"No, he's not. You just don't know the half of it." I took a handful of beans and began stringing them on the newspaper. "He's been sending flowers, for one thing. Well, you've seen them. They're all over the house."

"That's 'cause he know you sad an' lonesome with Miss Hazel Marie and Little Lloyd gone to live with that Mr. Pickens. He know you miss 'em, an' he tryin' to cheer you up."

"That's probably true." I nodded in agreement. "But *one* arrangement and *one* potted plant would've been a gracious plenty for any cheering up he wanted to do." I dropped snapped pieces into the bowl and reached for another handful of beans. "About the time one arrangement begins to wilt, here come two more. And the notes, Lillian, you just haven't seen those notes."

"No'm, 'cause you won't let me."

"No, and I'm not going to. Or anybody else, for that matter. Embarrassing is what they are."

Lillian cut her eyes at me, then laughed in the old way, her gold tooth shining. It struck me that she'd done precious little laughing since Hazel Marie and Little Lloyd had packed most of their belongings and moved in with Mr. J. D. Pickens. Just to see if it'd work out, Hazel Marie'd said. Mr.

Pickens was that private investigator I'd once hired, who set about winning Hazel Marie's heart without one word being said about making the situation legal. Except by me, who'd had plenty to say on the subject. Believe me, I won't ever employ a handsome man with a roving eye and an aversion to matrimony again.

"What them notes say?" Lillian asked. She got up to turn down the heat under the pot where she'd put a chunk of streak-of-lean on to boil.

"Never mind what they said. But you'd be worried about him, too, if you knew." I took a trembling breath, recalling some of the poetic passages that had accompanied the flowers, all in Sam's handwriting. "Then, Lillian, he calls me every day, just wanting to talk, he says. Now, you know how I hate talking on the telephone when nobody has anything to say. At all hours, too, as if some people aren't already in bed or busy with important matters." I stopped, then went on to tell it all. "And another thing. He drops by to see me without a by-your-leave or anything, just shows up right out of the blue. To see how I'm doing, he says. You've noticed that, Lillian, don't tell me you haven't."

"Yessum, I have. But you and Mr. Sam got so friendly at Miss Binkie and Coleman's weddin', I jus' figured things was pickin' up."

"What things are you talking about?" I demanded, readying myself to refute any assumptions she might have made.

"Well, you know. Maybe that weddin' put you in mind of another one." She came back to the table and started stringing green beans again, as innocent as you please.

"My Lord, Lillian, another wedding is the last thing on my mind." I said, throwing another handful of beans in the bowl. "Unless it's Hazel Marie's. Whoever heard of moving in with a man for a trial period, anyway?"

"Lots a people, that's who. An' it nobody's bus'ness but hers," Lillian reminded me, as she often did when she thought I was beginning to meddle. "Now, look like to me all Mr. Sam doin' is bein' nice and friendly."

I dropped the beans that were in my hand, and covered my face. "Oh, Lillian, it's not only what he says, but the way he says it. I don't know what he means, or if he means anything at all."

"I 'spect you figure it out, you put your mind to it."

I ignored that because, all along, I hadn't wanted to delve too deeply into what was behind Sam's unnerving attentions. Once burned, twice shy, you know, and after my previous less-than-satisfactory experience with a husband, I intended to steer clear of another one.

I propped my chin on my hand, my elbow on the table, and put the focus back on Sam where it belonged. "I'm afraid something's wrong with him, Lillian, and that's the truth of the matter. The way he's acting is just not like him. You know how he is. Usually, that is. So polite, so much of a gentleman, courtly even, and now . . ." I lifted my head as a sudden thought came to me. "You know who he reminds me of? Mr. Pickens, that's who. He flirts, Lillian, and says the most outrageous things you've ever heard."

"That don't sound so bad to me."

"But it's not like Sam! I tell you the truth, I think he's entering his second childhood. He's old, you know."

"Not much older'n you," Lillian reminded me.

I glared at her. "Age affects different people in different ways. You won't catch me wearing cowboy boots and blue jeans and whispering things in somebody's ear."

"Wouldn't hurt you to try; might even do you some good. Seem like to me you be noticin' you not gettin' any younger.

I know lots a ladies be real happy to have a well-set-up man like Mr. Sam whisperin' in they ear. You keep on like you doin' an' he gonna turn his eye somewheres else."

I blew out my breath in exasperation. "Don't get me started on all the widows in this town who'd do anything in the world just to get married again. I know how they carry on. Just as soon as somebody's wife dies, there they are with casseroles and cakes and pies and invitations to dinner. I tell you, they don't know when they're well off."

"Lemme get these beans on," she said, pushing herself up from the table and carrying the bowl to the stove. "This meat done boiled down enough."

"You're not helping me, Lillian. I'm really worried about him. At first I thought he was suffering a midlife crisis, except he's too old. Maybe he's getting senile."

"Well, which is it? He in his chilehood or his old age?"

"I don't know," I said, slumping back in my chair. "And to tell the truth, I don't know which would be worse."

A sudden whining and growling began building up from out on the street and, as I jerked upright, the racket seemed to fill the whole room. "What in the world is that?"

I started out of my chair as the commotion got louder and louder, and nearer and nearer. Clamping my hands over my ears, I ran to the window.

Lillian dumped the beans in the pot and slung the bowl on the counter. As she hurried to the window beside me, my first thought was that a swarm of hornets had nested in my front yard, ruining my boxwoods.

Realizing that we couldn't see from the kitchen window, Lillian and I pushed and shoved each other in our hurry to get through the house to the front door. The clattering, rumbling din was painful to hear as we got closer to it.

"What is it? What is it?" I gasped as we both reached for the door knob, our hands fumbling for purchase.

"Oh, my Jesus!" Lillian cried, her voice cracking as she panted for breath. "It's the Rapture! Here I am, sweet Jesus, I'm a comin'!"

"Lillian, for goodness sakes. Get hold of yourself and get this door open."

She took a deep breath and came down to earth. "Maybe a UFO's squattin' down out there."

Before I could say what I thought of that, she pushed my hand aside, got the knob turned, and opened the door. When we rushed out onto the porch, I'd have opted for any kind of flying object other than the one that greeted our eyes. A rumbling, whining, two-wheeled machine slued out of my yard onto Polk Street, then swung wildly around the street and headed back into my driveway, sideswiping the plastic roll-out trash container perched on the sidewalk. Then, weaving up the driveway, it sliced through a pile of leaves, sending them swirling and scattering in the air. As we watched, open-mouthed, the loud, grumbling thing took its rider between two boxwoods, grazed the limbs of a crepe myrtle, and chewed up my grass as it skidded in a mighty half-circle before coming to rest in the middle of my yard.

"My Lord," I gasped, taking a firm grip on Lillian's arm. "Who's driving that thing?"

"Look like it drivin' itself," Lillian said.

As the machine whined down, it gave off a few nerve-shattering pops and backfires. A black leather–clad figure swung a leg off the pile of steel, chrome and exhaust pipes, kicked down the kickstand, and turned to face us.

At least, I guessed he was facing us, for his head was encased in what looked like a shiny black bowling ball with a dark visor. Removing the black gloves, the figure creaked and squeaked its way toward the porch, steel-toed boots clanking on my concrete walk.

"Is that Mr. Pickens, Lillian?" I asked, trying to peer past the black face-covering. "Is that who it is?"

"No'm, I don' think so. This 'un not as spry as Mr. Pickens."

Whoever it was stopped at the foot of the steps and pulled off the helmet, leaving a few sprigs of silvery hair standing straight up, looking for all the world like Little Lloyd's cowlick. Tucking his helmet under his arm, Sam stood there, grinning at us. If there was ever any proof that my concerns about Sam's mental condition had a solid foundation, it was right smack in front of us.

"See, Lillian!" I whispered, rounding on her, although if Sam heard me I didn't care. "That's what I'm talking about! If it's not one crazy thing, it's another. And now he's running around on a two-wheeler like a maniac. Sam," I raised my voice and turned to him with my hands on my hips, "the very idea, coming around here disturbing the peace and giving me a heart attack with all that roaring and popping and carrying on. What will the neighbors think, I ask you."

Before he could answer, Lillian said, "Don't be jumpin' on him, Miss Julia. He havin' the time of his life." Her smile was as big as his. She'd certainly changed her tune from when she'd been expecting the end of the world hardly a minute before.

"I say, the time of his life. He's on the way to ending his life with that thing. At his age, he ought to know better than to run around on such a contraption." I crossed my arms over my bosom and glared at Sam as he came toward us. He was grinning with a mixture of pride and what should've been embarrassment after that less-than-graceful entrance. "Senile old fool," I mumbled.

"Hello, Julia, Lillian," Sam said, still smiling as he walked up the steps to the porch and stopped next to me. "How you like my new toy?"

I declare, I never knew how the smell and sound and look of leather could overpower a person as unaccustomed to such attire as I was. Sam seemed twice his size—and he wasn't a small man to begin with—as he stood close, breathing in and out from the exertion of steering a machine with a mind of its own. I took in all that leather smell and the preponderance of zippers on his jacket as he leaned over me and said, "Well, Julia, what do you think?"

I took a step back. "I think, Sam Murdoch, that you have lost your mind."

Chapter 2

"Now get in the house," I said, "before half the town sees you in that get-up." I opened the door and gave him a little push toward it. It was the first time I'd been on the porch without having a sinking spell at the sight of Pastor Ledbetter's Family Life Center looming above us from across the street. I'd been too taken up with the amazing spectacle that Sam had presented to give the building a second thought. Not that it deserved one, for it was the bane of my existence.

"I can't stay, Julia," he said, going in anyway. "I just came by to show you my new Harley-Davidson Road King."

"I've seen it, which is more than I ever wanted." I motioned him to my Duncan Phyfe sofa, now covered in a bright yellow chintz instead of the maroon velvet that my lately deceased husband, Wesley Lloyd Springer, had thought appropriate for our living room. I sat in the matching Victorian ladies' chair across from Sam and studied him. "What in the world has possessed you, Sam, to get on such a machine as that life-threatening thing out there?"

"Oh, just one of those things I've always wanted to do," he said as he leaned back and made himself comfortable.

"And I decided that if I don't do some of them soon, I never will. We're not getting any younger, Julia. Have to do them while we can."

"Well," I said, with a glare at Lillian, who was standing in the arch to the dining room, still admiring Sam's leather outfit. "That's the second time today I've been reminded of my age, and I'll thank you not to bring it up again."

Sam laughed. "That's the thing, Julia. We're both healthy and active and interested in what's going on in the world. But if we just sit down and rest on the past, we'll grow old in a hurry. So I decided to try something new and fun for a change." He patted the helmet in his lap and smiled in a dreamy sort of way. "Always wondered what it'd be like to take a Harley out on the open road and ride with the wind, free as a bird."

"I say, free as a bird." I shook my head at such an irresponsible notion. "You are a grown man, respected and admired by everybody who knows you, and by many who don't. And to suddenly want to have *fun,* why, Sam, that is not the be-all and end-all of life, as you well know. Why in the world would you want to turn back the clock and turn yourself into a Hell's Angel or something?"

"Lots of people ride, Julia, and they're not all Hell's Angels—or anything like them. I'm joining a motorcycle club that has a lot of professional men in it, all just liking to ride and enjoy the great outdoors."

My skeptical look must've stirred him, for he went on. "They do a lot of good, too. They have charity runs, for instance, raising money for any number of good causes like St. Jude's Hospital for Children and Toys for Tots around Christmas. You'd be surprised at what all they do."

"I probably would, seeing that I've read about those so-called motorcycle bashes in the newspaper. You know what I'm talking about, don't you, Lillian?"

I turned to her for confirmation, but she just shrugged her shoulders and said, "I got beans to see about," and left for the kitchen.

"Now, Sam," I continued, knowing that he needed some straight talking to get him back on track. "That's not the kind of thing you ought to be involved with, I don't care how many good causes those people support. They used to have those Woodstock kind of conventions over near Asheville until the city council put a stop to them. Thousands of motorcycle people from every state in the union gathered at a campground, and they just tore up jack. I saw it all on the news, so I know what I'm talking about. I tell you, they disrupted the whole city something awful, all that loud music and swarms of cycles roaring and popping on the roads, tying up traffic and, would you believe, cutting up with such antics as coleslaw wrestling and wet T-shirt contests and other unsavory things I won't mention, like beer belly contests. That's just common, Sam, and you shouldn't be associated with such a bad element. Like I tell Little Lloyd, you're judged by the company you keep. I think you ought to turn that thing in and get your money back."

Sam laughed again—or maybe he hadn't stopped. "I'm not planning to go to a rally, Julia. Put your mind at rest. The club I'll be in rides mostly on weekends in groups of ten or so. We'll go up on the Parkway or stay on the interstate, not in residential areas. Besides, this is the best time of the year to ride—leaves're turning, the weather's fine and just cool enough. I tell you, it'll be something to see the mountainsides with all the colors, then pull off for some barbeque or a picnic. You'll enjoy it, I promise you will."

"And I can promise I won't. Because I'm not about to get on that thing." If he expected me to participate in such an unseemly activity, that just showed how far from normal his mental state was.

"Why, that's why I came around, Julia. I want to take you for a ride. Now, wait," he said, as I reared up in my chair. "We'll just go around the block and let you get used to it."

"Yes, and throw me off when you try to stop it, too. No, Sam, I'm not riding on two wheels, no matter who's trying to drive it. Besides, there's nowhere for anybody else to sit, and if you think I'd sit on your lap, you'd better think again."

"That's not a bad idea, but there's a passenger seat on the back with armrests and everything. It'll be like sitting in your easy chair, and I've got a helmet for you, too."

I just looked at him, as visions of me straddling that monster with my shirtwaist dress hiked up and flapping in the breeze, holding onto Sam for dear life, flickered through my mind. "You didn't need to waste your money on any kind of get-up for me, Sam, because it'll be a cold day before you get me on that machine.

"The idea!" I went on, as his assumption that I'd just be thrilled to grab onto all that leather and go flying off who-knew-where on a loud, open-air, souped-up piece of machinery struck me as the height of wrong-headed thinking. "How you could even think I'd be interested in such an undignified activity is beyond me, Sam Murdoch. In fact, it's beneath me and, if you want to know the truth, it's beneath you, too. No," I said, shaking my head, "you can just forget about it. I'm not about to swing my . . . my . . . *self* on that contraption."

"Well, I'm not giving up on you, Julia," Sam said, getting to his feet with those layers of leather creaking with every movement. "I'll admit, I need a little more practice on it, but

I need a partner on that backseat, too. All the other riders in the club bring their wives and girlfriends with them. You wouldn't want me to be the only one without a good-looking woman perched on the back with her arms wrapped around my waist, would you?"

I rolled my eyes, seeing no need to answer such a question. I didn't care if he never had a woman, regardless of her looks, clinging to him. Well, I'd have to rethink that when I had the time to give it adequate attention.

"Now," Sam said, looking toward the kitchen. "I need to speak to Lillian a minute. A legal matter she's concerned about."

"Why, what?" I asked, immediately disturbed that I didn't know that Lillian had any legal matters. "Is she in trouble? Is it her family? What's going on, Sam, and why hasn't she said anything to me?"

"I don't know, Julia," Sam said as he headed out of the room. "But right now, she wants to speak to me in private. Besides," he said, turning back to give me a sly grin, "maybe she'll ride with me if you won't."

I started to follow him as he pushed through the door to the kitchen but stopped, brought up short by Lillian's desire for privacy. That worried me. I thought that Lillian and I had no secrets from each other. At least, she knew all of mine.

But what did I know of hers? Very little, if the truth be known. Oh, I knew that her nephew had been arrested a few times and was now serving time for theft. And I knew both of her daughters had had children out of wedlock, then had left the grandbabies for her to raise while they went up north to find work. And I knew that Lillian'd had at least two husbands, but that neither of them had stayed very long. From what I'd gathered, one had taken off years ago without a word to her, and she'd kicked out the other one. And, wouldn't you know, but the one she'd sent on his way was the one she talked about and still longed for.

I knew, also, that Lillian was strong in her faith and within herself. She'd lived her life pretty much on her own, raising two daughters and two granddaughters with hardly a lick of help from anybody, and without one word of complaint. Furthermore, I knew that I had her to thank for keeping me on the straight and narrow every time I was about to bounce off the ceiling. And I knew that I respected and admired her for her sense of fairness and for her honesty, although on occasion I wished she would keep her opinions to herself, and let me do what I wanted to.

But I didn't know a thing about any legal problems. Even more worrisome was why she'd want to talk to Sam about them. Sam had retired from the practice of law a few years back, so he couldn't give her any official help. And if his current interests in motorcycles, flowers and poetry were any indication of the way his mind was working—or not working—he could even give her bad advice. And Lillian would follow it because she thought the sun rose and set on him.

The fact that she hadn't confided in me could've hurt my feelings if I'd let myself stew over it. The thing to do, I resolved, was to find out just what was going on that worried her enough to turn to a lawyer who I had plainly told her was more than a little addled in the head. And without saying word one to me.

~ *Chapter 3*

By the time Sam came back into the living room to say that he wasn't giving up on me as his backseat partner and I'd told him his foolishness was giving me a headache, I'd decided to tackle the immediate problem that he presented before dealing with Lillian's legal concerns. First things first, I always say, and my fear for Sam was more pressing than the nagging worry over Lillian.

I stood on the porch watching as Sam switched on that monster, revving it up and raising so much Cain that the noise reverberated up and down the street. When he got it going to his satisfaction, he guided it, wobbling as he went, out on the street. I gasped as he sped up, overtaking a car, then whipping back in front of it.

"He's going to kill himself," I said, biting my lip as the roar of the motor diminished in the distance.

Shaking my head in dismay, I wondered how much he was going to enjoy the great outdoors when he was laid up in the hospital in a full-body cast.

The thing to do, I determined, was to get somebody to talk some sense into him. It was a settled fact that he wasn't going to listen to me. All he'd done was laugh at my concerns, which was one of the few normal things he was still doing.

The first person I could turn to was Deputy Coleman Bates. Sam might listen to him and take heed, since Coleman had honored Sam by asking him to be the best man at his wedding to Binkie. And, besides that, Coleman was a law enforcement officer who could warn Sam in ways that I couldn't. Maybe describe some accidents he'd seen; tell him what happens to a rider when there's nothing between him and the pavement or a logging truck. Lord, Sam would be nothing but a greasy spot if he had a wreck on that thing.

With such worrisome thoughts in my mind, I went upstairs to use the telephone by my bed, not wanting Lillian to overhear me. If she could have secrets, so could I. Besides, she'd seemed too entranced with motorcycles in general to be worried about who was trying to steer one, and who was doing a poor job of it, too, I might add. Even I, with no experience of those two-wheeled machines, could tell that.

Well, wouldn't you know it, but Coleman was on patrol and couldn't be reached.

"Could I leave a message, then?" I asked the dispatcher.

"We can't take personal messages on this line," he informed me. "Is it urgent?"

"Well, I should say it is," I snapped. "If an inexperienced and disturbed individual weaving in and out of traffic isn't urgent, I don't know what is."

"Somebody's driving while impaired?"

"That's it! I would certainly say he is impaired, and Coleman needs to straighten him out before he kills himself."

"Where is this individual, ma'am?"

"Oh, he's home by now, so just tell Coleman to call me first, then go on over there. He knows where Sam lives."

"Uh, ma'am, this wouldn't be Mrs. Julia Springer, would it?"

"Why, yes. How did you know?"

After leaving a message for Coleman to call me, I hung up, thinking again of how pleasant it was to live in a small town where everybody knows everybody and their business. Of course it had its drawbacks, too—especially when you didn't want everybody knowing your business.

Disappointed not to get Coleman, I went to the next person who might be able to get through Sam's hard head. As I dialed, I thought again of how empty the house seemed without Little Lloyd in it. Not that he was a boisterous child, not at all, just as quiet and mannerly as anybody could want. But he filled up the spaces just by being around, and I missed him something awful.

"Hazel Marie," I said when she answered, "I need to speak to Mr. Pickens. Is he there?"

"No, not yet. He'll be home about suppertime. At least, he said he would. Anything I can do?"

"I wish there were, but I'm afraid not," I said with a sigh. "Oh, Hazel Marie, it is just so pitiful. I never thought I'd live to see the day when an active, intelligent man started down the road to wrack and ruin."

"Oh, Miss Julia, who's in that kind of trouble?"

I could hear the immediate concern and sympathy in Hazel Marie's voice. She was so pleasing in that respect, her heart always going out to whoever was suffering or in dire straits.

"It's Sam," I said woefully, as the thought of the deterioration of that great and decent man overwhelmed me. "You won't believe what he's up to."

I went on to tell her what he'd taken to wearing, what

he'd bought to ride on, and what he expected me to do with him on it. "And Hazel Marie, he's spending a fortune on flowers, and he's writing some of the worst poetry you'd ever hope to read, and changing his manner of dress, and coming over here every time I turn around, and just making a plain nuisance of himself."

There was dead silence on the line, then some muffled noises as she struggled to get her breath.

"Hazel Marie!" I said. "It's nothing to laugh about. This is serious, I tell you."

"Oh, Miss Julia," she gasped, as if she'd half strangled herself. "I hate to tell you, but we already know about it. The motorcycle, that is." She stopped while laughter bubbled out again. "I didn't know about the flowers and poetry, though. I think that is so sweet."

Sweet! I should've known that would be Hazel Marie's response. She was so easily taken in by men. Just look at her situation now, to say nothing of her previous one with my husband. Which is exactly what I'll do—say nothing of it. "I'm worried about him, Hazel Marie, and in spite of all the indications of encroaching senility, he's been giving legal advice to Lillian, and you know she'll do whatever he tells her to. And no telling what that'll be in his current state of mind."

"Why does Lillian need legal advice? Is something going on with her?"

"Don't ask me," I said, disturbed again at the thought of Lillian's secrecy. "I tell you, Hazel Marie, there's more than one person around here who's acting strange. Now, listen. I want you to ask Mr. Pickens to talk to Sam and get him off that motorized death trap before it kills him."

"I don't think J. D. would be much help, Miss Julia. You

probably don't want to hear this, but it was J. D. who helped Sam pick out that motorcycle. He's got one, too, you know."

"No! I didn't know that. But come to think of it," I went on, "it doesn't surprise me. That's exactly the kind of thing I'd expect from Mr. Pickens. But it *does* surprise me that you'd let him do it."

"It's not so bad," she said. "In fact, I kinda enjoy it, too. We've been riding on the weekends, and Little Lloyd just loves it."

"Hazel Marie! You let that child get on the thing? Oh, my goodness, he's going to be damaged for life. You've just got to put a stop to it before something awful happens."

"Now, Miss Julia, of course he wears a helmet, and J. D. is real careful when Little Lloyd rides with him."

"Thay Lord," I said, holding my aching head, "I know how that man drives a car. No telling how he drives a motorcycle."

"I tell you what," Hazel Marie said. "Why don't we come over this weekend and let J. D. show you how safe it can be? Once you ride on one, you'll feel a whole lot better about them."

I couldn't believe what I was hearing. Here was somebody else who was trying to get me on the back of one of those things. And if Hazel Marie thought she could do it, then Sam wasn't the only one not clicking on all cylinders.

Well, no help from that quarter, I thought as I hung up the phone. I should've known better than to expect anything sensible from Mr. Pickens.

Then Binkie came to mind—and just as quickly left it. Ordinarily, she'd be the one I'd turn to about Sam, since he thought so much of her that he'd arranged for her to take over his law practice when he retired. Those two were as close as two peas in a pod, and Binkie could've given him some straight talk about peril to life and limb, to say nothing of the liabilities he could be stuck with.

But Binkie was out. That girl was so close to giving birth that she could hardly walk. In fact, the last time I'd talked to her, she'd told me that she was only working part time now. Too tired and uncomfortable to make a full day, she'd said. So she was going home around three o'clock instead of the usual seven or eight.

I just couldn't add another burden to the one she was already carrying. So who did that leave?

Lillian, that's who. I'd just have to make her understand that Sam needed our help, and that she should be cautious about taking his advice. That way, I could kill two birds with one stone and, between us, we could look after him and talk him into some sedate activity more suited to his age.

A sudden image of the local shuffleboard court filled with senior citizens flashed in my mind. I shuddered at the thought, but if that's what it took to get Sam off that death trap, I'd learn to wield one of those sticks with the best of them. At least there'd be less danger from a wayward puck than from a motorcycle flipping in the air.

What I had to do was ease into a general conversation with Lillian, then gradually persuade her to tell me what was bothering her. I felt justified in using such a tactic because she didn't need to be taking half-baked legal advice from Sam when I was perfectly willing to help with whatever she needed.

Maybe I should let her read some of that pitiful poetry he'd sent, and if that wouldn't make her think twice about consulting him, I didn't know what would.

Chapter 4

I didn't want to be too obvious about delving into Lillian's business. She had every right to keep her own counsel if she wanted to. But of course, that didn't mean I had to like it if she did.

The thing to do was to come at it sideways, so she wouldn't think I was being meddlesome. Still, I couldn't imagine why she hadn't confided in me before now.

And that disturbed me all over again. Why was she keeping something from me? Didn't she trust me? And if she didn't, what did that say about all we'd been through together for, lo, these many years?

So I walked into the kitchen and, before I could help myself, just came right out and said, "Lillian, I want to know what kind of trouble you're having. I want you to sit right down here and tell me. I declare, to have to learn that you have a problem from somebody else is more than I can stand."

"Miss Julia," she said, drying her hands on a dish towel as she stared out the window. "They ain't nothin' you can do. Ain't nothin' nobody can do, look like. So no need to worry you with it."

"Listen to me, Lillian," I said, pulling out a chair for her at the table. "Anything that worries you, worries me. Whether I know what it is or not. So I might as well know about it. Now, you've been moping around here for I don't know how long, and I thought it was because you were missing Little Lloyd."

"Well, I was, an' I still do. But you been doin' some mopin' yo'self 'bout the same thing."

"I know it, but that's not all that's been bothering me, as you well know because I told you how concerned I am about Sam. Now I find out that missing Little Lloyd is not all that's bothering you, either. Tell me, Lillian, and even if I can't do anything to help, at least you'll have somebody who can still think straight to talk to."

"Might as well, I guess," she said as she sank into a chair with a heaving sigh. Then she started up again. "Lemme get us some coffee."

"Just as long as you're not trying to put me off. I tell you, Lillian, I'm not going to give up until I get to the bottom of this."

She didn't reply because she knew I meant it and she might as well resign herself to it. She brought the coffeepot that we kept replenished throughout the day while I got down two cups and saucers.

When we were both settled at the table again, I said, "All right, let's hear it."

"Well, it's like this, Miss Julia." She stopped, added more sugar to her cup, and stirred her coffee a considerably longer time than it needed.

"I'm waiting."

"Well, it's that Mr. Clarence Gibbs," she said, as if it hurt her to say his name. Then, in a rush, she got it all out. "An' I know he a friend of yours, which is why I didn't want to tell you, an' I don' want to say nothin' 'gainst him, but he bringin' down a peck of trouble on us."

"Clarence Gibbs!" I cried. "He's no friend of mine. Where in the world did you get that idea?"

"Well, I know he a member of the Presbyterium Church over there, an' I know he had some proppity dealin's with Mr. Springer 'fore he passed, so I figgered you still doin' bus'ness with him."

"You figured wrong, then," I said. But I had to stop and study the matter. I declare, when you have a husband suddenly expire on you and leave you with a theretofore unknown number of acquisitions, both real and personal, it's a wonder if you know who you're doing business with. I'd have to talk with Little Lloyd about it, too. The child had taken a precocious interest in real estate recently, which I'd encouraged. The reason being that he would come into a goodly number of properties when he grew up, and even more when I passed on. Which I didn't intend to do anytime soon.

"I'll have to check some of Mr. Springer's holdings," I went on, "but I know I've had no personal contact with Clarence Gibbs. Oh, I see him at church occasionally, but just to nod to. He is a deacon, you know."

"Yessum, I know. An' he known 'round town, too. But, Miss Julia, that deacon fixin' to put us out." She leaned her head on her hand and covered her eyes.

I leaned closer, not fully understanding what she was telling me. "Put who out? And from where?"

"Our whole street, that's who. He own all the houses on it, an' now he say he need that proppity, an' he not renewin' any rents, an' we all got to move."

"You mean," I said, leaning back in my chair, "he just all of a sudden told everybody they have to move without giving any reason whatsoever?"

"Well, he say the town council done voted us out 'cause them houses too far gone for anybody to be livin' in 'em, which can't be no news to any of us. An' the sheriff, he say the same thing 'cause the Reverend Mr. Abernathy, he went down an' talk to him for us. An' the sheriff say he sorry but he got a 'viction order he got to carry out."

"Well, I say," I said, stunned that Clarence Gibbs had been able to get the town council to condemn those houses, and not a word in the newspaper about it that I'd seen. He was fairly tight with a couple of the councilmen, so he could pretty much push through anything he wanted. "How long have you lived there?"

"All us been livin' there a long time," she said, wiping her face with her hand. "Some of our people livin' there 'fore even the courthouse got built, but they all dead now. An' used to be all them houses was owned by whoever lived in 'em. But Mr. Gibbs, he always knowed when folks havin' troubles, an' he come 'round offerin' to take them houses offa folkses' hands. He handin' out money to buy 'em, then he rent 'em back to whoever owned 'em." She reached for a napkin to do a better job of drying her face. "So now he own 'em all, 'cept maybe one or two, an' he want them, too. He say they all have to sell or they be settin' in the middle of something they don't like."

"Like what?" I asked. "What's he planning to do with that land?"

"We don't know. Don't nobody tell us nothin' but get up and move." Tears welled up in her eyes again and she covered them with the napkin. "Miss Julia, we got a graveyard back up there by that ridge. Nobody use it now, but they's folks buried there a hundred years ago."

"Well, he certainly can't put anything on that spot," I said. "There are laws protecting cemeteries." At least I thought there were.

I couldn't stand the thought of Lillian being taken advantage of, and the idea of the likes of stoop-shouldered, hooded-eyed Clarence Gibbs being the one to do it just tore me up.

"Seems to me," I said, throwing out a few terms that I didn't know the meaning of, "that you and your neighbors would have eminent domain or squatters' rights or something. How can he just move everybody out, lock, stock and barrel?"

"I don' know, but look like he can. That 'viction notice come a few weeks ago, an' we s'posed to be out this week."

"This week! Lillian! Why didn't you tell me? I might've done *something,* at least I'd have tried to."

She bowed her head, mumbling, "We was hopin' Mr. Gibbs have a change of heart, but don't look like it gonna happen."

I frowned, trying to think what Clarence Gibbs might have in mind. With his reputation for slick business practices, there'd be money to be made somewhere.

"What about your leases?" I asked. "Surely, as permanent as that street is, you all have long-term leases."

"No'm, it always been week to week. He send somebody ever' Friday to pick up the rent money."

I thought for a minute, picturing in my mind the street where Lillian lived. It was an unpaved offshoot of a road right outside the town limits, no more than a lane where a few grandchildren played hopscotch and jumped rope in the thick dust of summer. As I recalled, there was an empty field, what might have been a pasture at one time, where the lane ended in a dirt turn-around. The field ran some distance beyond the houses, ending in a wooded ridge that didn't seem suitable for any kind of development to me. But then, developers see possibilities where most folks see cliffs and gullies and sheer mountainsides.

Willow Lane, I thought, and not a willow in sight. Large oak trees lined the street, their branches forming a shady canopy overhead. The small houses, no more than four or five on each side, were all alike: shotgun style with small banistered porches. They were made of weathered clap- boards, many of them listing to one side or the other on foundations of stacked rocks. I'd often driven Lillian home, so I knew the place well. Her house, at least from the out- side, was well cared for. Flowers blooming in pots and cans on her front porch testified to that, as did the dirt yard that was kept raked in neat lines, reminding me of a Japanese garden I'd once seen. And, knowing her, it would be just as well-kept on the inside.

The more I thought about it, the madder I got. From the looks of those houses, Clarence Gibbs had not put a nickel into their upkeep, letting them deteriorate year after year. No wonder he was able to get the town council to condemn them.

"I just wish I knew why he suddenly needs that property," I said, trying to figure out what scheme Clarence Gibbs had in mind.

"They no tellin', Miss Julia, but we seen him walkin' 'round up on that ridge back of us, goin' in an' out the trees. He bring some men one time with him, look like they mea- surin' something."

"Surveying, sounds like," I said.

I thought about that for a minute, bringing my newly realized—as of Wesley Lloyd's passing—business sense to bear. "It's got to be something commercial," I said. "Nothing else would be worth more than residential rentals."

"I don' know, Miss Julia," she said, looking as unsettled as I'd ever seen her. "All I know's we got to move, an' the time comin' up on us fast. But they's nowhere to go, 'cept places that cost more'n anybody got the money to pay."

"Oh," I said, taken aback at the reminder that not everybody could just write a check for whatever they wanted. Of course, I knew what Lillian had to live on because I knew what I paid her. I'd been proud of myself for raising her salary after Wesley Lloyd's demise, and I'd given her bonuses and raises every year since. Yet when I mentally compared her income to my own, it didn't amount to a hill of beans.

Because of my late husband's estate, I could do whatever I wanted, and I was often brought up short when I realized that that wasn't the case for everybody.

Still, not everybody'd had to put up with Wesley Lloyd Springer and the shame he'd left me with, so I considered his estate a just compensation.

"Well, you certainly have a place to go. I want you to move in here, right up there in Coleman's rooms which he no longer needs, and you can stay as long as you want."

"That's real nice of you, Miss Julia, an' I thank you for it. But I don't know what ever'body else's gonna do, an' you know I want my own place."

"I understand that, but at least you have somewhere to come to until you find something. Oh, Lord, Lillian," I said, overwhelmed with what she'd been holding inside. "I am just so sorry this is happening. But, now listen, all is not lost. There may still be some legal avenues to look into. Still, though, if you only have a day or two, we need to get you packed up and moved. Then we'll see what can be done."

She just shook her head. "I think it too late, Miss Julia. Coleman, he been comin' by, an' he all tore up 'cause the sheriff sent him to serve that notice."

"My Lord," I said, realizing that I'd been doing an awful lot of calling on the Deity lately. But I certainly needed to call on somebody, since no one had had the decency to let me know what was going on. "Well, what's done is done. Now we have to think about your furniture and all your things."

"Coleman been helpin' me," she said, wiping her face again with the napkin. "I been packin' an' tho'win' out an' givin' away all kinds a stuff. Hardly nothin' left but my bed an' all them boxes." She heaved a heavy sigh. "I tell you the truth, Miss Julia, it make me happy to move outta that ramshackle house if there be a decent place to go to."

I sat and stared at her, torn between pity and anger. Anger won out. "I still can't believe that you've let things come to such a pass and not told me a word about it. I declare, Lillian, I am hurt, *hurt,* that you'd keep this from me."

She wrung her hands, looking at them instead of at me. "I know you got yo' hands full, an' I thought somethin' might turn up or Mr. Gibbs change his mind or somethin'. Coleman, he been helpin' me look for a place to move to, but all them others what live there, they in the same fix."

"Thay Lord," I said, just about done in for going on my merry way while Lillian'd been losing her home. "How many others are there?"

"They nine houses on that street. Used to be ten, but the roof of one give way. Some people live by theyselves, like me, now my grands is grown an' gone. Some're married folks, an' Mr. William an' his wife, they have her ole daddy livin' with 'em. Lot of 'em have they chil'ren come stay when they lose a job. Nobody have a place to move to, 'cept the Whitleys, who already gone to Durham. They daughter, she got a good job workin' at the Duke Hospital."

Well, my goodness, I thought, running my mind over the housing possibilities for that many people. There wasn't much in the way of affordable housing in Abbotsville, especially for the financially handicapped.

I leaned toward her. "What did Sam say about this?"

"He say he gonna look into it, an' talk to Mr. Gibbs, see he can work something out. But he say since we don't have no leases, Mr. Gibbs might can do whatever he want."

"Well, we'll just see about that," I said, ready to get on my high horse. "Lillian, far be it from me to undermine Sam and his advice, but I've already told you that I'm worried about his mental state. You need to take whatever he tells you with a grain of salt."

Lord, I hated to tell her that, it seemed so hurtful to Sam. But I couldn't just let her be evicted from her home while Sam piddled around, looking into it.

"We gonna have a meetin' tonight," Lillian told me, pushing away her cup of cold coffee. "The Reverend Mr. Morris Abernathy, he gettin' all us what live on the street together to talk about what we can do. He ast Mr. Gibbs to come to the meetin', too, but Mr. Gibbs say he don' think he can make it. He got bus'ness to tend to, an' can't be 'spected to come to no meetin' that can't change nothin', no way."

"Well," I said, standing up and pacing around the table. "He's got a nerve. Lillian, you can't just give up. If there's anything that can be done, you've got to do it."

"I tole Mr. Sam 'bout the meetin', an' he say he be there an' tell us what he find out. Maybe somethin' come up outta that, 'cause he gonna be lookin' into it today. Proppity records and such like, down at the courthouse. Mr. Sam put a stop to it, if anybody can. We countin' on him."

"Good," I said, wanting to encourage her, but hoping that Sam was up to the job. From what I'd witnessed of him lately, though, I wouldn't want to depend on him, as Lillian clearly was doing. "I think I'd better be there, too. That be all right with you?"

"Yessum," she said, smiling at me. "You more'n welcome, 'cause we gonna need all the help we can get. I don' know what some a them folks gonna do; they gonna be out on the street without no place to lay they heads."

"We'll figure something out," I assured her, wondering where in the world we could find housing for that many evicted families. "In the meantime, you tell Coleman to bring all your things over here and store them in the garage. There's plenty of room, and my car can sit in the driveway. And," I went on, pointing my finger at her, "you are moving in right upstairs, and I don't want to hear another word about it."

~Chapter 5

I sent Lillian home early that afternoon, knowing that she had a lot on her mind and needed to get ready for the meeting. There were some, she'd told me, who weren't sure they wanted to go, fearing that Clarence Gibbs wouldn't like it.

"Lord, what else can he do to them?" I'd asked her. "And who cares whether he likes it or not? I hope you can get them all there, Lillian. This needs to be a team effort, maybe a class-action lawsuit or something." I didn't know what I was talking about, but it seemed to me that if they were all being evicted, then they all needed to hold together. "You want me to pick you up?"

"No'm, I thank you, though. I'm goin' with Miz Causey, she live next door, an' we gonna take some a them what might not go 'less we get 'em there. I'll wait for you in front a the church, an' we can go in together."

Telling her that I'd be there a little before seven, I locked up behind her and fixed an early supper for myself. Since night fell so quickly this time of year, it didn't seem all that early to be eating. After I finished, I went upstairs to put my feet up before getting ready for the meeting to save Lillian's home.

The sound of a car pulling into the driveway startled me, and I got up to look out the window.

"Why, what in the world?" I asked myself, watching as Hazel Marie climbed out of the car and slammed the door with such force that her feet almost slid from under her. She stomped across the yard to the front porch, Little Lloyd tagging along behind her.

I hurried downstairs and opened the door as she rang the bell. She stood there, her face flushed with more than the amount of makeup she usually wore, huffing like she could hardly get her breath. Little Lloyd moved slowly up the steps, his head lowered and turned away.

"Hazel Marie . . . ?" I started, holding the door open.

"Can we come in, Miss Julia? I've left J. D."

"Why, of course you can," I said, stunned at this sudden turn of events. "But what happened?"

"Don't ask." She barrelled into the living room with a full head of steam. Then she turned on her heel and headed out the door again. "I forgot our suitcases."

Little Lloyd followed her, giving me a shoulder shrug as he passed. I held the door for them as they came back, lugging suitcases and grocery bags of shoes, hair rollers, and various and sundry beauty aids.

"You sure this is all right, Miss Julia?" Hazel Marie asked as she passed me on her way in again. "We can always go to a motel."

"You know it's all right. Your room is just as you left it. Little Lloyd, I need to put fresh sheets on your bed, but you can go on up." I tried to pull myself together as I closed the front door. I was of two minds about their return—pleased that I had the two of them under my roof again, and disturbed that Hazel Marie had no staying power. Although, to be fair, she had told me that living with Mr. Pickens would be a temporary arrangement, so he'd see the benefits and advantages of marriage. Have you ever heard of anything so foolish? I could've predicted what would happen, but far be it from me to bring that up in her present frame of mind.

I watched Little Lloyd trudge up the stairs, lugging a suitcase, with his backpack full of books on his shoulder, and my heart went out to him. No telling what he'd witnessed between his mother and Mr. Pickens if Hazel Marie'd gotten mad enough to leave. I had to shake my head at the pity of it all, as I looked at those skinny little legs of his in the short pants that came all the way to his knobby knees.

"I'll be up in a minute," I told him.

Then, heading toward Hazel Marie's room, I heard her slam a dresser drawer shut, then clomp across the floor.

"Hazel Marie," I said as I stood in her door. "What in the world is going on?"

"I don't want to talk about it," she said, slinging clothes out of the suitcase. "J. D. Pickens is without a doubt the most aggravating man who ever lived."

"Well, I know that, but what happened? Did you have a disagreement?"

"I have just had it with him," she fumed. "Believe me, Miss Julia, I've learned my lesson, and now I'm going to teach him one." She slammed a hairbrush on the dresser.

Wondering how she intended to do that, I decided to let her cool down before finding out what else she didn't want to talk about. "I'll just go up and see about Little Lloyd."

When I got upstairs, I found the boy looking out the front window of his room. The streetlight on the corner had already come on, early as it does on fall evenings.

"Little Lloyd," I said, "why in the world is your mother so upset with Mr. Pickens? Did he do something to her?"

He turned from the window, but stayed beside it. "Yes, ma'am, I reckon he did. But he didn't mean to."

I knew better than to expect him to tattle on his mother, but I couldn't resist trying to get a handle on the situation. "Well, what did he do?"

Little Lloyd was staring out of the window again. He shrugged his shoulders and said, "I don't really know. Mama picked me up from school, and when we got home he was just sitting at the table talking with somebody, and Mama sent me outside. And the next thing I knew, she was throwing suitcases in the car."

"Well, I say," I said. "And she didn't tell you why?"

"No'm," he said, shaking his head and watching the street from the window. "She just said if she never saw Mr. Pickens again, it'd be too soon for her."

"I don't expect she meant that," I said, wondering what he was looking at out on the street. Trying to distract himself, I surmised. "Let's get this bed made up. You take that side and I'll take this one. Then it'll be ready when you are." I removed the coverlet and began to unfold the bottom sheet that Lillian had left beside the bed. "You know, Little Lloyd, I know this is all pretty upsetting for you, but I'm glad to have you back. I've been needing some help with first one thing and another. That trailer park, for instance, and there's a building on Main Street that's coming on the market soon. We ought to look into that and see if it's worth buying." It'd been my habit to take the child into my business confidences here lately to prepare him for the day when I wouldn't be around to help him with monetary decisions.

"Yes, ma'am," he said, and tore himself away from the window long enough to help me make the bed.

"Now," I said, straightening up after a final smoothing of his sheets. "Go ahead and unpack your suitcase. I'll go see how your mother's doing."

I walked slowly down the stairs. Lord, I didn't know what to think. Here I'd thought Hazel Marie was settled, lacking a marriage certificate, of course, but headed that way with a decent, if somewhat unmanageable, man.

Approaching her room through the back hall, I was relieved to hear none of the slamming and banging she'd been doing. When I tapped on her door, I saw her sitting on the bed with her head bowed and her hands twisting in her lap.

"Hazel Marie," I said, "come on to the kitchen and let me fix you something to eat."

"I don't think I can eat anything." She looked up at me with fierce eyes. "But," she said, getting to her feet, "I'll sit with you a while. I'm too upset to eat."

When she was settled at the kitchen table in her usual place, I made a peanut butter and jelly sandwich and put it and a glass of milk in front of her. "Eat," I said. "You'll feel better."

"I feel fine, now that I've done what I should've done in the first place, tell J. D. Pickens to get out of my life and stay out." She frowned as her eyes darted around the room, and I prepared myself to endure another fit of temper.

"You weren't feeling that way when I talked to you on the phone earlier today," I reminded her.

"I didn't know then what I know now, and that man has tried my patience for the last time." She reached for the sandwich, but instead of picking it up, she put her palm on it and mashed it. Grape jelly oozed out the sides. "You won't believe what he was doing when I came home today. I wanted to smack him to kingdom come, and I may still do it." Her clenched fist slammed down on the table—some little distance from the sandwich, I'm happy to say. "But," she said, "I don't want to talk about it."

"All right."

"Oh, Miss Julia," she went on, "you just don't know what I've been through with him. He thinks he's God's gift to every woman he sees, and I've had my fill of it."

Ah, I thought to myself, that's what I was afraid of. Mr. Pickens was a world-class womanizer, and I'd warned Hazel Marie of those tendencies of his long before this. Of course, you can't tell people what they don't want to hear; they have to find out for themselves.

"Some men are just like that, Hazel Marie."

"Like what?"

"Why, like Mr. Pickens. Running after everything in a skirt."

Well, that certainly opened the floodgates. She covered her face with her hands and began to sob. "Oh, Miss Julia, I thought I could change him, he *said* he would change, but he hasn't and I don't think he can." She gave a mighty sniff, grabbed a napkin and wiped her nose. "And it's too late, anyway."

Now, I hadn't had much experience with men in general, but I knew enough to know that trying to change one was an uphill job, and Hazel Marie hadn't stood a chance of changing the stripes of a man like Mr. Pickens. Women just melted when he turned those black eyes on them and smiled that wicked smile of his. Maybe he couldn't help what he did to women. Some men can't, you know.

"Hazel Marie," I said, wanting to offer something to ease her heartache. "I don't think he means a thing by it. I've never seen a man so taken with anybody as he is with you. I watch him, you know, and he can't keep his eyes off you."

She gave me a teary smile. "You think so?"

"I know so. The man's in love, Hazel Marie, and it looks like you're just going to have to put up with the way he attracts other women." I said this even though I couldn't've done it myself.

Hazel Marie sniffed again, picked up the sandwich, then put it back down. "One thing I'll give him, he knows how to treat a woman."

Intrigued, I longed to ask just what that treatment consisted of, since I'd never had any of it, and probably wouldn't recognize it if any ever came my way.

But I held my peace as tears began to spurt out of her eyes again. Ignoring them, she picked up the flattened sandwich and finally took a bite. Chewing and sniffing as she wiped her eyes with a napkin, she went on, "He can be so sweet and thoughtful and kind and considerate." She swallowed hard. "And I could just knock him winding."

"I don't blame you. I'd want to do the same." I thought of how I'd wanted to take the hide off Wesley Lloyd Springer when I found out that one woman hadn't been enough for him.

"Oh, Miss Julia," Hazel Marie suddenly wailed. She put her head down on her arms and began crying like her heart was breaking. I took the sandwich from her hand and put it on the plate. "It's even worse than you think."

"What is?" I said, leaning close. "What in the world could be worse?"

"He . . . ," she sniffed, her voice muffled against the table. "He, he's married."

"Married! To *who?*"

"To *two!*"

I reared back in my chair and grasped the edge of the table with my hands. "He's married to two women? And leading you on at the same time? Why, Hazel Marie, the man's a bigamist! I can't believe this. That sorry thing needs to be in jail, and I've a good mind to put him there."

"Well," she said, straightening up and wiping her face. "He's divorced from both of them, so I don't guess they'd put him in jail for that."

After the stunning revelation of two Mrs. Pickenses, I had to heave a sigh of relief. Mr. Pickens was at least free of criminal intent, legally speaking. But divorce? And two of them? That didn't say much for Mr. Pickens's qualifications for another stab at marriage.

"You just found out about this?" I asked.

"Yes! And I wouldn't have found out at all if one of them hadn't come to see him today. Just showed up out of the blue, and he had the nerve to invite her in and be sitting at the table drinking a Coke with her when I walked in. Can you believe that? There they were just talking and laughing, and she had her hand on his arm." She rubbed the napkin over her eyes, mopping up mascara-tinged tears, then plunged on. "And do you think *he* would tell me who she was? No, *she* did!" Then, mimicking somebody else's voice, she said, " 'Hi, I'm Tammi with an *i,* and J. D. and I were married for a short while. Too short, don't you think, J. D.? We didn't give it long enough.' Little red-headed witch, I could've snatched her bald-headed."

"And so you left?"

"I certainly did, and I'm not . . ." She stopped as we both looked up at the ceiling at the sound of Little Lloyd's footsteps running across the upstairs hall and galloping down the stairs to answer the front door.

"You stay here," I said, rising from my chair. "I'll see who it is."

When I got to the living room, Little Lloyd had opened

the door for Mr. Pickens. They stood together, with the child's arms around his waist and Mr. Pickens holding him close.

"Told you I'd come, didn't I?" Mr. Pickens said to him.

The boy looked up at him. "Did you bring Tammi, too?"

Mr. Pickens laughed and hugged him closer. "No, I didn't bring Tammi. She's long gone and good riddance. Don't you worry about her. Now, where's your mother?"

The child heaved a mighty sigh, and we all turned as the kitchen door swung open and Hazel Marie walked into the dining room, heading toward us. She looked a sight, with smeared makeup, tangled hair and red eyes. I don't think Mr. Pickens minded in the least. He walked over to her, crooning, "Hazel Marie, sweetheart."

She backed away from him. "Don't come around trying to sweet-talk me. I've had enough of it!"

"I know I should've told you, but I was afraid I'd scare you off," he said, holding out his arms. "Come on, sweetheart, let's just talk about it."

"I'm not about to talk about it," she said, tears coursing down her face. "How can I when I'm not speaking to you ever again? You might as well leave, 'cause that's all I have to say." And she stomped off to the kitchen, letting the door close in his face.

His shoulders slumped as he stared at the closed door. Then he glanced at me in a sheepish way, and said, "Guess I blew it this time." Then he took Little Lloyd's hand, saying, "Sit out on the porch with me, son, and we'll straighten this out between us."

Mr. Pickens's concern for the child's feelings confirmed what I'd always thought. He was basically a good man whose flaws all had to do with women.

I went back into the kitchen to see about Hazel Marie.

She was sitting with her elbows propped on the table and her face buried in her hands.

"You could've let him explain," I said, trying not to sound as if I were accusing her of being hasty. "Maybe he got married when he was young and didn't know any better. Or he could've been tricked into it. There could be a good explanation." Actually, I didn't know any really good ones, but I wanted to soothe her feelings.

"He could've told me, Miss Julia. Not just let me walk in and see the second Mrs. Pickens hanging all over him. It's obvious what she wants. I heard her tell him while I was packing that she'd just broken up with her latest live-in. She wants J. D. back. And she can just have him!" She rubbed at the tears that were welling up again.

"From what I heard," I said, "he doesn't want her back. He wants you."

"It doesn't matter. It's all ruined now. I'm not going to get into it again with a married man. Not ever, ever again." She covered her face with her hands, unable to look at me, as her words conjured up her previous relationship with my husband.

"Hazel Marie," I said as firmly as I could, "it's not the same. Mr. Pickens is divorced, even if he did have to do it twice. So unless there's another wife he hasn't told you about, he is unattached at the present time."

"But, but, remember Pastor Ledbetter's sermon on divorce, when he said, once married, always married? He said," she said, sniffing wetly again, "he said there's no such thing as divorce in God's eyes, so that means J. D.'s still married to his first wife. And, and, it means his second wife was just like me—a blamed fool for falling for him. No wonder they both threw him out."

"Oh, for goodness sakes," I said, just so put out at the damage Pastor Ledbetter seemed to wreak every time he opened his mouth. "Listen to me. I happen to know that the pastor himself has performed wedding ceremonies for people who've been divorced. So what does that say about his pronouncements from on high?" I thought for a minute, as what she'd just said came through to me. "They threw him out?"

"He said they did. And laughed about it. See, Miss Julia, he's just impossible."

"No, Hazel Marie, that makes him possible," I said, satisfied that I'd found the pastor's justification, as well as my own. I didn't know how I felt about divorce, except that some married people needed it, and those who seemed to need it the most rarely got it.

While I was musing over my sudden insight into how the pastor managed to overcome his objections to performing the second marriage of an elder's divorced daughter, I heard Little Lloyd close the front door and run up the stairs. So Mr. Pickens had had his talk and, if I knew him, he now had an accomplice on the inside.

"See, Hazel Marie," I said, putting my hand on her arm. "Mr. Pickens was the injured party." Though the Lord knows, I thought, it was hard to picture him in such an innocent light. "*He* didn't get the divorces, his wives did. So even Pastor Ledbetter couldn't argue with that."

"Well, but he should've told me before this." She took another bite of the sandwich, her eyes still swimming with tears, and chewed it as if it had little taste. Then she looked at me. "You really think it's all right that he's been married before?"

"Of course it's not all right," I said. "But what's done is

done, and he's not married now, at least in the eyes of the law. As to what he is in the eyes of the Lord, I don't have a clue, and neither does Pastor Ledbetter."

"I don't know what I'd do if he was." She began sobbing again between bites of the sandwich. "I just love him so, and I know he loves me. So, why, Miss Julia, *why* didn't he tell me?"

"There's no telling. I've given up trying to understand any of them." The thought of Sam crossed my mind—Sam and his unexplainable behavior of late. "Now, Hazel Marie," I said, glancing at my watch. "We'll deal with Mr. Pickens when the time comes, but right now I've got to see about Lillian."

"Oh," she said, swallowing hard, as immediate concern for another suffering soul distracted her. "What's wrong with Lillian?"

I gave her a long look, concluding that what she needed was something to take her mind off Mr. Pickens and his waywardness.

"I'll tell you in the car," I said. "Call Little Lloyd and tell him he'll need a jacket and some long pants. It's getting cool out there."

"Where're we going?" she asked, sopping up mascara-soaked tears as she started out of the chair.

"We're going to a protest meeting at the Reverend Morris Abernathy's AME Zion church."

Chapter 6

As Little Lloyd scrunched up between the bucket seats so he could hear better, I told Hazel Marie about Lillian's impending homeless state.

"That's just not fair," she said, righteously upset on Lillian's behalf. She gave an angry sniff—or maybe she needed to blow her nose again. "It's not right to put all those people out when they've lived there for so long."

"Amen to that, Hazel Marie," I said, heading the car toward the south end of town where Lillian's church was located. "Even though Clarence Gibbs may have the law on his side, we ought to be able to do something."

I turned the car down several streets lined with increasingly smaller and less well-cared-for houses, trying to figure out where the AME Zion church was. Several blocks closer to town than Lillian's street, I remembered, but off the beaten track since I never passed it when I drove her home. I knew it was in the same general area as her neighborhood, though.

"You know," I went on, "I've heard of landlords who collect cash rents every week, but I had no idea that Lillian lived under those conditions."

"I thought Miss Lillian probably owned her house," Little Lloyd said.

"I guess I did, too," I said, as a feeling of shame swept over me. "No, to tell the pitiful truth, I just never really thought about it."

"Well," Hazel Marie said firmly, her mind already taken up with Lillian's problem. "We have to do something. What can we do, Miss Julia?"

"I know," Little Lloyd said. "She can move in with us."

"She certainly can," I agreed. "And that's what she's going to do. But I'm afraid she'll only accept it as a temporary measure. She wants her own place, and I don't blame her. Hazel Marie, we'll just have to research places to rent and help her get resettled. And in a much nicer place, too."

"I think she ought to buy a house," Little Lloyd said. "Then she won't ever have to move again."

"I expect she can't afford to buy anything, honey," Hazel Marie told him.

I nodded grimly, doubting that Lillian had any savings, much less any collateral for a bank loan. Still, she seemed to've managed her affairs with care and prudence. Then again, what did I know about how she did it? I'd never asked, never thought it my business to look into hers.

Maybe I should have.

"I'll give her the money," Little Lloyd said, and I could've hugged him for his generous little heart. "Can't I do that, mama, out of what my daddy left me?"

Hazel Marie thought a minute, then said, "I don't know, sugar, if you can or not. We'll have to ask Mr. Sam."

Sam was the administrator of the child's trust fund, and I had a sinking feeling at the thought that Sam might not be able to administer anything for much longer.

"I'll take care of Lillian," I said. "Let's not bother Sam with that right now."

I pulled to the curb a few doors from the small brick church, where we could see a group of people standing around in the bare, leaf-strewn yard before going in to the meeting. A few clumps of bushes huddled next to the foundation of the church, throwing shadows from the light fixture over the church door. A pole lamp near the street gave off a meager light in the early dark of the Fall evening.

As we pulled our coats closer before facing the brisk wind, I said, "The only problem with whatever we do about Lillian is that she's as concerned about the other residents as she is about herself. It wouldn't surprise me one bit if she refused any help if it didn't include everybody."

"That sounds just like Lillian," Hazel Marie said as she opened the car door. "She's so good-hearted. But my goodness, Miss Julia, I don't think even you could take care of all of them."

"No, and I don't intend to," I said, pulling up my seat so Little Lloyd could get out of the back. "Jump on out, Little Lloyd." Then, looking at Hazel Marie across the roof of the car, I went on, "If all those people're put out on the street, it'll be a matter for the whole town to take on."

Little Lloyd ran up beside his mother and took her hand as we walked toward the soon-to-be-evicted crowd. I hoped to goodness that more people had turned out for the meeting than the dozen or so I saw standing around. Lillian caught sight of us, her face lighting up at seeing Little Lloyd.

"Why, baby," she called as she came toward us, "what you doin' here? Lillian so glad to see you. Miss Hazel Marie, I didn't 'spect to see you. Where you leave Mr. Pickens?"

"I just plain left him, Lillian," Hazel Marie said. Then,

seeing Lillian's frown, she went on. "But don't worry about him. We're worried about you."

"Lillian," I said, holding down my hair as the breeze blew it first one way, then the other. "I thought your whole church would turn out for this. I hope most of them're inside."

"No'm, look like it jus' us and the reverend. And you all, an' Mr. Sam, if he come," she said, a look of worry sweeping across her face.

"Did you get everybody here?" I was anxious for all the evictees to show a united front.

"Yessum, they all here. Come on over an' meet 'em."

We followed her into the small yard in front of the church, as I thought that I'd just as soon go on in and get out of the wind.

Lillian introduced us to several of her neighbors as they began walking up the concrete steps and into the church. They were friendly, but not overly so, which seemed appropriate to me considering their immediate concerns. In their place, I would've found it hard to welcome anybody, much less somebody who'd never darkened their door before. I was struck by the fact that not a one of them appeared to be under fifty. Many were white-haired and bent with age, one leaning on a cane and another trying to manage the steps with a walker. Some, though, seemed as strong and healthy as Lillian. They all looked worried.

Walking into the small sanctuary, I followed the others down the center aisle, hearing the soft shuffle of their feet and the tap of a cane on the uncarpeted floor. I glanced around at the furnishings, trying not to appear too curious. It was not what you'd call elegant or luxurious; more like bare and serviceable. The walls were painted white with dark shellacked wood trim that matched the pews. Three black wrought-iron sconces lined each side of the sanctuary.

There was a piano in the front with—Lord help us—a set of drums beside it.

As I slipped into a pew beside Lillian, I looked up at a figure of Christ painted on the wall behind the metal chairs in the choir. It was not my practice to be critical of other people's ways of worshipping, but I have to say that this picture had been rendered by a somewhat wobbly hand. Most surprising to me was the deep coloring of the skin tones. We Presbyterians don't hold with painted images, yet I'd seen many pictures and paintings of the Christ in Sunday School pamphlets and in Little Lloyd's Bible story book. All those pictures showed him as fair, some going as far as making him blond and blue-eyed, which everybody knows is far from accurate. But the more I looked at the figure on the AME Zion church wall, the more taken with it I was. It certainly didn't depict a fair-skinned individual, but neither was it real dark, either. Sort of Mediterranean, I guess, which, come to think of it, was probably closer to the real thing than any picture I'd ever seen before.

My thoughts of artistic license came to a sudden halt as the Reverend Abernathy stepped to the front of the church, standing below the podium where he was close to the pews. It pained me to see how frail he looked. He was thin and small in stature, with a lined face and a ruffle of white hair around his head. He had always seemed to me to be in need of a stout arm to lean on, but I remembered that he'd not looked any healthier at Binkie and Coleman's wedding. And he'd handled that just fine.

The Reverend Abernathy looked around at the meager showing, wondering, I should expect, why the rest of his congregation hadn't turned out in support. I was certainly wondering that.

Before speaking, the reverend lifted his hand to quiet the

soft murmuring as the people talked among themselves. Worried faces quickly turned toward him, some with hopeful gazes, others looking as if they'd already lost everything they had. Which they just about had.

"Before we begin, I'd like to extend a warm welcome to our visitors," he said in his quiet, unassuming way. He smiled at Hazel Marie, Little Lloyd and me. "Now let us look to the Lord for the guidance we all gonna need."

We bowed our heads as the reverend offered thanks for any number of blessings before finally asking that these precious lambs be led to make good and wise decisions. It was very close to a Presbyterian prayer in its length and coverage of every contingency anybody could think of.

When he allowed us to look up and get on with the business at hand, I glanced around to see if Sam had slipped in.

"Where you think he is?" Lillian whispered to me, for she was looking around for him, too.

"I don't have any idea," I whispered back. "But I don't like it, Lillian. I hate to think that it's slipped his mind."

She sighed as her face drooped in disappointment. I patted her hand as an elderly man took his place beside the reverend and began recounting what everybody already knew, namely, that Clarence Gibbs was evicting everybody and they didn't know what they were going to do.

A woman's voice interrupted him. "I think we need ourselves a good lawyer, is what I think."

"Now, sister," Reverend Abernathy cautioned. "Lawyers cost money, and that's the one thing we don't have."

Lillian gathered herself, took a few deep breaths, and, taking hold of the pew in front, pulled herself to her feet. I saw her coat trembling in her nervousness at speaking in public. "Reverend," she said, "Mr. Sam Murdoch say he gonna be here to help us, an' I don't know why he not here.

I already talked to him, an' he say he won't charge us. An' he'll help us, I know he will, 'cause he always a friend to the downtrodden."

Having had her say, she sat, and I put my hand on hers. Such loyalty, I thought. Then thought that I could wring Sam's neck for getting her hopes up, only to disappoint her by forgetting where he was supposed to be.

"Thank you, Sister Lillian," the reverend said. "We appreciate your remarks, and we look for Brother Sam to come walkin' in any minute and give us the help he's known far and wide for."

As I was mourning Sam's decline, the door at the back of the pews flew open, and a gust of wind blew through the church. I turned with a gasp and saw Sam closing the door behind him. Everybody turned to stare at him, and I thought to myself that I'd never seen him look so frazzled. His white hair was windblown, his lined face drawn, and his shoulders slumped with weariness. I started to rise as my heart went out to him in his confused state.

"Reverend," Sam said, as several others rose from their seats. "Sorry I'm late, but I've just come from meeting with Mr. Gibbs and, as hard as I tried, I couldn't get anywhere with him. He's bringing in the bulldozers and backhoes tomorrow, and they'll start work the day after. He's dead-set on bringing those houses down."

~ *Chapter 7*

Lillian gave out a low moan and leaned against me, as a chorus of anguished cries and calls to Jesus rose from the congregation. Sam walked down the aisle toward the reverend, touching Lillian's shoulder as he passed our pew.

"Reverend," Sam said, nodding to him. Then he turned to face us, holding up his hands for quiet. "Folks, let me talk to you a minute. I've tried everything I know to get Mr. Gibbs to delay clearing that property, but he says he's waited long enough. He wants you all out by tomorrow. Now, wait," he cautioned, as several people began to cry out again, and some moved toward the aisles to leave. "There's nothing you can do tonight, but we do need to talk about what you're going to do tomorrow."

The Reverend Abernathy started shaking his head. "This just bad doin's, Mr. Sam. Where these poor souls gonna go? All us here at the church been tryin' to find places for 'em to move to, but they few and far between."

"First of all," Sam said, as I marvelled that he was able to speak in such sensible terms. In fact, I was beginning to feel quite proud of his grasp of the situation. "I might've been able to get an injunction against that eviction order, if there'd been enough time. But even if we'd started earlier, it would've been a long shot. As you know, sentiment in this county is pretty strong on property owners' rights. I've tried appealing to Gibbs's sense of community responsibility, but I'll be honest with you; I didn't get very far."

"Oh, Lawd," one old man quavered. "Can't somebody do something?"

Sam shook his head. "If I'd had more time . . . maybe we could've done something. As it is now, Gibbs is making plans to put up a water-bottling plant on the site."

"A water plant!" a voice called out, echoing my thought. What in the world would Clarence Gibbs do with a water plant?

"Water-*bottling* plant," Sam clarified. "Seems he's found a spring up on the ridge that he thinks has commercial possibilities."

One man—it might have been Mr. Wills—started laughing, and he kept on at it so long that it began to infect the rest of us, a welcome relief from the rampant sadness. "Mr. Sam," he finally managed to get out as he struggled to his feet, "They been stories 'bout that ole spring ever since I was a boy, an' long before that. My granddaddy used to go get him a sip ever' now an' again, but too much of it'll fly back on you. I could tell some stories, uh-huh, I could. It strong stuff, so just a taste be all a man need to keep on a-goin' strong, don't matter how old he is. It keep on buildin' up his strength. 'Scuse me, ladies, I jus' tellin' what I heard. Never tried it myself. Never had no need to."

He sat down, still chuckling to himself. But another man chimed in. "I heard them tales, too, an' lots of people b'lieve 'em. You reckon he make a go of it, Mr. Sam?"

"Sounds pretty risky to me," Sam said, smiling. "I wouldn't want to invest in it."

Lillian leaned over and whispered to me. "I heard 'bout that spring, an' ever' man here an' a lot more's tried it out, I don't care what they say."

Hazel Marie leaned across me to ask, "Does it work?"

"Nobody say it do, an' nobody say it don't," Lillian said, covering her mouth to hide a smile. "They jus' so tired from trompin' 'round up on that ridge, they have to lay down an' rest when they get back."

A heavy-set woman stood up, ignoring the laughter around her. "Well," she said, her flower-laden hat quivering on her head. "All this talk 'bout springwater's not helpin' us right now. Don't look like nobody care but us."

"I wouldn't care myself, if I didn't live there," the woman with the walker said. "Them houses oughtta come down long time ago. They awful to live in, but they's nowhere else to go."

"Now, Sister Pearl," the reverend said. "You know the whole church been prayin' 'bout this matter. So don't you worry, the Lord gonna provide."

"He better get busy with it, then," a bent-over man said as he leaned on his walker. "If Mr. Sam right, we be beddin' down on the street tomorrow night."

Sam stepped up again and said, "That's exactly what we need to concentrate on, Mr. Washington. We need to find places, even if they're temporary, for each one of you and get you out of the way of those 'dozers. Now, how many of you have someone you can move in with for a while?"

The Reverend Abernathy said, "Pay attention now. Le's get ourselves organized an' see who needs what. I'm gonna start with one end of Willow Lane and go 'round to the end house on the other side. Sister Flora, you live in the first house on the left, don't you? You have some place you can move to?"

"I can go stay with my auntie," Sister Flora said. "But neither one of us too happy about it."

"We'll try to do better for you," the reverend said. "All right, who's next to you?"

"That's me," a man with a fuzz of white hair around his head said. "I live there, but look like not for long."

"You have somewhere to go, Brother Thomas?" the reverend said. "No? Mr. Sam, would you be so kind as to keep a record of who's going to need a place?"

Sam nodded and pulled a notepad and pen from his pocket and began writing.

People leaned toward each other and began talking among themselves, trying to decide where they could go. From the frowns and head shakes, it looked as if a goodly number of empty beds would have to be found before the sun set again.

The Reverend Abernathy said, "I can take four people, if two don't mind sleepin' double. An' I know we can call on Deacon Robert and Deacon Henry, they both got extra rooms. I need to get on the telephone an' see who else can take in somebody. I'll do that right now, Mr. Sam, if you'll keep on managin' the meetin'."

I could feel the anxiety level in the church rise as voices increased in volume. Some of the women dabbed at their eyes with lace handkerchiefs, and one man blew his nose long and loud.

As the reverend left to begin telephoning, Sam looked out at those upturned faces and said, "We don't want anybody to be left without a place to stay, so we need to know where you'll be. I can take some of you at my house."

"I got chil'ren in town," one man said in a mournful voice. "But I hope I don't have to stay long, they crowded enough as it is."

"I'll pass this notepad around," Sam said. "All of you who have a place to go, write your name and a phone number where we can reach you. Everybody else can be assigned to the extra beds that've been offered."

Sam looked over at me, raising his eyebrows. I nodded, knowing he was asking about Lillian. He jotted something on his pad, then began passing it around.

"Mr. Sam?" Sister Pearl said, as she stood up to get his attention. "You reckon they's insurance on our houses?"

Sam considered the question, but from the look on his face I could see the answer coming. "Mr. Gibbs may well have insurance on every one of them, but I'm afraid that will only benefit him. If you have individual homeowners' policies, though, that might cover the loss of any personal possessions that you can't get out. I'll have to look into it."

"I got burial insurance," she said. "Do that cover anything?"

"Sister," a hefty man in the front pew said loudly, "the only thing that'll cover is *you* when you pass over."

A few rueful grins and head shakes agreed with him.

It was at that point that I realized that Sam was dressed in his normal retirement clothing—khaki trousers, a flannel shirt, and a barn jacket that'd seen better days—with not a stitch of leather on him. It struck me at the same time that he also seemed his old self again—calm and in control. I just hoped it would last, for every person in the sanctuary, including me, was looking to him to tell us what to do.

"What you reckon them 'dozers gonna do, Mr. Sam?" the quavery-voiced man called out.

"I'm afraid they're going to push down all the houses, Mr. Wills. Then they'll load up what's left and clear the land."

"Can't we save anything?" That was from Sister Flora, I

think. "I mean, what we put in the houses ourselves? I put in a new water heater las' year, an' it not near paid for yet."

"That somethin' Mr. Gibbs oughtta've done," a man's loud voice called out. "He leave everything up to us, then snatch it out from under us. I tell you, anything be better'n what we been livin' with."

I had my arm around Lillian, feeling her tremble next to me, and Little Lloyd had come to sit on her other side. Hazel Marie was dabbing at her face as she mumbled to herself, "This has just been a terrible day. First, J. D., and now this."

"We'll get the water heater out for you," Sam said to Sister Flora as he walked closer to the pews to answer the question. "I called several people before I came tonight, and we're going to meet over there first thing tomorrow. We'll have some trucks, and we'll help you load up. The big problem is where we're going to store your things." He stopped for a minute, then went on as if it hurt him to say what had to be said. "I want you all to know that there're a lot of people in this town who want to help."

"Mr. Sam?" a white-headed man asked as he raised his hand. "What about that graveyard up a ways by the spring?"

Before Sam could answer, another voice chimed in. "Oh, Law, we 'bout to forget about that. I got a great-great-granddaddy buried up there. What I gonna do with him?"

Sam studied the matter for a minute. "I know where that is. There's, what? Some eight or ten graves? Got a fence around them, I believe."

"Splinters an' scraps!" a woman suddenly called out, a sob in her voice. "Mr. Gibbs jus' makin' kindlin' outta our houses an' diggin' up our bones!"

Then she got up and began pushing her way toward the aisle.

That started a rush of hysteria as another woman threw her arms out wide and collapsed in the aisle with an unnerving scream. The reverend hurried back in as the commotion began to get out of hand.

Several of the calmer ones went to the women, trying to settle them down. They helped the one on the floor back to her seat, then stood around patting and fanning her.

"Now, sister," Reverend Abernathy said, ushering the first woman back into a pew, "this is not helpin' anything. Jus' take your seats, everybody, and work with us here. Le's us thank the Lord for his goodness toward us, an' le's us think about what we can do to take care of each an' every one of you in this time of need."

The woman crumpled up, crying her heart out, as they finally got her and the wild-eyed man seated again. I began to tear up myself at the thought of what these people were losing.

I searched in my pocketbook for the Kleenex I always kept handy and passed some to Lillian and Hazel Marie. Then I dabbed at my own eyes.

"Listen, folks," Sam said, holding up his hands to try to bring some order to the proceedings. "There're laws that protect cemeteries, especially old ones. Gibbs can't do a thing to those graves, unless he digs them up and reburies them in a designated site. And if he does, it has to be done in a respectful way. Those graves will not be desecrated, I promise you that."

Sam's promise seemed to have a calming effect, but I could feel Lillian still trembling as I slipped my arm around her shoulders.

"Lillian," I whispered to her. "I know it's bad now, but we'll work something out."

She shook her head, as tears welled up in her eyes. "I

didn't think it come to this, Miss Julia. I been wantin' to move, but I ought not be pushed out by them bulldozers."

"I know, but we're not going to be sitting on our hands," I said, trying to encourage her. "You'll have a home, Lillian, and in the meantime, I intend to see what can be done about this travesty."

She squeezed my hand in response, as Hazel Marie leaned across me and said, "You're coming home with us tonight, Lillian. Isn't she, Miss Julia?"

"Of course she is. She doesn't need to be by herself." I was about to continue, but Sam began talking again.

"Now, folks," he said, "a whole bunch of people're going to show up in the morning to move you out, so be sure you label all your boxes and furniture, whatever you have, so it won't get misplaced."

"Oh, Lord," Lillian whispered. "It gonna be like startin' all over again. All my flowers be gone, an' my porch, an' my neighbors."

I tightened my arm around her shoulders and whispered to Hazel Marie, "Let's get her out of here. Little Lloyd, slip up there and tell Sam we're going home, and for him to come on over if he can."

As the child tiptoed up the aisle to give my message to Sam, Hazel Marie and I stepped to either side of Lillian and walked toward the door. Lillian stared straight ahead with a blank expression on her face.

As I marched down the aisle, I determined to turn the tables on Clarence Gibbs, just as he'd threatened to turn these people out of their homes and turn long-dead bones out of their resting places. And for a water-bottling plant, of all things. It perturbed me so bad I almost stumbled going out the door.

The three of us walked out onto the steps of the church

as Little Lloyd slipped out beside us, closing the door behind him. Gusts of wind whipped at our coats and hair, and I thought, what a terrible time of the year to be homeless.

I thought of Clarence Gibbs, who was probably tucked up in a warm bed in a mortgage-free house without a worry to his name. I wanted to snatch him out of bed and shake him till his teeth rattled for what he was doing to these people.

By the time we got in the car, I was so unsettled that it took me three tries to get the thing turned around and headed away from the church and toward my house.

Chapter 8

"Let's take her to the living room," I said to Hazel Marie when we got in the house. Little Lloyd held the door open for us, then ran ahead to turn on the lights. Lillian, still with that blank stare on her face, had not said a word all the way home. She'd just sat in the passenger seat, which Hazel Marie'd insisted she take, and looked straight ahead.

I figured she was in shock, which is where I'd be in her situation. We sat her in the Victorian chair beside the fireplace, and I turned on the gas logs to warm the room.

"Her hands're freezing," Hazel Marie said. "Lloyd, honey, run get that blanket off the foot of my bed."

"Just sit back, Lillian," I said. "You've had a shock and you need to rest." I took one end of the blanket that Little Lloyd brought and, together, we draped it around her shoulders and tucked it in tight.

Hazel Marie took off her own coat and laid it across Lillian's lap and legs. Then she straightened up and said, "I've got to call J. D. and tell him about this. He loves Lillian to death, you know."

I glanced at Little Lloyd and, as our eyes met, we exchanged knowing smiles. Hazel Marie didn't notice, which was just as well.

"And she needs something hot to drink," Hazel Marie went on as she headed for the kitchen. "I'll put on some hot chocolate while I'm calling."

"That's a good idea," I said, smoothing my hand over Lillian's blanket-covered arm. "We could all use some, I expect."

"Here, Miss Lillian," Little Lloyd said, sliding a footstool near her chair. "Put your feet on this." When she didn't move, he lifted one foot at a time and placed them on the stool. Then he pulled one end of his mother's coat down over her feet.

Hazel Marie returned with a tray loaded with mugs of hot chocolate. Putting down the tray, she took one of the mugs to Lillian and held it to her mouth. "Drink this, Lillian," she said. "It'll make you feel better. J. D.'s on his way, and he said for you to sit tight and not worry about a thing."

I couldn't help but roll my eyes at the arrogance of the man, but I didn't say anything. Besides, we could use all the help we could get, even if Mr. Pickens's help was unlikely to live up to its billing.

The three of us hovered over Lillian, patting and tucking and mumbling comforting words as she sipped the hot chocolate that Hazel Marie kept holding to her mouth.

"Now, Lillian," Hazel Marie crooned, "You're going to have all the help you need to finish packing. I've moved enough to know what a job it is. J. D. will be there if he can, and Sam, and Coleman, and whoever else they can get. We'll have you settled in here before you know it, won't we, Miss Julia?"

"We certainly will," I said, leaning over and peering closely at Lillian to see if she was looking any better. "Just don't worry about a thing tonight, and in the morning we'll go over to Willow Lane and move you out."

"You think she ought to go back?" Hazel Marie asked, poking the mug at Lillian's mouth again. "I mean, it might be too much for her, to see the actual moving. Especially with those big machines coming in to tear everything down."

"We'll see how she feels in the morning," I said. "Little Lloyd, are her feet warm? Maybe we ought to scoot the chair closer to the fire."

Lillian began squirming in the chair, and then, freeing one hand, she threw the blanket back and turned her head away from the mug. "Y'all keep talkin' 'bout me like I ain't even here an' treatin' me like I'm sick or something," she said, trying to shrug the blanket from her shoulders. "Jus' gimme some room so I can get outta this blanket. It about to strangle me to death."

We stepped back and watched as Lillian untangled herself and pushed the footstool away. As she straightened up, I think we all breathed easier, for her face was taking on some life and she was looking like her old self again.

"Well," she said with a heavy sigh as she leaned her elbows on her knees, "not no use cryin' over spilt milk. If I knowed some place to live, I jus' soon be shed of that ole shack, anyway. Though I don't know where any of us gonna go."

"Don't worry about that, Lillian," I said with a lot more assurance than I felt. "Everybody has a place to stay for the next few days at least. Then we'll have to regroup and see what can be done. Hazel Marie," I went on, turning to her, "we need to get one of the banks to open a special account so people can send in contributions. That's the way this sort of thing is done, isn't it?"

"Yes, ma'am, they do that all the time. The television stations are forever announcing one fund or another to benefit people who've had some tragedy, like a fire or a sickness of some kind. And I think turning people out of the homes they've lived in for years would certainly qualify as a tragedy."

"So do I. And if anybody disagrees, send them to me. I'll get that started in the morning and make sure the radio and television people know about it."

Lillian raised her head and looked at me. "I don't know as I like bein' talked about on the radio and the TV. Sound like I be askin' for charity."

"Now, Lillian," I said firmly, "they certainly won't mention any names. Besides, it would be for everybody who lives on Willow Lane because they're going to need a lot of help. So just put aside any prideful thoughts about charity, and let's start thinking of ways to raise money to house the homeless."

"I know one way," Little Lloyd said. "The young people's group at church can have a car wash. We raised fifty dollars the last time we had one."

"Oh, honey," Hazel Marie said, "that's a wonderful idea. Everybody needs to pitch in, and a car wash would be just the thing to get a fund started."

I smiled at Little Lloyd, gratified that he wanted to help, but I knew fifty dollars wouldn't be a drop in the bucket.

"Lillian," I said. "We ought to call your daughters and let them know what's going on. They'll be worried if they can't get you on the phone." I stopped and thought for a minute. "They may well want you to come live with them." Although that was the last thing I wanted her to do, and I don't think it was for purely selfish reasons. I'd miss her something awful if she went to live up North.

"Yessum, I call 'em tomorrow an' tell 'em. But I can't live up in that cold country, an' anyway they got all they can do to take care of they chil'ren an' they ownselves."

Then she leaned back in the chair and closed her eyes. She pulled the blanket back up around her shoulders, and I got worried about her all over again.

"Are you cold?" I asked.

"Yessum, I guess I am," she said without opening her eyes. "This whole thing jus' fly all over me again. It make me glad to move, but scared 'bout where I move to."

Turning to Hazel Marie, I said, "We need to get her to bed. I wish I had something to help her sleep because this is going to be running through her head all night long."

"I wish . . . ," Hazel Marie started, but stopped as we heard footsteps on the front porch. "Oh, maybe that's J. D." She hurried to the door, her face lit with expectancy.

Well, yes, it was, and he came in, windblown and frowning with concern. "Hey, sweetheart," he said to Hazel Marie, with what I thought was a little hesitancy, as if he weren't sure if she was still his sweetheart or not. He reached out a hand to her, but she stepped back from him.

"J. D.," Hazel Marie said—in a somewhat stand-offish tone, I thought, in spite of her earlier eagerness to welcome him in. "We're so glad you're here. Lillian needs your help."

"Miss Julia," he said, casting a worried glance at me with those black eyes of his and nodding as he walked over to Lillian. Lord, I couldn't help but look at him with narrowed eyes. All those women, I thought to myself, and he doesn't look a bit different.

Mr. Pickens brushed Little Lloyd's shoulder with his hand as he went past him. "Miss Lillian," he said, kneeling by her chair and taking her hand in his. "I'm so sorry to hear about your trouble, but you know what they say." He gave her a crooked grin. "Everybody ought to move about every five years, just to clear out the junk."

I frowned and opened my mouth to rebuke him, since

she didn't need to hear such nonsense at a time like this. But I restrained myself as Lillian smiled at him and patted his hand.

Then, just as unexpectedly, she covered her eyes with her hand and moaned, "Oh, Jesus, what I done to deserve this?"

"Not one thing, Lillian," I said. "It's all Clarence Gibbs's fault, which he is certainly going to hear about from me and everybody else in town. Now, Mr. Pickens, we think she needs to be in bed, if you'll excuse us."

"Sure thing," he said, getting to his feet, "but she needs a little something else first. Don't want her lying awake all night worrying herself to death."

"That's what we were just saying," Hazel Marie said. "Did you . . . ?"

"I did," Mr. Pickens said, and drew a small flat bottle of brownish liquid from the pocket of his coat. "Now, Miss Julia, before you get on your high horse, this is for medicinal purposes only, and I happen to know that the Bible recommends it."

I opened my mouth again to refute him but, on second thought, decided against it since I was well acquainted with Paul's advice to Timothy concerning his stomach problems. I was also well aware of the dangers in taking verses out of context, which untold numbers of people are inclined to do when they want something they oughtn't have.

But this didn't seem to fall in that category, so I said, "Well, Mr. Pickens, you might be surprised to learn that I am not averse to the proper and cautious use of alcoholic mixtures. I think a teaspoon or two in some sweetened hot water is certainly called for in this case."

"I agree, Miss Julia," Hazel Marie said, taking the bottle from Mr. Pickens. "I can mix a hot toddy that'll make anybody sleep like a baby." She patted Lillian's shoulder, as I wondered where she'd learned so much about the properties of alcohol. "Lillian, this is going to fix you up."

She headed for the kitchen, bottle in hand, with Mr. Pickens right behind her. To be sure she fixed it right, I expect.

"Little Lloyd," I said, concerned at what lesson he was learning about the use of strong spirits, "when the ox is in the ditch, it takes unusual measures to get it out."

"Ma'am?"

"Never mind," I said, not exactly sure of what I'd said, myself.

~ *Chapter 9*

Sam never came by, in spite of the fact that I waited up for him until almost midnight, long after the others had gone to bed. On the other hand, I'd thought we'd never get rid of Mr. Pickens. He'd lingered, trying to sweet-talk Hazel Marie, but she was having none of it. She kept slipping away from him, pretending not to notice his efforts, and finally telling him that he needed to be on his way.

She was playing hard-to-get, which I'd always heard was the way to keep a man's interest. But, considering the fact that she'd just left his bed and board, it seemed a little late for that tactic.

But Hazel Marie's ill-considered living conditions seemed a minor worry in the face of Lillian's problem. I sat by the fire in the quiet house, turning the possibilities over in my mind and trying to tell myself that something could still be done. I just didn't know what. That was the sort of thing I'd ordinarily depend on Sam for, but where was he when I needed him? Nowhere to be found, that's where.

I settled back in my chair with a sigh, knowing that it was all up to me. I knew I'd see to a new home for Lillian, but that wouldn't ease her pain at losing what she had, even if she knew it wasn't worth wanting.

Trying to keep my spirits up, I kept reminding myself that the big earth- and house-moving machines Clarence Gibbs was bringing in hadn't been fired up yet. Something might still be done to save those houses. My spirits didn't stay up long, though, for surely Sam would've called or come by to reassure Lillian if he'd thought of some last-minute legal tactic.

After checking the doors and turning off the gas logs and the lights, I trudged up the stairs to bed, trying to put aside my concern for Sam and focus on the problem I could do something about. One thing I knew for certain: the whole town needed to turn its hand to helping those needy people.

The churches, I thought, as I readied myself for bed. There were dozens of churches in the county, and more forming every day, it seemed like. Church members in Abbot County were a testy lot, quick to take offense and not at all averse to forming a new congregation at the drop of a hat. It didn't take much to set them off, either. A few would get mad at a preacher and try to run him off. If he wouldn't budge, then out they'd go to a new meeting place. Others would be led out by a preacher so exercised by the waywardness of a convention, an assembly or a committee that he'd hear the voice of the Lord calling him to raise money for another church building, free of liberal influences. Many of them declared that they were returning to the ways of the apostles, without ever considering the fact that the apostles never put one brick on top of another, much less installed stained glass windows or hooked on lapel microphones.

Perhaps the Reverend Abernathy would be willing to approach the churches. Maybe it could be arranged for him to fill a few pulpits in town on certain Sundays and present our case. A special offering could be taken up, although I knew that special offerings rarely brought in more than a dollar a family.

I fell asleep on that discouraging thought, just exhausted by the emotional distress I'd thought would keep me awake all night. But I awoke the next morning with an idea of how to get the town involved in a fund for Willow Lane. It was a grand idea, but it would take a lot of work, which I was most willing to do.

But first, it needed to be decided just what that fund would be funding. Maybe it should be called a rebuilding fund; if those houses were so run-down that the town council had to condemn them, then we could just build new ones or remodel the old ones to bring them up to code. But I certainly didn't intend to raise money to do anything on property belonging to Clarence Gibbs because everything would still belong to him, without a cent of his own being put into it.

The bottom line was that we needed to buy that property, then decide what to do about the houses. We needed to make an offer to purchase, and make it attractive enough to tempt the present owner.

I was brought up short, though, thinking of Clarence Gibbs's plan to commercialize the area. A plant to bottle water, no matter how special it was supposed to be, just seemed ridiculous to me.

I studied the problem as I tiptoed past the room where Lillian still slept. And no telling how long she'd be down, considering what Hazel Marie and Mr. Pickens had stirred together for her. By the time she'd finished one glass, Mr. Pickens had been right there with another, urging her to drink up, saying it was good for what ailed her. I'd wanted to caution him, but figured he knew how much of a dose she needed better than I did.

I started the coffee and kept on thinking about Clarence Gibbs. Lillian had said that he'd been tramping around, measuring and surveying the lay of the land. He could've been testing the volume and taste of that spring, or studying building sites. For all I knew, he could've been showing the property to a prospective buyer, the thought of which brought me up short again. If that was the case, I needed to get to him before he listed it with a realtor.

Lord, if Clarence Gibbs would entertain the notion of selling, maybe I could give him a down payment that would hold it until the town came through with enough to buy it.

I was more than willing to do that, but it just didn't seem to me that I ought to be the only one to help. Besides, I already had all the rental property I could handle and, believe me, it was a constant worry. If it wasn't one thing it was another, what with a roof leaking, walls needing paint, or a dead tree about to fall.

As soon as the coffee stopped perking, I poured a cup and turned around to see Little Lloyd coming through the door, still in his pajamas. As usual, his hair was standing on end, and he looked as if he needed coffee as badly as I did.

"Good morning," I said, although I don't much like cheeriness early in the day. I poured a cup for him and took it to the table, where I sat across from him.

He managed a small smile, which I took as a return greeting, and we sat in silence while trying to get fully awake.

"Little Lloyd," I said, setting my cup in the saucer, "I guess we have to face the painful truth this morning and go help Lillian clear out her house. I just hate the thought of it."

"I do, too," he said. "I dreamed about empty houses all

night long. I even got up one time and came downstairs to be sure we still lived here."

"Well, my goodness," I said, struck again at how sensitive the child was. Of course, he'd been moved from pillar to post enough times to make him feel a little unsettled. "I didn't hear you at all."

"I tiptoed so I wouldn't wake anybody up." He turned his cup in the saucer, then went on. "What're we going to do to help Miss Lillian and all those people?"

"I've been thinking about that. And the first thing I'm going to do is call Clarence Gibbs and see if he'll sell that property. If he will, then we need to think about how to raise the money to buy it." I thought about that for a minute, then said, "Of course, we'd then have to worry about how to fix the houses on it. But one worry at a time is enough."

"Maybe we could put some trailers on it," Little Lloyd said. Then, seeing my frown, he came up with another idea. "I know what we can do! Why don't we see if President Jimmy Carter and his carpenters would come build the houses? I think he likes to help people who need a place to live."

"That's an excellent idea," I said, surprised that I hadn't thought of it myself. "And we'll certainly pursue it. Well, on second thought, I think the people they build those houses for have to help with the building. From what I saw at the meeting last night, most of them wouldn't be able to hit a nail with a sledgehammer. But it's still a good thought, Little Lloyd. Maybe," I went on, musing over possibilities, "maybe there're individuals or groups in town who'd sponsor a tenant and help get a particular house built.

"Thurlow Jones, for instance!" I said with sudden inspiration. "Lord knows he's got the money, and this is just the sort of thing that might interest him. Although, with him, you never know."

"I don't mean to be disrespectful," Little Lloyd said, "but he's kinda strange, isn't he?"

"Well, he has his quirks, that's for sure. Still, he's worth approaching for a sizeable donation to our efforts. Although I'd hate to be the one to do the approaching."

"I bet you could talk him into it, if anybody could," he said, and I smiled because I thought I could, too. Then he propped his chin on his hand and went on. "Miss Julia? Do you think that spring they were talking about really can renew a man's strength?"

"Lord, Little Lloyd," I said, my mind going ninety miles an hour, trying to think how to answer him. I started to tell him to ask his mother about things like that, but that would've just piqued his interest even more. I just had to give him a straight answer and hope he'd let it drop. "Don't pay any attention to old wives' tales like that, or old men's tales, either."

"Well, I was just wondering if it would make your muscles bigger."

"I sincerely doubt it," I said, hoping he didn't have the specific muscles that those old men were referring to in mind. There are some things I just couldn't discuss, regardless of the company. "Listen, people're always looking for a quick fix and, believe me, they're not going to find it in water bubbling up from a cow pasture."

He grinned and said, "*I* sure wouldn't want to drink it." Then he got up from the table and put his cup and saucer in the sink. "I think I need some cereal. You want some, too?"

"No, thank you, but I'll fix us some toast. I declare," I said as I rose from the table, "we're going to need all the nourishment we can get to face this day. The biggest problem, Little

Lloyd, is going to be getting the whole town behind any kind of plans we come up with. Abbotsville is not noted for the kind of local charity we're thinking about. Everybody gives to the United Fund and figures they've done their civic duty."

Little Lloyd put down the cereal box and looked me straight in the eye. "Will it be because all those people on Willow Lane are black?"

"Oh, Lord, child," I said, just stunned at his prescience. "I hope not, but if it is, then all the more reason for us to show them that charity begins at home, regardless of who happens to live in that home."

I got the butter dish and a jar of grape jelly from the refrigerator, still thinking of the ugly problem that Little Lloyd had brought to the fore.

"You know," I said, turning from the open refrigerator door, "I really don't think that who those people are will affect the town's generosity. No, I think it's more likely that some will resent being asked for contributions of any kind, for any reason. There're some people who believe what they call hand-outs are inherently wrong and encourage divorce, delinquency and a general deterioration of the American way of life. Until, that is, they need some help themselves. Then they're quick to hold their own hands out."

I pushed the refrigerator door closed with my hip, almost dropping the butter dish in the process. "That attitude, Little Lloyd," I went on, "is what we have to overcome."

"Well, my word, Miss Julia. How're we going to do that?"

"It's what I've been studying on all night," I told him. "And I have at least one idea, which I'll tell you about when your mother comes down. I want to see what she thinks about it."

Chapter 10

Hazel Marie came into the kitchen dressed for the day in a dark green pantsuit with a matching sweater. Her blonde hair was pulled back and up, making her look trim and fashionable—a far cry from the way she'd looked before I'd taken a hand in her shopping habits. The 18-karat gold earrings and necklace didn't hurt her overall appearance, either, but none of it looked suitable for a moving day.

"Morning," she said, patting Little Lloyd's head as she passed him on her way to the coffee pot. "Lillian told me last night when J. D. and I took her upstairs that she'd been in such a turmoil that she'd packed up all of her clothes, and Coleman already loaded them in a truck he rented. So I'm going shopping for her this morning, but I'll need to make a list of the basics. Will you help me, Miss Julia, so I won't forget anything?"

"Of course, I will. But you mean she doesn't know where her clothes are?"

"Coleman must've taken them out along with the other boxes," Hazel Marie said as she reached for a cup and saucer. "And she doesn't want to ask him to unload everything to find the right box."

"Well, I wouldn't get too much if I were you, since we'll have to guess at sizes. Unless you think we should wake her up and ask her what she wears."

"I don't think so." Hazel Marie put a slice of bread in the toaster and waited for it to pop up. "I looked in on her before I came downstairs and she's sleeping like a baby."

"All right, then," I said. "If you'll take Little Lloyd to school on your way, I'll stay here until she gets up. Then I'll take her to Willow Lane and be sure those men get everything."

Little Lloyd looked up from his cereal. "I'd sure like to go and see Miss Lillian's house before it's gone."

"To tell the truth," I said, "I'm not looking forward to going at all. But I know Lillian needs to be there. I don't expect it'll be the last time we'll go, Little Lloyd, so you'll get your chance later today.

"Now, Hazel Marie," I went on, "I came up with an idea last night about how we can start organizing a community effort to raise money. What do you think of having a home and garden tour?"

"You mean of this house?"

"Well, of course this house would be included. But I mean having several of the nicer homes in town open to the public. For a fee, of course. People just love to see how other people live, what they have in their homes, how they're decorated and so on. What do you think?"

Hazel Marie brought her toast and coffee to the table and sat down. Then she drummed her fingers on the table and looked thoughtful. "You know, I've always wanted to see inside the Whitaker house. If we could get that on the tour, everybody would buy tickets." She picked up the toast and bit into it. "I think it's a wonderful idea. What other houses could we get?"

"We'll need to think about that. I know a lot of people who'd love to be included, but whose houses are just not up to par."

"Oh!" Hazel Marie said, apparently having a sudden inspiration. "Let's see if we can get that real modern house with all the windows, up on the side of the mountain. Did you ever find out who's building it?"

"Some retired football player, I heard," I said. "No telling how it's decorated, since it's so stark on the outside. It doesn't appeal to me at all."

"Well, me either," Hazel Marie said. "But if a celebrity has moved to town, we ought to try to get his house on the tour. Everybody'll want to see inside, even if it's awful." She chewed a bite of toast, swallowed, and grinned. "*Especially* if it's awful. And the publicity will be wonderful. Just think, we can say something like 'Visit the home of the Home Run King.' Everybody'll buy tickets."

"Ma-ma," Little Lloyd groaned, shaking his head. "You don't have home runs in football."

"Well, you know what I mean." Hazel Marie was not in the least abashed. She turned to me and said, "What do you think about trying to get that house? It is *the* most unusual house in town, and I think it would be a great drawing card."

"I expect you're right," I said. "More's the pity. I wonder about their yard, though. The last time I had my hair done, I heard that they're bringing in huge boulders for their landscape, which doesn't strike me as any kind of design at all."

"You're going to have gardens, too?" Little Lloyd asked. "Lots of leaves falling this time of year, and not much blooming. At least, not in our yard."

The child continued to amaze me with the things he came up with. "You're absolutely right," I told him. "And the

weather might not be conducive to wandering around outside, either. But we need something else to make the tour
really attractive."

"I know!" Hazel Marie said, splashing coffee as she set
the cup down. "It's not that long until Christmas. Why don't
we see if the garden club would decorate the homes for the
holidays?"

"Oh, that's wonderful! By the time we get this organized,
it'll probably be November, and that's perfect timing. And
I know the garden club would love to do it. We'll get the
newspaper to print pictures of the winning arrangements
and decorations. Most of the club's members already know
how to plan this kind of thing. You know, they used to have
their shows in various homes back when I was a member. I
need to call Helen Stroud. I think she's still their president."

"I didn't know you were in the garden club, Miss Julia,"
Little Lloyd said. "You don't do much gardening."

"Why, I certainly do. Don't you see me out in the yard
every time Raymond comes, telling him what to do?"

"Oh, yessum, I forgot about that."

"Besides, the reason I resigned was that it got to be too
much for me. They were into all these modernistic arrangements, with one stalk and one bud sticking up out of a piece
of driftwood. And some just wanted to talk about bonsai and
such. Nothing at all that would fit into my traditional decor,
so I just lost interest." I stopped, recalling some of the meetings I'd been to. "Then there were always some who were
into growing orchids and wanted every program on that.
And LuAnne Conover had a thing about African violets, and
I hope I never have to hear another word about African violets. Besides," I went on, smiling at Little Lloyd, "around
that time you and your mother came along, and I decided
I'd rather grow little boys than flowers any day. Especially

African violets, which always need more water, or less; I never could get it right."

Lillian pushed through the swinging door, drawing our attention. She looked considerably the worse for the wear, her hair frizzy and standing out from her head and the dress she'd worn to last night's meeting misbuttoned so that it hung crooked and off-center. Her eyes were puffy and red-rimmed, as if she'd not had enough sleep. But if the snoring I'd heard during the night was any indication, she'd had plenty.

"Y'all want some breakfast?" she asked, her hand reaching for the back of a chair to steady herself.

"We're having it," I said, getting up to lead her to the table. "It's you who needs feeding. Sit down here before you fall."

Little Lloyd jumped up to get her a cup of coffee, and Hazel Marie started two pieces of toast.

"You feel all right, Miss Lillian?" Little Lloyd asked as he put the coffee in front of her. "You don't look so good."

Trust a child to speak from the heart and tell the truth, for Lillian was nowhere near the neatly combed and pressed person she usually was. In fact, I'd never seen her in such an untidy state.

"I got a real bad headache," she said, leaning her head on one hand while pushing away the coffee cup with the other. "An' dizzy, my Lord, I might never get myself straightened out."

"You need some aspirin," Hazel Marie said, a tiny smile playing around her mouth, which I thought entirely inappropriate. "I'll get you some, and I think there's some tomato juice in the pantry. Little Lloyd, would you look for it and put some ice in a glass, while I get the aspirin?"

"You've had a shock," I told Lillian. "And it's no wonder you're feeling under the weather."

"I feel worse'n that," she mumbled.

"I expect you do. We're all feeling the effects. But Hazel Marie's going to get you some clothes, and when you feel up to it, I'll take you home for your last-minute things. Who knows, Lillian, you might enjoy moving to a new place, and all this anxiety will've been for nothing."

I stopped then, realizing that I was sounding like a Pollyanna, which was not like me at all. If there was one thing I'd prided myself on ever since Wesley Lloyd had been gone, it was seeing things as they are and speaking out on them when necessary. There's nothing worse, to my way of thinking, than someone who puts a happy face on reality and goes through life in a hypocritical haze.

I know what I'm talking about because I'd been one of those people for most of my life. But no longer, because if you can't face reality yourself, sooner or later somebody'll come along and shove it in your face, as happened to me.

"Lillian," I said, determined to help her rather than smooth over the truth with pious platitudes. "I'm going to quit downplaying what's happened. I think you're going to have to face the fact that your house is all but gone. Surely, Sam would've let us know if he'd come up with something to stop the destruction. So you've got to prepare yourself for the worst, and if it's better than that, well, that's all to the good."

"Here, Lillian," Hazel Marie said, handing her three aspirin tablets and a glass of tomato juice. "Take these and just sit still for a while. Then go up and take a shower. I promise you'll feel better before long."

"Yessum, thank you," Lillian said, obediently swallowing the pills and sipping the juice. "I jus' hope it all stay down long enough to do some good. I'm gonna tell Mr. Pickens I don't want him fixin' me nothin' else to help me sleep."

Hazel Marie laughed, then quickly sobered up as she remembered that she was put out with Mr. Pickens. "I don't blame you," she said. "His fixing doesn't always work, but I intend to fix him, if it's the last thing I do."

Little Lloyd, his head bent over his plate, looked up at me, a frown between his eyes. I nodded my head at him, hoping to assure him that things would eventually work out. And of course they always do, although nine times out of ten, not in any way, shape nor form like we want them to.

⌐*Chapter 11*

After Hazel Marie and Little Lloyd left, Lillian and I girded ourselves to face whatever awaited on Willow Lane. I got Lillian's dress re-buttoned and held her coat for her. She wasn't functioning all that well, for she kept taking deep breaths as if she couldn't get enough air. Her hands were trembling, too.

"Lillian," I said. "You don't have to do this. I can go over there and make sure the men get everything."

"No'm, I got to see 'bout it myself," she said, getting that blank look on her face again. "Not no use me settin' here doin' nothing. Might as well go ahead and face the worst."

So that's what we did. I drove through the streets, just dreading the empty feeling of emptying out Lillian's house. One good thing, the wind had died down during the night and it looked to be shaping up into a cool but sunny fall day.

As we turned into Willow Lane and drew near Lillian's home, we saw several pickup trucks and U-Haul trucks and trailers backed up to the porches. Men walked to and from them, carrying boxes and manhandling appliances and yelling for dollies. Some of the women who lived in the houses stood on the porches or out in the yards, watching as their possessions were loaded up to be taken who-knew-where.

I parked beside an enclosed U-Haul truck with a ramp that extended onto Lillian's front porch. We got out of the car, but Lillian just stood for a minute, taking in the house she'd lived in for years, as if she were memorizing it. I walked over to stand beside her.

"Now, Lillian," I said, taking her arm. "Prepare yourself."

She nodded, but I purely didn't know how anybody could be prepared for the forcible loss of house and home. I tried to imagine it for myself, but I couldn't.

"Morning, Lillian, Miss Julia," Deputy Coleman Bates called out as he came through the front door lugging one end of a mattress. Behind him, on the other end of the mattress, Sam emerged, giving us a quick smile but too intent on holding on to do much more. They hefted the mattress up the ramp and into the truck.

When they came out of the truck, Sam was wiping his face with a handkerchief. "Hot work," he said, although it seemed too early in the day to be all that warm.

"Don't give yourself a heart attack, Sam," I said, concerned that he would overexert himself. I declare, there's not a man alive who'll ever admit that something is too much for him. I eyed Sam carefully, trying to determine how well his mind was working. It seemed to come and go, you know.

Sam laughed. "It's good for me, Julia. Lillian, I sure do hate this, but we're doing the best we can for you."

"Yessir, Mr. Sam," she said. "I know you are, but it real hard to take."

"We need you to come on in here, Lillian," Coleman said, as he leaned on the porch banister. "We've just about got everything, but you ought to look around behind us."

"Yessir, an' I need to sweep and mop when ever'thing get out."

"For pity sakes, Lillian," I said. "The last thing you need to do is clean this place up. It's all going to the dump, anyway."

Then I realized that I could've chosen a kinder way of reminding her of what was going to happen. Lord, I could've throttled Clarence Gibbs, as I stood there wracking my brain for some way to stop him.

"I misspoke, Lillian," I told her. "It's just that I don't want you doing any extra work. Now, let's go inside and see what else needs to be done."

Easier said than done, for the truck's ramp covered the narrow front steps, and there was no way for us to climb up on it.

"Back door's open," Coleman said, so I took Lillian's arm and we walked along the side of the house toward the back.

"There's my Rose of Sharon," Lillian said, sniffing as we passed a bush in a mulched bed. "Miz Thompson give me a cuttin', oh, Law, how many years ago? An' it been bloomin' ev'ry year since. Now it gonna be gone, too."

"We'll get it out," I said. "If the men are too busy loading up everybody, there's no reason we can't do it. In fact, we'll bring Little Lloyd over after school and he can do the digging. You just decide what you want to save, and I'll get Raymond to heel them in behind the garage. He'll look after them until we can transplant them to your new place." Wherever that'll be, I added to myself.

She seemed to brighten at that. "Can Little Lloyd and me come back over here after he get home from school?"

"Of course you can. You can stay all day if you want to, and I'll drop him off as soon as he gets out. I want you to take all the time here that you need."

As we reached the back steps, she stood for a minute and

looked around the small yard. There was a privet hedge along the back, with a few azaleas and rhododendrons in the corners of the yard. A clothesline was strung from two wooden posts, but I knew she often spread her washing across the bushes to dry.

"Well, no use lingerin'," she said with a sigh that seemed to come from her feet. "Le's us get at it."

There wasn't all that much to get at when we got in. A kitchen with a sink on exposed metal legs, one built-in cabinet, and a stove that'd needed replacing years ago.

"Is that your stove, Lillian?"

"No'm, it here when I moved in. I guess it belong to Mr. Gibbs. Maybe we ought to move it for him."

"We certainly will not," I said, and right smartly, too. "We're not about to ask Coleman and Sam to move that heavy thing. If Clarence Gibbs wants it, he can get it himself."

Hearing the footsteps of Coleman and Sam on the wooden floor of the front room, we walked on in. Lord, the place was empty. Except, of course, for pages of newspaper, dust, and lint that had gathered in the corners during the packing process. And a telephone on the floor by the front window. I'd put that in for her when I discovered after Wesley Lloyd's passing that she didn't have one. I'd paid the bill every month, too, telling her that it was all for my convenience so she'd let me do it.

"Lillian," Coleman said, laden with three paper sacks filled with oddments of all kinds. "We're about finished here, but check your closets and all the rooms. Be sure we've got everything. Oh, and," he said, turning back to her, "is there anything under the house we ought to get?"

"I got a leaf rake an' a snow shovel under the porch, an' they's a tub and a washboard out on that ole table by the back door. But I'll get 'em."

"No, you won't." Coleman grinned at her. "We're the movers around here. You just be sure we get everything, that's all you have to do."

Lillian nodded, tears beginning to shine again in her eyes. Then she walked into the two bedrooms and looked around. I stayed where I was, figuring she needed time to herself. I try to be sensitive to the needs of others whenever I think about it.

When I thought she'd had enough time to say good-bye to the room where she'd slept for so many years, I called to her. "Lillian, do you want to stay here for a while? Or go on back to the house?"

"I ought to stay," she said, coming back into the former living room. "See I can he'p some a the others, but Miss Julia, this all 'bout done me in. Seem like I can't hardly drag one foot front of the other."

"Well, no wonder," I said, looking sharply at her. She had that same dazed look she'd been getting off and on since the previous night. "You need to rest yourself, so let's go on back. I've got a number of things to see to myself, and I ought to get to them. Sam," I said as he came in, brushing his hands from the last load. "We're going on back to the house, so we'll be there when you and Coleman come to unload."

"Okay, Julia. Park your car on the street so we can back up to the garage. Ready, Coleman?"

"Yep," Coleman said. "I think we've got it all, Lillian. But let us know if we've missed anything. As soon as we unload, Sam's coming back to help at the other houses. I'll be back, too, after I check in with Binkie. She was feeling a few twinges this morning."

"Law, Coleman," Lillian said, her spirits noticeably rising. "Miss Binkie 'bout to have that baby? You ought not be here helpin' me, if she havin' that baby."

"No," he said, shaking his head and smiling at Lillian. "It's still a little early for the baby. But I have a pager, if she needs me."

As Coleman and Sam started toward the cab of the rented truck, the grinding of many gears drew our attention to two long flatbed trucks that were turning into Willow Lane. Everybody on the street stopped to watch as the heavy trucks maneuvered their ponderous way down the lane, across the turn-around and into the field beyond. The trucks themselves were unlikely enough on the narrow street, but it was what was on them that brought us all to a stunned stop. If Little Lloyd had been there, he could've told me the names of the big yellow machines that were chained to the flatbeds. Two of what had to be instruments of destruction were offloaded into the field. They both had tracks like tanks, and one had a big shovel on the front, while the other had a scoop with teeth. It took only a little imagination to see them chewing up these defenseless little houses.

"Don't look, Lillian," I said. "Let's get away from here before we both break down and cry." As Coleman eased the rental truck away from the porch, I took her arm again to lead her down the front steps.

We'd barely gotten in the car good when one of those machines fired up, emitting a cloud of black smoke and a nerve-shattering roar. It turned on its track and began following two men who directed the driver with arm signals. The yellow monster headed toward the last house on the left of Willow Lane, the abandoned one with the caved-in roof. With pincers opened wide, it sunk into that shell of a house and took a huge bite out of it. Then it spun on its tracks and dumped its mouthful into the back of a truck.

At the sight and noise of the thing, everybody who was moving and being moved came out into the street to watch the destruction. Others hurried back inside to grab their possessions for fear that, once started, the machine would continue up and down the lane, gobbling up houses as it went.

"Oh, my Jesus," Lillian gasped. "That thing eatin' up houses, an' not everybody moved out yet."

"Somebody ought to stop it," I said, staring with my mouth open. "They weren't supposed to start today. Oh, look, Coleman's walking down there. He'll straighten them out."

And apparently he did, for after leveling the house and dumping the remnants in the truck, the driver cut the motor and climbed out. Just getting a head start on his demolition work, I guessed. Amazed at how quickly the house had been leveled, I had a mind to organize everybody and form a living line around the rest of the houses. I'd read about those protester types who stretched out in front of trucks and tanks or chained themselves to trees, and I wondered if the same tricks would work here. We'd probably just be arrested like they'd been, and I'd have to go everybody's bail.

There had to be another way to stop it but, for the life of me, I couldn't come up with one.

❧

Soon after we arrived at home, Coleman and Sam drove up and began unloading Lillian's household goods and stacking them in the garage. On our way into the house, she and I stopped and peeked in at the accumulation of a lifetime.

"Sam," I said, "Lillian's clothes are packed up somewhere in there. Have you or Coleman come across them?"

Sam stopped and looked at Coleman, the one who'd been helping Lillian pack. Sam said, "I've not seen any clothes, except a couple of sweaters that were hanging in the closet. Have you, Coleman?"

"I sure haven't. What were they in, Lillian?"

"I don't much 'member," she said. "All them boxes you brung me look alike. But if you find anything for me to wear, I 'preciate you let me know."

"Don't worry about it now, Lillian," I said, turning her toward the house. "Hazel Marie's getting some things for you."

She smiled as she reached for the screen door and, with a touch of her usual humor, said, "That's what I'm afraid of."

I helped her get her coat off and said, "Why don't you go up and lie down for a while?"

"No'm, I think I'm gonna make us a cake. Or a pie. Or maybe both." And she headed for the sink to wash her hands.

"You don't need to be doing any cooking, much less making a pile of desserts. I think you need to rest."

"Cookin' help me rest, Miss Julia," she said. "It take my mind off all them troubles. I jus' hate to do it in my church dress, though. 'Course, it my *only* dress, since no tellin' where the rest of 'em be packed up."

"Not for long," I told her. "If I know Hazel Marie, she'll come back with an armload."

Lillian took an apron from the pantry and wrapped it around herself, tying it in back. Then she brought out three cake pans from a cabinet under the counter. "I'm gonna make us a three-layer white cake with pineapple fillin' and seven-minute frostin', an' that'll take up half the day. After that, I'm gonna use them Granny Smith apples I got yestiday an' make a apple pie. Or maybe that lemon pie what Coleman like so much. By that time, maybe this first day of havin' no house be done an' over with."

"Oh, Lillian," I said, clenching my fists. "Believe me, something will be done about this, and I'm going to start in right this minute."

As I turned to leave, we heard the truck start up, and Lillian said, "Coleman comin' in."

That handsome young man walked in, looking considerably different in his blue jeans and flannel shirt than he did when he was in his uniform, with his law enforcement paraphernalia strapped everywhere around him.

He walked over to Lillian and put his arm around her. "Lillian, I know that moving's no fun under any circumstances, but this way is just . . . well, I just hate it for you."

Lillian patted his arm. "I be all right, Coleman. Don't you worry 'bout me. I got so many frien's I can't even count 'em all. Why don't you call Mr. Sam in here, an' let me fix you something to eat."

"I can't, Lillian," he said. "I've got a wife so pregnant that I'm afraid to linger anywhere. Now, Lillian, since I'm the one who didn't pay attention to the boxes, you'll need some clothes. Let me help you with that." And he reached for his wallet.

"Hazel Marie and I are taking care of it," I told him. "But we're putting together some plans to raise money to get new homes for all those people, so we'll be contacting you and Binkie pretty soon. Then you can open up that wallet."

"Great," he said, hugging Lillian again. "Just let us know. I'll be around, Lillian, if I can do anything for you."

And with that, he left to check on his heavy-laden wife. And I left to go upstairs, just as heavy-laden with money-raising schemes running around in my head.

～Chapter 12

Reaching my bedroom upstairs, I sat down in the easy chair by the window and pulled the telephone close to dial Sam's number. I couldn't figure why he hadn't come in with Coleman, unless he was in a hurry to help the rest of the Willow Lane folks so he could get on that motorcycle again.

As I listened to his phone ring, I thought again of how much I depended on him—his good common sense, his reasonable approach to every problem, and his indulgence of me when I began to bounce off the walls. I knew that in his current condition, in spite of the good front he'd put up the night before in the church, I might not be able to depend on him. But like always, he was the first one I turned to.

But not today, for James, when he answered the phone, told me that he didn't know where Sam was or when he'd be back.

"I know where he is, James," I said. "He's helping the Willow Lane folks. But didn't he tell you how long he'd be?"

"No'm, I jus' seein' after Mr. Wills and Mr. Washington, what spend the night here. Mr. Sam, he tell me to feed 'em good an' he be back sometime."

"Thay Lord," I said. "Well, tell Mr. Sam when he does

89

come home that Lillian's making cakes and pies right and left, and that we'll expect him to come over tonight and help us eat them."

"Yessum, I do that."

"Oh, and James," I said, right before hanging up. "I am so glad that you didn't live on Willow Lane, and therefore don't have to look for a place to live."

"Yessum, me too. I been livin' over Mr. Sam's garage a long time now, ever since he retired. But I sure do hurt for Miss Lillian. You tell her that for me, won't you?"

"Yes, I will, and I know she'll appreciate it." Again, I almost said my good-byes, but another thought came to me. "James, have you noticed any changes in Sam lately? I mean, anything that we ought to be concerned about?"

There was silence on the line, and I prepared myself for a dire diagnosis. Then he said, "No'm, I don't see no changes, 'cept for that motorsickle he got out there, what pop an' growl an' carry on loud enough to wake the dead. But he like it, so I get used to it, too."

"Ah, well," I said, knowing I shouldn't say more and put ideas in his head. "I worry about him falling off the thing, but just give him my message, James, and I'll talk to you later."

I did get off the phone then, and sat for a minute trying to decide what to do next. I knew what I should do, which was see if Clarence Gibbs would sell the property instead of erecting a bottling plant on it, which, if you want my opinion, was the most foolish idea I'd ever heard. There was no way I could see that he'd ever get a return on his investment. He needed to have that pointed out to him, so he'd listen to an offer to purchase.

But before tackling Clarence Gibbs, I looked up Helen Stroud's number and called her.

"Helen, this is Julia Springer," I said. "I have a proposal for the garden club, and I hope you'll give it serious consideration. Now, I know I'm no longer a member, but I left in good standing, so I hope you won't hold that against me."

"Why, Julia," she said, just as gracious as she could be. "Of course not. We do miss you, but I know you have your hands full now." Then she quickly moved past that since she was, like so many people, uncomfortable with bringing up Hazel Marie and Little Lloyd and how they came to live with me. "Now, what can we do for you?"

I told her about the soon-to-be destruction of Willow Lane, which she already knew about from a number of other telephone calls, and about my idea for starting a rebuilding fund for the people who'd lived there.

"Oh, it is just so unfair," Helen said. "You wouldn't believe how upset people are about it. Why, Marlene Nixon called a while ago, practically in tears because the lady who does her washing and ironing is moving to Brevard to stay with family over there, and Marlene doesn't know what she's going to do about her laundry."

"Well, I think we need to set our sights a little higher than Marlene's laundry problems," I said. "Now, Helen, if people want to help, and I certainly hope the garden club does, here's one way we can do it."

I told her about the home tour that Hazel Marie and I had come up with, and she was just delighted with the idea. "Oh, Julia, I love that idea. I've long thought that the club ought to be doing more for the community than just planting bulbs at the Town Hall."

"That's wonderful," I said, much relieved that maybe this would be one thing I wouldn't have to do. "I know that the club will do a marvelous job, and I can leave the planning, the ticket sales, the advertising, and the actual tour entirely up to you. In the meanwhile, I'll see that one of the banks sets up an account for the fund, so it'll be ready for all the deposits we'll have."

I'd probably said enough, but then thought I'd better let her know what else I expected from the club. "Oh, and Helen, I don't know which houses you'll want on the tour, but I was thinking that the Whitaker house would be good, and that modern thing somebody famous is building up on the mountain. And, of course, my house would be available. You know, I've completely redecorated the living and dining rooms since the garden club met here a few years ago, so everything is fresh and very different from what it once was. I know people will want to see it."

She thought those were great ideas, as I'd known she would. We finished our conversation and I was able to turn my mind to other things, knowing that the home tour was now in good hands. One thing I've learned in my years of volunteer work, if you want something done and done right, give it to a group of women to do.

As I finished my task I heard Hazel Marie drive in and car doors slamming, so I went downstairs to see what she'd bought for Lillian. I probably should've stayed where I was.

"Just wait, Lillian," Hazel Marie was saying as I entered the kitchen and saw her dump a pile of boxes and shopping bags on the table. "Wait till you see what I got you. Now, of course, if something doesn't fit or you don't like it, I'll take it back."

Her eyes were sparkling at having had a successful shopping trip. I'd never considered shopping anything but a chore, but Hazel Marie enjoyed it ever so much now that she had the wherewithal to do it.

She turned to me. "Come look, Miss Julia. I got her the

prettiest things I could find, and I want you to just see the lingerie I bought."

Lillian stood by the kitchen counter, frowning at the pile on the table.

"I don't know 'bout no lingerie," she said. "I usually jus' wear underwear."

"Oh," Hazel Marie said, laughing, as she began to dig into the boxes and bags. "That's what I mean. But there's no reason not to have on something pretty underneath. It makes you feel so, well, nice."

"I don't know I want no underwear makin' me feel that way," Lillian mumbled, still standing some way from the table.

"Miss Julia," Hazel Marie said, paying little attention to Lillian's hesitancy. "I went by the uniform shop, too, but they were out of white ones in Lillian's size. They'll call us when they come in. They had her size on file, but I'd already done most of my shopping by the time I got there, so I might've gotten things a little on the small side. But," she quickly added, "we'll exchange whatever doesn't fit. Now, Lillian, I want you to try everything on so we can see what needs to go back."

"Well, I better watch these cakes I jus' put in the oven," Lillian said. "I don't want 'em to burn."

"I'll watch them," I told her, going over to her and placing my hand on her arm. "Lillian, you know you need clothes, so let us do this for you. You see the pleasure Hazel Marie is getting from this, and we want you to enjoy it, too."

She turned away, saying, "I know, Miss Julia, and I 'preciate it more'n I can say. It jus' do me in that I too worriet to know what I was doin' when I packed ever'thing."

"I'd have been just as bad, or worse," I assured her. "But

run on, now, and try them on. And don't hesitate to say if you don't like something." Then, in an effort to lighten her up, I went on, "I'll tell you the truth, I'd hate to have Hazel Marie picking out clothes for me. She'd probably come back with a miniskirt and a halter top, and wouldn't I look a sight then?"

The picture I conjured up brought us all to laughter, which was what I'd intended. Hazel Marie handed Lillian an armload of boxes and shopping bags and, taking some herself, they left to go upstairs for a formal fitting. I glanced through the glass door of the oven at the cake layers that were just beginning to rise, then began to rinse the mixing bowls Lillian had used, wondering what else I could do to lift her spirits.

Hearing Hazel Marie and Lillian coming down the stairs, I quickly put the last mixing bowl in the dishwasher, and prepared myself to witness Lillian's new wardrobe. Hazel Marie was chattering on in a reassuring way, telling Lillian as they passed through the dining room that she shouldn't worry, she'd exchange everything. Lillian was uncommonly quiet.

"I declare, Miss Julia," Hazel Marie said as they came through the swinging door. "I can't believe how far off I was. Lillian always looks so slim and trim that I thought I could guess her size." She laughed, trying to put a good face on the fact that Lillian had been considerably larger than all of Hazel Marie's selections.

Well, that wasn't exactly true, for as Lillian trailed in behind her, I heard a swish with every step. My mouth dropped open as she came into full view. My word, she was a sight in one of those nylon sportswear suits that people run around town in, trying to sweat off their extra pounds. It was navy blue with a red stripe down the side of each leg and a zipped-up top. The expression on Lillian's face made me close my mouth and try to pretend that such a getup was perfectly normal for her size and shape. I gaped again, though, as I noticed the huge tenny-pumps on her feet. They looked like boats, but then, they did on everybody else who wore the things, too.

"Don't you say nothin', Miss Julia," Lillian warned me, as she lifted her head high and sailed over to the oven to check on her cakes, that nylon material rustling between her thighs with every step. "This the only thing what fit, an' leastways I won't mess up my good church dress."

"It's very becoming," Hazel Marie said with a tiny frown on her face. "Don't you think, Miss Julia? Everybody wears them, you know, because they're so comfortable."

"You look fine, Lillian," I said, lying through my teeth, just as Hazel Marie was doing. "Hazel Marie, why don't you go ahead and take the other things back and get the right sizes? No matter how good this outfit looks, she's going to need something else to wear.

"But before you go," I went on, "what do you think of getting Sam and Mr. Pickens, and Coleman, and maybe Binkie if she feels up to it, over here tonight to discuss what we can do to get the fund drive off the ground? We're going to need help to eat all this food Lillian's fixing, anyway."

Hazel Marie twitched her face into a thoughtful expression and said, "Well, I want to do whatever I can to help, so I'll call Sam and Binkie and Coleman for you if you'll call the other one."

"What other one?"

"Why, J. D., of course."

"Don't you want to call him?"

"I'm not speaking to him."

"Oh, I forgot. Well, I hope you can put up with his presence because I need a calm head to deal with Sam." I stopped, struck with the thought that I wouldn't ordinarily describe Mr. Pickens as having the calmest head around. Still, if you kept him away from trashy women and pitchers of beer, he could pretty much be counted on.

"I been tellin' you," Lillian said as she began to peel apples at the sink, "they ain't nothin' wrong with Mr. Sam, an' you need to quit thinkin' they is."

"Well," I said and let it drop. I knew what I knew, and I knew that Sam needed some careful watching, which I intended to provide regardless of what anybody else thought.

~Chapter 13

After going upstairs and making sure no one could hear me, I nervously called Clarence Gibbs and made an appointment with him. Then I got in the car and backed out of the driveway in my usual careful manner. Two cars, one coming from each direction, had to wait for me to straighten out and get in my lane, but drivers on Polk Street were accustomed to doing that.

I parked and walked into Patrick's Pancake House, some little distance from the three blocks of downtown. Since it was mid-afternoon and long after breakfast time, the place was practically empty, so I had no difficulty finding Clarence Gibbs in the red leatherette booth at the far end of the restaurant. Why he'd wanted to meet in such a place, I didn't know, but I'd learned since Wesley Lloyd's demise that business is often conducted in unlikely places.

He elevated himself slightly from his seat as I approached, giving me the simpering smile that he bestowed on all the women at church. I'd never had any dealings with the man before, so I tried to make a quick assessment as I took in his tan, silky-looking suit, narrow tie, and white no-iron shirt. I declare, I know better than to judge people by their looks, but what else do you have to go on when you don't know a person? Trying not to stare, I took in his five o'clock shadow, even though it was barely mid-afternoon, and the dark circles under his eyes. And his posture! Even seated, his shoulders slumped over the coffee mug in front of him, and I knew, having seen him walk down the aisle at church often enough, that his coat tail hiked up in the back from the way he carried himself.

"Mrs. Springer," he acknowledged me with a nod. Then he settled himself again after his gesture of courteousness and motioned me to the opposite seat. With another gesture of considerably less courteousness, he raised his hand toward the waitress at the cash register and called out, "Another cup over here, Miss."

"No need to order for me, Mr. Gibbs," I said, placing my pocketbook by my side and loosening my coat. "I've come to talk business."

Nevertheless, a mug of steaming coffee suddenly appeared before me as the waitress said, "You want anything else, hon?"

Taken aback at the express service, I managed to say, "No, thank you."

Mr. Gibbs's eyes sparkled as he watched me with that little half smile that verged on a smirk. "I tip heavy," he said, as if explaining something to a socially inept person, which I most certainly was not.

"I daresay," I replied, pushing the mug away. "Now, Mr. Gibbs, I'm here to talk about that property on Willow Lane. I've been over there this morning, and I'll tell you it is a doleful scene with all those people being turned out on the street and those wrecking machines already working away."

"Well," he said, his face drooping in what I might have mistaken for concern if I hadn't known he was the cause of the problem. "It is a shame, and that's a fact. I didn't expect 'em to wait till the last minute, though. I give 'em plenty of time to find somewhere to move to."

"Yes, I'm sure the law requires you to do that. But, Mr. Gibbs, you of all people know how few places there are to rent in this town—especially for those who can't afford much. Those people are surely up a creek, and it seems to me that you'd want to keep those houses up, refurbish them a little, and continue to have a nice income."

He began shaking his head before I'd even finished. Then he picked up a salt shaker, turning it around and studying it. "I got no plans to stay in the rental business. Why, I couldn't remodel or replace those houses and get a good return on 'em to save my life." He pursed his lips and shook his head again. "No, ma'am, a bidnessman got to look after bidness first and foremost. Now, I'm sorry for those folks, but . . ." He shrugged his shoulders and turned his attention to the salt shaker again.

"But what will they do?" I asked. "You performed a real community service, Mr. Gibbs, by providing affordable housing for people who don't have much, and I'd think you'd at least consider their present plight."

He tried to straighten up but his shoulders wouldn't let him. "Now, Mrs. Springer, I'm sure you understand that I'm not in the bidness of community service any more than you are." I reared up at that, offended at being categorized as a business-at-any-cost property owner. But before I could set him straight, he went on. "I pay my taxes just like everybody else, and I say let the gov'ment worry over this. They got every kind of program you can think of—which is paid for by you and I—and I just don't think I ought to be doin' any extra subsidizin'."

"I understand that," I said, and I did. I'd resent it, too, if anybody expected me to replace a government program. "So that brings me to this question. Would you consider selling the property and, if so, for how much?"

His eyes narrowed as he studied me. "You interested?"

"I could be."

"Well, selling is an option, I grant you." He rubbed his fingers across his mouth as he gazed out at the blacktopped parking lot, then at the scrubby bushes next to the sidewalk and the cars passing beyond that. Then he turned back to me and said, "But I been working on plans for that piece of property."

I let out a long breath. "I've heard, Mr. Gibbs. Everybody's talking about that water you're planning to bottle out there. But do you really think that's a good business move?"

"Yes, ma'am. With the right kind of marketing and advertising, it'd be worth a fortune."

"Yes, and what will all that cost you? Besides, if you market that cow pasture water as being beneficial to men only, you've cut your customers in half right there." I was most uncomfortable touching upon such delicate matters, but he needed to see what he was up against. "Consider that against a quick return if you sell the property. Money in your pocket, instead of a constant outgo for the next several years. Now, what would you take for it, if you decided to sell?"

"I don't know," he said, still giving me the occasional sharp glance. "I had it surveyed not too long ago, and there's ten acres out there, more 'r less. Plus, it's not zoned so it can be used for anything. That makes it a real desirable piece of real estate."

I knew what he was doing—building it up before hitting me with what he'd take for it.

"It's right next to a residential area," I reminded him, "which limits its uses."

"Not necessarily." He raised a finger, not quite pointing it at me. "It includes that old pasture, which I own, too. So, you put all that together and you got a real nice piece of property. Not another one that size anywhere close to town."

"I'm not talking about the pasture, which, if I recall from the heavy rains we had a few years ago, is partly in a flood plain. Plus, it's a burial site. You can keep that. I'm talking about two acres, more or less, where the houses are."

"Can't do that," he said, shaking his head in a sorrowful way. "We got to talk the whole parcel, which means the whole ten acres."

"I declare, Mr. Gibbs," I snapped. "You could break it up into two parcels if you had a mind to. In fact, I expect it's already listed that way down at the courthouse."

"It don't matter since I own 'em both. If I want to sell as one package, I got ever' right to do it. *If* I decide to sell."

It was my turn to stare out the window, as I cogitated over how to proceed. If he'd set a reasonable price, maybe the fund drive could afford to buy it all, then sell off the pasture to help fix up the houses. Of course, we didn't yet have a fund to be able to afford anything.

"All right," I said, turning back to him. "What's your price?"

"Well," he said with a dramatic sigh, like I was pushing him to his limit. But I could see the way his eyes glinted. He thought he had me where he wanted me. "I hadn't really given it much thought."

Hah, I thought. That's all he'd been thinking about ever since I'd walked in.

"Name it," I said.

"I got to think about it," he said, frowning as he put on a show of serious consideration. "I don't much like selling what's already owned free and clear. And I had that property a long time now, so it's hard to let something like that go. They're not making any more real estate, you know."

"Mr. Gibbs," I said, trying to break through all that put-on resistance, when we both knew he'd sell his own mother if he could get a good price. "I'm acting in good faith here, and I expect you to do the same. We've been sitting here discussing that property, me with an eye to purchase and you with an eye to sell. Now, let's quit beating around the bush and get to what you'll take for it."

"Let me give you some advice, Mrs. Springer," he said, hunching over the table. "When you're negotiating a piece of property, you don't want to jump too quick to talkin' money. You miss a lot of the fun that way."

"You may be looking for fun, Mr. Gibbs, but I assure you I am not. We've got good and decent people about to be without homes, and I'm trying to help them out. Now, set your price."

He stared at me, but I didn't think he was really seeing me. I could see that he was running figures through his head, even though I figured that he already knew what he wanted for it.

"Mr. Gibbs," I said before he could commit himself. "I would not exactly be the sole purchaser of your property. We're getting a community effort together, and I know that you'll want to take that into consideration in your asking price."

"If that's the case, I could make a donation down the line somewhere. Right now, I'm thinkin' bidness."

I sighed in exasperation, but what can you do with a businessman who has something you want and knows it? "All right, then, talk business." I almost said 'bidness,' but caught myself in time.

"Two hundred and fifty thousand dollars," he said, all too promptly, "and worth every penny."

I was stunned. That property, in that part of town, with houses in the shape those were in, couldn't be worth more than a hundred thousand, which was more than a gracious plenty. I'd been hoping against hope that even if he'd wanted to engage in a little gouging, he'd not go higher than one-fifty.

"And another thing," he said, "if you want it, you got to go ahead and take it. I can't be waitin' around for fund drives and evaluations and bank approvals. I got plans in the making and deadlines to meet."

"Why, Mr. Gibbs!" I said, just so provoked I didn't know what to do. "I can't possibly buy that property anytime soon. There are people I have to consult, and, well, we've barely started the fund drive. We're going to need a few weeks just to come up with a down payment."

"Well, I'm sorry, Mrs. Springer, but I can't let these things hang fire." He smiled, and it was a sorry sight to see. "Unless, of course, you want to put a little sweetener in the pot."

"I don't know what you're talking about."

"I'm talking about something that'll make it worth my while to wait. Say, you put up something of value, like your house, for instance, and I'll give you three weeks to get up the money for the Willow Lane property. You raise the money, you keep your house and you get the property." He shrugged his shoulders and splayed out his hands. "You don't, and I get both."

"Why . . . why," I stammered, staring at him as if he'd lost his mind. "I have never heard of such a thing. *My* house? I can't possibly do that."

He smiled. "Real estate investors make this kinda deal all

the time. If they want to hold something bad enough. So," he said, shrugging and splaying out his hands, "I guess it depends on how bad you want Willow Lane."

I slid out of the booth and struggled to my feet. "I'll be in touch," I said, holding on to the table to steady myself. "Two days, Mr. Gibbs. Give me two days to come to grips with this. Will you do that?"

"Won't be easy," he said. "But I will."

I managed to get out that I'd give him my answer in the time specified.

I started to leave, simply stunned by his proposal that I put up my home as surety of the sale. Then I turned back. "In the meantime," I said, "I sincerely hope you'll make your position a matter of prayerful reconsideration."

Chapter 14

My home! I thought as I drove away from the pancake house. I'd never heard of anything so outrageous. He ought to've been thrashed through the streets for suggesting such a thing. Taking advantage of a poor widow woman, that's what he was trying to do.

Well, there were other ways to skin a cat. And with that thought, I drove directly to Binkie's office to find out what they were. By the time I got there, parked, and walked along the sidewalk, I'd calmed down somewhat. Clarence Gibbs's proposal was simply out of bounds, no two ways about it. Still, I couldn't help but store it in the back of my mind as a last-ditch option, if all else failed.

But I had no intention of telling Binkie about it. I knew she'd hit the ceiling and spin around a few times. And in her condition, she didn't need that kind of excitement.

"Binkie," I said, as I sat in her client's chair, my hands folded on top of the pocketbook in my lap. "I declare, I think that baby's found a home." I didn't want to make too big an issue over her size, since that's as impolite as commenting on someone's food, but I was awestruck. "You think it's ever going to get here?"

"Doesn't look like it," she said, blowing her hair out of her eyes. "I'm just getting bigger and bigger, and slower and slower. Why, I haven't seen my feet for weeks now."

She laughed, then squirmed in her chair behind the desk, trying to find a comfortable position. "I tell Coleman it's all his fault."

"Uh, yes, I imagine so." As a sudden image came to mind of just how Coleman managed that, I hurried on to the purpose of my visit. These young women today don't care what they say. "Now, Binkie, I wanted to ask you about liquidating some of my assets so I can help those poor homeless folks who live on Willow Lane. We're starting a fund drive, you know."

"Yes, I've heard about it, and I think it's a fine idea. Coleman and I will certainly contribute, so you can count on that. Now, as far as you're concerned, Miss Julia, let me see." She opened the folder that Mary Alice McKinnon, her office assistant, had brought in, and pulled out several papers. "I wouldn't recommend selling any stock at this time. I'd rather see the market settle down a little."

"And I'd rather get out of the market altogether," I said, never having put my total trust into something so much like a game of chance. As I'd reminded Sam, we Presbyterians are generally opposed to putting money in risky ventures, and I'd never understood why Pastor Ledbetter hadn't included the stock market the Sunday he took off on the evils of gambling. He'd gotten stirred up when the sewing group that met in the Fellowship Hall once a month asked if they could use the church bus to go over to the casino at the Cherokee Indian Reservation.

She glanced up at me. "Well, we can certainly discuss that, but you have some fairly liquid assets already, and all kinds of real estate. I'd hate to see you sell any of that, though. Here's a sizeable money market account that you can draw on, but you don't want to touch the annuities. How much do you think you'll need?"

"Enough to build a house for Lillian," I said. "And I may be forced to buy that property from Clarence Gibbs, who has set an unreasonably high price on it. The more I think about that man, the more I'd like to pinch his head off."

I told her what he was asking for the property, omitting any mention of the so-called sweetener, namely my house.

Binkie just stared at me over her reading glasses. "He doesn't want to sell it," she said flatly, which I'd already figured out for myself. "Now, look, Miss Julia," she went on, "you can certainly build a small house for Lillian with no problem, and more power to you for doing it. But I wouldn't recommend that you buy all of that property yourself. It's way overpriced, and not a good business move for you to try to replace all those houses. What I recommend you do is find a small lot and build on it for Lillian; or you might find a house she likes that's already built."

"But Lillian's concerned about the others," I said, all the while knowing that Binkie was giving me good advice. "I think she'd feel so guilty about them that she wouldn't let me do it just for her. Of course," I added, "that's why we're starting a fund, so the whole community can own that property in common."

"Better let me think about that," Binkie said, leaning back in her chair and squirming some more. "You're going to need some legal guidelines on exactly who will own it. Maybe form a corporation, or turn it over to the town council. *If* you're able to buy it. You could get into a real mess if you're not careful. I'm surprised that Sam hasn't cautioned you about it."

"Well, Sam," I said, letting my eyes wander around the

room, "That's another matter. Binkie, I didn't want to say anything, but I'm a little worried about Little Lloyd's estate."

"What?" She sat up in her chair and leaned as far over the desk as the mound in front of her would allow. "You don't suspect Sam of . . . ?"

"No. Oh, no," I quickly interrupted her. "Absolutely not. It's just, well, Sam's acting a little strange every now and again, and I couldn't help but wonder. He's aging, you know. And he might not be quite up to par, what with that motorcycle and, well, with some other things I've noticed."

Binkie started laughing, pushing her hair off her forehead. "Miss Julia, don't tell me you think he's getting senile. Listen," she said, stacking the papers and putting them into the folder. "Sam can run rings around both of us any day. You don't need to worry about him."

"Well," I said, somewhat offended at having my concerns given so little credit, "I just feel a responsibility to make sure Little Lloyd's assets are safe."

"They are," she assured me. "I look over everything every year at tax time and, believe me, nobody could do a better job than Sam is doing."

"That's reassuring, then," I said, preparing myself to leave. "But I'm telling you, Binkie . . . Well, I don't guess I will, if you think everything's fine. But let me know how much money I'll have available for Lillian, and I do want to make a contribution toward the purchase of the property." I sighed and got to my feet.

"Well," I said, disappointed that I couldn't immediately lay my hands on enough money to call Clarence Gibbs's bluff. What's the use of having wealth if you can't get at it when you want it? "I guess that's it, then."

I caught my lip between my teeth, as Mr. Gibbs's proposal concerning my house loomed ever larger in my mind.

It was certainly one way to buy time until the fund kicked in and got me out of the hole. "So," I said, hating to just let it drop, "you don't think I ought to buy it myself?"

"Absolutely not. But I'll look over things, and if I come up with some other ideas, I'll let you know."

"Don't wait too long," I said, standing and putting on my coat. "That baby's going to be here any day."

"Today wouldn't be too soon for me," she said with a smile, as she rubbed her stomach. "Oops, I just got kicked."

I turned away, never very comfortable with this modern tendency of discussing every little detail of our inner workings. I mean, just think of some of those television ads they have now—like the one with a woman high-stepping down the street singing, "I feel good," because she had a movement that morning.

"You never did find out if it's a boy or a girl, did you?" I asked.

"No, Coleman and I want it to be a surprise."

"Well, I can tell you it's a girl because you're carrying it high. That's what Lillian says, and," I said with a laugh, "she's right about half the time."

—◆—

I pondered what Binkie had told me as I drove home, finally deciding that it was best to put aside any idea of buying that property myself. What I had to do was concentrate on raising money from other people, while at the same time making sure that Gibbs gave us enough time to raise it.

I parked the car in the driveway and, without giving it much thought in case I talked myself out of it, walked across the street to the church. My chest tightened up every time I looked at or passed by that Family Life Center, which we'd gotten whether we wanted or needed it. I walked through the back door of the church and on through the Fellowship Hall that was under the sanctuary on the main floor.

Poking my head into Norma Cantrell's office, I saw with some pleasure that the gatekeeper was not at her desk. So I marched across the room and tapped on Pastor Ledbetter's door.

"Who . . . ?" he started to ask, as he opened the door, a frown of annoyance on his face. I knew that he did his sermon preparations mostly in the mornings, but didn't like disturbances anytime. Too bad.

"Oh, Miss Julia," he said, quickly smoothing out his broad face. He looked around for Norma, wondering, I guess, how I'd gotten past her.

"I expect Norma's in the ladies' room," I said, moving past his large frame and into his office. I declare, the man could use some time in that gymnasium he'd built next door. "I just need a minute of your time, Pastor."

"Always glad to see you, Miss Julia," he said, slipping on his suit coat and sliding his tie up. "Always have time for you." Neither of which I believed for a minute, but I let it go.

"Pastor, I'm here about those poor, evicted folks on Willow Lane, who the whole town ought to be exercised about. Lillian's one of them, you know."

"Yes, I know, and they've been weighing on my heart. I've had them all in my prayers ever since I heard about it."

"I'm sure you have," I said, taking the damask-covered wing chair, in front of his desk, which I noticed he'd not offered to me. "But it might've done some good if you'd had a word or two with Clarence Gibbs, as well. Now, I'd like to know what the church plans to do for them. It could come under the heading of Mission Outreach or some such."

"Why, Miss Julia," he said, as he settled himself in the executive chair behind his desk. "You know that our budget is set up to take care of overhead here in our own church first. Then everything else goes toward our evangelistic endeavors, both at home and on the mission field—a step that the session took a few years ago when it became apparent that the liberals in Congress were turning this great country into a welfare state."

"Well, Pastor, disregarding the liberal threat for a minute, these are our people, and they're in great need. I'd think that the church would want to do something to help them. We're supposed to feed the hungry and clothe the naked, and it would surprise me if housing the homeless isn't included in that."

He shook his head tiredly. "You've let the social gospel confuse you, Miss Julia. You can't just look after the body and overlook the soul. That's not the way of those of us who obey the Great Commission. We go into all the world and preach the Gospel. But don't despair," he added, seeing my mouth tighten, "I'm sure that many in the congregation will give generously on an individual basis, but the church itself, well, it's not our policy to rob Peter to pay Paul." He smiled. "So to speak."

This was the man, as I recalled, who'd put a stop to the Boy Scout meetings in the Fellowship Hall on the basis that the Scouts were not a Christian organization. And he'd proclaimed his justification for it some years later when there was all that uproar over perversion and deviant lifestyles and such as that, which I hadn't wanted to hear, neither then nor now. In fact, there was a time not too long ago when certain words, like *pregnancy*, were only whispered in polite company. And when other words in the same general category happened to be mentioned, I hadn't known what half of them meant. Now, I could just about count on hearing many more such previously unmentionable words flung out in his newsletters and from the pulpit almost every Sunday that rolled around. And Pastor Ledbetter, who'd improved *my* education considerably, was one of the loudest opponents to teaching the same subjects in our schools.

"I guess, then," I said with a mighty sigh as I rose from the chair, "that you wouldn't object to our asking individual members for donations. Over-and-above giving, I believe it's called, as you yourself have asked for on occasion."

"Of course not," he said expansively, getting up to hurry me on my way. "Our members are free to do as they're led with what the Lord has blessed them with. And, to show that our hearts are in the right place, Emma Sue and I will pledge a hundred dollars to your fund. But, Miss Julia," he held out a cautionary hand, "I know some people count their donations to the United Fund, the Red Cross, and other worthy causes as part of their tithe, but I hope you won't encourage that kind of thinking. The church needs every penny it can get to carry on the Lord's work of evangelizing the lost souls of the world."

"It's not my intention to interfere with the Lord's work," I said, heading for the door. "All I'm asking is for him to help me with mine."

As I walked back across the street, I was pleased that the pastor had not raised my blood pressure all that much. I'd pretty much suspected all along what his response was likely to be, and I hadn't been wrong. Still, I'd felt led to give the church an opportunity to help with our fund-raising. So it was done, and now I wouldn't have to put up with Pastor Ledbetter trying to run everything, which was a considerable compensation for his refusal to get the church officially involved.

Chapter 15

Lillian turned from the stove and looked at me as I entered the kitchen. "Miss Julia," she said, as she took a deep breath. "I been thinkin' 'bout all this, an' I never take charity before, nor nobody else on Willow Lane. We always take care of ourselves, an' that's what we ought to do now."

"For goodness' sakes, Lillian, what we're doing is not charity. If we can figure out what to do, you'll be paying rent just like you've always done. And, besides, you're all going to be helping with the fund-raising, aren't you? And speaking of that," I said, not giving her a chance to discuss it any further, "I need your help with something I may have to do."

"I don't know I want to hear what. But what?"

"Let me think about it a little longer. I'll let you know. Now, have you heard from anybody about tonight?"

"Yessum. Mr. Sam comin' an' Mr. Pickens. Coleman, he call an' say Miss Binkie still got the twinges an' they better not come."

"My land," I said, "she seemed fine just this afternoon. I tell you, Lillian, this is not a good time for her to be out of commission having that baby. I might need her again at any minute."

"I 'spect that baby not worriet 'bout what you need."

I had to laugh at myself. "I expect you're right."

We both looked up as we heard Hazel Marie's car pull into the driveway and her footsteps on the back stoop. She came barreling into the kitchen, her face as red as fire. She kicked the door shut behind her and announced, "I'm so mad I could spit."

She dropped the packages she'd exchanged for Lillian onto the table, ignoring the one that fell to the floor. We couldn't do anything but stare at her as she threw her pocketbook on top of the packages.

"Whatever is the matter, Hazel Marie?" I asked, ready to take cover if she continued to throw things around.

"You won't believe what I saw downtown," she stormed. "Just guess, Miss Julia. Take a guess, Lillian." Then she threw herself into a chair and crossed her arms over her chest.

Before Lillian or I could venture a guess, Hazel Marie told us. "J. D. and Tammi, that second wife of his!"

"Law!" Lillian yelled, throwing her hands in the air. "Don't tell me that man be married!"

"Now, Lillian," I cautioned, "she didn't mean it that way. He was married once, I mean, twice, but he's not now. Hazel Marie," I went on, turning to her, "where did you see them?"

"In the tea shop, that's where!"

I frowned, thinking how unlikely it was that Mr. Pickens would be in the tea shop. Somehow the two concepts didn't go together. But then, if you wanted a cup of coffee downtown, it was either that or something in a styrofoam cup at a filling station.

"Maybe they just happened to run into each other," I suggested, trying to put a better face on it than the one Hazel Marie had in mind.

"No, ma'am," she said, huffing up even more. "You wouldn't think that if you'd seen them. There I was," she said, standing up and stomping around her chair, "minding my own business and dropped in for a minute, and there they were, leaning over a table with their heads practically on top of each other."

"What did you do?" I asked, almost afraid to hear the answer. When Hazel Marie got hot, she could evermore cut a wide swath.

"I turned right around and left," she said, and I sighed with relief that the tea shop had suffered no damage.

Lillian had been following this, her eyes going back and forth, and finally she said, "Did they see you?"

"J. D. did," she said with some satisfaction. "I walked down the sidewalk right past the window where they were sitting. When he looked up and saw me going by, he jumped up so quick he spilled coffee on himself." She managed a vengeful smile. "Served him right, too. I hope it scalded him."

Well, this was certainly a pretty come-off. I couldn't imagine that Mr. Pickens would continue to pursue Tammi with an *i* after his last contact with her had resulted in Hazel Marie's leaving him flat. Unless, that is, he wanted Tammi back, just as she seemed to want him.

I wasn't about to suggest such a thing to Hazel Marie, though. There could still be a perfectly understandable reason for the two of them to be together, although for the life of me I couldn't figure what it could be.

And here I'd been thinking that Mr. Pickens knew women backward and forward. But if he thought he could juggle two women and keep both of them happy, he certainly didn't know Hazel Marie. I knew she'd had her fill of sharing a man.

"Now, Hazel Marie," I started, but was interrupted by the doorbell. "Who in the world is that? We don't have time for visitors."

"I get it," Lillian said, pushing through the dining room door.

"Hazel Marie," I began again. "I think you ought to talk to Mr. Pickens before you go off half-cocked. There might be a legitimate reason for the two of them to be together. The thing to do is give him a chance to tell you what it is."

She frowned and screwed up her mouth. "You wouldn't think that if you'd seen the way she looked at him. She's after him, Miss Julia, and I'm not going to sit around and wait for him to decide between the two of us."

"Well, now listen. . . ."

Lillian came to the kitchen door and poked her head inside. "Miss Hazel Marie, you got comp'ny."

"The nerve of him!" Hazel Marie stormed. "Showing up here like nothing's happened. Tell him I don't want to see him."

Lillian frowned and said, "It not Mr. Pickens, if that who you talkin' 'bout. It some red-headed lady I never seen."

Hazel Marie looked as if she'd been slapped in the face. She went white as a sheet, her hands knotted up into fists, and her whole body began to shake. Gritting her teeth, she stomped out of the kitchen, her shoulders hunched up like she was ready to take on the world.

"Come on, Lillian," I said. "We'd better not leave those two alone."

Taking her arm, I led Lillian after Hazel Marie. I wanted to see this famous red-headed Tammi with an *i,* and I certainly got an eyeful.

So this had been one of Mr. Pickens's unfortunate marital choices, I thought as I stared at the woman. I couldn't say much for his taste. She looked only an inch or two taller than Hazel Marie, although she had so much teased and tousled orange hair that she might well have been an inch or two shorter. It must've taken her hours to get that hair in such a state, and I am talking *big* hair. She was of a firm and athletic build, making Hazel Marie, who stood glowering at her, look fragile beside her.

"What're you doing here?" Hazel Marie said through clenched teeth. "How did you know where I live?"

"Oh," Tammi said, "I asked around. Look, I just came by to tell you that J. D. and I have a history together, which I thought you ought to know about so you won't keep on embarrassing yourself. No hard feelings, okay?" The woman smiled in such a smug way that—even as even-tempered as I am—made me want to smack her good.

Hazel Marie was breathing so deep that I could see her chest rise and fall. She was doing her best to hold her temper, and I admired her for it. Although I must say that Hazel Marie had not extended the courtesy of inviting Tammi in, for both of them were still standing by the door.

"No hard feelings?" Hazel Marie repeated in a tone that made me want to find a place to hide.

"No," Tammi said. "We could even be friends. Compare notes, so to speak."

Oh, Lord, I thought, Hazel Marie's going to blow sky high. "Uh," I said, thinking to avert a catastrophe, "won't you have a seat, Miss . . . Ms. . . . ?" For the life of me, I couldn't call her Mrs. Pickens.

It didn't matter, for neither of them paid me any mind. Hazel Marie was strung so tight that I could almost hear her thrum. Lillian picked at my sleeve, feeling the tension and wondering what we should do.

"Friends!" Hazel Marie screeched. "Compare notes! You

get out of this house and don't you ever come back, you, you home-wrecker, you!"

"All right, honey," Tammi said, sneering right in Hazel Marie's face. "I've tried to be nice about it, but you just keep your sticky hands off J. D. Pickens or you'll live to regret it."

"I'll show you sticky hands!" Hazel Marie cried. She reached up and grabbed the top of Tammi's head. Then, giving a yank, she came away with a handful of orange hair. Hazel Marie stared at it, as shocked as the rest of us.

Tammi screamed, Lillian yelled, and I lost my breath.

Lord, Hazel Marie'd snatched Tammi bald-headed, just as she'd said she would.

"Law," Lillian shrieked, throwing up her hands. "She done scalped that woman!"

I dashed to get between Hazel Marie and Tammi, expecting the stronger-looking woman to retaliate with a cat fight to end all cat fights. And in my living room, too. But Tammi was clutching the top of her head, cowering behind her hands, realizing that her Texas-sized coiffure had been mangled beyond repair.

Lillian, still shrieking, ran over and put her arms around Hazel Marie. "Oh, Miss Hazel Marie! They put you in jail, you pull out that woman's hair!"

"Lillian!" I called. "It's just a hairpiece!"

Hazel Marie looked again at the clump of hair in her hand, then threw it back at Tammi. "Take it and get out."

And Tammi did, calling out, "You'll regret this, see if you don't." She scrambled out onto the porch and down the steps, trying to mash the hairpiece back on her head as she went. It kept sliding around as she ran to her car, slammed the door, and pulled away from the curb with a chirp of the tires.

"Law, Miss Hazel Marie," Lillian said, looking at her with awe. "You fix her wagon good."

"Yes, and I'll do it again if she messes with me."

I had no doubt that she would, but the thing to do was to get her calmed down. "Hazel Marie," I said, "why don't you go lie down? All this upset is not good for your system. You run along and I'll bring you a nice cup of tea."

She drew in a deep, shuddering breath and said, "I can't calm down until I fix somebody else's wagon." She whirled on me, and went on. "Have you ever seen the like, Miss Julia? Didn't she have a nerve, coming here and telling me to leave J. D. alone? And then saying we could be friends!"

Hazel Marie suddenly stopped, her eyes widening as a new thought came to her. "Did J. D. suggest that? Did he send her over here to give me the news? He didn't have the courage to tell me to my face, did he? That was it, wasn't it?"

"I'm sure I don't know, Hazel Marie," I said soothingly. "But I doubt he'd do a thing like that. Mr. Pickens always seems to be able to handle his own business. I don't think he'd send in a substitute."

Hazel Marie barely heard me. She'd taken to pacing back and forth across the living room, muttering to herself about that low-down, two-timing, double-dealing, sneaking, no-good rat who couldn't be trusted as far as she could throw him.

As she passed the front window, she came to a dead stop. Then she ran to move aside the lace undercurtain and stared outside. With a gasp and an ugly word I won't repeat, she dashed to the door, flung it open, and ran out onto the porch.

Lillian and I looked at each other, then hurried out after her. Coming down the front walk was Mr. Pickens himself, sauntering along with one hand in his pocket. I couldn't help but notice a large wet spot down the front of his trousers. It would've looked mighty suspicious if Hazel Marie hadn't told us he'd spilled coffee on himself.

When he saw Hazel Marie running out to meet him, he stopped and opened his arms to receive her. A smile of greeting lit up his face as she ran toward him.

Before he could clasp her in his arms, she wound up her arm like a softball pitcher. Then she hauled off and socked him across the chin as hard as she could. He was so surprised that he had to take a step back to keep his balance.

Then she turned on her heel and, without a word, stomped back into the house, passing Lillian and me on her way.

Mr. Pickens blinked a couple of times and worked his jaw back and forth. "What brought that on?" he asked, somewhat pitifully, I thought.

"She just had a visitor," I told him. "One of the ex–Mrs. Pickenses. And she's not in the best of moods."

"Man," he said, rubbing his chin. "I guess she's not."

"I declare, Mr. Pickens," I said, "you need to get your personal business straightened out. Hazel Marie's mad as thunder, and you're not doing a thing to help matters by huddling up all over town with another woman."

"She's pretty upset, huh?"

I couldn't help but roll my eyes. "If you didn't get the message when she up and moved out on you, then I have nothing but pity for you."

"Well, she never gives me a chance to explain," he said, feeling sorry for himself. "Tammi still owns half of my house and she wants me to buy her out. That's all that's going on."

"Oh, no, it's not," I said, and right strongly too. "Tammi came here not ten minutes ago and told Hazel Marie that the two of you were getting back together. And Hazel Marie's supposed to bow out gracefully, so she and Tammi can be friends. Do you understand now, Mr. Pickens, the gall of that woman and why Hazel Marie's so upset?"

He held his head in his hand and moaned. Then I learned where Hazel Marie'd picked up her store of ugly words, for he said one under his breath. "What am I going to do?" he said, but I don't really think he was asking me.

I answered him anyway. "Get rid of Tammi, for starters. Then you'd better do some heavy-duty courting, and if I have to tell you how to do that, you're not the man I thought you were."

He grinned then, that same white flash under his mustache that captivated women, young and old. "Think she'd talk to me now?"

"No, and I wouldn't recommend trying. I'd stay out of her way, if I were you. You're invited to dinner tonight, though, so we can discuss ways of raising money for the Willow Lane folks. I'll tell her that we need your help, and she has to at least be courteous to you. The rest is up to you."

"Think I'll be safe?" And he laughed outright, shaking his head at the thought of it.

"Maybe she'll be calmed down by then," I said, turning to go inside. Then I stopped and looked back at him. "Far be it from me, Mr. Pickens, to comment unfavorably on a person's clothing. But, if I were you, I'd change trousers before parading around in public. The location of that stain might well give pause to whoever sees it."

~ *Chapter 16*

That evening, we all—except for Binkie and Coleman, who decided to stay home with a stopwatch—sat around the table trying to get ourselves and the fund drive organized. I told them about my meeting with Clarence Gibbs that afternoon, and the sky-high price he'd put on Willow Lane, leaving out his proposition concerning my house. That amount of money put a sudden damper on the conversation, as we all considered what we faced.

I sat there, my nerves getting more and more strung out, knowing that I had the solution at hand if I could bring myself to put my home at risk.

All I wanted was for someone, Binkie or Sam in particular, to tell me it was a good idea. But I held my peace, knowing that they'd tell me I was foolish and rash and lacking any business sense whatsoever.

Nobody was saying anything, just sitting there playing with the silverware and turning coffee cups in their saucers.

"All right," I said, breaking the silence. "So I shouldn't have let him know we were interested. It's all your fault, Sam, for not being home when I needed you. And Binkie's, too, for being practically out of commission." Then I leaned my head on my arm, which was propped on the dining room table. "No, the plain truth is that it's my fault. I jumped the gun and just pushed too hard."

I looked around at Sam, Mr. Pickens, Hazel Marie, Little Lloyd, and Lillian, hoping that one of them would disagree with me.

"He's a hard man to deal with," Sam said, "and I doubt anybody else could've done any better."

I wasn't sure of that, but I appreciated Sam's support.

"I better clear off this table," Lillian said, reaching for my plate. I'd insisted she join us while we ate all the desserts she'd spent the day making. She'd made so many, in fact, that she'd forgotten to cook a meal. The table was cluttered with the remains of take-out pizza, my least favorite attempt at a meal in the world, and the remnants of seven-layer cake and the last sliver of apple pie, which Mr. Pickens had been eyeing. And I kept eyeing him, his various marital escapades tumbling about in my mind. He and Hazel Marie had had a long talk in the living room before we ate, but from Hazel Marie's stony silence I guessed he'd not made much headway.

"Sit down, Miss Lillian," Mr. Pickens said, "and let those dishes alone. We need to come up with something here."

Lillian eased back into her chair and left the dishes alone. It surprised me that she hadn't taken a leaf from Hazel Marie's book and stopped talking or listening to Mr. Pickens after the way he'd gaped at her when he first came in that evening. He'd stood in the middle of the kitchen, his eyes wide and his mouth open, staring at her swishing nylon getup and huge running shoes, while she grinned at his foolishness.

"Lillian," he'd said, after making a thorough fool of himself, "that outfit was made for you. I've never seen anything like it." And of course he hadn't. Nor had anybody else, for that matter. I could've smacked him for bringing up what the rest of us had been trying to ignore, but Mr. Pickens wasn't known for his tactful ways. What surprised me, though, was that Lillian had taken no offense; she had just been tickled to death with his attention. Which just goes to show what a man who has a way with women can get away with.

Little Lloyd suddenly sat up. "Two hundred and fifty thousand dollars? Why, that's more than twenty-five thousand an acre, which is what those view lots up on the mountain're going for."

Lillian groaned at the thought, knowing as we all did that there were no views on Willow Lane.

"How can Mr. Gibbs do that?" Little Lloyd asked.

"He knows what he's doing," Sam said, frowning as he considered the matter. "Although that water-bottling notion of his beats all I've ever heard of. I wouldn't put it past him to have something else up his sleeve."

Yes, he did, and I knew it was my house, but I wasn't about to mention it.

Mr. Pickens turned to Sam and said, "You know Gibbs better than any of us. You think he'd listen to a counter-offer?"

"We could make one," Sam said, "but he won't take it. He's known for setting a price and sticking to it."

Sam looked across the table at me and smiled. "Don't beat yourself up about it, Julia. I've got a feeling he doesn't want to sell at all. He's set an unrealistic price on it to discourage us, while at the same time appearing to cooperate with a community effort. He's never much cared what the town thought of him but, in this case, he might."

"I'd hate to tell you what *I* think of him," I declared. "It's not like he'd just want to sit on empty land when there's money to be made. And how in the world he can think he'll make money on bottled water, I don't know."

Sam shook his head. "It doesn't make good sense, does it? What's likely is that he's had an offer for less than he quoted you, and he's trying to jack us up to get a better one."

"Well," Hazel Marie chimed in, "why don't we meet his price? I don't see why we can't raise two hundred and fifty thousand dollars, and besides, we wouldn't have to have that much up front, would we? I mean, we could get a bank loan to make up the rest."

"Somebody's got to be good for the rest of it, sweetheart," Mr. Pickens said. Hazel Marie bit her lip and looked away.

"But she's right," I said, coming to her defense. "Why couldn't the property itself be collateral for the major portion of the loan?"

"Ordinarily it would be," Sam said. "Except it's not worth that much. Look at the condition of those houses, for one thing. And anything in that section of town wouldn't be highly valued by any bank. They'd know it's way overpriced."

"Well, what're we going to do?" I asked, just about at my wit's end with every idea being shot down.

"Raise the money," Little Lloyd piped up. "And we can do it if everybody pitches in. We're going to have our first car wash this weekend, and the Scouts're going to rake leaves and donate what we make."

"Bless your little heart," Lillian said, reaching across his chair and hugging him.

"And remember the house tour," Hazel Marie said. "That'll bring in a good bit."

"Not nearly enough, though," I said. But fearing that I was throwing cold water on their optimism, I went on. "But every little bit will help."

"What we need," Sam said, "is some big money-raising

events, something that'll get the whole town involved, maybe even bring in people from out of town."

Hazel Marie's eyes widened as a thought came to her. "Maybe something like a basketball game between the doctors and the lawyers," she said. "Or a talent show with a big-name performer. Or a music festival! Oh, I know, maybe some country-western star like Alan Jackson would come and perform for us. That'd be a sell-out like you wouldn't believe."

Mr. Pickens smiled at her in the way I occasionally did at Little Lloyd when he had some high-flown idea. "That'd be great, sugar, but I doubt Alan Jackson would come to Abbotsville, regardless of how worthy the cause."

"Well, he might." Hazel Marie couldn't help but pout, but at least she'd spoken to him.

"A charity golf event might work," Sam offered. "Maybe get a few professionals to play with us amateurs—if, that is, the weather will cooperate."

"We may have to schedule that for spring," Mr. Pickens said. "Or we'll be shoveling snow to find the cups."

Little Lloyd giggled at the thought.

"One thing we can do starting right away is call some of the movers and shakers in town," Sam said. "Both individuals and businesses. First thing tomorrow, I'll start on a list of the folks who're well-heeled enough to make sizeable donations. That ought to prime the pump for the rest of the town."

"That's good, Sam," Mr. Pickens agreed. "That'll be where the big money is. But we need to get as many people involved as we can. I mean, have things that appeal to different interests, if you follow me."

"Like what?" I asked, beginning to feel some hope that

we really could raise that money. And if we could do it within three weeks, there'd be no risk in putting up my house to hold off Clarence Gibbs. My heart began to thud at the possibility, both of making it happen and of losing it all.

"Well, like a Poker Run, for instance; that'll bring out a whole 'nother segment of the population." Mr. Pickens grinned in that devilish way he had. Hazel Marie cut her eyes at him, unable to resist, and Sam perked up considerably.

I was afraid to ask, but I did. "What in the world is a Poker Run?"

"Oh," he said airily, waving his hand as if it wasn't important. But the way those black eyes of his glinted in the light of the chandelier put me on my guard. "It's just a way for us motorcycle types to raise money for charity."

Lillian frowned at the word *charity,* while I frowned at the word *motorcycle.* She mumbled something under her breath, but I spoke right up.

"Sam," I said, "whatever he's got in mind, I want you to stay out of it. I've seen how you drive that machine, and you don't need to be playing cards at the same time." I stopped as they stared at me, then went on. "Besides, we Presbyterians don't believe in gambling, and you know it."

Mr. Pickens's shoulders began shaking as he leaned his head practically on the table. Sam was trying not to laugh, but was having a hard time holding it down. Little Lloyd had a little smile on his face, but was too polite to laugh out loud.

"Well, what's so funny?" I demanded.

"Oh, Miss Julia," Hazel Marie said, ignoring Mr. Pickens and his antics. "You don't play cards while you're riding. It's more complicated than that. It's like, well, you ride to different places and draw a card at each stop. Then at the end of the run, you see who has the best hand, and that's the winner."

"I never heard of such," I said, still mortified at being laughed at. "How in the world does that raise money? Sounds more like just an excuse to ride around on those things to me."

"There's some truth in that," Sam agreed, his face now composed into a kindly smile. "But we could get sponsors beforehand, and the riders could make bets based on the cards they draw at each stop. Then, of course, all the players have to ante up, so with a good cause like we have, there'll be a lot of money to start with. And whoever wins the hand will donate whatever's in the pot."

"The pot," I repeated, not understanding the terminology. "Then why would anybody want to play if the winner doesn't win anything?"

"It's like you said, Miss Julia," Mr. Pickens said, still trying to get himself under control. "It's an excuse to ride and do some good, too. Besides, we could have a prize of some kind for the winner. Some kind of bike accessory, maybe, or a free tune-up." Then he seemed to get serious for a minute. "Too bad it's not warm enough for a Bikini Bike Wash."

"It's a lot of fun," Hazel Marie assured me, while ignoring him. "J. D. took me on a short one a few weeks ago, and I enjoyed it ever so much." She bounced a little in her chair, as the idea began to appeal to her. "Listen, you wouldn't believe the amount of money that could be raised. We only went with a small group and they raised several thousand dollars. If we get a whole big group of riders, why, no telling what we'd bring in."

"Really?" I asked, perking up at the thought.

Mr. Pickens eyed Hazel Marie warily, then ventured, "You'll ride with me, won't you, sugar?"

Hazel Marie flounced herself, swished her hair a little, then settled down with a martyr's sigh. "I guess I could, for Lillian's sake. But you better behave yourself."

Mr. Pickens smiled like a milk-fed cat. "You're on my backseat, then. Sam," he went on, "who's going with you?"

I glanced at the wistful look on Little Lloyd's face, knowing that he wanted to go. I held my breath, hoping that he'd be preserved from risking life and limb. I was ready to put my foot down if Sam wanted to take him. It was bad enough, to my mind, that Sam was considering the perilous venture for himself. I wouldn't be able to stand having the both of them in the way of danger.

"Julia," Sam said.

"Yes?" I responded.

"I'm answering J. D.," he said. "He asked who I'm taking, and I said you."

"Oh, no, Sam Murdoch. Nobody's taking me anywhere. I wouldn't get on that thing for all the tea in China."

"I'll go, Mr. Sam," Little Lloyd said.

"You're going," Mr. Pickens said, smiling at the boy. "We just have to work out the seating arrangements."

"Hazel Marie," I began to protest, "you can't . . ."

"Miss Julia," she said, "I promise you he'll be safe. But we really want you to go. You'd love it, I know you would. But first, we'd have to get you some pants so you can straddle the backseat."

I reared back in my chair. "If you think I'm going to pull on a pair of pants and hike myself astride one of those machines, why . . ." I nearly choked at the thought. "I can't believe you'd think I'd do such a thing. No," I said, shaking my head, as determined as I'd ever been in my life. "No way in this world would I ever consider it."

"I know what'll solve that," Sam said. He looked at Mr. Pickens. "J. D., will my Road King take a sidecar?"

Mr. Pickens's white teeth gleamed against his tanned face. "It sure will, and that way, Miss Julia, you can wear whatever you want." He looked over at Lillian and winked. "Although I was really looking forward to seeing you in one of Lillian's running suits."

Lillian began to laugh at that unlikely event, and everybody except me joined in. I didn't see a thing funny in the idea.

Sam looked at Little Lloyd. "That'll work out so all of us can go. You can ride behind me, and Julia'll be in the sidecar. How about that?"

The child nodded his head up and down like a yo-yo, delighted to have his place confirmed.

"Sidecar, backseat, or running board," I said. "I'm not getting in or on any of them. And I'm not gambling my money in any kind of card game. So just leave me out of your plans, and that is that."

I stood and began to gather the dishes, then I stomped out to the kitchen. But not before seeing another wink exchanged between Sam and Mr. Pickens.

Chapter 17

I made an effort and recovered myself enough to be pleasant for the rest of the evening, but I refused to listen to any further plans that included me as part of that outlandish Poker Run idea. Except at one point when Sam sidled up to me as we adjourned to the living room, saying that he really wanted me to go with him.

"You've threatened to take Lillian in my place," I told him. "So why don't you do it?"

"No, ma'am!" she said, as silverware clattered on a tray. "Don't be makin' no plans for me to go on that 'sickle. I'd as soon live in a tent as get a house on the back of one a them things."

Then she realized that she might have sounded somewhat ungrateful. "I mean, Mr. Sam, I sure do 'preciate what y'all tryin' to do, but me an' that machine not cut out for one another. Why, I'd prob'bly mash them tires flat if I got on it."

"No fear of that, Lillian," Sam told her. "You should see some of the riders in our club. They'd make three of you, and they haven't flattened any tires yet."

Then Mr. Pickens added his two cents' worth. "I can put a sidecar on mine, Lillian, if you want to go. Hazel Marie can ride behind me, and Lloyd behind Sam, and you and Miss Julia can ride in style in the sidecars."

"Nossir," she said, shaking her head. "Y'all got to count me out. 'Sides, I got the high blood, an' crawlin' on one a them things make it shoot up outta sight."

Oh, Lord, I thought, she's right. I knew Lillian had high blood pressure because she took medicine for it, and I knew she didn't need any stress beyond what she already had. In fact, just the thought of riding on a motorcycle made my own heart race and my mouth go dry. No telling what it would do to her.

"Just leave Lillian alone," I said. "Neither of us is going with you, and as far as I'm concerned, the whole idea is ill-conceived and mortally dangerous."

That pronouncement didn't have the effect I'd hoped it would, which was to stop the whole thing in its tracks. I sat in the living room, holding my peace, while the others continued to make their plans, discussing what route they would take, how many miles they'd go between stops, who would want to join them, what supplies to put in the storage bins on the back, where they'd rendezvous at the end, and how much money they might raise.

I watched Sam as closely as I could without attracting his attention, looking for evidence of diminishing faculties, not wanting to find any, but, on the other hand, thinking that any suspicious sign just might keep him at home. But he was talking sensibly with Mr. Pickens, answering Hazel Marie's questions in his usual courteous manner, and making plans with Little Lloyd on how they'd load the Road King.

I declare, I thought to myself with a sudden start, what am I thinking of? There I was feeling reassured about Sam's state of mind by the way he was participating in a conversation, when the whole conversation was on a subject that indicated a state of dementia in the first place.

Yet I couldn't discount their efforts out of hand. If I made that agreement with Mr. Gibbs, I'd have to support whatever fund-raising idea they came up with—even a Bikini Bike Wash, as long as I didn't have to wear one.

It wasn't long before Sam got up to leave, saying that he had house guests to see to. I'd heard Lillian go up the back stairs to her room, and he'd probably taken that as a signal to end the evening.

He started for the door, winked at me, and cocked his head at Mr. Pickens, who'd been edging closer and closer to Hazel Marie until she was mashed up against the arm of the sofa.

I followed Sam to the door, realizing as he had that those two wanted some time alone, which suited me fine, except Hazel Marie didn't seem to be that eager for it. But she'd fooled me before where Mr. Pickens was concerned.

I put my hand on Sam's arm, hoping to get in another word to dissuade him from pursuing the reckless idea of running around on two wheels. I wasn't against the idea, I was just against his participation in it.

Instead, he sidetracked me by saying, "Julia, if you know anybody who might make a sizeable donation, you might want to go ahead and approach them about it."

"I've been thinking of that," I said, handing his jacket to him. "And I have an idea or two. I went to see Mr. Benton down at the bank this morning about setting up an account for the funds we raise, and he told me he'd make sure it was done. He said he'd make the first donation himself, which I thought was nice of him, but no more than I expected." I paused, thinking of the bank that Wesley Lloyd Springer had owned, which had passed to me for the short while between his passing and Binkie's unloading it for me. I'd not foreseen any trouble setting up the account, nor of having everybody who worked there make a donation to it. After all, I still had a considerable interest in the bank, and none of them wanted to get crosswise of me. "And," I went on, "I made my donation, too, which I can increase if need be."

Then I led Sam closer to the door and said, "But I've also done something I'm not sure about, Sam, and if you don't think it's right, I hope you'll go to the bank tomorrow and straighten it out."

"I can't imagine what you've done," he said, with that smile that made me a little weak in the knees.

"I let Mr. Benton put my name on that account. Well, I mean as treasurer of the Willow Lane Fund, which is the name we came up with. I put Mary Alice McKinnon's name on it, too, since she's so good with figures."

"That's perfectly all right, Julia. Somebody has to be able to access the account, and I expect people think both of you are as trustworthy as they come."

I smiled, proud of my reputation in town. "Well, I didn't want anyone to think I'd overstepped. I'd just not thought about it until I got to the bank, and that seemed the easiest thing to do at the time."

"If it makes you feel better, I nominate you for treasurer, and I'll second the motion, as well."

"Now, one other thing," I said, smiling at his idea of Robert's Rules, which I was familiar with from my association with any number of women's organizations. "I'd like you to talk to Little Lloyd and Hazel Marie about their contribution." I stopped, bit my lip for a moment, then plowed right ahead. "Maybe you ought to talk to Binkie, too. Let her look over Little Lloyd's assets with you, before you do . . . I mean, before you let him do something rash. That's something Binkie can help you with."

He looked at me, a little smile on his face. "You can trust me with his welfare, Julia."

"Oh, I know I can," I said, somewhat flustered at being caught out. But the truth of it was, I didn't know if I could or not. "I didn't mean to imply . . ."

I finally got out of that embarrassing moment, but not before having another one.

"I tell you what, Julia," he said. "When we get this fund off the ground, why don't you and I go over to the Grove Park Inn? I've had dancing on my mind for a while now, and I've even bought some dancing pumps. Black patent leather that'll knock your eyes out."

I just stared at him. Why in the world he'd think of such a thing as dancing in black patent leather pumps was beyond me. It certainly wasn't my cup of tea and, as far as I knew, it'd never been his either.

Unwilling to get into it with him, I just said, "We'll see," bade him good-bye, and took Little Lloyd by the hand. We went upstairs to bed, leaving Hazel Marie alone with Mr. Pickens, the man she wasn't speaking to. And she might well not've been, for it wasn't long before I heard the front door close again and her lonely footsteps going back toward her bedroom.

❦

I came downstairs the next morning and was walking through the living room when the front doorbell rang.

"I'll get it," I called back to Lillian and Hazel Marie. They'd just gotten Little Lloyd off to school, and Hazel Marie was making out some kind of motorcycle accessories list.

I opened the door to be greeted by two huge floral arrangements, which hid the face of the delivery person from The Watering Can.

"Morning, Mrs. Springer," a voice said. "Somebody's real popular 'round here today."

"I daresay," I said, just so put out with Sam's continued foolishness I could hardly stand it. "Put them here on this table, if you will."

I stepped back to let him in, thanked him, then went to call the others to witness more evidence of Sam's carelessness in throwing money away on spring flowers on a brisk October day.

"Oh, they're beautiful!" Hazel Marie said. "Who're they from?"

"Guess," I said dryly.

"He send you two at a time now?" Lillian asked, eyeing the flowers and probably wondering, as I was, where we were going to put them.

"Yes, and it's proof of what I've been concerned about," I told her. "He probably forgot he'd ordered one, so he turned around and ordered another one."

"Oh, look!" Hazel Marie sang out, as she unpinned an envelope from one of the arrangements. "This one's for Lillian!"

A look of disbelief and delight swept across Lillian's face. "No! Nobody be sendin' me flowers."

"Look right here," Hazel Marie said, holding the envelope out. "There's your name, plain as day. Open it. Let's see who sent them."

Lillian's fingers trembled as she took out the card. "Oh, my goodness. They from Miss Binkie and Coleman. I think I jus' about cry." And she sniffed to prove it, at the same time reaching out to touch one of the flowers.

"What does the card say?" I asked, somewhat chagrined by my assumption that both arrangements were for me.

"It say they thinkin' 'bout me."

"That is just so sweet," Hazel Marie said. "Now let's see who the other one's for." She plucked the envelope from the other arrangement and handed it to me with a knowing smile. "For you, Miss Julia."

I pulled out the card, and then quickly shoved it back into the envelope.

"Who it from?" Lillian asked. "The same one what been sendin' 'em?"

"Well, yes."

"What does the card say?" Hazel Marie said; she should've known better than to ask such a question.

"It says . . . well, it's personal," I said, and slipped it into my pocket.

"I bet," Hazel Marie teased.

"Well, not *that* personal," I said, anxious not to let on what I'd seen at first glance, which was *Roses are red,* after which I'd stopped reading. "Sam's a gentleman, and he's just thanking us for dinner last night. Even if it was take-out pizza." Then, to change the subject, I said, "Hazel Marie, we need to help Lillian with dinner tonight. Little Lloyd needs a balanced meal, and you do, too, Lillian. We don't want you getting sick from all the worry you have right now."

"Yessum, we all need one. I ain't never forget to cook supper before. I don't know what got into me."

"Oh, Lillian," Hazel Marie said. "You had a lot on your mind, and it was our fault for not realizing it. I'll tell you what. I'll cook supper tonight."

I rolled my eyes just the slightest bit, for Hazel Marie was not all that adept in the kitchen. But then, neither was I.

Chapter 18

Lillian took her flowers to the kitchen, grinning all over herself. I stayed in the living room, pacing back and forth and glancing occasionally at mine, while Hazel Marie took herself on another shopping trip.

Pacing and thinking, I went around and around, trying to decide what to do. If I could muster the courage to put up my house for three weeks, we could stay Clarence Gibbs's hand. He couldn't sell the Willow Lane property to anybody else, and he couldn't proceed with his water bottling plans.

But could we raise two hundred and fifty thousand dollars in that amount of time? Frankly, I didn't see how we could, no matter how lucrative a Poker Run would be. Maybe, I thought, I could unload some of my other real estate within that time. There was the convenience store on the highway near the edge of town and, Lord knows, I'd be happy to be rid of that trailer park out in Delmont. Why in the world Wesley Lloyd ever invested in such as that, I'll never know. Of course, they brought in regular income, which was nice to have, but I also knew that neither of them would sell quickly.

Of course, Binkie would have a fit if I put them on the

market. But I had to have a backup plan, or I'd be out on the street with Lillian.

Well, there was nothing to do but get at it, and start bringing in some money, some way, somehow.

With that decided, I pushed through the kitchen door. "Lillian, I'm going to pay a visit to old man Jones, and I want you to go with me."

Her eyes got wide and her mouth gaped open. "Ole man *Thurlow* Jones?"

"Yes, and don't look at me like that. He's got enough money to afford a big donation, and I intend to get it from him."

"Miss Julia, you can't go see that ole man. He crazy. No tellin' what he do, you go over there."

I clicked my tongue. "He doesn't bother me. Besides, he's not really crazy, he just likes to act that way. Says it keeps the riffraff away."

"You better not go see him. Let Mr. Sam go, he know how to handle him."

"Oh, Lillian, he does not. Thurlow Jones takes great pleasure in getting the best of any man in town. Don't ask me why, but he is much more amenable to women. At least, he'll be courteous to me, whereas he'd turn Sam down flat before he got in the door."

"Yessum, that why you ought not go. I hear how he be with the ladies."

"He's not interested in women my age," I said, waving my hand. "Listen, Lillian, that old man is so cantankerous that he won't give a cent to the church or to any other kind of normal fund. But he *does* give money—lots of it—to the craziest things. Why, LuAnne Conover told me that he gave five thousand dollars to some educational program about African violets, and they only needed a couple of hundred. And Binkie says he gives thousands of dollars every time elections roll around to anybody who's running against an incumbent. And I know he gave an untold amount to a group of women who call themselves goddesses after some preacher wrote a letter to the editor complaining about them. You remember that, don't you? It was all in the paper."

"Yessum," she mumbled, still unconvinced. "I guess. But that don't mean he listen to us." She stopped, then began to smile, her gold tooth gleaming. " 'Less he think you an' me look like a goddess." She bent over, laughing at the thought.

I laughed, too, and when we'd recovered, I said, "So you'll go with me?"

"Guess I will, if you bound an' determined. But I ought not go in this athaletic suit. Maybe Coleman come over an' help me move them boxes till I find somethin' else to put on. Miss Hazel Marie, she 'changed some of them things what was too little. But, Miss Julia, don't none of them fit, either."

"You look fine in what you have on," I said, although I'd dressed carefully that morning in a light wool mauve dress, the one Hazel Marie said complemented my coloring. My winter white coat set it off perfectly.

"When you plannin' on goin' to Mr. Jones's?" Lillian asked.

"Right now's as good a time as any," I said, looking at my watch. "I don't want to lose my nerve. One other thing, Lillian," I went on, "this visit to Thurlow Jones has to be our secret until it's successfully completed. Don't tell anybody. Now, do you think I ought to wear a hat and gloves? I want Mr. Jones to know that I mean business, and I want to look like it."

She looked me over, while I was doing the same to her. I wished I hadn't brought up the subject of clothing, for she was in another nylon running suit purchased by Hazel Marie. This one was green with yellow stripes, and she was still wearing those huge boat-like tenny-pumps.

"No'm, I don't think so. He might think you there on church bus'ness, an' that turn him off good."

"You're right. Well, get your coat and let's go."

"I wouldn't do this," she mumbled as she slipped into her winter coat, " 'cept I know you do it anyway by yo'self."

As we drove the few blocks to Thurlow Jones's once-stately brick house, I grew more nervous. I'd known him for years, but we were not what you'd call close acquaintances, much less friends. Of course, with my unassailable position in town, he would know about me, just as I knew about him. But just what would he know? That I'd been the duped wife of a man who carried on a secret life right under her nose? Lord, he could well laugh me off his porch before I got into the house. I ground my teeth together and pulled into his long driveway.

"Look at that, would you?" I said, looking around at the poorly maintained yard, full of weeds, dying grass, and fall leaves. A shutter hung halfway off one of the front windows, and a torn screen flapped in the breeze. "You'd think he'd keep this place up. He certainly has the money to do it."

"Yessum," Lillian said. I knew she was none too happy to be there, which meant that I had to keep my own spirits up.

"All right," I said, opening the car door. "Let's go."

I marched up the walk to the front door, my pocketbook gripped under my arm, and banged the knocker. Lillian breathed heavily behind me.

"Nobody home," she whispered. "Le's us go."

I shook my head. I'd gotten this far on pure nerve, and I might not be able to work up enough of it to try again. This had to be it. Just as I lifted the knocker again, the door flew open and there he stood.

"I don't want any, whatever you're sellin', givin' away, or witnessin' to," he all but shouted in my face. Then we both stood there and stared at each other.

He was a small man, short and skinny as a rail, and dressed in a white shirt that was none too clean. A sprig of white chest hair peeked out of the shirt's open neck, a most unappetizing sight. His trousers hung low on his skinny hips, the cuffs drooping down over leather bedroom slippers. I took all that in, then lifted my eyes to his thinning white hair that badly needed barbering and his sunken and unshaven cheeks that gleamed with white bristles, and stared through his glasses into his fierce blue eyes.

"Well, now," he said before I could get a word out. "Who is this? It couldn't be the Lady Springer, could it? Here with her handmaid? How do I rate such an honor?"

I drew myself up, determined not to let his sarcasm disturb me. "Good morning, Mr. Jones. I am Julia Springer and this is my friend, Lillian. We're here on an urgent mission, and wonder if you'd allow us a moment of your time."

"Come in, come in," he said, smiling widely and clicking his upper plate firmly in place. "My god, I haven't had a surprise like this in a coon's age." He stepped back and waved us into a dark, musty-smelling hall.

We followed him into an equally dark parlor, filled with too much tapestry-covered furniture, old newspapers, and a foul-smelling Great Dane. Lillian hummed deep in her throat as she walked in behind me, and I knew she was liking none of it.

"Have a seat," Mr. Jones said in an immoderately loud voice. "Take any of 'em, I don't care." Then, raising a newspaper at the Great Dane, he yelled, "Get off of there, Ronnie! Let the ladies have that settee."

The dog lumbered off the sofa and curled up by the sooty fireplace.

I sat gingerly on the still warm sofa, and patted a place beside me for Lillian. She didn't much want to take it, but I glared at her, so she did. I needed her close by.

"Well, here we are," Mr. Jones said, his eyes glinting from behind his glasses as if he were thoroughly enjoying this break from his morning's routine. He settled himself into a recliner that was long past due for reupholstering. "Just what can I do for you, Lady Springer?"

Determined to put a stop to his ragging and get down to the business at hand, I said, "My name is Mrs. Julia Springer. And I'd appreciate your addressing me as such."

"Hah!" He threw his head back, seemingly tickled to death at being corrected. "A woman with spirit! I like that. Go on, *Mrs.* Springer, I know you want something from me, so let's hear it."

"Well, Mr. Jones, it's like this," I said, gathering myself to present my case.

"I can't wait," he said, fidgeting in his chair to let me know how eager he was. "This'll be good, I know it will. Now, Mrs. . . . *Julia,* can I call you Julia? You wouldn't mind, would you? First-name basis, that's what we need here."

"Of course," I said, although I most certainly did mind. But when you're on a begging mission, you have to put up with more than you ordinarily would. "Now, Mr. Jones," I began again.

"Thurlow!" He said, grabbing the arms of his recliner and leaning toward me. Little specks of spittle flew toward me as he spoke. I leaned back out of the line of fire. "Call me Thurlow. Don't know when I've had such a handsome woman in my house. We got to get to know one another and do it fast. I'm on my last legs here, god doggit."

"Oh, I wouldn't say that," I said, anxious to placate him and get what I was there to get. "You look in fine shape to me."

"I knew it!" he boomed, then pulled a lever so that both he and the chair reclined with a thump. "I knew it soon as I set eyes on you. We're gonna get along just fine. Now whatta you want?"

Lord, his moods seemed to go up one side and down the other. Lillian was trying to make herself smaller as she scrunched down on the sofa, her breath catching in her throat every time he switched channels.

So I told him what I wanted, running as fast as I could through the catastrophe that had befallen the people on Willow Lane, Clarence Gibbs's plans for a plant to bottle cow-tainted water, and our need to help the people who had helped build our community.

"Clarence Gibbs," he said, running a hand across his mouth as his eyes wandered around the room. "Never had much use for that sneaky sonuvabitch."

"Mr. Jones!" I rared back, shocked by his use of profanity in mixed company. Then, on second thought, I decided to make use of his openly expressed feelings. "Ah, well, many others might agree with you. Although perhaps not in such terms. Now, what we need to do, Mr. Jones . . ."

"Thurlow. Call me Thurlow," he reminded me, but not as strongly as before. He appeared to have his mind still on Clarence Gibbs.

"Thurlow," I said, almost choking on it, "we need to buy up that property and prevent Mr. Gibbs from proceeding with his own plans. It's for sale for a period of three weeks only, so we have to raise the money before then. I know you'd like to help, Thurlow, so what can we count on you for?"

I wasn't good at asking for money and it grated on my soul to have to do it. He was still musing over something in his own mind and didn't appear to have heard me. So, figuring if I ground my teeth much more I'd have to make a dental appointment, I gritted them once again and leaned over to put my hand on his arm.

I smiled my most winning smile. "Thurlow? The people on Willow Lane really need your help."

He glanced at my hand, then leaned close, the bristles on his face shining whitely. He blew out his breath from behind those false teeth, and it was all I could do to keep a smile on my face.

"One thing I'll have you know, little lady," he said, offending me something awful—I'd easily make two of him. I took my hand away, wishing I could smack him with it, and prepared myself to leave. But he wasn't through. "I'm not in the habit of giving money to every Tom, Dick, or Harry who shows up on my doorstep."

Then in a sudden change of mood, he demanded, "Who else have you hit up for donations? If you expect me to be the Lone Ranger on this, you got another think coming."

"Everybody," I assured him. "Everybody in town is participating. Why, Mr., I mean, Thurlow, the children are contributing, banks, businesses, individuals—just everybody—and we want you to be a part of it. Why, just listen, the garden club is having a home tour, the Boy Scouts are raking leaves—which you could take advantage of; your yard badly needs it. There's talk of a bake sale, a talent show, a basketball game and . . ." I turned to Lillian, using the opportunity to slide away from Mr. Jones's vicinity. "What's the name of that other thing Mr. Pickens was talking about?"

"A Poker Run," she mumbled.

"What's that?" Mr. Jones leaned forward, cupping his hand around his ear. "Speak up, I didn't hear you."

"A Poker Run," I said, in a voice somewhat above my normal tones. "You know, it's something having to do with cards and motorcycles."

"Hah!" he cackled, throwing himself against the recliner so that both feet came off the floor as it sprang backward. "I'd like to see that!"

"Well, you'll certainly have the opportunity. Now, Thurlow, how much can we expect from you?"

He raised himself to a half-sitting position, fastened his eyes on me, and said, "You ridin'?"

"Oh, no, not me." I twittered at the thought. Everybody and his brother seemed to think I belonged on a motorcycle. "No," I said, shaking my head as if I purely regretted my inability to straddle and ride. "That's not the sort of thing I do."

"I dare you," he said, taking an inordinate amount of pleasure in doing so.

"Absolutely not."

"Hah!" he yelled, jerking his chair upright so that he was almost catapulted off of it. "Double-dog dare you."

I'd had almost more than I could take from Thurlow Jones, so I gripped my pocketbook and prepared to rise.

Then, squinching his eyes as a beam of sunlight in the darkened room flashed on his glasses and cocking his head in a calculating way, he said, "I'd give money to see it."

I gasped, struggling to maintain my decorum as I balanced my strong aversion to motorcycles in general, and to me on one in particular, against my even stronger desire for a large check from Thurlow Jones. He watched me carefully, as if he could see the battle in my mind. I settled back on the sofa.

"How much?" I whispered, the battle now won.

"How much what?"

"How much would you give to see me on one of those death machines?"

"Hah!" he yelled, springing back in the chair again, his legs spraddled out so that one slipper went flying, landing on Ronnie, who passed gas in surprise.

I ignored the faux pas, as any well-bred lady would under the circumstances. Lillian looked as if she were about to pass out, but then she was closer to the dog.

"Behave, Ronnie," Mr. Jones yelled. "There's ladies present. Now, Ju-u-lia," he crooned, moderating his voice and turning to me with what looked like a salivating grin on his face. "I'd give one hundred thousand buckeroos to see you ride in that Poker Run. How you like them apples?"

I couldn't get my breath. A hundred thousand dollars. Lord, that property was as good as ours. A quick thought of what I'd have to do for it passed through my mind, and I just as quickly let it pass on out. I'd face that when the time came.

"I like them just fine. Now, if you'll just give me a check."

"Not so fast, little lady," he said, that grin still on his face. "I got to see it before you get it. You might cash my check and then back out on me."

"Indeed, I would not," I said, ruffled that he would impugn my given word. "But, now that you've brought it up, how do I know *you* won't back out on *me*? I'm the one risking my life, here. To say nothing of the impropriety of it all."

He cackled again, seemingly delighted to have someone stand up to him. "We better come to terms then, hadn't we? You wanna sign an agreement?" He hopped up and scrounged around on a littered desk in the corner, then swung around with a sheet of paper and a pen in hand. "Your woman," he said, pointing the pen at Lillian, "can be a witness. We can get it notarized, too, if you want to hold me to the fire."

"That won't be necessary," I said, aghast at taking such an agreement downtown for some notary to look at. Even though they're not supposed to read a document, you know they do. "No," I went on, "what you can do is give me a down payment today, and we'll both sign an agreement that upon my completion of the Poker Run, you'll hand over the remainder."

His eyebrows went up and a look of absolute pleasure passed across his face. "A looker *and* a businesswoman! God dog, you don't meet many of them," he said, then he turned to Lillian. "That's a fine-looking woman, ain't she?" Lillian nodded, too mesmerized to speak. "Yessir," Mr. Jones went on in a satisfied way, "a handsome woman with a head on her shoulders. Holds herself well, too, don't she? A little age on her, though, but beggars can't be choosers, can they?"

Lillian was nodding, then shaking, her head, her eyes wide and round. I sat there while my qualities were being analyzed as if I were an object up for sale.

Lord, I thought, that's exactly what I am.

Then, waving the sheet of paper, Mr. Jones said to me, "Come on over here, I'm gonna write this up right now. Can't let you get away without signing it."

"And you need to sign your check," I said, as sharply as I could between gritted teeth. "Make it out to the Willow Lane Fund."

He laughed, his narrow shoulders shaking. "Tell you what

I'll do," he said, holding up the pen. "I'll write out a check for fifty thousand, and give it to you today. Then I'll write another one for the same amount, but I'll hold onto it till I see you come sailing in on a motorcycle. That'll make a cool one hundred thousand. Now, wait, I see you gettin' all huffed up, but I ain't finished." He looked off into the distance as his mind turned over some other crazy notion. "Here's the deal," he finally said. "Listen up, now. What I'll do is donate ten thousand more dollars for every female you can get to ride in that Poker Run. And I mean *quality* ladies. I'm not talking your usual run of Harley mamas."

I needed a fan to stir up enough air to breathe. Other ladies? Who? And how in the world could I talk anybody into doing what I so feared to do myself?

I narrowed my eyes, thinking LuAnne, maybe Helen Stroud, and certainly Hazel Marie. Several young women in the church came to mind.

"How many would you have in mind?" I asked.

"However many you can get. Hell, it's only money." He watched me, his eyes glinting behind his glasses. "But let's make it interesting. Any woman under fifty won't count."

There went more than half the women I'd come up with, but there were still plenty who could meet the age requirement—if they'd admit it. "Write out the agreement and the down payment check," I told him. "And sign both of them. I'll deposit the check, and the other one better be waiting for me when I come off that Run."

And he did, laughing to himself and mumbling about how he liked a woman who knew her own mind. And he had certainly met one today, although I feared that I might've lost it, too.

I took the signed check and a copy of the agreement and

walked toward the door, Lillian close behind. Mr. Jones hurried in front of us, almost skipping in his eagerness to be a gentleman.

As he opened the door, I spoke as formally as I could under the circumstances. "I can't tell you how much your generosity is appreciated, Mr., I mean, Thurlow. You are to be commended for the greatness of your heart."

I stepped aside so Lillian could precede me, as I knew she was anxious to get away. While she hurried to the car, I turned and offered my hand to Mr. Jones.

"Thank you again," I said stiffly, wanting to leave the impression of a cool and self-possessed businesswoman. "And, Thurlow, if you know what's good for you, you won't even think of stopping payment on this check."

"Dear lady, you have cut me to the quick," he said, taking my offered hand with one of his, while the other one slid around my waist. Before I knew it, his bony fingers had nipped through wool coat, wool dress, and silk underclothing to a most tender and private spot.

"Mr. Jones!" I shrieked, backhanding him with my pocketbook and scurrying out the door. I could hear him cackling as I steamed my way to the car.

"Lillian," I said, breathing heavily as I locked the car door behind me. "You won't believe what that old goat did."

Chapter 19

"Don't you tell a soul," I said to Lillian, as we got to the house. I was so glad to be home and away from that offensive old man I didn't know what to do.

What I did was take off my coat and try to calm my jittery nerves. "Let's have some coffee, Lillian. I declare, I have never been subjected to such an outrage in my life."

I sank down into a chair at the table and covered my face with my hands. "Such presumption," I moaned. Then I took my hands down and looked at her. "Say something, Lillian."

"That ole man need a whippin', is what I say. An' nobody gonna know anything 'bout it from me. But what you gonna tell Mr. Sam about how you gettin' them checks?"

"I'll just tell him that we asked him for a donation, and he gave us one. The other one, the one we'll get if I ride that machine, well, I'll think of something when the time comes. Just don't let on that he's paying to see me on a motorcycle. And, whatever you do, don't say a word about him pinching me, it's too humiliating."

Lillian set a cup of coffee in front of me and said, "You don't need to tell me more'n oncet 'bout that pinchin', but you better make out like you change yo' mind 'bout that

Poker Run thing. An' Mr. Sam gonna want to know why you change it. An' something else you better be thinking about is how you gonna get some of them quality ladies on a motorsickle."

"I'm trying to think of how to present it to them." I picked up the cup, then set it back down. "Oh, Lord, Lillian, you know what this means, don't you? I have been bought and paid for. That's why that repulsive old man thought he could put his hands on my person and get away with it. He paid for the privilege. What if he tries to pinch every woman who climbs on a motorcycle?"

"I 'spect he won't try long 'fore somebody take a broom to him." She put her hands on her hips and laid down the law. "Now, I want you to quit carryin' on like you doin'. All he done was put up money for that Poker Run thing to help us all out. It don't buy him nothin' else, so you jus' set him straight on that."

I started laughing, though I felt more like crying from the shame of it all. "Oh, Lillian, I think I did. I whacked him good with my pocketbook, and it certainly set him back a step or two." I wiped my eyes, trying to see the humor of being pursued by a disreputable old man with false teeth that kept loosening up on him. For all I knew, Sam could be just as crazy, but at least he had his own teeth. And he was tall.

I shuddered at the thought of that grizzled old man with his wet, shiny lips getting close to me again. It was beyond me why such a short, repulsive man found me so attractive. For once, I could understand why widows wanted to remarry so quickly. They couldn't stand being pawed at by men who swarmed up from the bottom of the barrel.

"Okay, Lillian," I said, having had enough of ruminating over such unappetizing matters. "I'll call Sam and see if he'll have dinner with us. And I might as well call Mr. Pickens, too, whether Hazel Marie wants him here or not. Though she probably does. He was the one with the Poker Run idea, so we need to get that started. I declare, I feel like we're feeding them every night."

"That's jus' about what we doin'," she said. "But they batchin' it, so we he'pin' 'em out. What you want me to fix?"

"I don't know. What about a pork tenderloin? And some sweet potatoes, and whatever else. That's a good fall dinner."

She nodded and went toward the pantry to see what she'd need from the grocery store. I left to do the telephoning, determined to be happy about the money I was raising without worrying too much about the way I was getting it.

When I dialed Sam's number, it was a relief to catch him at home. I realized that I hadn't heard from him all day, and wondered if he'd been lying on the side of the road somewhere. "Sam," I said, "where have you been?"

"Collecting money, Julia. Why? You worried about me?" I could hear the smile in his voice, which got my back up.

"Not one bit. I just thought you'd check in sometime today, since hardly a day goes by that you don't."

"Day's not over yet, Julia."

"I know that, but here's why I called. How are you doing with your collecting? Are people responding like they should?"

"Pretty well, I'd say. But we've got a long way to go. I thought I'd talk to Gibbs and see how much time he'll give us."

"Oh," I said, trying to think fast. "I wouldn't do that, Sam. I'm still negotiating with him. In fact, I'm supposed to call him tomorrow morning to see if we can come to some agreement."

"That's fine, then. If he'd give us six months, I know we could come up with his price."

"Hold on. I've got to sit down," I said, and did. Six months, I thought. Lord, we had to do better than that. Clarence Gibbs would have both my house and his water-bottling plant long before then. "He gave me the impression that he won't wait that long. He wants to get started on something."

"The only thing we can do is just keep raising the money," Sam said. "I might as well warn you, though. There's all kinds of talk around town. I've heard that he's listing it with a realtor, that he's thinking of an asphalt plant, or maybe an office building. And the word is still going around about a water-bottling plant."

"Oh, Sam, we have got to nip all of that in the bud," I said, wishing I could strangle Clarence Gibbs for his under-handed way of doing business. He was supposed to be giv-ing me a little time, and instead he was letting the rumors run rife. And I knew why—to make me anxious enough to seal an agreement concerning my house.

Sam said, "You'll be happy to know that I got pledges of about thirty thousand today, and Binkie has the fund set up, with you as the treasurer. It's all legal and safe-guarded, so we can begin funneling donations into it any time."

"Good. But, Sam, pledges're not good enough. We have to have the money in hand. You know how people are about pledges; they tend to put off paying them. That's the way it works for the church, anyway."

We chatted a little while longer, and several times I was on the verge of telling him about my visit to Thurlow Jones. But each time I opened my mouth to do it, I closed it again, or filled it with something else. I knew Sam would tell me I shouldn't have done it, not that that would've stopped me, but still. I didn't want him to know exactly how I'd been able to extract a hefty donation from the most unlikely source he could imagine.

"I fixed you a sam'ich for lunch," Lillian said as I walked into the kitchen.

"Oh, thank you, I do need to eat something. Now, Lillian," I said as I sat at the table, "there's something else I need to do, and I'll need you to help me."

She hung a dish towel on the rack, and said, "Ever'time you want me to help with something, you get us in trouble. You not aimin' to go see that ole man again, are you?"

"Lord, no," I said. "I'm as through with him as I can get. No, Lillian, I need to make a trip up to that spring so I can see just what kind of water is in it. I need to know what we're up against. For all I know, Clarence Gibbs is bluffing, trying to make out like that land is more valuable than it is. I aim to call him on it."

"Well," she said, turning away. "I kinda thought when Little Lloyd get out of school, we'd go over to my house one las' time. That Rose of Sharon need diggin'."

"Oh, Lillian," I said, just done in by my own thoughtlessness. Of course, her plants could stay right where they were, if I played my cards right. But I didn't want anybody to know what kind of hand Clarence Gibbs had dealt me. "I'd forgotten about moving your plants, being so taken up with all this fund-raising. We'll pick up Little Lloyd at school and go right on over there."

She glanced back at me. "I don't want to mess up yo' plans if you need to see 'bout that water."

"My plans can wait, but not for too long. Besides, it might be better to make that trek to the spring after dark, anyway."

"After dark?" She stared at me, her eyes wide. "Le's do it in the mornin', if you have to do it."

"No, it'd be better if nobody saw us. I tell you, Lillian, you don't know what kind of man I'm dealing with in Clarence Gibbs. It wouldn't surprise me one little bit if we got up there and found nothing but a mud puddle, with him carrying on like he's Moses getting a miracle out of a rock. We'll run up there as soon as Sam and Mr. Pickens leave tonight."

She didn't look too happy about the prospect of traipsing around after dark, but I couldn't help that. It had to be done before I risked my house the next morning.

Lord, when I drove up and parked us in front of Lillian's house that afternoon, I was overcome with the sense of emptiness of the whole street. There were no chairs or swings on the porches, no hanging baskets, no dogs lying in the shade, no curtains on the windows. The little houses looked so weather-worn and lonely as they waited for the yellow monsters parked in the field beyond, that I wondered how wise it was to've brought Lillian back.

Still, I didn't blame her for wanting one last look around before the wreckers reduced her house to kindling. It was heartbreaking, though, and I could've cried for her. Although I will say that if you looked with cold business eyes at the shape the houses were in, you'd have to admit that leveling them would be a decided improvement.

And that made me mad all over again, for it was Clarence Gibbs who'd let them get in such a state. Right then and there, I decided that Little Lloyd and I would make a tour of inspection of all our rental property and make sure we weren't letting them deteriorate as he had let his.

Still, as I looked closer at the houses, I could see possibilities for refurbishment. The houses were not as far gone as Mr. Gibbs had made out when he'd had them condemned. Do a little masonry work on the foundations, replace a few roofs, and put on a coat of paint, plus upgrading the interiors, and those houses would be fit to live in. It would cost time and money. But, then, what didn't?

"Well," Lillian said as she opened the car door and maneuvered both the hoe she'd been holding and herself out. It wasn't easy to do with her huge pocketbook gripped under her arm. "Settin' here ain't gettin' it done."

"I sure don't like this," Little Lloyd said, stepping out with a shovel in his hand. "I mean, I sure don't like that you have to move, Miss Lillian. But I'm glad we can take your flowers with us. Come show me what you want dug up."

"They 'round yonder in the back," she told him. And the two of us followed her around the house. "I sho' hate to leave my apple tree an' the grape arbor back there, but they too big to take."

"Yes," I agreed. "And I doubt we'd get them in the trunk, either."

They both smiled at that, but we were a serious trio, as we trooped to the back of the house.

"What all you want, Miss Lillian?" Little Lloyd asked as he surveyed the side yard, which was lined with a chicken wire fence, overhung with ivy and honeysuckle.

"That Rose of Sharon right there." She pointed to the bush. "An' my snowball bush, if we can get it outta the ground. An' maybe one or two of them daylilies. We don't need many of them 'cause they spread out an' grow by theyselves. An' if you not too tired, Little Lloyd, my penny bush. I already cut it back, so it won't take up much room."

"Penny bush?"

"Peony," I whispered, but he didn't know the difference, so I needn't have bothered.

"Oh, my goodness," I said, beginning to wonder if I'd started suffering from a mental weakness of my own. "Lillian, I need to put something in the trunk of the car, some plastic or something. I completely forgot about that."

"Yessum, that car be ruint we put all that dirt in there."

"Well, I'll run to the hardware store and get something. Little Lloyd, you go ahead and start digging, and I'll be back in a few minutes."

"Yes, ma'am. And maybe you ought to get something to tie down the trunk. We're going to have so much, it might not close. Good thing, though," he said, as he pushed the shovel with his foot into the soil, "that the leaves're all gone. They might not've fit in the trunk at all."

As I turned to leave, Little Lloyd called out, "Miss Julia, you might better bring back a mattock, too. This ground is pretty hard."

I waved, not too sure what a mattock was, but sure that someone at the hardware store would know. I heard Lillian caution Little Lloyd against cutting any roots, as she began hacking at the daylily bed with the hoe.

I left them to it, and drove to Prince's Hardware. It was not my favorite place to shop since I didn't know one thing from another in it. But it was far and away better than one of those huge sprawling things outside of town where you had to dodge some old man wanting to hug you and where you couldn't find anything or anybody to help you. Give me a business that's family-owned and operated anytime. And I'm talking about a local family, not one that lives in Arkansas.

Clabe Harris greeted me as soon as I stepped inside the store, but he did it without running at me with arms out-spread. He knew I'd not tolerate any such familiarity, nor would any other well-positioned woman in town.

"Mrs. Springer," he said. "What can I do for you today?"

I looked around at the baskets of nails of all sizes, the

stacks of shining snow shovels ready for a change in the weather, the shelves of sorted hinges, bolts, screws, and other hardware oddments. A man I didn't know was examining a leaf blower with the help of another clerk, and I hoped to goodness he wouldn't fire it up. The noise of those things could deafen a person.

"How do you do, Mr. Harris," I said, noting his thinning hair, his checked sport shirt, his khaki trousers, and his running shoes that looked enough like the ones Hazel Marie had bought for Lillian to've been their twins. "I need something called a mattock, and something to put in the trunk of my car to hold some plants we're digging, and something to tie the lid down if it won't close."

"Yes, ma'am, you want a liner and a tie-down. We got 'em right down this aisle." He led me past shelves filled with plumbing apparatus to an area with all kinds of gardening equipment. "Now, what size mattock you want?"

Not knowing that they came in different sizes, I thought for a minute and said, "Boy size."

He picked up a yard tool that I immediately recognized, hefted it, and said, "I think this'll do you. Just right for a youngster or a lady gardener."

"It's not for me," I informed him, but then thought I might have to use it if Little Lloyd and Lillian gave out. I'd do it, too, because I intended for Lillian to have what she wanted from that yard. "It's for Little Lloyd, at least for a start. Do you think he can manage this thing?"

"Sure he can. Y'all plantin' bulbs? We got some real nice Dutch tulip bulbs over here. They'll make a pretty show, come spring."

"Not today, Mr. Harris. We're moving some of Lillian's plants before those bulldozers tear up everything in sight, which I understand will be first thing tomorrow."

Clabe Harris's shoulders seemed to sag in concern. "That's bad doin's, Mrs. Springer. I was sorry to hear 'bout it. But," he said, straightening somewhat, "business has to go on. Who knows? Clarence Gibbs may make a real economic impact on the town that'll benefit a lot more people than the few who have to move."

"What kind of economic impact?" I asked, wanting to know what he'd heard about Clarence Gibbs's plans.

"Well, I don't know for sure, but word is that he's found some kind of spring or well up on the ridge of that field, and Willow Lane's the only easy access to it."

"Well, my goodness," I said, trying to downplay my interest in the matter. "What's so wonderful about a spring that he has to tear down people's houses in order to get to it?"

"Word is, he's gonna channel that water and build a bottling plant. Then he's gonna put it on the market. I'd kinda like to invest in something like that."

"Why, Mr. Harris, that doesn't make sense. There's already more bottled water on grocery shelves than anybody could want. And I wouldn't want any of it. Why in the world would Clarence Gibbs think he's got something the others don't have?"

Mr. Harris's eyes slid away from mine, and a flush of color ran up his neck. "I don't know too much about it, but the way I hear it, that water's real good for your constitution."

"Really?" I asked, as if it was all new to me.

"Well, uh, I might've heard wrong."

"Oh, I doubt that. If Mr. Gibbs has to move a bunch of old people out so he can put that water in a bottle, I'd like to hear what makes it so special."

"Well." Mr. Harris was finding a shelf of garden pest killer mighty interesting by this time. "Way I hear it, that water acts kinda like a tonic for some folks. Gibbs has had some doctor or laboratory-type person analyze it, and that's all I know. You might want to ask somebody else, Mrs. Springer. We better ring these things up. I'll put the liner in the trunk for you."

And he headed off toward the cash register, leaving me to follow in a state of frustration. That's the way a bandwagon gets started. Some superstitious nonsense that'd been circulating for years, with nobody really believing it, and now, all of a sudden, a sharp businessman makes noises as if it's a wonder-working cure-all, and normal, everyday people start opening their checkbooks. For my money, if anybody's constitution needed help, they could buy some vitamins or take a tonic to clear out their systems.

I huffed all the way to the cash register, thinking that Clarence Gibbs had a nerve depriving Lillian of her home just to get tired people's hopes up. Of all the snake oil promises I'd ever heard, this one took the cake. It was as bad as all those companies selling cosmetics that promise to cure face wrinkles, and charging you an arm and a leg for it without doing one blessed thing that I'd been able to tell.

Chapter 20

The trunk lid bounced and Lillian's big satchel clanked every time I hit a pothole on the way back to the house. But we'd gotten her plants in the trunk, and I hoped they'd survive the digging, pulling, and shoving that we'd subjected them to. Both Lillian and Little Lloyd were dirt-smeared and worn out by the time we got home.

"There's Coleman," Little Lloyd said, sitting up in the backseat as I pulled into the driveway. The garage door was open, and most of Lillian's household goods had been unstacked and pulled out in front.

I could see Coleman's head bobbing up from behind boxes, a chest of drawers, and a rolled-up rug that he'd moved out of the garage.

"Oh, that pore man," Lillian said. "He been movin' stuff all day, an' I bet that clothes box right on the bottom."

"I hope he's got enough energy to help with the plants," I said, somewhat concerned at how tired Little Lloyd looked.

I needn't have worried, though, for the child hopped out of the car and hurried to help Coleman. Coleman was like a tonic to him, a much better one than any Clarence Gibbs could bottle.

"Lillian," I said, as we got out of the car, "now that you and Little Lloyd have some help with clothes and plants, I'll run on in and set the table."

She nodded and, brushing at her nylon outerwear, went into the garage to search through boxes.

The smell of the pork tenderloin that Lillian had left cooking in the oven filled the house and made my mouth water. I called to Hazel Marie from the dining room as I hurriedly set the table.

"We're having a meeting tonight," I said as she came into the room. "I hope you don't mind, but Mr. Pickens is coming, too. I want to get that Poker Run idea of his moving." Having run through my mind the number of ladies who'd meet Thurlow's requirements, I figured it to be our best hope for raising money on a grand scale.

She smiled a little, then quickly became businesslike. "I don't mind. I'll give him credit, he's good at that sort of thing. But do I have to sit next to him?"

"Hazel Marie, I declare, we need to put aside personal animosities and pull together on this. You don't know what's at stake here."

"What?"

"Well . . . oh, there's the phone. Would you finish the table for me?"

I hurried to the kitchen and answered the phone, only to hear an unwelcome voice.

"Mrs. Springer? Clarence Gibbs, here."

"Why, Mr. Gibbs, how nice to hear from you." I glanced toward the dining room door, hoping Hazel Marie would stay behind it. "I hope you're calling to say that you'll give us more time, and that you've reconsidered your ill-advised proposal concerning my house."

He didn't answer right away, but he breathed so that I

knew he was there. "No, that's not why I called. I just want you to understand that I'm going the extra mile for you, and honoring your request to give you until the morning for your decision. I tell you right now, Mrs. Springer, things're moving, and you're going to have to, too, if you want to take advantage of this opportunity."

I felt weak, afraid to make the commitment and afraid not to. "I'm thinking, Mr. Gibbs," I said. "And one thing I thought of is to offer you a very nice trailer park out beyond Delmont in place of my house. Wouldn't that be sufficient to hold the Willow Lane property for maybe sixty days?"

"No'm, it would not. First off, three weeks is my limit. And second off, I don't want a trailer park. It's your place or nothing."

"But I don't understand why you want this house. You already have a lovely home."

He made a noise that might've been a low laugh. "I don't want to live in it. It's in a business zone, so I'd tear it down and put up an office building. It's close enough to Main Street and the courthouse to be fully rented before the paint dries."

My knees wobbled at the thought, and I had to clear my throat before I could answer. "You'll have my answer in the morning." I cleared my throat again and said, "You're a hard man, Mr. Gibbs."

He said good-bye with a lilt in his voice, and I do believe he took my comment as a compliment.

I hung up, just so provoked with myself for begging him to allow me enough time to put my own home in peril. But the fact was, I had to make up my mind, and do it soon. That made it imperative that I find out just how effective that water was up on the ridge. And if, by any remote chance, it did have something in it that men would pay good money for, then all the more reason for me to push that motorcycle cal-vacade for all it was worth.

~

Mr. Pickens scraped the last crumbs of Lillian's pineapple upside-down cake from his plate, and said, "I've already talked to Red Ryder, and he's all for it. We decided on the last weekend in the month. That'll give us time to get notices and flyers'll out, so we'll have a lot of riders."

"I thought he was a cowboy," I said. I was mentally counting the days, trying to picture the calendar. Three weeks would be up the Monday after the last weekend.

"Who?" Mr. Pickens, his bushy mustache twitching, glanced across the table at me.

"That Red Ryder person you just mentioned."

He gave me a quick grin. "No, this Red owns a motorcycle shop and restaurant, Red Ryder's Shop, Stop and Eat, out on 193, this side of Delmont. He organizes several runs every year, so he knows how it's done. Now here's the good part," Mr. Pickens said, leaning on the table so that I got a whiff of his new aftershave—lemon and mint and who-knows-what else—designed, I speculated, to lure Hazel Marie back. From the tantalizing aroma that swirled around my head, he was going to lure not only Hazel Marie but every other woman within smelling distance. I leaned back to clear my head as he went on. "The motorcycle club has agreed not to take a cut of the pot. Every cent will go to the fund, and Red thinks there'll be a good response. The only thing he asks is that we start and end at his place."

"And eat there when we get back," Sam said with a smile. "Well, that's the least we can do. Food's not bad, either."

"I like his barbeque," Hazel Marie said. I noticed that she'd kept her place next to Mr. Pickens, in spite of what she'd said earlier. Every time he moved, she was being engulfed with waves of that sweet-smelling cologne emanating from him. She'd close her eyes and sway like she was being carried away every time a wave of the stuff broke across her brow.

"It concerns me a little," Sam said, "that we're doing this so late in the year. These things're usually held in the summer, aren't they?"

"Yeah, usually." Mr. Pickens finally gave in and helped himself to another piece of cake. "But if the weather holds and we get one of our clear Fall days, they'll come out in droves." He forked up a bite of cake. "Only problem is, I don't think a Bikini Bike Wash would be a good idea, and that'll be a disappointment."

"Oh, J. D." Hazel Marie said, "I wish you'd get bikinis off your mind."

He grinned at her, then took up where he left off. "But we can count on the beer flowing freely any time of the year, and when the crowd's had enough, we can pass the hat for more donations."

"Now, let's get one thing straight," I said, deciding that this was as good a time as any. "I do not intend to dine with a bunch of intoxicated and unruly carousers, no matter how much money they give."

"Why, Julia," Sam said, his eyebrows lifting in surprise. "I wouldn't expect you to drive out there and join us. It'll just be the riders who come in off the run. Of course, if you want to, you're welcome to meet us there."

Lillian slid her chair away from the table and made as if to rise. I declare, the woman couldn't stand being around deceitful activities of the least kind. I put my hand on her arm to keep her seated.

"I'll be riding with you," I said, folding my napkin and laying it beside my plate, as calmly as I would announce I'd be going to church on Sunday.

There was a moment of dead silence, and I felt every eye in the room staring at me. Mr. Pickens's fork stopped halfway to his mouth and Hazel Marie tipped the sugar spoon she was holding, spilling sugar on the table.

"Oh, boy," Little Lloyd said, being the first to recover. "We'll have a lot of fun now."

"Oh, Miss Julia, are you sure?" This worried question was from Hazel Marie, no less. The one who'd told me I'd enjoy riding if I'd just try it.

Mr. Pickens's surprised look shifted into that wicked grin, which I was convinced had enticed many a woman off the straight and narrow. "That's my girl," he said, so that I couldn't help but preen a little at his approval. "This is gonna be a ride and a half."

Sam hadn't uttered a word, and I'd carefully avoided looking at him. Now, I slid my eyes to him, deciding not to wait for his response.

"Now, Sam," I said with enough force to brook no argument. "I'm doing this entirely for Lillian's sake." I felt her stir in the chair beside me, so I hurried on. "But I want to get back in one piece, so you better get to be a better driver than what I've seen so far. And I want a side seat, too. I'm not about to perch myself on the back of that thing."

"Julia," he said, reaching over to take my hand. I took it back. "If you'll ride with me, you can have anything you want. I've been taking a safety course, so you don't have a thing to worry about."

"And," Little Lloyd said, squirming with excitement, "he's joined the H.O.G.s, too."

"Please, Little Lloyd," I said. "Not at the table."

"Harley Owners' Group, Miss Julia," Mr. Pickens said, enlightening me, but not by much.

Sam leaned over and said, "What made you change your mind, Julia?"

"Well," I said and hesitated. Now was the time for a big, fat lie if there ever was one. I could pretend I wanted to experience that freedom of the road Sam had talked about. But I didn't think I could pull it off—Sam wouldn't believe me and Mr. Pickens would laugh. They'd all know I had as much freedom of the road as I wanted, tooling around in my little sports car. "It's occurred to me that there might be some professional and business people and the like who would be willing to sponsor teams of riders. Especially if those teams were made up of, well, let's say, unusual combinations. Like, for instance, if women of a certain age and status who wouldn't ordinarily be caught dead on a motorcycle teamed up with your average biker-type drivers. I'm thinking of LuAnne Conover, for one, if we could find someone for her to ride with."

"Big Bill Beasley!" Hazel Marie shouted, nearly bouncing out of her chair. "He'd be perfect for her."

Mr. Pickens almost choked on the cake he was shoveling in, as he began laughing his head off.

"Then," I said, encouraged by Hazel Marie's immediate grasp of the possibilities. "We might be able to talk Emma Sue Ledbetter into going with us. If we present it to her in just the right way."

Mr. Pickens sputtered and finally managed to say, "The club has a chaplain. Maybe she'd ride with him." Then he broke up again.

"Oh, wow, Miss Julia," Hazel Marie said. "The whole church would turn out for that."

"I sure would," Little Lloyd said.

My mind was really revved up by then, calculating the ages of my friends, as well as increments of ten thousand dollars. "How about Norma Cantrell? Wouldn't she be a good one?"

Sam threw himself back in his chair, laughing and wiping his eyes. "Oh, Julia, that'd be great, but how would you talk them into it?"

"Sponsors," I said. "We'll challenge the ladies in town to get sponsors. And," I went on, leaning on the table to better present my points, "and to make it interesting, we could set a minimum, maybe a high minimum, like a thousand dollars they'd have to donate before any lady would get on a motorcycle. And it's possible that each one would have several sponsors."

"But what if they don't play fair?" Little Lloyd said. "What if a lady doesn't want to ride and she doesn't even try to get sponsors?"

"I think we could manage that," Hazel Marie said, her eyes sparkling with insider knowledge. She knew those women almost as well as I did, by now. "All we have to do is advertise the names of the ladies who've agreed to this, and sponsors will line up for the privilege. Then they'd have to ride whether they wanted to or not. Miss Julia, I think this is going to be the most fun of anything we do."

"What about you, Sam?" I asked. "You think it'll work?"

"You better believe it'll work. If, that is, the bikers' wives and girlfriends would be willing to sit this one out."

Mr. Pickens leaned close to Hazel Marie and whispered something about a little hair-pulling, but she swished her hair in his face and he pulled back, laughing.

"And," Sam went on, "if you and Hazel Marie can get those ladies to hold up their end of the bargain."

"They will," I said. "Especially when they hear that I already have a sponsor. Purely out of the goodness of his heart, Thurlow Jones is putting up one hundred thousand dollars to see me . . . I mean, to make our Poker Run fundraising a success." I reached in my skirt pocket and pulled out half of his donation and put the check in front of Sam. "You can deposit that. The other half will be handed over as soon as the run is over." I stopped and bit my lip, and in the silence my announcement had created, I went on. "I guess that means we'll have to invite him to Red Ryder's Shop, Stop and Eat for dinner."

Lillian said, "I thought you not tellin' how you got that money."

"I changed my mind," I said. "It's always better to be open and forthright, Lillian."

She mumbled something under her breath, but I ignored her. "Well," I demanded, "isn't anybody going to congratulate me? This almost guarantees we can buy that property."

My eyes slid to Sam and I saw him looking down at the check, shaking his head from side to side. "Julia," he finally said, "how in the world did you get this much money out of Thurlow Jones? I know he's unpredictable and about half crazy, but this kind of money is unheard of, even for him."

"It wasn't any problem at all," I told him as coolly as you please. "I just asked if he'd like to sponsor me in a motorcycle card game, and he was ever so agreeable. And deeply concerned about the plight of the people on Willow Lane. Now, Sam," I went on, taking a deep breath as I prepared for the big one. "I've heard the stories about him, but, I must say, I think the man's misunderstood. His behavior was impeccable. He was a perfect gentleman in every way."

Lillian couldn't stand any more. She hopped up and headed for the kitchen, taking not one dish with her.

"Did you go see him by yourself?" Sam asked, his eyes boring into mine, now that I'd found the courage to look at him.

"Why, no. Lillian went with me, and she can testify to the propriety of the whole episode." There was a crash of pots and pans in the kitchen, right by the dining room door where Lillian was undoubtedly listening. "Now, Sam, quit giving me the third degree. I need to know how to prepare for this road trip we're taking."

Mr. Pickens put his hands against the table and tilted his chair back. "Lord help us," he said, pretending to be awestruck. "Miss Julia's gonna be a biker chick."

"Hush, J. D." Hazel Marie said. "Now, Miss Julia, we need to get you outfitted." Her eyes were shining with the thought of another shopping spree. "I'll show you what I'm going to wear—it's all leather, and that's what you need, too. And some boots so your feet will stay warm. We'll be going up on mountain roads where it'll be chilly, so you'll need some long underwear. It'll be fun, Miss Julia, you won't believe all the different outfits that're available, but most everybody likes the plain black ones."

I couldn't help it. My eyes rolled up in my head at the thought of a leather outfit outlining my lower limbs and various other parts. "Hazel Marie," I said, "get that idea out of your head right now. I intend to do this only one time in my life, and I don't need to spend a fortune just to have the right costume. Besides, I'm not in the habit of wearing pants, slacks, or trousers, much less any made of leather, so I'll just wear an everyday dress and a heavy coat. Since I'll be sitting in a little car on the side, that should be sufficient."

Mr. Pickens started laughing, and so did Sam. I gave him a glare but it didn't stop him. "You ought to reconsider, Julia," Sam said. "You'll be much more comfortable in slacks of some kind. You'll have to climb in and out of the sidecar, you know."

"I'll manage," I said. "Especially since I don't aim to climb in and out more than one time each. And if I ever get out, I won't be getting back in."

Mr. Pickens had leaned his head on his hand, still laughing at my intention of maintaining my dignity in spite of the upcoming indecorous conditions that I'd taken money to take part in.

Little Lloyd said, "We just don't want you to get cold, Miss Julia. It'll be breezy, you know."

"Thank you for your concern, Little Lloyd," I said, smiling at him. He was the only one besides Lillian, who was still hiding out in the kitchen, who was not finding humor in the situation. "But I'll take a lap blanket, some gloves, and a head scarf. I'll be all right."

Lord, I hoped I would. Here they all were, so worked up over my having the proper costume, while I was worrying about getting home with all my body parts intact. And, I suddenly thought, enduring the certainty that I was going to be the laughingstock of the town.

But I had no intention of being the only one. If I could dare LuAnne, Emma Sue, Norma, and a few others who came to mind to perch themselves behind burly, bearded, and tattooed bikers, nobody'd even notice me.

But even if they did, I reminded myself, it was for Lillian's sake, and for the sake of all those others who were homeless and helpless. Let them laugh then; I knew my heart was in the right place, even if my person would be strapped to the side of a Harley-Davidson Road King driven by a novice driver whose internal sparkplugs might not be firing as they should.

Chapter 21

I came close to being as inhospitable as I'd ever been in my life by practically pushing Sam out the door soon after we finished eating. He'd wanted to linger and quiz me about Thurlow Jones, but I was having none of it.

"Sam," I said, after he'd taxed my patience by going on and on about how I needed to keep my distance from that crazy man, "give me some credit. I'm not studying Thurlow Jones, and you don't need to be, either."

"Well, but he may be studying you, Julia," Sam said with a worried frown. "I may have to have a talk with him."

"No, just leave him alone." I said, fearing that he'd ruffle Thurlow's feathers and make him go back on his promise for further donations. "He's not bothering me and, if he does, I'll take care of him."

"That's what concerns me, Julia," Sam said, showing it by putting his arm around my shoulders. "I might have to call him out."

I slipped away from him and shooed him out the door, telling him I'd let him know if I needed any help. My mind was so much on our ridge-running plan that I didn't want to think about anything else.

Hazel Marie helped implement my plan, although she didn't know it, by reluctantly agreeing to ride with Mr. Pickens to Binkie's to see how she was doing. I don't think Hazel Marie would've done it if Lillian hadn't made Coleman's favorite lemon pie and wanted to get it to him. She was worried that the way Mr. Pickens drove, the pie would end up on the floorboard.

"Well, I'll go," Hazel Marie said, flouncing around without a glance at Mr. Pickens. "But just to hold the pie. Seems to me there'd be a better way to get it there."

Of course there was. Her own car was right out in the driveway, but I didn't mention it to her. I was too concerned about Coleman being on duty that night, shuddering at the thought of Binkie in the house alone with Lillian's Lemon Chiffon pie. Believe me, she didn't need to put on another ounce, even if she *was* eating for two.

As soon as they all left, I shifted into high gear. "Lillian, Little Lloyd, let's get a move on. We need to check out that spring."

"It real dark out there," Lillian said as she looked at her reflection in the window. "We might not ought to go up there, it so dark."

"It's not that late," I said. "Why, it's barely eight o'clock. We need to do it when nobody's there, so this is a perfect time."

"Yes," Little Lloyd said, agreeing with me. "And remember, Miss Lillian, we saw Mr. Gibbs and some other men up on that ridge while we were digging your flowers."

"You did?" That just strengthened my intention to get to the bottom of that spring. "Who were they?"

"I don't know, but some of them looked like they were surveying, and they came out of the woods from the top of the ridge. Then I saw Mr. Gibbs down in the pasture, talking for a long time with another man. I thought it was Pastor Ledbetter at first because he had on a raincoat just like his. You know, the kind with the special plaid lining? It wasn't him, though, because the man had on a little felt hat, and the pastor never wears a hat. Him and Mr. Gibbs kept walking back and forth, both of them just talking away."

"Mr. Gibbs and he," I corrected him, distractedly, as the pastor's Burberry raincoat came to mind. "I wonder if that means Clarence Gibbs is cooking up some other scheme."

"Law," Lillian said. "Look like he have enough on his plate without comin' up with something else."

Then Little Lloyd said, "We need to find out what he's doing. But I don't think we ought to go in through Willow Lane. Somebody might see us, and the pasture's full of earth-moving machines. We could break our necks. You think we could come in from the other side of the ridge, the way those men did?"

"Let's think about that, Little Lloyd," I said, as I tapped a finger on the counter, trying to picture in my mind what was on the other side of the hill. The streets in Abbotsville were so curvy and winding that it was hard to figure out where you might end up.

"Don't you be doin' no thinkin' an' get yo'self in trouble," Lillian said. "They's nothin' you can do 'bout that spring 'cept look at it. An' it too dark to do much lookin'."

"I intend to get a sample of it," I told her. "So let's take a Mason jar or something. I don't know how we could get it tested. Lord knows, I wouldn't drink it. But we can at least see what it looks like."

"I bet if we went up Mountain Lake Road, we'd see a turn-off somewhere," Little Lloyd said. "Those men I saw had to've walked in from there because they sure didn't come in from Willow Lane. We'd've seen their cars if they had."

"You're right," I said and headed for the catch-all drawer next to the refrigerator. "We need to look at a county map and figure out how to get in from the other direction."

"I bet there's even a trail we can follow," Little Lloyd said.

"This chile don't need to be followin' no trail in the middle of the night," Lillian said. She glared at me, but she didn't know the time constraints I was under.

"I bet it's easy to get in from the other side, Miss Lillian," Little Lloyd said. "We won't have any trouble."

"Yes," I said. "And equipment means they were doing something up there."

Lillian was about fed up by this time. "Y'all don't listen to nothin' I say."

Little Lloyd patted her shoulder. "Yes, we do, Miss Lillian."

"Of course we do," I said. "I hear every word you say and almost always take it into account. But Lillian, we can't just sit back and hope everything'll work out. Sometimes you have to take a hand in things and *make* them work out." I'd found the county map by this time and began spreading it out on the table. "And I intend to find out what Clarence Gibbs is up to before I climb on that motorcycle with Sam Murdoch or anybody else."

Lillian still wasn't happy about it, and she let me know it by refusing to look at the map.

"Lillian," I said, hoping to bring her around. "What if I rode on that thing, then found out that Mr. Gibbs wouldn't sell to us? What if, after risking my very life, he announced that he was going to do something else with that property? Believe me, I would be hard to live with if that happened."

"You not all that easy to live with now," she said, cutting her eyes at me. Then she laughed. "Well, Law, I 'spect I better go on an' go with you. I ain't never argued you out of nothin' anyway." Then she frowned, thinking up some other argument. "I feel better, though, if you let Mr. Sam or Mr. Pickens know what you doin'. Even Miss Hazel Marie, who get us some help if we need it."

I just let her ramble on. I wasn't about to be deterred or made to listen to reasons why I shouldn't go. Which was exactly what Sam would've given me, and exactly what I didn't want to hear. "I'm going up to put on my galoshes so I won't ruin my shoes."

"Well, if I gotta do this, I gotta change outta this new uniform I just got," Lillian said as she headed for the back stairs. "Miss Julia, you oughtta get you some long britches, you gonna be tromping through the woods like you plannin' to do."

"I don't know why everybody's so worried about my clothing," I mumbled, hurrying out to change my footwear.

We gathered back in the kitchen to study the county map again to make sure we had our bearings. I was somewhat taken aback when Lillian appeared in her nylon running suit with, of course, those thick-soled blue and white boats on her feet. Lillian had already cut slits in the sides of both of them to make room for her corns, and now said that they were the best walking shoes she'd ever had, but she didn't aim to do any running in them, regardless of what they were made for.

I leaned over the table and peered at the tiny lines running every which way. "I can't make heads nor tails of this thing."

"Here's Polk Street," Little Lloyd said, pointing to a line that ran east-west across Main Street. "And here's Willow Lane." He pointed to a thin line that just ended, without joining up with anything else. "Now, this area here is that old pasture and, look, Miss Julia, here's the ridge."

I followed his finger as he moved it across the map. "Find Mountain Lake Road for us," I said, moving my head up and down as I tried to bring the map into focus. It was my experience that the printing on anything I picked up, from maps to telephone books, had gotten smaller every year. And it wasn't all due to my eyesight. "I declare, I don't know why they don't print these things so a person can read them."

"Here it is," Little Lloyd sang out. "See, Miss Julia, it's this twisting line here, the one that goes up the mountain. Now let me see." He bent his head closer. "Right here. See this little bitty line? It comes off Mountain Lake Road and looks like it ends up on the other side of the ridge." He looked up at me. "It might be an old logging road because it's not even named. I bet that's it."

"Let's try it," I said, straightening up with a hand on my back to help me do it. "But if we're going to go, we'd better go now before it gets any later." And before Mr. Pickens and Hazel Marie get back, I thought to myself.

"We could still go in the mornin'," Lillian said.

"Lillian, I have no intention of running into Mr. Gibbs in broad daylight," I said. Not to mention that by daylight, I had to give him an answer.

"We better take some flashlights," Little Lloyd said, running to the pantry where we kept the necessities for power outages in the winter. "We'll need 'em." As usual, the child was thinking ahead and preparing for all contingencies.

I pulled onto a weed-filled dirt road off Mountain Lake Road and parked the car a few feet in. There was no sign of any other cars, so I figured that whoever had been on the ridge that afternoon was long gone. The night had fully settled in, with only our headlights cutting a tunnel through the blackness. The thick stand of pines on each side of the rutted road enclosed us in a deep darkness. I was beginning to think that this might not have been the best idea I'd ever had.

"You have our sample jar, Little Lloyd?" I asked, preparing myself to brave the wilds.

"Yessum. Right here."

"Let's go, then."

"I don't much like this," Lillian said, looking out from one side of the car to the other. "I jus' been thinkin' 'bout that ole graveyard out yonder. We ought not be 'sturbin' no haints in the middle of the night."

"Lillian," I said. "You know better. We're not going to bother them, and they won't bother us."

"It'll be all right, Miss Lillian," Little Lloyd said as he opened the car door. "Just shine your flashlight in front of you so you won't trip on anything."

"You can stay in the car, if you want to," I told her, but she pushed up the front seat and got out beside Little Lloyd, mumbling that she wasn't about to stay by herself.

It was fairly easy walking along the old logging road, but I was glad I'd had the foresight to wear my galoshes. The weeds rustling against my feet and lower limbs would've ruined my stockings.

I held up my hand and whispered, "What's that noise?"

We all stopped in our tracks and listened. "I don't hear anything," Little Lloyd whispered back.

"Me neither," Lillian said, swallowing hard.

"Well, now I don't, either," I said. "Let's keep going."

But as soon as we started walking again, I heard a rhythmic rubbing noise as if something or someone were following alongside of us. I swung the flashlight beam on each side of us, but the trees were too thick to see anything.

I stopped again, as did they, and the noise stopped, too.

"What's it sound like?" Little Lloyd whispered, his voice slightly on the quavery side.

"Like somebody's rustling through the leaves, making every step we make," I answered. I didn't want to scare him or Lillian, but I was on the verge of being unnerved, myself.

"I think it me," Lillian said. "See, this be what you hearin'." And she walked a few steps as we stood watching her. Sure enough, the nylon fabric of her running suit sliding between her lower limbs with each step made the noise that had given me such a turn.

"Lord, Lillian," I said with a nervous laugh. "You need to do something about that. Anybody could hear us coming a mile away."

"They's not nobody out here anyway," she said. "Ever'-body in they right mind be home eatin' they supper."

Little Lloyd had walked a few feet beyond us and was shining his light along the left side of the road. "There's got to be a path somewhere," he said. "This road just stops on the map and doesn't go over the ridge at all. There has to be a way for those men to cut across the ridge to get to where we saw them."

We kept on walking, pulling our coats closer as the autumn cold began to seep around us and the night kept getting darker. I glanced up and saw one lone star twinkling in the deepening night. About the same time, I began to realize that the left side of the road was getting steeper as the ridge rose beyond it. We watched for a path that had to branch off the dirt road.

"Here it is," Little Lloyd called out, pointing his light into an area of flattened weeds. "This has to be it. You want to follow it, Miss Julia?"

I pointed my light into the narrow opening among the

trees and rhododendron thickets, and saw how the path an-gled upward. "Well, we've come this far, so I guess so. I just hope it's not too steep."

"We can always turn back if it is," Little Lloyd said as he plunged in. I followed with some trepidation, and Lillian brought up the rear.

"Don't y'all go too fast an' leave me," she said.

The walk was easier than I had feared, though I wouldn't've wanted to do it every day. The path soon leveled off as we followed it along the top of the ridge. I could see a sprin-kling of lights from the town through the trees.

"Be careful here, Miss Julia," Little Lloyd said. "And you too, Miss Lillian. We're starting to go downhill now."

It wasn't long before I could smell a dampness in the air and, in spite of the noise Lillian's running suit was making, hear water bubbling and trickling.

"Hold up," Little Lloyd said, stopping so that we al-most ran into each other. "There're rocks and boulders along here." He threw the beam of his flashlight around so that we could see a rocky incline. The sound of water was louder, and Little Lloyd's light finally steadied on a small, noisy rush of water that seemed to seep from among some large rocks above us, then fall in a miniature waterfall to pool at the bottom.

"This must be it," I said, not at all impressed with its size. "The one Mr. Gibbs wants to bottle and sell, if anybody can believe that."

Lillian peered over my shoulder. "It don't look no differ-ent from any other spring, an' I seen a million of 'em."

"Slip down there, Little Lloyd," I said, not wanting to slide down the incline. "Scoop up some of that water for our sample, while I hold your flashlight."

As I lit his way, the boy slid down to the little basin below the spring. He knelt down and filled the jar, then turned to climb back up.

As he reached us, Lillian drew a sharp breath and said, "You hear that? I think them haints is movin' 'round."

Before I could answer, Little Lloyd grasped my arm and whispered. "Turn off your light."

I did, Lillian did, and he'd already done his. I was blind as a bat in the sudden darkness.

"What is it?" I whispered, feeling the child edge closer to me and Lillian reach for him.

"I don't know," he said. "Something."

"Oh, Jesus," Lillian said under her breath. "They be comin' up from they graves." I could feel her trembling behind me. Or it could've been my own shivering.

As the three of us huddled together on the path, fearing even to breathe, a bright light from the other side of the spring suddenly spotlighted us. I nearly fainted.

"Well, as I live and breathe," a voice I could've done without hearing called out. "I do believe that's Mrs. Julia Springer and her entourage out gallivanting after dark."

Of all the people I hadn't expected to run into, Thurlow Jones was the most unlikely. "Turn that light off," I snapped. "You're about to blind us. And get out here where we can see you." I flicked on my flashlight as soon as the bright beam swung away from us. "What do you mean jumping out at us like that?"

Thurlow Jones moved his scrawny self out from behind a large boulder on the other side of the pool, his flashlight in one hand and a quart Mason jar in the other.

"I could ask you the same thing," he said. Our lights glinted off his glasses, and I thought to myself that he looked even crazier than when I'd last seen him.

"But we didn't scare *you* half to death, Mr. Jones," I reminded him. "And I don't appreciate being sprung at like you did. What're you doing here, anyway?"

"Same thing you are, little lady. Testing the waters."

I drew myself up tighter and taller, taking offense at his term of address, as well as his assumption of my mission. "I'll have you know that I have no interest whatsoever in testing water from a cow pasture."

"You don't know what you're missing," he said, holding up the Mason jar. He gave the jar a shake so that the water in it sloshed around. "It's supposed to give a man a new lease on life and, as I've already had a jar full of it, I can feel it doin' its work. Stand back, folks, I'm coming across." And he backed up on the slippery bank to get a running start to jump the stream.

"Run!" I yelled, grabbing Little Lloyd's hand and pushing Lillian to lead the retreat.

As we scrambled back up the path, we heard a slithering of rocks, the shattering of glass, and a small splash. The beam of a flashlight flickered wildly through the treetops, and Thurlow Jones yelped, *"God doggit!"* But we neither lingered nor looked back.

"Turn off the lights!" Little Lloyd called out. We did and were plunged into darkness. Our sudden blindness didn't stop Lillian. I don't know how she did it, but she kept us on the path up the ridge, across it, and down the other side, all of us panting and wheezing as if the devil himself was after us. And for all I knew, that's exactly who it was. As for Little Lloyd and me, we had it easier than Lillian, who had to keep on the path by instinct. The child had me by the hand, pulling me along the narrow way, as he took aim on the reflecting strips on the heels of Lillian's running shoes.

How she did it, I don't know, but she guided us straight to the car.

I cranked the car with shaking hands and backed out from the logging road onto Mountain Lake Road, gratified that I'd managed to go in reverse without hitting anything.

"At least we got our sample," Little Lloyd said. "Some of it sloshed out, though. I should've brought a lid."

"Just so we have enough to look at," I said, straining to keep the car on the twisting road. "But I don't think it's going to matter. Image is everything when you're selling something, Little Lloyd. And if big talkers and big spenders like Mr. Jones think there's something special about that water, then everybody else will, too."

I bit my lip, thinking hard as we coasted down Mountain Lake Road. For all I knew Thurlow Jones might throw in with Clarence Gibbs and put that stuff on the market. We'd never get Willow Lane if that happened. It looked as if the only way to stop Clarence Gibbs was to put my home in jeopardy, and I determined then and there to just do it.

But there was something else I could do, as well. "Lillian," I said, "how close would you say that cemetery is to the spring?"

"Not far," she said from the backseat. "Them graves be under that oak tree on the edge of the pasture. Nobody been buried in there for a long time now, so it won't get no bigger. Them headstones be crooked an' fallin' over, an' they 'bout a hundred years ole."

"It just occured to me that Mr. Gibbs couldn't sell a drop of that water if people knew it came from under a graveyard."

"Oh, yuk," Little Lloyd said.

"It don't run under that graveyard," Lillian said. "Them graves be downstream."

"I know," I said, "but how many others know that? If

Clarence Gibbs tries to back out of selling to us after we work so hard to raise the money, I'm going to see to it that everybody knows where that water comes from."

"Oh, Law, Miss Julia, he gonna sue you."

"Let him try," I said. "Sometimes, Lillian, you just have to hold a man's feet to the fire."

Chapter 22

"My goodness!" Hazel Marie said, as the three of us burst into the kitchen. She jumped up from the table, her eyes wide with concern. "What happened to you?"

We'd recovered from our run, but not from the scare that Thurlow Jones had given us. Wanting to appear somewhat collected, I put my hand up and smoothed back my tangled hair. Little Lloyd made an effort to keep from laughing, but Lillian was still puffing and blowing from our flight through the woods.

"Why, nothing," I said as I removed my coat. "We just took a little walk, and it took longer to get back than we'd expected."

Little Lloyd couldn't help it. He began to laugh out loud. "It didn't take any time at all, the way we were moving. I think we set a record, Mama."

Nothing would do then but to tell Hazel Marie all about our scouting expedition, the upshot of which was that we'd learned little more than we'd known before we went. Well, we'd located the spring, but knew nothing more about the water spurting from it—other than Thurlow Jones's testimony, which could be thoroughly discounted by reasonable people. But reasonable people are few and far between, as everybody knows. I shivered again at the thought of Thurlow's bony fingers reaching for a tender spot on my person. Unaccustomed as I was to footraces and already feeling the consequences of running that ridge, I would do it again in a minute if that fool started after me again.

Hazel Marie was properly impressed with our daring and said that the next time she wanted to go with us.

"I doubt there'll be a next time," I said, pulling off my galoshes and wondering if my feet would ever be the same.

Lillian began making hot chocolate and mumbling something about marshmallows to go with it. "Nobody gonna get me back up there," she said. "When that ole man jump out at us, I like to died right there."

"But, Mama," Little Lloyd said as he hung on her chair, "it was Miss Lillian who got us out of there. She was going so fast, you wouldn't believe. And if it hadn't been for those shoes you got her, me and Miss Julia would've been left in the dark."

Lillian smiled to herself, then said, "That the truth, an' I didn't even know 'bout them headlights on my heels."

"Let's look at that sample, Little Lloyd," I said. "Though I don't know what it can tell us without microscopes and laboratories and such."

Nonetheless, we all gathered around the kitchen counter as Little Lloyd set the jar in front of us. We peered at it, shook it, and watched as something flickered in the murky water.

"Law!" Lillian said. "That thing alive!"

"It might be a tadpole," Little Lloyd said, shaking the bottle again.

"Too cold for tadpoles, I think," Hazel Marie commented. "Don't they hatch in the spring?"

"I don't know," I said. "But I know this, I wouldn't drink that stuff for anything in the world."

"Mr. Jones say he did," Lillian said, her eyes big at the thought. "Wonder he get sick from it?"

"It'd serve him right," I said, still smarting from the fright he'd given us. "Little Lloyd, you better run up and take a shower in case any of it splashed on you."

After we finished studying the water without coming up with any possible benefits to either man or woman, Hazel Marie and I lingered at the table. Lillian followed Little Lloyd upstairs to prepare for bed.

"Hazel Marie," I said. "I hope you don't think I put Little Lloyd in danger by letting him traipse all over that ridge. Thurlow Jones may be crazy, but I don't think he'd hurt a child."

"I don't ever worry about him when he's with you," she said, with that innocent trust she extended to everybody. I couldn't help but wonder if it was justified when it came to me, since more than once it'd been the child who'd taken care of me, rather than the other way around.

"I appreciate that," I said. Then I sighed and leaned my head on my hand. "I declare, Hazel Marie, I think Sam may be right, as much as I hate to admit it. That old man is after me, and if he hadn't fallen in the creek he might've caught me. I don't know what I'm going to do about him."

She smiled and reached out to pat my arm. "You're an attractive woman, Miss Julia. It wouldn't surprise me a bit if half the older men in town were after you."

"Huh," I said, straightening in my chair. "I can see what's in the mirror, and it's Wesley Lloyd's estate that's attractive, if anything is."

"Oh, Miss Julia, that's not true." Hazel Marie frowned. "Look," she said, leaning her arms on the table, "Thurlow

Jones doesn't need your money. He's got more than the U.S. government already. And look at Sam. You think he's after your money? Uh-uh, no way. What I think you ought to do is loosen up and enjoy the attention."

I started to tell her that if she knew the kind of attention that'd put a bruise on an extremely personal area, she wouldn't be talking enjoyment of any kind.

"Speaking of Sam," I said, ready to turn the conversation elsewhere, "I wish I could quit worrying about him."

"Now, look," she said, with what seemed to me some exasperation. "There is not a thing in the world wrong with him. And I don't know where you got the idea that there is."

"Why, Hazel Marie, you've seen the stuff he keeps sending, the flowers and that unfortunate poetry he tries to write. And look at what he's wearing, and that lamentable motorbike or whatever it is. And now he's talking about going dancing, of all things. He's just not himself, and whenever I think about it, I get sick with worry." I drew a deep breath, as my heart seemed to drop down inside of me. "And now, having gotten myself into that Poker Run mess, I'm going to have to put my life in his none-too-reliable hands."

"Oh, Miss Julia, please don't worry about that. J. D. says Sam's as safe a driver as he is." At my skeptical look, she hurried on. "The things you're worried about come from only one thing: Sam Murdoch is in a courting mood, and that's all that's wrong with him."

"Well, my word," I said, as her words sunk in and a warm flush filled my face. Lord, I thought, could a courting mood be all that was wrong with him? Had romance on his mind made him get decked out in blue jeans, leather jackets, and cowboy boots, then lead him to put his thoughts into verse? It was hard to believe that a sensible man like Sam could act in such a way, regardless of his inner urges—the thought of which sent a shiver up my spine.

I have to admit that I'd had a sneaking suspicion that there might've been another explanation for Sam's behavior. But I hadn't been able to let myself believe it for fear that I'd be wrong and make a fool of myself as a result. I mean, courting at our age? It was so unseemly.

"Well," I said, hoping that Hazel Marie hadn't noticed my long silence. "If that's the case, which I seriously doubt, you'd think he'd dress appropriately for it."

⟶

I was on the phone first thing the following morning, calling Clarence Gibbs. Sometime during my restless night I'd confirmed my decision to expose my home to his greedy grasp. What else could I do? The people on Willow Lane wanted to keep their homes, and it seemed to me that we should honor their wishes and not go looking for another place that we thought more suitable for them. I'd had some experience with somebody—namely Wesley Lloyd Springer—asking what I wanted, then deciding on his own that I'd be better off with something else. Why ask, if you're going to make the decision on your own, anyway?

Besides, Sam and Coleman had been looking for another piece of property, and all they'd found was out in the county, far from grocery shopping, bus service, and their church. And every house would have to be built from scratch, the cost of which would be overwhelming. It had to be Willow Lane, if we were going to do anything at all.

And, since that spring might really be putting out a tonic of some kind, I had to tie Clarence Gibbs's hands, even if it was only for three weeks. I knew I was running a real risk, for we might not be able to raise enough money in the time allotted, but if I didn't act now we'd lose out completely. As soon as Gibbs put the first dollar into a bottling plant, that property would be gone forever.

"Mr. Gibbs?" I said as soon as he answered the phone. At the sound of his voice, my hand jerked so bad that I almost dropped the phone. Then I had to clear my throat several times before I was able to go on. "I guess I'm ready to sign that agreement, although I must say that I'm not at all happy about it."

He sounded absolutely delighted, as well he should've. He had a very real prospect of ending up with both properties— mine *and* his. "I'll meet you on Willow Lane in thirty minutes, and we'll wrap it up."

"One more thing," I said before he could get too carried away. "That wrecking machinery must not touch another one of those houses. Is that understood, Mr. Gibbs? I am agreeing to purchase both the property and whatever is on it as of this minute."

He sucked his breath between his teeth, and finally said, "Do you know what it costs to rent those 'dozers? Every day they sit out there is costing me money. I need 'em to get the job done so I can turn 'em back in."

"It's not my problem if you got ahead of yourself," I said, trying to sound as firm as I felt. "I'll just call off the whole deal if you destroy those houses."

I listened to him breathe some more, then he said, "Okay, I'll send 'em back, but in three weeks those houses're coming down."

Not if I can help it, I thought as I hung up. I thought also that I'd finally gotten Clarence Gibbs's number. He was playing both ends against the middle, trying to have his cake and eat it, too, and risking a little to gain a lot. The bottom line was that he wanted it all, and thought he'd found a way to get it by stringing me along. But if I had anything to do with it, he was heading for a fall he wouldn't soon forget.

That's what I had to keep my mind centered on—outwitting Clarence Gibbs—and not on the very real possibility of my home ending up as a pile of rubble. I leaned back in my chair, thinking, Oh, Lord, if I only had someone to tell me I was making a good move. But I knew there wasn't a soul who would back me up. I could just see Binkie springing out of her chair, saying, "You did *what?*" And Sam, he wouldn't believe I could be so headstrong. Lillian would likely cry and call on the Lord. Even Hazel Marie, who wouldn't know a good business deal if it hit her on the head, would be stunned. So I had to either do it or not do it, all on my own. And I was going to do it.

Then I leaned my head on my trembling hand, wondering what in the world I was letting myself in for.

❧

As I drove through the streets toward Willow Lane, I felt myself becoming more and more unsettled. It's not every day that you decide to gamble with your own home, but I had my back against the wall. That Poker Run, backed by Thurlow Jones to the tune of one hundred thousand dollars plus the money for however many fifty-year-old quality ladies we could round up, was our best bet for raising the money, and to save my house, we'd need every cent we could get. Which meant that I had to personally hit the road on a motorcycle—the last thing in the world I ever thought I'd do. When I'd been bargaining with Thurlow, it had seemed far off in the future, something that might not even happen.

I'd been so thrilled with getting those checks from him, all but assuring that we'd be able to buy the property, that the fact that I would have to actually crawl on one of those machines was something I hadn't wanted to think about.

I wondered if there were any way to get out of it. *And* keep Thurlow's money. *And* keep my house. *And* purchase Willow Lane. Maybe I'd get sick or break some little bone or something so I'd have a doctor's excuse. Maybe Sam would have a spell of some kind so that Mr. Pickens would judge him unfit to drive a motorcycle. That would do it, I decided, and then I could be so disappointed because I wouldn't be able to participate, either. And nobody would blame me for dropping out.

Oh, Lord, that wouldn't do it. They'd just assign me to Big Bill Beasley, whoever he was, or somebody of equal quality, and there I'd be, hanging on to a half-naked, tattooed driver who didn't have a sidecar and wouldn't use it if he did.

No, better to take my chances with Sam, failing though he might be.

I turned into Willow Lane, stopped the car, and stared at what used to be a place of activity, home to people who'd lived there for years. Now it looked cold and lonesome, with no one at home.

But Clarence Gibbs was there. He got out of his car and walked over to my window. He was wearing another one of his shiny suits, but this time with heavy brogans on his feet. They were much more appropriate for the surroundings, I had to admit, than my Red Cross lace-up oxfords. He leaned over as I rolled down my window. "You want to walk the property lines, Mrs. Springer? See what you might be getting?"

"I'll walk out in the field with you, and you can point out the boundaries." I got out of the car and walked along with him on the proposed demolition site.

"Careful, now," Mr. Gibbs said, taking my elbow. "Don't want you to turn an ankle or something."

Thinking that that wouldn't be the worst thing to happen, I said, "How far back does the property run?"

He pointed to the west. "Up over that ridge, there's a logging road. The line runs along it."

I nodded, not mentioning that I'd become acquainted with it the night before. He continued talking as I walked carefully over the rough grade of what had once been the site of the fallen-in house, and on over to the grassy pasture. Wondering if cows had left any calling cards, I picked my way alongside of Mr. Gibbs, just about ruining my shoes and working up a head of steam about what I was fixing to do.

As I sidestepped a large clump of weeds, I decided to try one last time to dissuade him from attaching my house.

"Mr. Gibbs," I said, "I wish you'd just outright sell this property. There's no reason in the world to include my home of almost fifty years in the bargain. But if you must have something to bind our agreement, I'll offer any other piece of property I own."

"Well," he said, shrugging his shoulders as we stood in the middle of the pasture. "I guess it depends on how bad you want this property, as to what you're willing to do to get it. I'm already about to regret giving you three weeks, even with your house thrown in. And there's nothing else you have that I want, so it's take it or leave it."

I didn't believe for a minute that there wasn't something else I owned that he'd want. I was convinced that he'd lit upon my house in an effort to make me refuse the bargain. Then when I surprised him and accepted it, he must've realized what a good deal it was for him. I knew he didn't think we could raise the money. I intended to give him another surprise.

"I heard the rumors about bottling that water up there," I said, delaying the moment I'd have to sign the agreement. I figured it wouldn't hurt to create a little doubt in his mind as to the value of the property.

He slid his eyes away from me, a know-it-all half smile on his face. "Maybe. Maybe not. I got several irons in the fire. I could pull one out any minute."

"Oh, for goodness sakes, Mr. Gibbs. Just tell me what's going on. I'm not about to risk my home if you're cooking up something behind my back."

"I'm a public-spirited citizen," he said, still playing with me. "And I told you it would be on the market long enough to give you folks a crack at it. But, even with your house as a sweetener, three weeks is pushing it for me."

"Let's sign that agreement," I said, resigning myself to whipping along a mountain road in Sam's sidecar.

"Before we do that," Gibbs said, abruptly stopping, "I need to know how you folks plan to raise enough money to buy this place."

"That, Mr. Gibbs," I said, "is not your concern. We either raise it or we don't. And if we don't, you'll end up with two pieces of property instead of one. You are running no risk at all."

He gave me a sharp glance. "How much y'all raised so far?"

I opened my mouth to tell him we had pledges for almost half of his asking price, then thought better of it.

"It's not going so well, I'm sorry to say," I said, figuring that I could poor-mouth as well as he could. Besides, no good businessman or -woman tells everything he or she knows.

And there was one thing I was convinced of: if Clarence Gibbs knew how close we were to meeting his price, he'd renege on the deal so fast it'd make my head swim.

"That's too bad," he said, giving me a full-fledged smile. Then he took my arm and began walking me back toward my car. But not before I got a glimpse of two men up along the ridge, carrying some tools or instruments or something.

Before I could ask him what they were doing, he said, "I had the agreement drawn up yesterday." He pulled out a sheet of folded paper from the inner pocket of his jacket and handed it to me. "You might want to look it over."

"I certainly do," I said, unfolding it and taking note of his lawyer's letterhead. It was written in fairly plain English for a change but, even so, I longed to have Sam and Binkie look it over. I'd never before done anything of a business nature without good legal advice, but I determined to do this for Lillian and, if I lost my house because of it, then I'd just have to live with the consequences.

I read the thing over again, then laid it on the hood of my car. I took a deep breath to steel myself, then signed my name before I lost my nerve.

After a few strained pleasantries on my part, I got in my car, knowing that I'd just committed myself to the worst business deal of my life. And knowing that I was going to have to ride that motorcycle if it killed me, which it just might do.

Chapter 23

When I got home, I went straight to the telephone, bypassing Lillian and Hazel Marie. I had to get things on the road, in more ways than one. Quality ladies, I thought, as I looked up phone numbers. What other kind did Thurlow think I knew?

I called LuAnne, Emma Sue, Norma, Helen Stroud, and, to be on the safe side, Mildred Allen. Every one of them met the age requirement, which I didn't intend to mention. I couldn't imagine Mildred Allen would want to climb on a motorcycle. She was a heavy-set woman, don't you know. But she was a woman you didn't want to leave out of anything, even something she was unlikely to be interested in. She was bad for passing along her own speculations on matters that she knew nothing about. And as everybody knows, speculations soon take on a life of their own.

I invited them all to my house later in the morning to discuss an urgent matter having to do with the people of Willow Lane. They all agreed, each one wanting me to tell them on the phone what urgent matter I had to discuss. I didn't fall for that, knowing none of them would show up if they knew what I was going to propose.

After reaching the last one, I hung up the phone and sat for a while, wondering if there were anyone else I should call. It just did me in that Binkie was in no shape to ride with us; her enthusiasm for all things different and unusual would really put us over the top. It was my bad luck that she was in an expectant condition just when I needed her. Of course she wasn't old enough to qualify for a donation from Thurlow, but she would've had a ton of sponsorships from the sheriff's department and the lawyers in town.

"Hazel Marie," I called as I approached her room, where she was changing the sheets on her bed. I took a seat in the chair by the window and watched her flip the spread and smooth it out. "They're all coming, and I hope I haven't forgotten anybody who ought to be in on the planning stages. Now, Hazel Marie, I'm counting on you to help me present this idea in a way that they won't reject it out of hand."

"If they'd just try it one time, I know they'd love it." She suddenly straightened up, a new idea lighting up her face. "I tell you what! Let's get J. D. to come over and ride each one around the block, just to give them a taste of it."

"Why, you know, that is a fine idea," I said, thinking that Mr. Pickens had a good bit more experience with two-wheelers than Sam, and therefore a better choice not to scare anybody to death before we could sign them up. Then again, he had a somewhat more persuasive way about him than Sam did, when it came to the ladies. Though, on second thought, Sam was hardly a slouch in that department. "Why don't you call and ask him to be here, say about eleven? That'll give us enough time to present it to them, serve refreshments, and let them go to the bathroom before they climb on."

"I guess I could call him for that," she said, musing over

the propriety of talking to him when she wasn't speaking to him. "I'll just keep it on a businesslike basis."

"Good. Now, Hazel Marie, help me go over this before they get here. I asked LuAnne because she's an old friend and she'd be hurt if I didn't include her. Besides, I've noticed in the past that she's not averse to an occasional flirtation, as unbecoming as that is in a woman her age. Which might make her open to what she'd call an adventure." I stopped, recalling LuAnne's attraction to a certain race car driver of our acquaintance. Maybe a motorcycle driver would have the same effect.

"Oh, yes," Hazel Marie agreed. "If anybody'll do it, she will. In fact, I bet she'll be the first one to ride with J. D."

"And the others won't want to be outdone," I said. "Except Emma Sue. I can't imagine she'd do anything that's not church-related, but I had to ask her to keep her from crying all over town because she was left out." Emma Sue was known for her propensity for crying whenever her feelings got hurt, which meant she overflowed about every other minute, since her tender feelings were so easily damaged.

"Well, I don't know. She might surprise you, especially if you present it so that she can see it as an evangelistic enterprise." Hazel Marie took her lip between her teeth, and began to think. "You know, there is such a thing as a Christian Motorcycle Club. I don't know exactly what they do, other than ride together like any other club, but maybe they go somewhere and preach when they get there."

"Oh, excellent, Hazel Marie. Let's tell her that the riders she'll meet all need to hear the Gospel." I paused, considering the notion. "And I don't have a doubt in the world that it's true. The thing about it is, we need both her and Norma Cantrell. If the two of them won't bring every Presbyterian out of the woodwork, I don't know what will. A few Baptists and Methodists, too, I expect, just to see the spectacle."

"What will Pastor Ledbetter think?"

"He's Emma Sue's problem, not mine. Thank goodness. Anyway, my thinking is that each one of these women has contact with others who might volunteer to ride, too. Half the garden club will sign on if LuAnne and Helen Stroud do. And if Emma Sue rides, well, just think how many women in the church would follow her lead. And who knows, her example could bring in some other preachers' wives in town. Then," I went on, sighing as I did so, "there's Mildred Allen. I had to invite her over because she knows everybody in town and would bad-mouth us if I left her out. She won't ride, though."

"She might," Hazel Marie said. "If we could find a bike with a wide enough seat for her to fit into. Well," she said, as she picked up the phone, "let me call J. D. I declare, I hope he doesn't think I'm forgetting about his past, just because we need him to help us out in the present."

I opened my mouth to tell her that I didn't know what she hoped to accomplish by playing hard-to-get. I mean, the man couldn't go back and undo two marriages. Well, any more than he'd already done with two divorces. But the doorbell rang, interfering with any advice I was about to give.

We both went to the door, to be greeted by a young man who identified himself as the delivery man from Perkins Drugs.

"You must have the wrong house," I said, wondering who on our street was sick enough to need a delivered prescription. "I didn't order anything."

"No'm, I'm supposed to deliver this box to this address." He handed me a large, flat box wrapped in white drugstore paper.

I thanked him and turned to Hazel Marie. "Who could be

sending us something from the drugstore? Maybe it's for you, Hazel Marie."

"Not me," she said. "Maybe Lillian ordered something."

"Let's go see," I said, and we both trooped into the kitchen, where Lillian denied ordering anything.

"Jus' open it up, an' see who it for," she said.

So I did, and it nearly did me in.

"A Whitman's Sampler!" Hazel Marie exclaimed. "And it must be the biggest one they make. I love this candy. May I try a piece?"

I nodded as she searched for a caramel and held out the box to Lillian. I was busy looking for the name of the sender, although there could be little doubt as to who it was from.

"Who's it from, Miss Julia?" Hazel Marie asked. "And don't hide it from us."

"Mr. Sam, he mus' be switchin' off of flowers," Lillian said, her gold tooth shining. "Maybe he think candy sweeten you up some."

I opened the enclosed envelope, read the card, and flopped into a chair. "This is absolutely unbelievable," I said, patting my breast in my agitation. "I'm sending it back right this minute."

I gathered the wrapping paper, then stopped as Hazel Marie held up a piece of candy with a bite already taken out. "Uh-oh," she said. "I'm real sorry, Miss Julia."

"Me, too," Lillian said around a mouthful of chocolate. "Guess you got to keep it, seein' we already into it. You don't want to hurt Mr. Sam's feelin's nohow."

I leaned my head on my hand and tried to calm my rapid breathing. "Sam didn't send it," I said, realizing that I was going to need their help to handle a new and completely un-suitable suitor who was looming on the horizon. "Listen to this."

I unfolded the card and read:

"My heart will know no bounds
When you come riding around.
Whether you do it for love or money,
Thurlow'll want you for his honey."

"Oh, Lord," I said, my head sinking down on the table. "Have you ever heard anything so awful? I could just expire right here and now. Oh, the shame of it, being courted by that repulsive old man. What in the world am I going to do?"

"Just ignore him, Miss Julia," Hazel Marie advised. "He'll soon get the message and quit bothering you."

I looked up at her, frowning. That's what she'd been doing to Mr. Pickens, in the hope that he'd get the opposite message.

Lillian reached for another piece of candy. "Look like to me, we ought to eat all we want, then send him the empty box an' say we had our fill an' don't want no more."

Hazel Marie bent over the box, deciding what to try next. "Wonder what Sam's going to say when he hears about this," she said, as if she were talking to herself.

Lillian started laughing, and I threw up my hands. "Sam wouldn't care one way or another," I said, and started out of the room.

"I think he ought to know he has a rival, don't you, Lillian?" Hazel Marie said, as I took myself off.

With Hazel Marie's words still ringing in my mind, I went upstairs to face an unpleasant task that simply had to be done. I sat down at my desk and, sighing, drew out an informal with my initials engraved on the front. I declare, I hated writing a thank-you note to someone I couldn't stand, but one does what one knows is the proper thing to do. Even if one would like to wring the recipient's neck.

Gathering my thoughts and taking pen in hand, I wrote:

Dear Mr. Jones,

On behalf of the residents of Willow Lane, I want to thank you again for the generous donation you have made and also for the additional one you will make upon completion of my promised excursion. Pursuant to that, it is my pleasure to invite you to dine at Red Ryder's Stop, Shop and Eat, where the presentation of said promised donation can be made to the acclaim of all present.

Thank you also for the Whitman's Sampler box, an entirely unnecessary but appreciated gift. Lillian and Hazel Marie enjoyed it ever so much.

Cordially,

I signed my name with a flourish and a sigh of relief at having the chore over and done with. After addressing and stamping the envelope, I congratulated myself on doing the correct thing, difficult though it had been, and also for writing a formal and dispassionate note that ought to serve to cool Thurlow Jones's jets, as Little Lloyd would say.

"One thing is for sure," I mumbled, wondering what I had done to be on the receiving end of such unwanted attentions, "I am not eating any of that candy."

When the phone rang on my desk, I picked it up before Lillian could get it downstairs.

"Julia?" Sam said. "How are you today?"

"I'm fine, Sam." Well, as fine as I could be after my meeting with Clarence Gibbs, and after receiving an unwanted box of candy, but he didn't need to know about either one. "How are you?"

"Not so good." He breathed long and deep, and I began

204 ⟶ *Ann B. Ross*

to worry that something else was wrong with him. "Julia," he went on before I could ask about it, "I've been thinking about that big donation from Thurlow Jones. He's an odd bird if there ever was one, and I hope he didn't get the wrong idea when you went to see him."

"I don't know what kind of wrong idea he could've gotten, Sam," I said. "My request to him was straightforward enough."

"Well, but you don't know him like I do."

"That's what you keep telling me, but you don't need to warn me about him." I rubbed a certain spot on my back side, but I wasn't about to mention that. "I'm well aware of what he's capable of, but so far he's been nothing but generous and thoughtful. Why, Sam, he even sent us a box of candy this morning." I don't know why I told him that. I hadn't intended to; it just popped out.

"Candy!" Sam said, in a voice raised louder than I'd ever heard it. "What is that fool doing sending you candy? Send it back, Julia. You can't encourage him or you'll never be rid of him."

"I can't do that, Sam," I said, a little smile playing around my mouth as I realized that Hazel Marie's assessment just might be right. "It would be so ungracious of me. Besides, a lady can accept certain attentions without implying any reciprocation. And, if I started sending things back, I'd have to employ a whole messenger service to return all the other gifts I've received."

"Who else has been sending you gifts? Julia, listen to me, you can't go around accepting things from every Tom, Dick, and Harry. It gives the wrong impression."

"Oh, Sam," I said, glancing out my window to see some of the ladies coming up the walk. "You worry too much. Look, I have guests coming in, so I have to go."

He didn't much like it, especially since I now had him thinking that every unattached male in town was showering me with presents. Well, just as Hazel Marie'd said, it wouldn't hurt him to think he wasn't the only one in the running.

When the doorbell rang downstairs, I prepared myself to meet my guests. I had to show them by my comportment that participating in this endeavor would not in the least be unusual or inappropriate, while hiding the fact that to me it was simply outrageous. It was imperative for my peace of mind that I talk them into signing up for the thrill of their lives, so I wouldn't be the only one making a fool of herself. Misery loves company, you know.

Chapter 24

It wasn't the ladies at the door, but Mr. Pickens, who'd arrived much earlier than we'd expected. Hazel Marie had let him in, and they stood together just staring at each other. I did a little staring, too.

Lord, the man exuded masculinity and lemon cologne in enough quantities to make my head swim. Leather does something exceptional to the men who wear it, especially when made up into tight-fitting pants and heavy boots with silver buckles. Because it was an Indian summer day, as he'd pointed out—although I thought it was just an excuse—he wore only a leather vest over a T-shirt with the sleeves cut out. I couldn't keep my eyes off those highly visible muscles and, particularly, that ugly scar on his upper arm. To have something like that made me wonder if his profession of looking for missing persons and tracking down insurance fraud was much more dangerous than I'd thought. Or maybe one of his wives had lit into him, leaving something to remember her by.

And, Lord, when he turned I saw a tattoo on his other arm—some kind of bird. An eagle, maybe. Or a chicken. I'll tell you, with all that ornamentation, Mr. Pickens cut a dashing and somewhat dangerous-looking figure.

He had come riding up on what he called his Harley Softail, a most inappropriate name in my opinion, and I hoped he wouldn't mention it again. He did manage his machine, however, with a great deal more skill than Sam had displayed on his.

As the ladies arrived, each pair of eyes popped out at the sight of Mr. Pickens's unclothed arm muscles. LuAnne immediately started flapping her hands, as she does whenever she gets excited, and at one point I thought she was going to reach out and rub her hand over his scar. LuAnne tended to lose her head when she was in the presence of a certain virile type of man. But, given Leonard's usual somnolent state, I guess she had to make up for it somewhere.

Mr. Pickens took all their wide-eyed stares in stride as if he were used to that kind of adulation. He was just as charming as he could be, greeting them and complimenting each one so that he quickly overcame any trepidations they might've felt. They were so taken with him, in fact, that they hardly partook of Lillian's offerings from the kitchen, standing around him and asking questions about the motorcycle parked in my front yard.

Every once in a while, he'd look over somebody's head and wink at Hazel Marie, letting her know that she was his one and only. I would've had my doubts, if it'd been me.

I finally got them seated and quickly presented our idea of the leading ladies of the town riding with an experienced biker in order to raise money for the Willow Lane folks. I explained how we'd get sponsors, spelled out in glorious detail how exhilarating and healthy a ride would be, and how much good we all could do.

No one said a word for a long minute, then Mr. Pickens stood up. "Ladies," he said, his white teeth gleaming from under that black mustache. He looked directly at LuAnne, and I heard her catch her breath. "Ladies, let me reassure you about a couple of things. Everybody you'll be riding with is highly safety conscious, and you won't be in any danger at all. Another thing, forget all you've ever read or heard about bikers. You won't meet a nicer or friendlier bunch of people anywhere. There won't be any fussing, fighting, or brawling; just a lot of good, clean fun."

Emma Sue Ledbetter sniffed and Norma Cantrell, taking a cue from her, twitched her shoulders, but Mr. Pickens pretended not to notice. "Now," he said, "I've brought my bike and I'd like to ride each one of you around the block to let you see what it's like." Then, looking deep into the eyes of each woman there, he lowered his voice and said, "I need somebody to go with me. Who wants to be first?"

He smiled that heart-melting smile right in LuAnne's face, and she jumped right up. "I will!" Then she stopped and looked down at herself. "But I have on a skirt. Hazel Marie, can I borrow a pair of your pants?"

Before Hazel Marie could answer, Mr. Pickens said, "We can fix that. I'll tuck you in good, and we won't go fast, anyway."

We all went out on the front porch to watch the performance. Lillian, not wanting to miss anything, edged out behind us. Mr. Pickens helped LuAnne put on the extra helmet he'd brought, then assisted her onto the backseat—what he called the saddle. Then, to her great delight, he carefully tucked her skirt around her so that it wouldn't blow up. Then he adjusted his own helmet and climbed aboard, giving the machine a kick that started the motor with a great roar. LuAnne shrieked and grabbed his waist.

Then he propelled the two of them out of the yard in the most careful and sedate manner possible.

"I can't believe she'd do that," Emma Sue said, a disapproving frown on her face. "What is Leonard going to say?"

"Leonard's not going to say anything," I said. LuAnne's husband seemed half asleep half the time.

While we waited for them to circle the block, I noticed a long, black car parked at the curb, not quite in front of the house but near enough for me to see a man sitting in it. I thought he was going to get out, but the spectacle LuAnne and Mr. Pickens presented may have caused him to think better of it. Probably a sales-type person, I thought, wanting to demonstrate a vacuum cleaner by throwing dirt on my Orientals. It was just as well that he kept his seat, for I never welcomed salespeople inside my house. When I want to buy something, I go to the store and get it. I don't need to be talked into something in my own living room.

I forgot about the salesman when Mr. Pickens guided the cycle back into the yard and helped LuAnne off in a gentlemanly fashion. When she took off the helmet, her face was lit up with excitement.

"That was wonderful!" she crowed. "I'm ready to go again. But somebody else take a turn. You'll love it."

When nobody volunteered, Mr. Pickens scanned each face, then pointed at Helen Stroud. "How about you? Wouldn't you like to ride with me?"

Well, put that way, what woman wouldn't? With a giggle, Helen took LuAnne's place and soon she and Mr. Pickens were roaring out into the street. She yelped as a sudden gust of wind blew her dress over her head, and I thought Emma Sue was going to die laughing on the spot.

LuAnne chattered on about the thrill of it until Helen was deposited back into the yard. Strange things must happen

under that helmet—or from holding onto Mr. Pickens—
because she was just as flushed as LuAnne had been.

Mr. Pickens put down the kickstand and walked up onto
the porch. Mildred Allen backed away, saying, "I would, but
I won't fit on that back seat." And she was right, for the seat
was molded across the back and along the sides, and even if
she'd been able to fit into it, she'd've been wedged in for life.

"We can fix something up for you," Mr. Pickens said.
Then, noticing her self-consciousness, he sidled up to her
and said, "Bikers go crazy for full-figured women."

She turned as red as a beet, while I rolled my eyes. Mr.
Pickens had no shame at all. But he turned his black eyes
on Emma Sue, smiling at her and ignoring her tight mouth
and frown of disapproval.

"Mrs. Ledbetter," he said, "you're the one I particularly want because you have the influence to make or break
this charitable enterprise. I know people look up to you, so
your approval would mean everything in making the Run a
success."

Her mouth loosened just a little, as she nodded her head.
"That may be true, Mr. Pickens," she said, "but I am totally
dedicated to Christian work alone. I just can't spread myself
too thin, you know. This sort of thing, even if it is for a good
cause, would take time and effort away from spreading the
Gospel."

"Ma'am, I'm glad you brought that up," Mr. Pickens said,
as if it'd just occurred to him. "See, there'll be riders from local Christian motorcycle clubs joining us. A good many of
them, in fact. You won't believe all the good they do, witnessing and testifying and preaching and teaching the Bible
everywhere they ride. You really ought to meet them. They'd
open up a whole new field ready for harvest and waiting for
someone like you."

I glared at Mr. Pickens, trying to warn him not to try to fool her with all that pious talk, but Norma Cantrell chimed in. "I've heard of them," she said. "Emma Sue, I think that new preacher out at Pine Grove Baptist is a member. And so is his wife. I heard that his congregation wasn't too happy at the thought of their preacher running with a motorcycle gang, especially since he'd already bought a red Trans Am and put headers on it. But he explained that it was all part of his ministry, and now I understand that almost all his deacons are bikers."

"Yes," Helen Stroud said, nodding her head vigorously, "and I heard they have a Sunday School class just for Harley owners. Harleys for Heaven, they call it."

"Is that right?" Emma Sue murmured, eyeing Mr. Pickens's motorcycle with increasing interest. "It *would* be a new field of endeavor, wouldn't it? And, you know, if I could say that I'd ridden a motorcycle, I'd really be able to reach young people."

"They'd think you were the greatest thing on two wheels," Mr. Pickens said, flashing that smile of his, knowing he'd talked another woman into doing what he wanted her to do. "Let's try it. Want to?"

And she did, shrieking and laughing and gripping Mr. Pickens's waist as they took off down the street. I wondered if Pastor Ledbetter could hear her, and what he'd do if he did.

By the time they got back, Mr. Pickens had another convert, for Emma Sue was ready to be catechized and baptized into motorcycle heaven. If there was such a thing.

Our only semi-failure of the day was Norma, who didn't mind the ride but hated the helmet. It mashed her teased hair down flat, and she was considerably upset about it, stomping off to the bathroom when she dismounted to back-comb it again.

I gave Mr. Pickens credit for convincing the ladies that motorcycle riding was not only safe and fun, but charitable and evangelistic. I didn't know another man in the world who could've done it.

In spite of having achieved what we wanted, though, I noticed that Hazel Marie had been unnaturally quiet during all the time Mr. Pickens was working his wiles. Women who used the same methods to get their way had nothing on Mr. Pickens, who could wrap a woman around his finger when those black eyes lit on you and his muscles started rippling and when, well, he moved his heavily cologned presence next to you. No wonder Hazel Marie'd held her tongue; he was a wonder to behold.

Chapter 25

"We need to get the word out," I said to Hazel Marie's back. She was still gazing pensively out the window long after Mr. Pickens had disappeared from sight, although the noise of his departure lingered on behind him.

"Advertisements, radio announcements, and what-have-you. You're good at that sort of thing, Hazel Marie; why don't you take that on?"

Tearing herself away from the window, she agreed to word the announcement to go in the newspaper and on the flyers that we intended to distribute around town.

"Let's get their names out as soon as we can," I told her, "before they have second thoughts and decline the honor. Be sure to put in that any other ladies who want to join in are welcome, as long as they get sponsors."

"Okay. But, Miss Julia," Hazel Marie said, a worried frown on her face. "I've been worrying about something J. D. said last night."

"Lord, Hazel Marie, it's a wonder you don't worry about everything he says, day or night."

"Well, I do, sometimes. But he mentioned that we might

have a problem with the bikers' regular riders, their wives and girlfriends. How're they going to feel if they're replaced by other women? They might not like it." She stopped, frowning even more. "I don't think I would."

I didn't doubt that a minute, given the fact that she couldn't trust Mr. Pickens around other women as far as she could throw him.

"What we have to do, Hazel Marie," I said, "is give those displaced riders something else to do. You know, make them feel that they're contributing something by not riding. What could it be?"

"Well, they usually have contests of some kind set up where the runs end. I know Red will have something in mind, maybe like a Burnout Pit. That's where they rev their motors and burn the rubber off the back tires. The one who creates the most smoke is the winner, and a new tire is usually the prize. He might have a Slow-Ride Contest, too, to see who can go the slowest without falling. Maybe even a Wienie-Bite Contest, but J. D. won't let me enter that."

I thought it best not to inquire about the last-named contest. If it was too much for Mr. Pickens, I didn't want to hear about it.

"And, Miss Julia," she went on, "there'll be vendors selling souvenirs, like stuffed teddy bears and bike replacement parts and so on. And bands playing, and people singing and dancing, all kinds of things for everybody to do."

"Since the displaced riders are all women, maybe they could help with the food," I said, then bit my lip. "No, let's not suggest that. Sounds too much like church. I tell you what, why don't we get Mr. Pickens to come up with something? From what I've observed, he can make a woman love something she doesn't even like." Then I realized that that wasn't the most tactful thing I could've said, but Hazel Marie didn't take offense at hearing the truth.

"Well," she said, "he's probably the best one to do it. Maybe he can put them in charge of the contests. You know, deciding the winners and handing out the awards. Oh, I know! He could have a Best-Dressed Female Biker Contest. They'd love that." Hazel Marie's face lit up, just like it did every time she had an idea. "I'll call him and suggest it, but first, I'd better get something ready for the newspaper."

"Well, I'll leave you to it," I said, and took myself to the far side of the house.

❦

That afternoon, while I busied myself counting up the donations we were likely to get, LuAnne called me.

Before I could thank her for her willingness to ride in the Poker Run, she took off on the latest news. "Julia, have you heard about Thurlow Jones? He's in the hospital, sick as a dog."

"No!" I said, sitting up with the sudden fear that he wouldn't be able to fulfil his promise. "What's the matter with him?"

"Nobody knows," she said, her voice quavering with the excitement of her news. "But I've heard he's on complete bed rest. Can you believe that?"

"Oh, LuAnne!" I said, patting my chest. "You scared me to death. I thought he was dying, the way you sounded."

"Why, Julia," she said in a sly tone, "I didn't know you'd be so concerned. Anything you want to tell me?"

"Not a thing. It's just that he's made a pledge to the Willow Lane Fund and, as long as he's not broken his check-signing hand, I don't care what he's done."

"Well, believe me, it's not his hand, and it's not broken." Then she giggled and, lowering her voice, went on. "Don't tell anybody I told you, but what I heard is that he's had a sudden spurt of growth in an unmentionable area of his anatomy. They sat that every doctor and nurse in the county has dropped by to see it."

"What are you talking about?"

"Use your imagination, Julia." She smothered another bout of laughter.

I suddenly realized what she was talking about, then wished I hadn't. There are certain things that a decent woman simply does not nurture in her mind.

"Is it catching?" I asked, wondering if the hospital was equipped to handle an epidemic of disabled men.

"What?" LuAnne asked. "Oh, what he's got? No, I heard that they think it's some kind of allergic reaction to something he ate or drank. They're giving him megadoses of one of those killer antibiotics."

"Oh, my Lord," I gasped, as a jolt of fear shot through me. "LuAnne, I've got to go. I'll call you back."

I slammed down the phone, cutting off her questions, sprang from the chair and nearly broke my neck running down the stairs.

"Lillian!" I called, dashing through the dining room and pushing through the kitchen door, my breath catching in my throat. "Lillian! Where is it? What'd you do with it?"

"What?" she asked, turning from the counter to stare at me. "What you talkin' about? What's wrong?"

"That jar! The one we took to Clarence Gibbs's spring! Where is it? Oh, Lord, tell me it's still here!" I grabbed the back of a chair with one hand, patting my chest with the other, so afraid I was trembling.

"What got you so het up 'bout that jar? They's nothin' in it but some ole cloudy water."

"Oh, I hope! I hope it's still full. Where is it, Lillian? I've got to see for myself."

"It right there in the pantry on the top shelf, waitin' for you to get it tested or whatever you gonna do with it."

I ran to the pantry, jerked open the door, and saw the jar. Relief flooded through me. I got it down and examined it closely, holding it up to the light to determine if the water level was the same as it had been.

"Little Lloyd hasn't been into this, has he?"

Lillian frowned at me. "What he wanta be doin' that for?"

"I don't know, Lillian," I said, collapsing into a chair. "It's just that little boys are likely to have a scientific turn of mind, and I was afraid he'd try testing this himself." I held the jar up for her to look at it. "There's not any of the water missing, is there?"

"You think he drink that stuff!" Lillian said, staring at me as if I'd lost my mind. "He got more sense than that."

"I had to be sure. Lillian, I hate to admit this, but it looks like Clarence Gibbs is right. This water is potent beyond belief." And I went on to tell her of the horrific growth potential lurking in the water of the spring, resulting in Thurlow Jones being the subject of widespread medical curiosity.

"Law!" she said, her eyes big enough to pop out of her head. "He musta drunk a bait of that stuff. All I ever heard was it took just a little sip to young a ole man up." She stood looking off for a minute as she studied the matter. Then she started laughing. "That Mr. Jones, he sho' got more'n he bargained for this time. I mean, he mighta wanted to jack things up a little, but how he think he gonna manage if he got to have a wagon to carry it around in?"

"Well, I expect he's learned his lesson," I said, still feeling weak from the fright I'd had. "Now, Lillian, we have to get rid of this. I'm not going to have it in the house a minute longer."

"Th'ow it out in the yard," she said, "an' put the jar in the garbage. I don't even want it in the dishwasher."

"I agree, and I'll do it right now."

I went out into the backyard, holding the jar as far from myself as I could. We now knew the water's baleful effect on the masculine half of the race, but who knew what it'd do to the other half?

I gingerly unscrewed the top and, walking over behind the garage to get as far from the house as possible, slung the water out around one of Lillian's transplanted bushes. Let it do some good somewhere, I thought, and disposed of the jar in the trash container. Then I went back inside and thoroughly scrubbed my hands. No use taking chances.

I stopped and turned to Lillian, my hands still dripping. "I just thought of something. Thurlow not only drank from that spring, he fell in it. What if it works from outside in, instead of from inside out? Oh, my goodness," I moaned, as I leaned against the sink. "What if Little Lloyd got some of it on him? I couldn't stand it, Lillian, if something happened to that child."

"Don't you worry 'bout him," she told me. "He stay in the shower more'n half a hour that night, an' come out all shriveled up."

"Good!"

❦

Still recovering from my fright, I pulled myself up the stairs to call LuAnne back. I needed to soothe her hurt feelings after I'd hung up on her.

"LuAnne," I said, sinking into my easy bedroom chair, "I apologize for being so abrupt, but there was a crisis in the kitchen and I had to see about it."

"Oh, that's okay," she said, though she sounded a bit miffed about it. "Well, now that I've got you, let me tell you about the home tour. We've decided on a Christmas vacation theme. Each house on the tour will be designated a Christmas vacation spot, and yours is going to be Christmas at the Beach. Don't you just love it?"

Well, no, I didn't. I let the silence drag out as I fumed at the idea of bringing in sand and driftwood arrangements to go on my mahogany tables.

"Now, I know," LuAnne said, trying to forestall my objections, "that a beach theme doesn't sound like much, so I thought we'd change it to Christmas at *Palm* Beach. That'd be so much more elegant."

"Maybe it would, LuAnne," I said. "But I don't know a soul who's ever been to Palm Beach, much less at Christmas. So nobody's going to know the difference between Palm Beach and Myrtle Beach."

"Oh, Julia," LuAnne said, exasperation clear in her voice. "Don't you read *Town and Country*? Palm Beach means polo and international society. Tiffany's and pearls and jewelry of all kinds, charity balls and lots of wealth. Why, I bet the arrangements in that category will be everybody's favorites."

"Good. Then you won't have any trouble assigning it to somebody else's house."

"Now, don't be that way," she pleaded. "I'll tell you what. I'll enter that category myself, and decorate a tree with all kinds of jewelry. You know, pins and necklaces with colored stones and strings of pearls and gold bracelets and little twinkling lights. Oh, I can picture it now. It'll be gorgeous, Julia, I promise you that."

"Well," I said, with a martyr's sigh, giving in for Lillian's sake and feeling a tiny bit better for it. "But I'll tell you this, LuAnne: those arrangers better not come tracking sand in my house and ruining my Orientals."

⟵

Keeping Lillian in mind with an effort of will after we hung up, I talked myself into being resigned to the beach theme, Palm or otherwise. I wouldn't have minded so much if I'd thought the tour would bring in any appreciable amount, but I knew it wouldn't. Still, I'd agreed to it, and I would endure it with my usual composure. But I didn't have to be happy about it, and I wasn't.

When I went downstairs, Lillian announced that she had to run to the grocery store. "I used ever' bit of sugar in the house when I went on my cake- and pie-cookin' spree."

"Let me go instead," I said. "I need to get out a little, anyway. After talking with LuAnne, I need some fresh air to cool me off."

⟵

When I returned from the store, lugging several bags of groceries, which always happens when you go for one item, Lillian said, "Some man come see you while you gone."

"What'd he want?"

"He don't say. I tell him you gone to the grocery store, an' he say he come in an' wait for you."

"Well, my word, Lillian, I hope you didn't let him."

"No'm, I say you likely be gone till suppertime, an' he oughta call 'fore he come back."

"Good."

"Yessum, he real pleasant, say he like our house."

"Typical salesman," I said. "Trying to flatter so you'll be in a good mood for whatever he's selling. I'm going upstairs, Lillian, and work on the fund-raising books."

As I turned to leave, she said, "I notice he have on one of them raincoats like yo' pastor have. You know, with that plaid linin' on the inside, an' he have on a fancy hat with a little feather on it. Don't nobody 'round here wear a hat like that. Baseball cap's the best they do."

That stopped me on a dime. Little Lloyd had seen a man in a Burberry raincoat and hat with Clarence Gibbs. I would've bet money—although that was not a custom of mine—that Gibbs had sent somebody to check out the property he already considered as good as his own. An appraiser, maybe, or some kind of inspector, either of which raised my blood pressure considerably above the normal.

"Lillian," I said, irate now at the nerve of that arrogant and overconfident weasel, "if that man comes back, you send him packing. I don't want him putting one foot inside this house."

"Yessum, I will. But what if you home, an' he asts to see you?"

"Then I'll do it myself. Believe me, he is up to no good, and we don't want him anywhere around here."

I went upstairs, still fuming, and thinking of calling Clarence Gibbs and blessing him out for overstepping himself. Then I thought better of it.

Better to let him assume that I didn't have a chance of redeeming my house and buying Willow Lane. I smiled to myself as I estimated the donations and sponsorships that were bound to come rolling in. He just didn't know who he was tangling with.

It was a settled fact that I wasn't one to count her chickens before they hatched, but if Thurlow Jones's condition didn't completely maim him, we had a good chance to meet Clarence Gibbs's price, as well as his deadline.

So, in a fit of compassion undergirded by my own ulterior motives, I called The Watering Can and ordered a plant garden to be sent to Thurlow's hospital room.

Chapter 26

With the house tour and flower show fairly well under way, I was free to turn my mind to other aspects of our fundraising efforts. Number one on my list was bringing in the pledges and seeing where we stood on our journey toward our goal of two hundred and fifty thousand dollars.

When I went down to breakfast Saturday morning, I found Hazel Marie still in her robe, drinking coffee at the table and looking through the morning paper.

"Where is everybody?" I asked. I'd expected Lillian to be making a big breakfast for Little Lloyd, as she usually did when he didn't have school.

"Lillian and Little Lloyd decided to walk over to Willow Lane," Hazel Marie said as she smoothed out the paper.

"My word, it must be two miles over there."

"Well, I think they both just wanted to get out. Lillian said something about visiting with one of her neighbors who's staying with a family near Willow Lane."

I made toast and poured coffee and, offering more to Hazel Marie, sat at the table with her.

"Oh, look," Hazel Marie said as she turned a page of the

newspaper. "Look at this. They've got our ad in here. A whole half page."

I looked over her shoulder and read with increasing agitation the huge, attention-grabbing ad:

POKER RUN!!
Sponsored by the Abbot County H.O.G.s Chapter
and
Red Ryder's Stop, Shop & Eat
to benefit the Willow Lane Residents
ALL BIKERS WELCOME

Then, right below that in smaller letters, but not that much smaller, was a list of names of the leaders of local society—that's what it said, "leaders of local society," of all things. And heading the list was my name, as clear as you please. And beside my name were the words *Sponsored by Thurlow Jones, Sam Murdoch, J. D. Pickens, Deputy Coleman Bates, Sheriff Earl Frady, and Lieutenant Wayne Peavey.*

I found it hard to get my breath. "Hazel Marie! My name wasn't supposed to be in there! Who's responsible for this?"

"Well, I put it in, Miss Julia," Hazel Marie said. "You asked me to, remember? I didn't know I was supposed to leave your name out."

I put my hand to my forehead and moaned. "But what about all those sponsors? Thurlow Jones's name beside mine is bad enough, but the rest of them? That's false advertising, Hazel Marie."

"No, it's not," she said, beginning to smile at my distress. "They've all donated at least a thousand dollars in your name, and some of them even more. I'll tell you, the money is rolling in for you. Although Emma Sue Ledbetter would be a close second if you hadn't gotten Mr. Jones as a sponsor."

Leaning over to read the ad more closely, I said, "Well, at least you didn't put the amounts that the sponsors have given. I'd never live it down if this town saw how much Thurlow Jones gave. They'd be speculating on what else he was buying."

"Oh, you worry too much about what people say," she said with an airy wave of her hand, as if she had not been the major topic of whispered conversation for years. "Now, listen, there're five or six more women who've volunteered to ride since I sent this to the paper. A couple of doctors' wives, a lawyer's daughter, the Lutheran minister's wife, and a judge's wife. And they've all got sponsors. This thing is really rolling, Miss Julia."

"How old are they?"

"I don't know," she said. "They're mostly in their thirties and forties, I would imagine. Why?"

"Oh, no reason," I said. "I'd just prefer not to be the only elderly woman to make a fool of herself." Then, turning to the phone, I said, "I better call Sam."

"He's not home. I talked to J. D. before you came down, and he's going with Sam to have the sidecar put on. Then they're going to ride for a while to see how the bike handles. And I think J. D. wants Sam to get in a little more practice before the big run."

"From what I've seen, he needs it," I said. "When did you talk to Mr. Pickens? I didn't hear the phone ring."

She ducked her head and said, "Well, I called him. Just to tell him the ad would be in the paper. He might've missed it, you know."

"If he had, somebody would've told him. This is going to be the talk of the town, if it's not already."

"Oh, look, Miss Julia," Hazel Marie said, holding the newspaper up. "They've got a separate article about the Poker

Run in here. Red Ryder's quoted, and so is Sam. Oh, my goodness, they've even interviewed Emma Sue. Listen to this: 'I go wherever the Lord tells me to go, whether I like it or not. And since he wants me on the back of a motorcycle, that's where I intend to be.' " Hazel Marie stopped and pondered Emma Sue's words, then, looking up at me, she went on. "Do you think the Lord really told her to ride?"

"For goodness sakes, Hazel Marie," I said. "If you listen to what Emma Sue says, you'd think she has a face-to-face conversation with the Lord every day. With coffee and doughnuts. The one thing I know for sure is that the only word I got about getting on a motorcycle came in the form of a check from Thurlow Jones, who is as far from being a conduit from heaven as anybody I know." I reached for my coat and began putting it on. "Now, I'm going over to Willow Lane and try to catch Lillian and Little Lloyd before they have to walk all the way home."

I closed the door behind me and got into my car, and didn't get five blocks from the house before I met Little Lloyd and Lillian walking home.

I leaned over and opened the passenger door. "I came to give you a ride."

They piled in, bringing cool air with them. "That take my breath away, Miss Julia," Lillian said. "Seein' how lonesome it look."

"I know, Lillian. But just think how much easier they'll be to repair with everybody moved out."

"Yessum, all us Willow Lane folks been prayin', hopin' we get to go back."

"You will, Miss Lillian," Little Lloyd said, patting her shoulder. "Mama said that since Miss Julia and all the other ladies're riding in the Poker Run, donations're coming in faster than she can count."

Well, let us hope and pray, I thought as I pulled into the driveway. I took a long, sorrowful look at my house, thinking what a shame it would be if it went the way of Lillian's house, and Clarence Gibbs put up another monstrosity like the Family Life Center across the street.

～

The next morning, being Sunday, Little Lloyd, Hazel Marie, and I walked across to the church for morning services. I was pleased that Hazel Marie had joined us, since she'd been avoiding church during her time of cohabitation with Mr. Pickens. I'd not said anything to her about it. It'd been my experience that the more you told somebody that they ought to go to church, the less likely they were to show up. Better to wait and let their own conscience do its work.

I was proven right by the fact that, without a word from me, she'd arisen, readied herself, and followed us into my usual pew, four rows from the front on the aisle.

But after commending myself for handling Hazel Marie in such a way as to bring her back into the fold, I soon wondered why I was there myself. Pastor Larry Ledbetter, in his black robe, cut loose on us with a sermon the likes of which I'd not heard in a month of Sundays. He took as his text half of a verse from Proverbs: *A prudent wife is from the Lord.*

"Prudence," he declaimed, lifting up a finger at each point he made, "means having discretion in all things." One finger went up and pointed at us. "It also entails exercising good judgment when it comes to making decisions." Another finger sprang up. "And common sense when it comes to practical matters." A third finger went up, and he leaned over the podium to make sure he had our attention, putting power behind his final point. "And *circumspection* when it comes to one's public behavior!"

As I reared back in the pew from that last onslaught, it came through to me that he was highly exercised over the plans of certain wives in the congregation to cling to strange men and ride behind them on Harley-Davidson Road Kings and Softails.

"It is incumbent," he said, using one of his favorite words, "upon Christian wives to conduct themselves in such a way as to give no offense, shame, or humiliation to their husbands or to those who look to them as examples and models of Christian behavior." He took a deep breath, leaned on the podium, and lowered his voice. "I say to you wives, nay, even to all women, you are commanded to be under obedience, as the law saith."

I looked around to see how Emma Sue was taking such a public dressing down, but she was nowhere to be seen. I poked Hazel Marie and nodded toward Emma Sue's empty place. Even though Emma Sue was not one of my favorite people, I couldn't help but feel sorry for her. If her husband could speak so forcefully about her behavior to the congregation, and I expect everyone there knew who he was talking about, then there was no telling what he'd said to her in private. I sat back, satisfied and content that I no longer had a husband to berate me when I didn't follow his directions.

Then Pastor Ledbetter switched from wives to widows, and I took immediate offense. If he wanted to preach about his own wife's shortcomings, that was one thing— unattractive though it was—but now he'd gone to meddling. I sat there, getting stiffer and stiffer, as he took off on something that wasn't one bit of his business.

"Widows," he exhorted with authoritative power, "are to occupy themselves with their own homes and the Lord's work, taking care to refrain from idleness."

Well, I couldn't disagree with that, even though I could

think of any number of worthwhile occupations for widows besides house and church work. But then he started going far afield. "There are those widows," he thundered, "who have nothing to do but be busybodies. They wander from house to house, stirring up discontent and speaking things they ought not.

"Paul writes," the pastor went on, quoting his favorite writer, "that they ought to be teachers of good things to the younger women—good things like being discreet, chaste, keepers of the home, and *obedient* to their husbands. This is what widows and aged women ought to be occupied with, instead of," he paused, then lowered his voice again for effect, "instead of running around enticing others onto the highways and byways of evildoers."

My word, I thought, hoping to goodness there were no visiting bikers who'd take offense at being publically named as evildoers on the highways. For all I knew, they'd be enraged enough to call out the pastor, after which we'd have to form a search committee to find another preacher.

But I was so mad by that time that I didn't much care what happened to the pastor. I didn't know where he'd gotten his information, but *I* certainly had not gone from house to house stirring up anything. They'd all come to my house, and it had been Mr. Pickens who'd done the enticing, not me. Furthermore, there was not one soul who could accuse me of being a busybody. Of all the people who minded their own business, it was me. I wanted to stand right up and tell him so, but then he'd have grounds for another sermon, about women keeping silence in the church.

It was all I could do not to get up and leave. Hazel Marie put her hand on my arm to calm me down, and Little Lloyd kept glancing up at me as I became more and more insulted at the pastor's effrontery. How dare he blame me for his own wife's conduct! Then, having a flash of insight, I realized I was not only personally insulted, I was insulted for Emma Sue's sake.

That was a change in my viewpoint, but as we rose to follow the choir in its recessional, I determined to do everything in my power to make sure Emma Sue crawled on that motorcycle and had the time of her life doing it. And Pastor Ledbetter could either like it or lump it, I didn't care which.

Chapter 27

Well, of course we had the pastor for dinner, and I don't mean we invited him to dine with us. Hazel Marie and I, with Little Lloyd and Lillian listening with wide eyes and open mouths, discussed him up one side and down the other. I was still so mad that it was hard to swallow either his sermon or my food.

"Lillian," I said, "what did the Reverend Abernathy preach on this morning?" I had driven Lillian to the AME Zion church earlier, and had picked her up after we returned from our services. The reverend always went longer than Pastor Ledbetter, although the pastor went plenty long enough. And, for my money, he'd've done better that morning to've quit before he started.

"The reverend," Lillian answered, "he preach on our home in heaven, that we not to worry what man do to us down here, we got us a heavenly home jus' settin' up there waitin'."

"That's beautiful, Lillian," Hazel Marie said. "And so true."

I agreed, thinking that I'd much rather have heard that sermon than the one I'd been subjected to, although if, like

Lillian, I didn't have a roof over my head to call my own, I'd've found it cold comfort.

"What're we going to do, Miss Julia," Hazel Marie asked, "if Pastor Ledbetter's sermon makes Emma Sue and the other women in the church pull out of the Poker Run? We've already got lots of donations for them, so if they don't ride, we might lose every penny of it."

"I know," I said, nodding wearily. I was tired to my bones of the pastor poking his nose in my business every time I turned around. "But I just don't see how they could pull out now. I mean, it would be a public embarrassment for them to say they'd changed their minds."

"If I understood what the pastor said this morning," Little Lloyd chimed in, "they've already been publicly embarrassed."

"You're right, Little Lloyd," I said. "That whole sermon was humiliating, to say the least, and I don't intend to sit still for it. The very idea," I went on, as the words of that sermon rolled over me again, "referring to me as a busybody, telling me I ought to stay home and not lead younger women astray. Besides, Emma Sue's not that much younger than I am."

"But Miss Julia," Little Lloyd said, frowning, "I didn't hear him say anything about you."

"He didn't have to, honey," I said. "That's his way. He makes sure everybody knows who he's talking about without naming names. Then he can deny it if somebody calls him on it. Typical preacher, is what I say."

"But not all preachers are like that," Hazel Marie said, and I appreciated the correction. Like her, I didn't want to overly influence the child against preachers in general. Most of them did enough of that on their own.

"Still," I said, "we need to do something. The whole

thing's going to be a flop if Emma Sue and LuAnne and Norma pull out. But it's Emma Sue we ought to concentrate on. The others will follow her lead. Let's invite her over and see if we can undo some of the damage Pastor Ledbetter did this morning."

"That's a good idea," she said. "But the pastor'll be home this afternoon, so Emma Sue wouldn't dare come over here."

"He probably wouldn't let her," I said, with some disgust. Remembering with even more disgust my own submission to Wesley Lloyd's authority, I didn't think Emma Sue would defy her husband and walk out. She'd not come as far as I had. But then, her husband was still alive. "I'll talk to her to-morrow," I said, wondering if I could wait that long to counteract the pastor's attack on us. "But if any of the others call to say they're dropping out, just refuse to discuss the matter. Say we have to get together before anybody makes a decision about anything."

She nodded, her face a study in worry and concern.

*

The pastor showed up at the church bright and early Monday morning, which I knew because I'd watched for his car from my upstairs window. Then I'd hardly completed my toilette before Emma Sue was knocking at the kitchen door. Lillian let her in and, when I came downstairs, she was at the table nursing a cup of coffee.

"Why, Emma Sue," I said, "I didn't know you were here. I didn't hear the doorbell."

"I parked around on the side, Julia," she said, her eyes darting to the window as if she expected to see someone looking in. "I thought it'd be best if Larry didn't know I was here. Now, Julia," she went on, beginning to get teary-eyed, as she was wont to do, "I hate to let everybody down, but I won't be able to participate in the Poker Run, the very name of which sets Larry off like you wouldn't believe."

I pulled out a chair, sat down across from her, and propped my elbows on the table. Lillian edged toward the back staircase, aiming to leave us to talk alone. But I wanted Emma Sue to know who she was jeopardizing. "Lillian," I said, "I need you to stay here in the kitchen, if you will. Now, Emma Sue, just why are you backing out at this late date?"

Emma Sue began to raise and lower her eyebrows and squinch up her eyes, nodding her head toward Lillian, who was now busying herself at the sink. Emma Sue whispered, "Let's go in the living room."

"We're fine right here. Besides, Lillian's interested in why you've decided not to do what you promised to do, as will be all the Willow Lane folks. Emma Sue, you gave your word and put your name on the list, and it's been published in the newspaper for all to see. And I'll tell you something else, you have brought in more pledges from sponsors than anybody else, except me. And I'm ahead of you only because of a fluke of nature, namely Thurlow Jones, who may be a freak of nature by now, if all I've heard is true. There're going to be a lot of disappointed people if you drop out. And remember what Mr. Pickens said. He said that you're a leader, so if you don't ride, what do you think LuAnne and Norma and two or three others from the church are going to do? You'd ruin the whole thing."

While she dabbed at her leaking eyes, I had a sudden vision of a wholesale dropout by not only the women from our church, but also by the Baptist and Methodist women. Once they heard that the Presbyterian minister's wife had decided not to ride, on the grounds of its unbecoming nature, there might be no one left on a motorcycle but yours truly.

I got a sick feeling in the pit of my stomach.

"Emma Sue," I said, determined to talk her into staying the course, "do you let your husband tell you what to do? Don't you have a mind of your own?"

"The Bible tells wives to submit themselves to their husbands," she said, "and that's what I try to do."

"Very commendable, I'm sure," I said. "But what if a husband is wrong?"

"Oh, Julia, I don't know," she wailed, laying her head on the table as the tears gushed out. "I have wrestled with that problem . . . oh, you just don't know." She raised her head as Lillian set a box of Kleenex beside her. Grabbing a handful, she mopped at her face. It was a good thing that Emma Sue didn't believe in makeup, else it would've been smeared from here to yonder. "Because . . . because sometimes he *is* wrong."

"Well, of course he is. He's human, after all," I said. "And a man." I took the wet wad of tissues from her hand and gave her some dry ones. "Now listen, let's look at this and see if we can figure out why he's so upset. Because remember, Emma Sue, he wasn't just talking about you, but all of us. Are you listening?" She nodded. "The whole purpose of the Poker Run is to help others, isn't it?"

She sniffed and nodded. I went on, "And helping others is the Christian thing to do, isn't it?" She shredded the wad of Kleenex and nodded again. "And you wouldn't be doing it for your own pleasure, would you?" She shook her head. "So what is his problem?"

"He said," she said, sniffing wetly, "he said it would be unbecoming for a minister's wife. And embarrassing to him."

"See!" I said. "It's himself he's concerned about. How it would look for *his* wife to do something he disapproved of."

"But, Julia, he's supposed to have the authority over me. Paul said that, you know."

I clicked my tongue against the roof of my mouth. "Paul said a lot of things, and a lot of them, by his own admission, were his own opinions. Who's to say that that wasn't one of them?" I leaned toward her, wondering if I was indeed leading her astray. Still, every time I thought of myself being the only woman to climb on a Harley come Motorcycle Saturday, I felt a renewed urgency to talk her into climbing on one, too. "Look, Emma Sue, use the common sense that God gave you and expects you to use. If you think there's nothing wrong with participating in a fund-raising ride, if you know it would mean the world to a lot of homeless people, if you believe in your heart that it would be a Christian act, then just do it."

"But what would Larry say?" she cried, as tears ran down her cheeks again. "Oh, Julia, you don't know what he said when he saw me making a pair of pants."

Emma Sue prided herself on being a seamstress, making all her clothes and occasionally a few blouses, scarves, and embroidered handkerchiefs for gifts. I happened to know that she'd once made a leisure suit for the pastor, which he'd never been known to wear.

"Well, it seems to me," I told her, "that he's already said everything he has to say. And if you're worried about what he'll do, he doesn't believe in divorce, so he's lost that foothold. Think about it, what's the worst that could happen?"

She covered her face and mumbled, "He could just stay mad and not talk to me forever."

"Uh-huh," I nodded, remembering one of Wesley Lloyd's

favorite ways of showing disapproval. "So let him sulk while you bask in the approval of the whole town, and in the knowledge that you've extended a helping hand to those who need it."

"But Julia, a *motorcycle?*" she said. "Maybe Larry is right. It's not exactly the sort of thing a woman in my position ought to be riding on. And I know that you're not too thrilled about it, either."

"No, I'm not. But I've set my eyes on the prize that lies ahead, not on what it takes to get it. Emma Sue, think about this: Jonah rode in the belly of a whale, Elijah rode in a chariot of fire, Paul rode on a ship that sunk, and Jesus rode on a donkey." Actually, it was an ass, but that's a word I rarely use. "Don't you think if a Harley-Davidson had been around in those days that at least one of them would've ridden it?"

She frowned, studying the problem. "Well, I can see that Paul might've. He traveled so much, you know." She shredded another handful of Kleenex. "Oh, Julia, I've never out-and-out defied Larry before. I don't know if I have the courage to do it."

"You forget that I've seen you in action," I said, remembering the many times that Emma Sue had ridden roughshod over whoever stood in her way. "You're a woman who does what she knows is right, regardless of what others think."

"But what would I tell Larry?" she asked, and I knew I'd turned the tide. But it didn't feel so good. Who was I to encourage a woman to defy her husband, and him an ordained minister of the Presbyterian persuasion?

Well, I thought, I was doing it for Lillian, and she was a good cause if I'd ever seen one.

"Don't tell him anything, Emma Sue," I said, thinking that

if I was in for a penny, I might as well be in for a pound. "Just go about your business and let him think what he wants to. Can you get away that Saturday without him knowing it?"

"I've already checked his calendar," she admitted with a little smile. "He has a wedding that morning, and another one that afternoon. He won't be home all day."

"Well, see?" I said, feeling no small triumph. "If that isn't a sign, I don't know what is. The Lord wants you on that motorcycle, Emma Sue."

"You know," she said, wiping the last of her tears from her face. "I believe he does."

When I saw her to the door and watched her slip around the back of the house, out of sight of the pastor's study window, I turned back to Lillian. "Don't you say a word, Lillian," I said. "Not one word."

"All I say," she said, "is you better watch out lightnin' don't strike you down."

Chapter 28

The dreaded day dawned cool and clear, at least overhead, where the sky was as blue as I'd ever seen it. Fall leaves glowed against the sky, and I knew the scenery would take my breath away up on the Blue Ridge Parkway. If, that is, the low bank of clouds to the north stayed where they were, and if I'd be able to unclench my eyes long enough to see anything. In spite of all my hopes for ice, snow, or broken bones, it looked as if I was going to have to park myself in that sidecar and pray for travel mercies.

Little Lloyd was up with the birds, so excited he could hardly stand it, and Hazel Marie wasn't far behind him. She was dressed in her black leather outfit, which molded her body in a way that made my eyebrows shoot straight up. I tried not to look too closely.

"Hazel Marie," I said, noting Little Lloyd's blue jeans and flannel shirt, "is that child going to be warm enough?"

"Yes, ma'am," she said. "He has on long underwear, and he'll be wearing the leather jacket J. D. gave him. You know, the one with the gold stripes and logo to match J. D.'s Softail. It looks so good on him." Hazel Marie's fashion sense didn't always match mine, but I kept my opinion to myself.

She turned to the child and said, "And gloves. Lloyd, don't forget your gloves."

As for myself, I'd blocked all efforts to get a pair of pants on my lower limbs. LuAnne had urged me to follow her lead after she bought a pair of what she called stretch denims. For my money, they needed a little more give to them.

"Now, Julia," she'd said as she turned to give me an eye-popping back view, "they're supposed to be a tight fit so they can hold you in. But my car coat covers what you're gaping at, so don't worry about it."

"I haven't said a word, LuAnne," I'd said, but I was thinking a lot.

As for my own attire, I was most concerned about freezing to death. Sam had told me that it would be breezy and that I should wear layers that could be taken off as the day warmed up. Which didn't make a lot of sense to me, as we were to gather at Red Ryder's a little after noon, when the day would be as warm as it would get.

My clothing consisted of an extra chemise under my slip, a woolen shirtwaist dress with a full skirt to allow freedom of movement, and a pair of thick cotton tights that Hazel Marie loaned me. As she was somewhat shorter than I, the tights had a tendency to creep down from their appointed place. My everyday winter coat, a pair of leather gloves, and a head scarf completed my open air ensemble. Plus a lap blanket.

As I gathered my things and prepared to go downstairs, I heard the back door slam and the sound of running feet.

"Miss Julia! Miss Julia!" Lillian's voice resounded through the house. "Come quick! Hurry, you got to see it!"

Hazel Marie and Little Lloyd ran out of their rooms in response to Lillian's screams, and I almost tripped in my haste to get down the stairs.

"What is it?" I cried as we met in the hall. "My land, Lillian, what is going on?"

She grabbed my arm and tugged me toward the door. "It takin' over ever'thing, Miss Julia! Hurry, you got to do something 'fore it get away from us!"

My heart thudded as I saw how frightened she was. Her eyes were popping and perspiration dotted her forehead.

"You want me to call the sheriff?" Hazel Marie asked, dithering around behind us.

"We don't know anything yet," I said. "Lillian, stop and tell me what's the matter."

But she was in no shape to tell me anything, for she pulled me outside and practically ran me to the rear of the garage. Hazel Marie and Little Lloyd followed, but we all came to a sudden stop as we rounded the corner.

"Jus' look," Lillian said, gasping for breath and pointing a shaking finger.

"My-y-y Lord," Hazel Marie said, absolutely awestruck, as was I.

"Goodness sake," Little Lloyd said, which almost made me laugh in spite of my shocked condition. "What happened to it?"

But I couldn't get a laugh or a word out; I just stood there and stared with my mouth open at the unprecedented development of one of Lillian's transplanted bushes. From a winter-pruned stub, the bush had put out one fat, upright shoot that reached all the way to the eave of the garage. Other branches, laden with lush green leaves, had sprung up from the root and now drooped over from the weight of round clusters of white flowers.

"Why, it looks like a banana," Little Lloyd observed. "Half-peeled."

"Let's not be making comparisons." I forced myself to

speak calmly, lest the child think of something else it resembled. "Look at all those blooms. And in October, too. That is the most unnatural thing I have ever seen. Lillian, that can't be . . . ?"

"Yessum, it is." Lillian's head bobbed up and down, her eyes fixed on the phenomenon. "Uh-huh. That my snowball bush what's growed all over itself."

"Look at that big stalk," Little Lloyd said, peering at it closely. "It's stiff as a board."

"Don't touch it, Lloyd," Hazel Marie said, pulling him back. "No telling what made it take off like that."

"None of them bushes got fertilizer 'round 'em," Lillian said. "Not since we dug 'em up an' put 'em here."

"Oh, my Lord," I gasped, leaning with my hand against the garage. "The spring water, that's what did it. I threw the whole jarful right under that poor bush. Oh, my word, first Thurlow Jones and now this."

Lillian's eyes got even wider. "You mean, Mr. Jones, he growed a thing like this?"

I shook my head. "I have no personal knowledge of his ailment, and I certainly don't want any. But I heard they had to rig up some kind of support for it." I walked around to view the aberration from the other side. "This violates every law of nature I've ever heard of. It is beyond belief."

Hazel Marie apparently didn't share my concern, for she stood gazing at the bush with something like admiration. "It sure did grow big snowballs, didn't it?"

"Hazel Marie, please." I aimed a pained look at her, but she was too taken with the overgrown specimen to notice.

Little Lloyd said, "I bet Miss LuAnne could use them in her flower arrangements."

"Don't suggest it to her," I said. "Now, Lillian, I hate to leave you with this, but we've got to go or we'll be late. Keep an eye on it, though, in case it keeps growing. I'll get some-body out here next week to get rid of it. I'm sorry about your snowball bush, but it will have to go."

"Yessum, I won't miss it. I don't want no snowball bush what grow worse'n a weed. An' a ugly one, at that."

Reluctant to leave such rampant growth for fear it would get away from Lillian, I nonetheless deemed it time to go. Not that I was that anxious to mount a motorcycle, but I'd made my bed and now had to lie in it. So to speak. So we went back into the house to get pocketbooks, keys, and coats, while Hazel Marie kept on murmuring about the size of those things.

⟶

"Lillian," I said, as we prepared to leave. "Are you sure you don't want to go?"

"I be out there when y'all get back. Miz Causey, she pickin' up sev'ral of us, an' we watch you come in." She stopped, started to say something else, then decided against it.

I walked over to her and said, "Now, Lillian, I don't want you to be worried about me. Sam's promised to go slow and not take any chances."

"Yessum, I know he take care." She gazed off into the dis-tance, the way she does when she has something on her mind. Or maybe she was looking to see if that snowball bush had sprouted up again. "It jus', well, Miss Julia, you think them biker folk know we be out there? They maybe not want us at they party."

"Oh, Lillian," I said, dismayed that the reputation of the biking community troubled her. Actually, it troubled me, but not for the same reasons. "Sam and Mr. Pickens both have assured me that all the riders know exactly who and what this fund-raising drive is for. Now, I know that bikers in general have a terrible reputation, but you can put your mind at rest about this particular bunch. They're all expecting a representative group of Willow Lane residents to be there, and *I* want you there. Who knows," I said, trying to laugh away my gnawing concern about personal safety, "I may need some help getting home. And remember, Lieutenant Peavey and a lot of deputies will be on duty. Some will even be riding with us. There's nothing to be concerned about, and I'm expecting you to be there, waiting for me."

Hoping that I'd reassured her, I followed Hazel Marie and Little Lloyd to the car. Sam had offered to come by for me on his Harley, but I'd said that I didn't want any more bareback riding than I'd already bargained for. Mr. Pickens had told Hazel Marie that he'd meet her at Red Ryder's, since he had to be there early to register the riders for the Poker Run.

I drove to LuAnne and Leonard's condo, where they'd moved when they sold their home of thirty years, and tooted the horn. LuAnne came running out, looking like a snowman in her white car coat and fuzzy white gloves. The legs of her stretch denims were jammed into a pair of white majorette boots with tassels that flipped with each step. I didn't have any idea where she'd found them; I knew for a fact that she'd never led a band in her life.

As she approached the car, I felt it necessary to caution Hazel Marie and Little Lloyd. "Don't say anything about that snowball bush around LuAnne. It'd be all over town before nightfall, and we've got enough to handle without announcing a botanical curiosity the equal of Thurlow's medical one."

"Well, but I still can't get over the size of those things," Hazel Marie mumbled.

"Miss Julia," Little Lloyd said. "I'll bet you're glad you didn't throw that water in the front yard."

"More than I can say," I said grimly, thinking of the crowds such remarkable growth would've drawn if it had been exposed to public view. Why, the way people are, they'd be looking for seeds and taking cuttings, and we'd have plants looking like half-peeled bananas all over town. "Remember, not a word to LuAnne."

LuAnne opened the car door and crawled into the passenger seat, which Hazel Marie had vacated for her. "I'm so excited," she said. "I can't wait to go zipping along the highway."

She and Hazel Marie chatted all the way to the Stop, Shop and Eat, while I nervously watched the increasing traffic and the clouds scudding overhead. I should've asked Hazel Marie to drive, but I didn't want to let on how nervous I was.

As we rounded a curve, Red Ryder's place came into view, along with long lines in both directions of pickups with motorcycles in the beds, pickups with trailers that had motorcycles on them, lots of cars, and more than enough impatient cyclists riding on the shoulders of the road—all trying to turn into the place of rendezvous. And, Lord, the racket of dozens of motorcycles already in the lot was enough to deafen a person. To say nothing of the vendor booths being hammered together, and what passed for music thumping loud enough to cause permanent auditory damage.

"Oh, wow," Little Lloyd said, straining against his seatbelt to see the spectacle.

I, for one, had never seen anything like it. Motorcycles of all stripes and kinds were swarming in from every direction. Little Lloyd started calling off their names. "Look, there's some Hondas, and a bunch of Suzukis. Oh, I think that one turning in is a BMW, and, man, look at the Harleys."

I couldn't tell one from another, and didn't care to learn. They came zooming in off the highway, some parking in rows in front of the long, low-slung building with beer signs flashing in the windows. Some machines rumbled slowly in and around the parking lot so their riders could see who else was there, and others were just revving up without going anywhere. Leather-clad people—you could hardly tell a man from a woman—waved and yelled back and forth, trying to be heard over the din. It was the most raucous conglomeration of men and machines I could imagine.

"Oh, my goodness," Hazel Marie said, with wonder in her voice, as she gazed out at the teeming lot. "Look! There's J. D. See, right there by the front door."

I nodded, unable to linger on the group that surrounded Mr. Pickens for fear that I'd clip the cycle that had wobbled into the path of our car. It was loaded down with a helmeted driver, a passenger who was wrapped around him, and what looked like saddle bags strapped to each side of the rear wheel.

LuAnne bounced in her seat with excitement. "LuAnne," I said, "if you do that once you're on a motorcycle, you're going to find yourself sitting on the highway."

She didn't even bother to answer, just flipped her hand at me.

A deputy standing in the middle of the road directed traffic, and I had to wait before turning in to let a stream of motorcycles go before me. Two other deputies were in the packed gravel parking lot, motioning cars to the back edge, where I hoped decent vehicles would be safe. Driving slowly through the crowd, toward the back of the building, I saw that the lot spread out on one side, forming a paved gathering place. People were swarming in it and a pall of smoke hung over the area, emanating from a pit that was covered with a sheet of tin. Stacks of firewood stood nearby, ready to keep the fire going.

"Oh, yum," LuAnne said. "Smell that barbeque."

"Mr. Red's been cookin' that pig since yesterday morning," Little Lloyd informed us. "We're going to have a real pig-pickin' when we get back."

My nerves were so knotted up by this time that I doubted I'd have the stomach for anything, much less pit-blackened pork.

I began fumbling through my pocketbook as if I were looking for something, but it was an excuse to bow my head and offer up a bargain.

Lord, I prayed, just let me get through this with some measure of grace and no injuries, and I promise to never undertake such a hazardous venture again.

Chapter 29

After pulling carefully into a parking space, I rested my hands on the steering wheel and sat for a minute as the others piled out. I drew a quivering breath, then stepped out of the car, telling myself that by sundown it'd all be over. If I lasted that long.

I pulled my coat closer against the chill in the air, as a cloud covered the sun. Shivering, I looked around, hoping somebody would call off the whole endeavor.

Little Lloyd spotted Sam across the lot and started toward him. "Come on, Miss Julia, that's our ride right over there."

Hazel Marie took LuAnne's arm and said, "Let's go around to the front. J. D.'ll be pairing up riders and passengers and setting up leave times. Gosh, there're so many here, we'll have a dozen different groups, all leaving at different times. Can't have us all on the highway in one big pack."

I heard LuAnne say that she couldn't wait to see who she'd be riding with, and Hazel Marie's response that J. D. would be sure she had somebody good. As little confidence as I had in my own designated driver, I took comfort in the fact that Mr. Pickens had no say about where and with whom I would ride. He had an unusual sense of humor that I didn't trust for a minute.

Left alone, I clasped my pocketbook close and hurried after Little Lloyd, taking my life in my hands as one motorcycle after another wove in and around the crowded lot. It was like a nest of hornets that'd been stirred with a stick. Noxious fumes from the growling machines nearly suffocated me, but I made an effort to maintain my composure as I walked across the lot amid the roar of dozens of unmuffled motors.

Sam, clad in his black, zippered leather outfit, looked up from his tinkering and smiled widely as we approached. "Hey, Little Lloyd. Glad to see my co-pilot's here." He looked over at me, still smiling, and said, "And here's my navigator. Julia, you are a good sport, and I'm proud of you."

"Hold your praise, Sam," I said, sweeping my eyes over the huge machine with the bullet-like car on the side. "I'm not in the thing yet."

"What can I do, Mr. Sam?" Little Lloyd asked. He was walking around the propped-up cycle, running his hand over the shining chrome and admiring the curved windshield and the dashboard, which had more gauges and switches and what-nots than my dearly bought foreign-made car, which itself had more than I had any use for.

"We're all set, Little Lloyd," Sam said. "Just waiting for time to get a map and draw our first card. Julia," he went on, turning to me. "You want to try out the sidecar before we start?"

"I'm not in any hurry," I said. "Little Lloyd, do you have to use the bathroom?"

"No'm," he said, then changed his mind. "Yessum, I guess I better." And he hurried off.

I turned to Sam. "Have you seen Emma Sue and Norma?" I asked, worried that they might've lost their nerve again.

Sam laughed. "They're here, and J. D. has them inside, where he can keep an eye on them. He's not going to let them sneak off. Besides, Emma Sue brought her Bible, and she's cornered a couple of long-haired dudes who can't get away from her. Helen Stroud's here, too, and that young Baptist preacher's wife. Several others, too." He pulled a black bubble-looking thing from the sidecar and held it out to me. "Want to try on your helmet?"

"Not until I have to," I said, drawing back.

"Well, look," he said, turning the thing upside down. "See this? It's your microphone. You'll be able to talk to me while we're riding, and you can hear me through these speakers, here."

I couldn't imagine having anything to say while enduring the next few hours other than "Look out," "Slow down," and "Let me off this thing!"

I nodded as he continued to point out the features of his Road King, showing me the gas tank, gears, brakes, accelerator and clutch—some on the handlebars, of all places—the purposes of the various gauges, the storage compartment, the passenger seat where Little Lloyd would ride, and I don't know what all. None of which was of lasting interest to me.

I kept glancing around, fearful of seeing somebody who knew me. All I wanted to do was hide my face and get the whole thing over with. As far as the eye could see on the back lot, there were clumps of leather and denim-clad people standing around or sitting on motorcycles. It was a hairy bunch, too; I'd never in my life seen so many beards, goatees, mustaches, stubbled chins, ponytails, and pigtails.

This was not the sort of social activity I was accustomed

to attending, as anybody who knew me could tell you. I felt ill-at-ease and overdressed, as if I'd misread an invitation. But because the event had been so thoroughly played up in the newspaper and on the Asheville television station, everybody in six counties was going to know I'd put in an appearance. I expected there'd be onlookers along our route and at every stop. So, as much as I dreaded putting on that helmet and looking like a space alien, I was thankful that the black visor would hide my face.

I was even more thankful for the helmet when I saw a television news van pull into the parking lot. A lot of yelling, catcalls, and the like greeted the cameraman and newscaster as they alighted from the van. Some people act like idiots at the sight of a television camera, thinking that a passing shot of themselves on the six o'clock news will turn them into celebrities.

Just as Sam finished his spiel about the wonders, plus options, of his machine, I happened to catch sight of an alarming figure walking somewhat stiffly around the side of the restaurant, threading his way around and through clots of cigarette-smoking and beer-sipping riders and spectators.

"Lord, Sam," I said, reaching for the helmet. "Put that thing on me, quick."

"Well, sure, Julia," he said, pleased that I was showing some interest. I grabbed the helmet and smashed it down on my head. "Careful, now. Here, let's pull up the visor."

"No," I said, putting up my hand to keep it closed. "I don't want anybody to see me."

He looked at me quizzically, probably wondering how I thought a helmet would fool anybody. And I wondered, too, for the visor did no more to limit visibility than a pair of sunglasses. But I'd not recognized Sam in the same get-up when he first rode into my yard; so, the thing blocked the lookee from the looker. Still, I moved to the other side of Sam, just in case, hoping his bulk would keep me hidden.

Peeking over Sam's shoulder as he continued his monologue on the virtues of open-road riding, I was dismayed to see the bandy-legged figure making a beeline for us. It seemed that Thurlow Jones had recovered from his crippling malady, but I preferred to keep my distance. For all I knew, it could strike again at any time.

"Sam," I said, clutching his leather-clad arm. "I've heard enough. Let's ride."

His eyebrows shot up in surprise. He'd thought he'd have to coax, beguile, and shoehorn me into the thing, and here I was, ready to jump in and hit the road. "It's not time to go yet, Julia. We won't be leaving until Pickens is ready, and that'll be with the last wave."

"I don't care. I need some practice time."

He grinned at my enthusiasm, delighted to show me the thrills of riding a Harley. He took my arm, pointed at a footrest, and said, "Put your right foot there, Julia, and swing on in. It's just like mounting a horse, only in reverse." Which didn't clarify a thing.

"Hurry, Sam," I said, holding on to his shoulder as I crawled gingerly onto the sidecar, then slid into the seat. It was lower to the ground than I'd expected. I scrunched down in it as far as I could, so that only the top of my bubble-encased head emerged from the top of the sidecar. I felt like Kilroy. "Let's get out of here," I said.

"Okay," Sam said, still bemused at my sudden eagerness to experience the freedom of the road. "Buckle up, and fasten your helmet. Little Lloyd'll find us when we get to the front."

Sam pulled on his helmet, walked to the other side of the motorcycle, and swung his leg over the seat. As he prepared to ignite the thing, Thurlow Jones presented himself alongside the sidecar.

"I be dog," he said, putting a hand on the sidecar by my shoulder. "I didn't think you'd do it."

I looked straight ahead, dismayed that he had so easily recognized me, but determined to ignore him. Which wasn't hard to do because Sam hit the ignition and a mighty roar filled the air. Thurlow didn't seem affected by the noise. He leaned down so that his face was right in front of my black visor.

"Knock, knock," he said, grinning like the fool he was. "Anybody home? Just want to thank you for the plant garden and the note."

I gripped the pocketbook in my lap and looked straight ahead.

"Hey, Sam," Thurlow yelled, his voice piercing the noise of the motor. Sam turned, saw him for the first time, and glanced down at me. He did something to the controls and quieted the motor to a throbbing rumble.

I heard Sam say, "What do you want, Thurlow?" It was hardly courteous, but Sam seemed to have something against him. I pretended not to notice a thing.

Thurlow yelled out, "Just came down to check on my investment, but I can't get her to talk to me. What's wrong with her?"

Looking neither to the one nor the other, I managed to see that Sam was sizing up the situation. "Maybe she can't hear you," Sam called.

"Well, hell, man," Thurlow yelled, bringing his face down to stare at me through the visor. "She can *see,* can't she?"

"We have to get with our group, Thurlow," Sam said, revving up the motor. "Glad to see you up and around again, but we have to go."

Thurlow Jones cackled and patted the top of my helmet. I ground my teeth and kept my eyes to the front.

"You better take care of this woman, Murdoch," the yellow-toothed wonder bellowed. "I got dibs on her."

To my relief, he began to turn away, thought better of it, and came back to lean across the sidecar. "I ain't sayin' you got to worry about this," he yelled at Sam. "But I seen Clarence Gibbs down the road a piece, hangin' around with a coupla Harley Fat Boys. They'll outrun this fancy thing any day of the week.

"An' another thing," he yelled, almost draping himself across the sidecar to make sure Sam heard him. As Sam revved the motor again to indicate his impatience, Thurlow jabbed his cocked thumb right in my helmeted face. "You tell her she's not seein' a penny more from me 'less she's back here by five o'clock. I already talked to Pickens and he told me that's the deadline, so all bets're off a minute after five." He stepped back, then thought of something else. "An' another thing," he bellowed, "she better make ever' stop and go the whole entire way. It don't count if she just goes a few miles an' comes back in." Then he leaned over, put his face right against my visor, and, grinning like an ape, yelled, "The whole way, woman! You hear me?"

Giving no sign that I had, I reached up, tapped Sam on the shoulder and pointed a stiff finger straight ahead. "Go," I said, although he couldn't hear me because my communications system wasn't hooked up.

But he got the message, twisting the handlebar controls so that the motor roared and the whole machine rocked on its wheels.

Thurlow Jones stepped back and bowed low, although some discomfort seemed to accompany the effort. But he grinned manfully and swept his hand in a broad gesture to wave us on. As Sam eased off the brakes, I felt a jerk in the mechanism, then it smoothed out and we were moving. I forgot about my pocketbook and clung to the sides of the sidecar with both hands, holding on for all I was worth.

Chapter 30

When I dared open my eyes, I could see that Sam was maneuvering slowly through the clumps of people and cycles, puttering around the building until we reached the far side at the front of the lot. He pulled up along the edge under a straggly tree that looked as if it had been stunted by years of engine exhaust.

Sam knocked on my helmet and motioned for me to elevate my visor. "If you're going to hibernate in there, let me hook up your microphone." He did, and the next thing I knew his voice seemed to come out of my own head. "We better go find Little Lloyd," he said. "He won't know where we are. And you need to play a hand, too, so you'll have evidence to show Thurlow."

I cocked my head close to the microphone and lifted my voice so he could hear me clearly. "I don't think I can get out," I said, and Sam almost levitated off his seat. I made an effort to modulate my delivery. "And you know I'm not a card-playing woman, Sam, so draw one for me."

"Okay," he said, looking as if he was having trouble keeping a straight face. Riding a motorcycle certainly put him in good humor. "You be all right by yourself for a minute?"

"Just don't be too long. And keep Thurlow Jones away from me."

"I'll try," he said grimly. "I don't know why he keeps hanging around you. What was he going on about, anyway?"

"Oh, Sam, the man's been sick, and he wasn't all that responsible before being struck down. Don't pay any attention to him."

Sam raised his eyebrows, acting as if he wanted to delve further into how much I knew of Thurlow's particular ailment, which I had no intention of discussing with him. It crossed my mind to tell him about the remarkable alteration of Lillian's snowball bush, but I didn't think I could bring myself to describe it.

But Sam let the matter drop, hung his helmet on the handlebars, and walked over to join the group around Mr. Pickens, who was now behind a table by the front door. I watched as riders lined up to register, receive maps, and draw cards from a deck on the table. Mr. Pickens and his helpers busied themselves sorting and writing down the results, then directing the various groups to their starting places. Then my attention was diverted from the mingling crowd by the unholy din of a half-a-dozen or more cycles revving up at the same time.

The racket increased to ear-shattering proportions as the first wave of riders roared out of the parking lot onto the highway. I gasped at the sight of LuAnne in her white outfit, clinging to a mountain of a man in a camouflage suit. His girth was such that she couldn't reach all the way around him. Big Bill Beasley, without a doubt.

Before the roar of that wave diminished to any appreciable extent, the next wave blasted my ears. Putting my gloved hands over my helmet, which didn't do a bit of good, I thought I recognized the Baptist preacher and his wife on their shiny purple machine, which Hazel Marie'd told me about.

Noticing a commotion at Mr. Pickens's registration table, I strained to see what was going on. Lord, it was Emma Sue and Norma raising a ruckus, unhappy about something. I started to climb out to see if I could help get them started, but a glimpse of Thurlow Jones kept me in my seat.

Before long, though, Sam and Little Lloyd dodged between the waiting riders and approached our parking place.

"What's going on, Sam?" I said, raising my visor.

Sam laughed. "Norma thinks her helmet's too small. She's worried about her hair."

Little Lloyd chimed in. "And Mrs. Ledbetter wanted to change partners. Mr. Pickens put her with Deputy Jim Daly and she said he wasn't old enough to be able to make wise decisions, and she wanted somebody with some experience to him. I think she hurt his feelings."

"Yeah," Sam said, chuckling at the thought. "And then half a dozen others volunteered, claiming all kinds of experience that I don't think Emma Sue understood."

"And then," Little Lloyd said, "when she looked at the choices, she didn't know what to do. But Deputy Daly told her that he might be young but he was a Christian, and Mrs. Ledbetter said that was a sign, so she'd ride with him.

"Oh, and Miss Julia," he went on as Sam handed him his helmet. "Coleman's here, too. Did you see him? He's not riding, just helping out with traffic duty, 'cause he might have to cut it short if Binkie pages him."

"Lord," I said, picturing the monumental mound on that girl, "let us hope that nothing happens till we get back."

That was an empty hope, for just then Coleman ran to his patrol car and took off out of the parking lot like he was going to a fire. As he passed us, headed back toward Abbotsville, he had both hands gripping the steering wheel and he was mortally flying.

"Uh-oh," Little Lloyd said. "I bet Binkie's in labor."

That shook me more than Coleman's abrupt departure. "What do you know about going into labor?"

The child's eyes darted back and forth. "Well, not much. I just heard you and Mama talking about it, and I figured that's what happens when a baby comes."

Sam started laughing as I glared at him. "Well, you're right, Little Lloyd," I conceded. "But it's not something you discuss in mixed company. Now, Sam," I went on, "I am absolutely torn. I need to be with Binkie in her hour of need, yet the other ladies might quit if I leave. What am I going to do?"

"You're going to stay right where you are," he said, giving me no room for argument. "Everybody's counting on you to go the distance. Besides, Binkie and Coleman will be all right by themselves."

If I could've flounced while sitting down, I'd have done it. He didn't have to remind me of what I'd gotten myself into. Now, I'd have Binkie, on top of everything else, to worry about every minute I was entrapped in the sidecar.

Another wave of riders took off, almost drowning out Little Lloyd, who yelled over the roar that he'd drawn the king of spades for me, but only the two of diamonds for himself.

"You can have my card if you want it," I said during a brief lull between waves of riders.

"No, Miss Julia, that's not the way you play. But guess what Mr. Sam drew—the queen of hearts, and he said if he was Mrs. Ledbetter, he'd take it as a sign."

"Oh, Sam," I said. But I had to smile at his foolishness in spite of myself.

Sam winked at me as he handed me a slip of cardboard

with lines on it. "Hold on to this, Julia. Thurlow's going to want to see it. Look, J. D.'s written in the king of spades on the first line, and initialed it. We'll get that done at every stop."

I put the card in my pocketbook, which rested on my lap.

Then Sam said, "Fasten your helmet and hop on, Little Lloyd. We're about ready to go."

Hoping that the motorcycle had enough power to pull the three of us, I took the time while they mounted to consider what Thurlow Jones had said about Clarence Gibbs and some fat boys lurking along the way. It was a worrisome matter, but I couldn't bring myself to get too excercised about it. I had too many other things on my mind, one of which was what Binkie was going through right at that minute, and Thurlow's threat that he wouldn't pay up if I didn't complete the course. That just made me so mad. There were a lot of things that could happen, acts of God and the like, that I had no control over. It was the intent of the heart that should count in such cases, but from what he'd said, Thurlow had no intent to give me any benefit of the doubt.

Another thing that burdened my mind at the moment was the sight of the same Burberry-coated man who kept turning up everywhere I looked. He'd just emerged from the restaurant, still in that nice raincoat, but in no way dressed to ride—not unless a suit and tie had become the order of the day. Just spectating, I guessed, but why anybody in his right mind would come out to watch a bunch of people he didn't know ride off on motorcycles was a mystery to me.

Just then a familiar car turned into the lot and pulled up just beyond us. I poked Sam and pointed at Pastor Ledbetter, who climbed out and jerked his coattail down before striding off toward the registration desk. He didn't speak to a soul, just scanned the crowd and found Emma Sue just as she was about to mount up behind Deputy Daly.

The pastor marched over to her, took her arm, and walked her back to his car. She didn't look too happy about the treatment, but she stood listening to him. I don't think he gave one thought to who else might be listening, as we certainly were, since they were hardly a stone's throw from us. But then, he could hardly recognize us, for one helmet-covered head looked pretty much like another.

"Emma Sue," the pastor started out, "get in the car. This is no place for you, and I'm taking you home."

When I heard that, I nearly came out of the sidecar. Sam put his hand on my shoulder to hold me down. "It's her decision, Julia," he said.

Well, I knew that, but we couldn't afford to have Emma Sue back out just because her husband thought riding a motorcycle would ruin her testimony. In fact, her testimony was at an all-time high, for almost every elder and deacon in the church had paid up to sponsor her, but only on the condition that their names not be made public. They knew the pastor's view on the subject and didn't want to cross him.

So I couldn't do anything but sit there and wait for Emma Sue to decide whether to obey her husband or make a decision on her own for a change. All I could think of was that if she got in that car, we'd be seeing all those sponsorship dollars—plus Thurlow's ten thousand—flying out the window.

Emma Sue squinched up her mouth, then blew out her breath. I knew it was her moment of truth, for she'd never bucked his authority in all their years together. I clenched my hands, waiting to see what she'd do. I think I even prayed that she'd work up a little gumption.

"I'm going to ride," she said, and seemed to gain some backbone just by saying it.

"You are not," he told her. I sucked in my breath when he reached in his car and pulled out his Bible. He leafed through it, then jabbed his finger at it. "You are told to submit yourself to my authority, which is given to me as the head of the household. Do you deny that, Emma Sue? Do you?"

"Not exactly," she said, but I thought she was beginning to waver. Then she called upon some unsuspected strength. "I just don't think it's relevant in this situation."

"Not relevant! What's happened to you, Emma Sue? *Everything* in Scripture is relevant. See, already your mind's been twisted from this association. Just look at yourself, Emma Sue. Here you are, parading around in tight pants and leather boots. What kind of witness do you think that is?"

Emma Sue glanced down at herself, taking in the corduroy pants she'd so proudly run up on her Bernini and the leather ankle boots that Hazel Marie had loaned her. I thought she was about to cry, and I wanted to give her some encouragement so bad I didn't know what to do. But Sam's hand was still on my shoulder.

Then she surprised me, and Pastor Ledbetter, too. She drew herself up tall, looked him in the eye, and said, "Oh, why don't you just stuff it." Then she swung around and marched back to Deputy Daly's machine. I watched her climb on without even a glance at her dumbfounded husband. He crawled back into his car and sat with his head bowed. Praying for her, I expect. I hoped he'd manage a mention of me, as well.

"Did you hear all that, Sam?" I asked, so proud of Emma Sue that I wanted to run over and give her a hug. But she and Deputy Daly were roaring out of the parking lot.

"Sure did. Little Lloyd, take a lesson, son. Don't ever tell a woman what she has to do."

Sam looked down at me and smiled, and Little Lloyd said, "Yessir, I see what you mean."

Sam made sure that the boy was ready, then he started the motor, letting it idle in a low rumble that I could feel more than hear. Wave after wave of riders roared out of the lot, heading west, so that there was a noticeable decrease in the number of people left. Most of those still milling around seemed to be spectators, neither being attired nor strutting around in the manner of your typical motorcyclist.

Mr. Pickens waved his hand, motioning to us, and Sam released the brakes of our machine. I heard Sam say, "About time we hit the road. We're the last ones."

As we moved over to the group we were riding with, Little Lloyd reached down and patted my helmet. I looked up at him, perched behind Sam, and we grinned at each other. At least I tried to. To keep his spirits up, you know. Lord, I hoped we were still able to smile by the time the afternoon was over.

As Sam moved us over to the group that we were to ride with, a black motorcycle with orange stripes zoomed into the parking lot at full speed. The black leather–clad rider brought the motorcycle to a careening stop, pivoting so that the back tire skidded around in a half-circle, kicking up gravel behind it. It was certainly a show-off's entrance, aimed to catch everybody's attention, which it did.

The driver dismounted, took off the helmet, and shook out a shock of orange hair. I gasped at the woman and her get-up—the stripes on her motorcycle and on her leather suit exactly matched the color of her hair. Halloween colors, but I doubted that she'd prove much of a treat.

And when I saw Mr. Pickens's face and heard Little Lloyd draw in a breath, I knew I was right.

"Is that who I think it is, Little Lloyd?"

"Yes, ma'am, it's Tammi," he said, looking around with a worried frown. "I wonder where Mama is."

I wondered, too, but I couldn't keep my eyes off that woman, nor could any man there. She was eye-catching— I'd give her that much—and she knew it. I could tell by the way she switched that head of hair around and by the way she swayed her hips as she walked over to Mr. Pickens.

She didn't come to a stop until she was right next to him. If either one took a deep breath, they'd be rubbing more than shoulders. Then the little hussy cocked her face up at him and smiled. We couldn't hear what she was saying, but any fool could understood what was happening. Tammi was talking and smiling, teasing him by running her hand over his chest, as he kept glancing up at the door of the restaurant. He should've backed off, but Tammi had him penned against his motorcycle.

Then of course Hazel Marie had to walk out of the restaurant, just at the most inopportune time. She took one look, turned on her heel, and slammed through the door on her way back inside. Mr. Pickens scooted sideways, jostling his motorcycle, and left Tammi in mid-sentence, so to speak. He ran into the restaurant after Hazel Marie.

"Uh-oh," Little Lloyd said. "Mama might not ride now."

"She better," I said, ready to come out of the sidecar and go after her. "I'm not doing this by myself."

"Stay here, Julia," Sam said, in that easy way of his. "They'll work it out."

I settled back in, none too anxious to hike up my dress and crawl out, then crawl back in. And sure enough, Mr. Pickens came out with his arm around Hazel Marie, who looked too rigid to move without help. He walked her over to his motorcycle, his mouth going ninety miles an hour, using, I guessed, his usual sweet-talking methods. Hazel Marie wasn't giving an inch, and she made that clear by glaring at Tammi as they passed. Tammi, in turn, just stood and watched them, a sly smile on her face. That woman was just asking for it, if you ask me.

Above the rumbling of the six motorcycles in our group—the last ones to leave—I could see Mr. Pickens's mouth still working—talking, talking, talking at Hazel Marie. She wasn't buying much of it, but she climbed into his passenger seat, crammed on her helmet, and folded her arms across her chest. She was determined not to touch him, I guess, in case he hadn't noticed how furious she was.

Mr. Pickens kicked the starter and took off like a shot, Hazel Marie's head jerking back from the momentum. The rest of us began moving out in a more sedate fashion, one after the other.

Just as Sam got us to the edge of the parking lot, I called out, "Stop! Don't go yet. I need to get fixed."

Sam stopped, letting the motor idle while the others in our group roared away, and looked down at me. "What's wrong, Julia?"

"Give me a minute, and don't look." Hazel Marie's tights were in an uproar, twisting around on me. There was no way I could ride for an untold number of miles with my circulation cut off. Covering myself with the lap blanket and lifting up off the seat, I commenced to squirm and tug and pull and straighten the things, to little avail. Nonetheless, I did get some relief, but I promised myself it was the last time I'd ever wear Hazel Marie's drawers, or anything else of hers.

"I'm ready," I told Sam. "I guess."

He revved the motor, twisting something on the handlebars, and before I knew it, we were cruising down the high-way at the tail end of a convoy.

When I could catch my breath and feel I could turn my head without endangering the balance of the machine, I looked back to see how far we'd gone. Instead, I saw Tammi's black-and-orange motorcycle nosing around the curve be-hind us.

Chapter 31

I didn't have the time or the energy to worry about her, and Hazel Marie was too far in front to be in danger of any hair-pulling, either from Tammi's head or hers. Still, I knew for a fact that Tammi had not registered for the Run, so what was she doing attaching herself to our outing?

But I was too worried about myself to give her much thought. Lord, I couldn't believe I was actually doing it—whoever heard of a woman of my age and position cruising along in a modern version of a rumble seat? I hardly dared breathe, much less do any moving around. It's so hard to balance on two wheels, you know, and I didn't want to upset the apple cart.

Nonetheless, I eventually dared a glance at the side of the road, and the sight of trees zipping along beside us was enough to make my stomach begin to heave. I hadn't thought we were going so fast until I saw that. I started to ask Sam what our speed was, but decided I'd rather not know. Then I took a chance and glanced down at the road, only inches away from where I was sitting, and the blur of it speeding by made my head swim.

After that, I just kept my eyes to the front and tried to

distance myself from the possibility of imminent peril by thinking pleasant thoughts. Which, if you want to know the truth, were few and far between, what with Thurlow Jones's unwanted attentions, the prospect of losing my home, a stranger in a raincoat popping up everywhere I went, the strange occurrence of unprecedented growth in unlikely places, Clarence Gibbs's sinister presence, and Mr. Pickens's second ex-wife hot on our trail.

"Sam," I said, speaking into the microphone. "Can you hear me?"

"Ten-four."

"What?"

He laughed. "Go ahead, Julia. I can hear you."

"You see that woman behind us?"

"I see her. I've been watching her in the side mirrors."

"Well, don't let her get past us."

"I'm not sure I can help it," he said. "If she decides to pass, there's not much I can do."

"Think of something. There'll be a wreck on the highway if she gets up close to Hazel Marie."

I declare if he didn't laugh again. There wasn't a thing funny about the situation, as far as I could see. And if I hadn't thought I knew better by this time, I'd've thought Sam was losing touch again.

Still, there wasn't much I could do about anything at the moment, so I tried relaxing in my little car seat. Not easy, since we were going up a noticeable incline that curved back and forth around a mountain. Sam and Little Lloyd leaned together as we went into a curve, straightened up, then leaned into another one. I held on tight. Both sides of the road were lined with wet-looking trees and fallen leaves. No houses, no businesses to be seen, and only an occasional farm truck or muddy car passing us, going in the other direction. Every rider, except me, raised a hand in greeting, getting a horn blast in return. It wouldn't've surprised me if everybody in the countryside knew who we were and what we were doing.

It did surprise me to suddenly notice water dripping down the windshield in front of my face. Why, it was raining, and I hadn't felt a thing. Actually, as I looked closer, it was more of a mist than anything else, a fairly common occurrence in the mountains. I pulled my lap blanket up to my shoulders and decided that if I hadn't known I was traveling near the speed of sound, my little nest would be quite cozy.

"You doing all right, Julia?" Sam's voice cut in.

"I'm fine. Just watch the road. This rain'll make it slick."

"I'm thinking of speeding up a little. We're so strung out, Pickens is probably a mile ahead of us."

That set me upright. "Oh, no. I'm just getting used to this speed. We've got plenty of time, so there's no need to get reckless." Then, as an added thought, I said, "Just so we make all the designated stops, we'll be all right. And besides, we need to keep an eye on that woman back there."

"Okay, I don't want to scare you. Maybe they'll wait for us at the first stop. That'll be coming up before long."

I settled back, relieved that the first leg was about over. I hadn't thought I'd be able to come this far unscathed, but it was proving to be not quite as terrifying as I'd feared.

Before long, we were approaching Delmont, and there was a noticeable increase in four-wheeled vehicles on the road. I began to get anxious again as cars passed on the left. Two cars trailed along behind us, and Sam had to slow to a crawl as we edged up to the rear bumper of a car in front. I cringed as we motored through downtown Delmont, for every person on the sidewalk stopped to stare and wave. And wouldn't you know it, we had to stop for both traffic lights on the main thoroughfare.

It was a relief to get through the outskirts and back out on the highway. I thought to myself, as trees started whipping by again, that if I'd expected to enjoy the fall foliage, I'd've been sadly disappointed. Mist and fog hung heavy over the mountains, and some of it had settled in the low spots on the road. I wondered if we had fog lights to go with the headlight that Sam had turned on when we started out.

Little Lloyd reached down and patted my shoulder, then pointed behind us. I risked another head turn and glanced back. Sure enough, she was still there, but she didn't seem to be overtaking us. Mr. Pickens and Hazel Marie were in the vanguard, while the rest of our group was strung out singly on the two-lane highway. We were the cow's tail, except for Tammi, who needed a switching for crashing our ride.

I sat up to look around when Sam flicked on his indicator, and I felt the motor decelerate. He turned us into a roadside park and pulled up beside a picnic table. Two women, both a little on the plump side and wearing what were undoubtedly stretch denims, scrambled out of one of the several pickups that were parked on the side.

"Time to draw our cards again," Sam said. "You want to stretch your legs, Julia?"

"No, let's just get this over with. Besides, I'm getting wet." It was the strangest thing that the drizzling rain hardly touched us while we were moving, but began to puddle in my lap when we stopped. Some kind of physics law, I guessed.

"I'll get you one of the ponchos," Sam offered, as he

reached toward the storage compartment below Little Lloyd's seat.

"No, don't bother," I said. "Let's just make our draw and be on our way. Thank you, though."

Sam and Little Lloyd drew cards from the deck that one of the women held out. "I'll draw for you, Miss Julia," Little Lloyd said, which suited me fine. "Look, you got the jack of spades! I bet you get a royal flush."

It didn't matter to me, but the child's disappointment when he drew a four of diamonds did matter. Sam drew an eight of diamonds, then patted Little Lloyd's shoulder. "Buck up, son. You know what they say; lucky in love, unlucky in cards." Which didn't seem to improve the boy's spirits.

We handed our scorecards to one of the women, who wrote down what we'd drawn, then gave them back to us. I made sure she'd initialed the jack of spades on my second line before putting the card back in my pocketbook to safe-guard it.

As she reshuffled the deck, she said, "Y'all want a cold drink? We got some in a cooler over there."

None of us did, but I took the time to ask that she write my name on her pad, confirming my presence, just in case a certain somebody decided to check it.

"The way Thurlow Jones was acting," I said, "I may have to offer double proof I was here. Let's go, Sam."

So he cranked us up again and off we went. I'd been afraid that Tammi would move on ahead of us while we were stopped, but she must've been biding her time. As we pulled out on the highway again, I looked back at an empty road. I wondered what had happened to her, but I soon put it behind me. As long as she left Hazel Marie alone, I didn't care where she was.

After a mile or so, I felt Little Lloyd tap me on the shoulder again. I glanced up to see him point behind us and, looking back, I saw Tammi some ways back, pacing us, it seemed to me.

"Sam," I said into the microphone. "That woman is still with us. What is her problem?"

"I don't know, Julia. Maybe she just wants to ride."

"In this weather?" I said. "No, I think she's looking for trouble."

Sam didn't answer for a few minutes, making me think that he agreed with me, but then he said, "I'm going to have to speed up, Julia. We're way behind, and the others are out of sight. I'm worried about the weather, too. The later it gets, the worse this fog will be, and we may have to turn back. Or stop altogether."

I almost rocked the boat, I sat up so fast. "Oh, Sam, no. We have to finish, and we have to make every stop. You don't know how much this means to me." My house, for instance, which I didn't mention.

"Go ahead, then," I said, resigned to my fate. "Put some speed on this thing. I'll bear up." Although high speed, fog, wet pavement, and two narrow wheels trying to stay on it were going to take a sight of bearing.

As we reached a straight stretch, Little Lloyd went to tapping my shoulder again. He pointed behind us and, as I glanced back, I saw not only Tammi but two other cycles behind her, and they were coming up fast.

"Sam," I said. "We've got company. Are they part of our group?"

"Don't know, Julia. I thought we were the last ones, but they could just be on their own business. They won't bother us."

But I wasn't too sure about that, for the two huge machines, their motors overpowering ours, pulled up alongside of us, riding side by side in the wrong lane. They both craned their necks at us but, with their helmets on, I couldn't tell who they were. I didn't like the way they both kept their heads turned toward us as they passed, nor the way they looked in general, which was just as I'd once thought all bikers looked—long hair dangling from under their helmets, big, beefy shoulders, barrel chests, and both of them hefty enough to squash the seats of their machines and overflow the sides. If they weren't the fat boys Thurlow mentioned seeing, I didn't know who they could be. They were scary looking, if you want to know the truth, and they kept revving up their motors, scooting ahead of us, then slowing down to our speed.

The one nearest us kept swerving from side to side, coming ever closer, so that Sam had to veer away from him. More than once, we came periously close to jumping the shoulder of the road and ending up in the ditch. I reached up with one hand and clamped down on Little Lloyd's leg to hold him on, while clutching the sidecar with the other.

"Sam!" I yelled into the microphone. "What're they doing?"

It took him a while to answer, so intent was he on holding us on the road. I don't expect my gasps and moans were much help to him, but my heart jumped up in my throat every time the cycle swayed. "Just hold on, Julia," he finally said, which I was already doing as hard as I could.

Then the lights of a car coming toward us appeared in the mist, which meant a head-on meeting with our tormentors fairly soon if something didn't give. I caught my breath at the prospect, but the two men swung into our lane, cutting in so close that Sam had to take evasive action. We wobbled all over the road, coming so close to a disaster that I probably lost a year of my life. As Sam fought for control of our vehicle, the two road hogs roared off, leaving us in the dust. Or rather, the exhaust.

When the danger was past, and I was trying to slow my heart rate, Sam said a word or two that I'd never heard from him before. I didn't rebuke him, for there were a few similar ones running through my mind. I reached up to Little Lloyd, patting him and reassuring myself that he was still with us.

What a relief to the see the last of those two. It was just as I'd always believed: regardless of what you're driving, it's the other drivers you have to watch out for.

~Chapter 32

The next stop was a closed-up fish camp on the side of the road. Babe's Fish Camp, to be specific, a shack peeling down to bare wood, a screened porch on the front, and a dock listing on a lake that rippled with raindrops, but not a soul there doing any fishing, boating, or camping. Two cars and a blue pickup were parked on the side and, as we pulled in, four women, waving and smiling, ran over to us.

"Running kinda behind, aren't you?" one of them asked, but in a kindly way. I declare, she didn't look like a biker chick to me, in spite of her leather jacket with its Harley emblem on the back. She looked like someone who ought to be home baking cookies, not standing out in the wet weather holding an umbrella and a deck of cards. But I'd already learned that the motorcycle culture attracted all kinds.

Sam drew an eight of hearts, and Little Lloyd, to his dismay, drew a three of diamonds. "Phooey," he said. "I'm not having any luck."

"Yes, you are," Sam said. "You're working on a straight flush. See, you've got the two, three, and four of diamonds."

"Oh, yeah, I do, don't I?" Little Lloyd grinned at his score card, delighted with the discovery. "And you have a pair, Mr. Sam. You beat me so far, but it's not over till it's over."

"Got that right," Sam said. "Now, Julia, let's see what you get." He drew a card from the deck that the woman held out. "Four of hearts. Not much help there."

"All I'm interested in," I said, "is getting her initials on my scorecard, so she can testify in my behalf, if it comes to that."

Sam double-checked the woman's official card, just to please me, I know, and it did. "How far ahead of us are the others?" he asked her.

"They left here, um-m-m," she said, gazing off in thought. "Maybe ten minutes ago. A good ten minutes, though."

"We better move on, then."

"Can we wait just a minute?" Little Lloyd asked. "I have to use the bathroom bad."

I was relieved to hear it, for I did, too.

"Sugar," the woman said, "I'm as sorry as I can be, but everything's closed up tight. You'll have to go in the bushes if you can't hold it."

That piece of intelligence put me temporarily on hold, since I preferred suffering to making use of an outdoor facility, but Little Lloyd said, "I can't." And he scampered off beyond the cars to relieve himself.

But little boys don't take long to do their business, and he was soon climbing back up behind Sam. Sam revved the engine and away we went again.

I declare, I was about to get used to the current method of travel. It didn't take any effort on my part at all. I just made myself comfortable, all scrunched down and covered up, reveling in the fact that we'd survived two legs of the trip. Only two more stops and we'd be completing the circle and on our way back to Red's Stop, Shop and Eat.

Sam pointed ahead, drawing my attention to beams of

the setting sun slicing through the fog, lifting my spirits immeasurably. Still, it was getting on in the day, which, with the early sunsets, meant that dark would overtake us before long.

"Next stop, eleven miles, Julia," Sam said through my speakers. "If Pickens isn't waiting for us there, I'm gonna have to whip him."

I smiled at the thought, though I was glad Sam couldn't see me. He wouldn't have appreciated it. Mr. Pickens, a former police officer and current private investigator, was a smooth operator from the outside. But for my money, he was rough as a cobb, and no retired lawyer who'd sat behind a desk all his life ought to think of tangling with him.

We met little traffic on the road, and no other bikers trying to scare us to death. But Tammi was still trailing us. She stayed some distance behind, but whenever I glanced back I could see her headlight beam coming steadily on.

Lord, if I let myself think about what was in front of us—two unknown bikers—and what was in back of us—Mr. Pickens's red-headed former wife with who-knew-what mayhem on her mind—I could've gotten quite agitated. So I didn't think about them. I thought instead of coming in with proof sufficient to snatch that check out of Thurlow Jones's hand so I could reclaim my house before Clarence Gibbs took a wrecking ball to it, putting Lillian and me both out on the street.

I was so taken up with these musings that it was a surprise to feel a deceleration in our forward movement and to see a number of cycles parked along the sides of a combination filling station and convenience store.

"Well, they're here," Sam said as he pulled us into the lot and parked along the side of the building, out of the way of any cars that needed to get to the gas pumps. So, I thought with a smile, Mr. Pickens has escaped a whipping. He would've been relieved, if he'd known about it.

"How about some coffee, Julia?"

"I'd love some," I said. "But first, you'll have to excuse me."

"Why?" Little Lloyd asked as he slid off the back perch. "What'd you do?"

"Nothing, yet. But I'm going to if I don't find a ladies' room. Preferably the indoor kind."

"Oh," he said, slipping off his helmet and running in to see his mother.

"Help me out of this thing, Sam, if you will." And with more help than I thought I needed, I landed on solid ground again. Lord, I was stiff from being cooped up in that little capsule, but the worst thing was the flattened condition of my hair when I took my helmet off. For the first time in my life, I sympathized with Norma Cantrell.

Walking stiff-legged while I ran my fingers through my hair to give it some lift, I followed Sam into the store. To our right, as we entered, we saw Hazel Marie, Mr. Pickens, and the others in our riding group clustered around a few tables. And to my surprise, there were some from the group who'd left before ours. I waved at two women from the church, and Mary Alice McKinnon, all of whom had brought in sizeable sponsorships. They were drinking coffee and eating hot dogs from the rotating cooker on the counter. The smell of coffee, so strong that it was probably burnt, filled the air. But burnt or not, I wanted some.

"Finally got here, huh?" Mr. Pickens called out to Sam, one of his teasing smiles on his face. "Pull up a chair."

Hazel Marie ran over to me. "Are you all right? We were about to get worried. I don't guess you've heard anything from Binkie, have you?"

"How could I, Hazel Marie? I've been on that machine, just as you have. And I'm fine," I said, grateful for her concern. "Mr. Pickens just went faster than I was prepared to go. Now, Hazel Marie, I need to visit the ladies' room. Where is it?"

"Come on. I'll show you." And she led me around a counter filled with all kinds of chips and toasted one thing and another, past another counter loaded down with Clorox, Tide, and Tidee-Bowl, and finally, next to a shelf filled with cans of motor oil and car wax, we located a door in the back with a female figure painted on it.

The door suddenly opened and out stepped Emma Sue Ledbetter. I declare, I'd never seen her looking so good, in spite of her homemade biker apparel. Her cheeks were rosy and her eyes were sparkling.

"Julia!" she yelled. "Isn't this the most fun you've ever had?"

"Well, hardly. But I'm glad you're enjoying it."

"Oh, I am," she assured me. "The only thing wrong with it is Deputy Daly, who wants to putter along like a Sunday driver. I say, if you're going to hit the road, you ought to hit it like you mean it!"

"The roads are slick, Emma Sue," I said, looking longingly at the restroom door.

"Look, Julia," she said, leaning close to me. "Larry's so mad at me that he may divorce me, in spite of his views on the subject. So, if I'm going to do this, I might as well get the most out of it. Now, I've got to go. We're pulling on out."

"My word," I said, thinking that the worm had certainly turned. As I watched her skip off, Hazel Marie drew my attention to the empty restroom.

"It's a one-holer," Hazel Marie said, "so I'll wait out here."

It was small, with just enough room to turn around between the johnny and the sink, but it was welcome none-theless. I soon rejoined Hazel Marie, feeling like a new woman.

Mr. Pickens made places for Sam and me at the tables and put steaming styrofoam cups of coffee in front of us. Little Lloyd already had a soft drink, which certainly wasn't good for him but I decided to overlook it. He'd found a seat on Mr. Pickens's knee, and it warmed my heart to see that strong arm around the boy's thin shoulders.

Hazel Marie got up again to make a purchase, and I took the opportunity to lean over to Mr. Pickens and whisper that his former wife was looking for him. He turned pale and looked around to be sure Hazel Marie was out of earshot.

"Don't worry," I whispered again. "She lays low when we stop, but she'll be coming around the mountain as soon as we start up again."

"Oh, Lord," he moaned, leaning his head on his hand. "I don't need this."

"This should teach you to look before you jump into something you can't get out of so easily," I said, feeling that he needed a lesson in exercising better judgment.

Since the rain had stopped and we were halfway along our route, some of the pressure to push on seemed to've lessened. Everybody was laughing and talking, discussing the rain and the road and the best way to handle both. Mr. Pickens seemed in no hurry to get started again, refilling his cup and telling some long story about a motorcycle police-man who lost control of his machine coming off a ramp in Atlanta, went airborne, and flew across three cars before landing in the back of a tomato truck. It seemed to me that he was taking some pleasure in lingering, knowing that since Tammi hadn't shown up here she was probably dawdling somewhere on the side of the road, feeling cold and miserable. But I may have misjudged him.

"Look, Mr. Sam," Little Lloyd said, pointing out the front window at the same time that the two bikers who'd almost run us off the road roared passed the store. "There go those Harley Fat Boys that passed us."

"Well, how about that," Sam said, frowning. "Wonder where they've been." I wondered, too, for they'd been ahead of us, and we hadn't passed them. Yet there they were, going past us again. I surely did not want to catch up with them, and was happy to see them moving on.

There was a great deal of cutting up as a deck of cards was brought out by the proprietor of the store. Little Lloyd was pleased with another diamond, but Sam drew a ten of spades, which didn't do him a bit of good. I drew a another jack of something, hearts, I think, but all I cared about was getting the proprietor's initials on my card. It crossed my mind that I should've brought along a notary public so Thurlow Jones couldn't question my participation.

Sam got up from the table, saying that he needed to check his gas tank, and Mr. Pickens went with him.

I watched through the window as Sam rolled his motorcycle to the front of the store, while he and Mr. Pickens talked. From Sam's hand motions, he seemed to be telling about the close call we'd had from those two fat boys who were now ahead of us.

By the time they came inside and returned from a visit to the men's room, the rest of us were getting up from the table and pulling on our coats. I dreaded crawling back on that machine, especially since it was clouding up to rain again. The lights around the gas pumps made the highway seem dark and gloomy, and the lateness of the day didn't help matters. But we were beginning the next-to-last leg, so it was downhill, so to speak, from then on.

As the other riders climbed on their cycles, I accepted Mr. Pickens's help to get back in my seat. "I'm going to stay close for the rest of the way," he told Sam. "With this weather, it'll be dark in a little while, and I don't want to lose you three slow pokes."

One motorcycle after another got kicked, cranked, and ignited, stirring up an awful noise. They moved out onto the highway and were gone in a minute. Mr. Pickens cranked his and sat idling with Hazel Marie hanging onto his waist, which I took as a sign that she was speaking to him again.

With all the commotion, I'd paid no attention to Sam's prolonged efforts to start our vehicle until Little Lloyd said, "What's wrong with it?"

Sam turned off the ignition, then switched it on again, with no resulting catch in the motor. All it did was grind like it wanted to catch, but just couldn't manage it. "Blamed if I know," he said. "It doesn't want to start."

Mr. Pickens left his bike and came over to ask an entirely unnecessary question. "Won't start?"

"No," Sam said with some asperity. He took off his helmet and wiped his forehead. "It turns over, but won't catch. You got any ideas?"

"Maybe," Mr. Pickens said as he squatted beside the cycle and surveyed the motor.

Hazel Marie left her perch and came over to see what was wrong. "Maybe it needs oil," she said.

Mr. Pickens looked up at her from his heavy eyebrows and grinned. "I bet that's it," he said, as he messed around with the motor, testing wires and such like. "Run bring me that tool kit in my saddle bag, Little Lloyd."

"Yessir," he said, eager to be of help.

Mr. Pickens said, "Crank 'er again, Sam, so I can hear what she does."

Sam turned the key in the ignition again, but nothing happened. Not a spark of life in it.

Hazel Marie watched all this, then she said, "I can tell you one thing that's wrong with it."

"What's that, sweetie?" Mr. Pickens asked, somewhat distractedly, I thought. He had his head practically inside the motor, fiddling around with the greasy thing.

Hazel Marie pointed at the back of the motorcycle. "It's got a flat tire."

We all turned to look, and Mr. Pickens sat down hard, just disgusted. "Well, dang," he said.

Sam came off his seat like a shot. "How'd I not see that?"

Mr. Pickens crawled on his hands and knees and examined the rear tire, while Sam and Little Lloyd hunkered down beside him.

"It's been slashed," Mr. Pickens said, running his hand around the tire. "And not long ago, or you would've known it."

Little Lloyd threw out his arms and whirled around. "This just bums me out!"

"Who'd do such a low-down, underhanded thing?" Hazel Marie demanded.

"Those fat boys!" I said, suddenly putting two and two together. "Why else would they pass us, stop somewhere, then pass us again? This . . . this *sabotage* was what they were doing in between."

"But why, Miss Julia?" Little Lloyd asked, sounding as if he wanted to cry. "Why would they try to hurt us when they don't even know us?"

"Well, that is the question, isn't it?" I said, but I was thinking of a few answers. "What do you think, Sam?"

"I think somebody doesn't want you to finish the Run."

"So do I," I said, darkly. "And, for my money, there're only two candidates for that dubious honor. Clarence Gibbs, who would give his eyeteeth not to have to sell to us, and Thurlow Jones, who's promised to give more than he wants to give."

And then there was Tammi, who'd certainly had the opportunity, but no motive, at least that I could see.

Chapter 33

"You may be right," Mr. Pickens said, as practical-minded as ever. "But a flat tire doesn't explain why it won't crank."

Sam had been giving the motor a closer examination, knocking and tapping at it. "Good Lord, Pickens. Look at this. Somebody's knocked the heads off every one of the spark plugs." He stood up and looked at me. "Well, Julia, I guess this is the end of our run. We'll have to see if Red can send a trailer to pick this thing up. It's gone its last mile today."

"Can't he send the parts so you can fix it?" I said, stung by the thought of giving up so easily. I'd risked everything—life, limb, and home—and come so close to winning the prize. The thought of losing practically at the last minute because of an unfair and criminal act was more than I could stand.

"Take too long, I'm afraid," Sam said, looking as discouraged as I felt. "We'd never make it back by five o'clock."

"Don't worry about a deadline," Mr. Pickens said. "It's not a race, so you can come in anytime. What counts is the best hand, and from what I've seen of yours, Miss Julia, you're pretty much out of the running anyway."

"No," I said, clutching my pocketbook because I needed

something to hold onto. "No, Thurlow Jones told me five o'clock. If I'm not back by then or if I've not made every stop, that check stays in his pocket. And," I took a deep breath, figuring they might as well know the worst of it. "And if I don't hand over two hundred and fifty thousand dollars to Clarence Gibbs by ten o'clock Monday morning, he'll withdraw his offer to sell and take possession of my house, as well."

"*What!*" I didn't know who said it, but probably all of them, for they were all gaping at me. Sam was the first to recover. "Tell me what you've done, Julia."

So I told him and said I was sorry for having done it, but it'd been the only thing I'd known to do. "It was for Lillian," I said, as Sam slowly shook his head and Mr. Pickens ran his hand through his hair in amazement.

I could feel tears welling up in my eyes, so I searched my pocketbook for a Kleenex. I felt so foolish and bereft and, well, homeless.

"It's all right, Miss Julia," Little Lloyd said, coming over to stand beside me. "We'll take care of you, won't we, Mama?"

"You bet we will," Hazel Marie said with such fierceness that we all turned and stared at her. "And the first thing we're going to do is get Miss Julia across the finish line. And I mean on time, too."

She turned to Mr. Pickens. "J. D., you're going to take her in. Sam, you and Lloyd'll stay here with me while we wait for Red. It won't matter if we don't finish. Well, J. D.," she said, her hands on her hips. "What're you waiting for? Put a fire under it, and get Miss Julia on the road."

"Oh," I gasped, trying to take in her meaning. "But he doesn't have a sidecar. Can we switch this one?"

"No time for that," Mr. Pickens said, springing to his feet, now that a plan was afoot. "Hop on, and let's ride."

I wasn't able to do much hopping, even in the best of circumstances, and these certainly didn't apply. "Hazel Marie?" I said, tremulously. "I don't think I can ride on the back of that thing."

"Yes, you can, and yes, you will. Now, come on." My word, but she was bent on getting that check in my hands.

"But I've got on a dress," I reminded her. "It'll be flying up over my head the way Mr. Pickens drives."

"Yes," she said, giving it some thought for a change. "And you'll freeze to death. Come on, let's go to the ladies' room. J. D., you have that thing fired up by the time we get back."

"Yes, ma'am," he said, giving her a little salute. Then he went to look over his motorcycle, belatedly realizing that it might've fallen into criminal hands, too.

Hazel Marie practically dragged me into the convenience store and through the aisles to the ladies' room. The man behind the counter called after us, "Y'all got trouble?"

"Nothing we can't handle," Hazel Marie answered without stopping.

She shoved me into the tiny room and mashed herself in behind me. When she closed the door, I thought I'd suffocate in the cramped space.

"Come out of that dress," she ordered as she threw her leather jacket on the toilet seat. Which was closed, thank goodness. Then she peeled out of her turtleneck sweater.

"Hurry, Miss Julia," she urged, unzipping her leather pants. "Get your dress off."

"Hazel Marie," I said as she bounced on one foot and stripped one leg of her pants off. Her elbow jabbed me as I mindlessly began unbuttoning my dress. "What are we doing?"

"We're changing clothes," she said, pulling off the other pants leg. "Or *ex*-changing them. Gimme that dress. Hurry."

"You know I can't wear your clothes," I said as she pulled my dress down my shoulders. "I'm two sizes bigger than you."

"They'll fit," she said through clenched teeth. "We'll make 'em fit. Step out of this thing."

I did, one foot at a time, as she jerked my dress out from under me. I stood there in my slip, stunned at the thought of inserting myself in those leather trousers.

Hazel Marie wasn't quite in a state of nakedness, having worn thermal underwear, but she was close enough. She threw my dress over her head and began buttoning it up. Then she tied on the belt and looked down to where her motorcycle boots peeked out under the hem of my dress.

"Let me have your slip," she said, reaching down and jerking it over my head, leaving me embarrassingly exposed. She wadded up the slip and stuffed it into my pocketbook. "I'll keep your purse for you. You can't hold onto it and J. D., too. Oh, but first, where's your card? You need to keep that with you. Now, get this sweater on." She pulled the sweater over my head. "Now, the pants."

Well, I'd put myself in her hands thus far, so I sat on the commode, removed my oxfords, and worked the pants over my feet. I never in this world thought I'd see the day I would, willingly and with aforethought, put on such a garment.

"Pull 'em up," she commanded. "They'll stretch a little." So I commenced pulling, while she knelt on the filthy floor and smoothed the leather up over my calves. We managed to get the material over my knees, where it bunched up and stopped. We'd hit a snag.

"Hazel Marie," I groaned. "It's no use. They'll never go over my hips."

"Yes, they will," she said, biting her lip, as determined as I'd ever seen her. "I'll pull the front and you pull from the back."

And so we did. I squirmed and wiggled, while Hazel

Marie wheezed and grunted with the effort of getting the things to a fitting place.

"Good enough," she said, taking the one step back that there was room for. "Whew, it's hot in here. Hurry, and let's go."

"I can't go like this!" I wailed. "Look, they won't zip up, much less button at the waist. Hazel Marie, they're not even up to my hipbone."

"Put your coat on," she said, as she shrugged into her leather jacket. "And button it up. Nobody'll know the difference. We'll meet back at Red's and change again."

"Oh, Lord," I moaned, feeling wrapped and bound. "This is just awful. I can hardly move, they're so tight and so . . . so unfitting."

She ignored me and knelt on the floor again. "Lift up your foot so I can get your shoes on."

"Thank you, Hazel Marie," I said, holding onto the sink with one hand and her shoulder with the other to keep from falling. "I couldn't bend over if my life depended on it."

She opened the bathroom door and stepped out. I clasped my coat together and began the mincing steps that were all I was capable of making.

"Wait, Hazel Marie," I said in a loud whisper. "Where can I put my card? I'm afraid it'll fall out of my coat pocket."

"In your bra. Here, let me help." She unbuttoned my coat and pulled up the sweater right there beside the Quaker State motor oil. "Slide it in. It'll be safe."

We started through the store again—one of us in a leather jacket and a dress that practically scraped the floor, and the other in a winter coat, leather leggings, and lace-up oxfords. If we weren't a sight, I didn't know what would be.

Hazel Marie banged through the door, yelling, "J. D., you better be ready, we're coming!"

I sidled out after her, coming to a stop at the top of the three steps to the ground. Lord, I was so bound at the place where my limbs needed freedom of movement that I didn't see how I could get down them.

"Hazel Marie," I quavered.

She came back and took my arm. "Step down sideways, Miss Julia. You can make it." I did, but it was hardly the most graceful descent I'd ever made.

I leaned over and whispered, "They're sliding off, Hazel Marie. They're inching down every time I move."

She motioned for Mr. Pickens to bring his bike closer and, as he did, she crammed my helmet on and pulled my coat closer. "You'll be fine. Once you're on the seat, they'll stay put."

Sam was yelling something to Mr. Pickens over the noise of the motor, telling him we'd meet up at Red's and not to endanger anything on his way. "Julia," Sam said, coming around to my side, "let me help you on."

"Oh, Lord," I said, turning away. "Hazel Marie, don't let him see me in this get-up."

"He can't see a thing," she said. "Put your foot on this peg, then hold onto J. D. and swing on up."

I tried, but the bunched-up leather wouldn't let my lower limbs separate enough to do any swinging. To my everlasting embarrassment, it took Sam, Hazel Marie, and Little Lloyd to lift me up and set me down on the seat behind Mr. Pickens. Mr. Pickens's eyebrows had arisen when I first appeared at the top of the steps, and by now they seemed to be stuck permanently in that position.

Sam stepped back and surveyed the way I was perched on the backseat. They'd plopped me on the seat so that I ended up sitting as prim as you please with my knees together, poking Mr. Pickens in the back. I knew my inflexibility concerned Sam, but I hoped he wouldn't mention it. I wasn't in the mood for explanations of a delicate nature.

Little Lloyd wasn't as tactful. He said, "You need to straddle it, Miss Julia."

I looked helplessly at Hazel Marie and she came to the rescue. "Give me your army knife, J. D." He didn't argue, just scrambled around in a storage compartment and pulled out a wicked-looking blade.

He handed it to her, saying, "Careful. It's sharp."

"That's why I want it," she said as he nearly twisted his head off, holding the handlebars steady, while turning to see what she aimed to do. She reached under my coat and came at me with the knife.

"Hazel Marie!" I gasped, my eyes on the knife as it approached a dangerous intersection.

"Mama!" Little Lloyd cried. "Don't cut Miss Julia!"

"What the hell are you doing?" Mr. Pickens said, amazement in his voice at the sight of mild-mannered Hazel Marie wielding a knife.

Sam was too awestruck to protest, which was just as well, for Hazel Marie paid no attention to any of us.

She grabbed a handful of leather where it'd slid down and bunched around my lower hips, then she sawed and sliced until I experienced a loosening of the bonds. "There," she said, reaching around and jerking the pants up so that they stayed up and might have even buttoned, if I'd had a mind to try.

Hazel Marie finished by tucking the sides of my coat under each leg, where I hoped it would stay, else everybody was going to get a glimpse of Christmas from the new opening she'd cut in her prized leather pants.

I was as settled as I'd ever be then, so I tapped Mr. Pickens on the shoulder, and called out, "What time is it?"

"It's after four," Mr. Pickens shouted, revving and rocking the motorcycle so that I had to clutch at him. "We gotta roll. You ready?"

"Ready!" I yelled back, thinking, Lord, I hope so.

I had every intention of waving as we left, but Mr. Pickens's machine took off with such a surge of power that I had to clasp my arms around his chest and bury my helmeted head against his back. We roared out onto the highway, slicing through wisps of fog in the diminishing light, the ends of my coat flapping in the breeze, and began eating up the miles.

Chapter 34

There was no talking en route on Mr. Pickens's cycle, since his helmet wasn't wired for sound, but that was all right with me. We were going so fast and my perch was so precarious that I had no heart for engaging in conversation. Believe me, this ride was considerably different than the one in Sam's sidecar. For one thing, Mr. Pickens was hunched over the handlebars, and I had my arms around him so tight that I was all but riding on his back. And for another thing, we were mortally flying—trees, fences, side roads, and the occasional barn flipping past in a blur.

The two-lane highway that we continued on took us down and around one mountain after another. We'd go into steep, curving declines, Mr. Pickens leaning into the curve—me along with him—with the sound of the motor whining and echoing from both sides. My breath caught in my throat so many times, I thought I was going to strangle myself.

Once or twice we passed some high country pastures opening out from the roadsides, so that I could see a few scudding clouds across the lowering sky. There was still some daylight when we weren't enclosed by thick stands of trees, but there wouldn't be for long. Lord, it'd be five o'clock any minute. One part of me wanted to urge Mr. Pickens to hurry, but another part already had the living daylights scared out of it.

As we leaned into an s-curve, the motor screaming between the mountainsides and me screaming inside my helmet, I caught sight of a lone headlight behind us.

When we hit a short, straight stretch, I risked patting Mr. Pickens's shoulder, then pointed with my thumb up beside his face toward the rear. I didn't want to distract him from holding us on the road, but he needed to know that someone was following us. He nodded his head and put on more speed, which I hadn't thought possible. Lord, the man could drive, or ride, or whatever he was doing.

Other than the one movement to warn him of impending danger, I don't think I moved an inch the whole twelve miles to the next stop. I feared I'd unbalance the vehicle, and we'd go flipping and skidding across the pavement, down an embankment to mire up at the bottom of a ravine, where not even the Mountain Rescue Squad could find us. Hazel Marie would never forgive me.

Mr. Pickens began nodding his head, so I lifted mine to peek over his shoulder. There, some little distance in front of us, I could see the cloud cover reflecting the lights of Abbotsville. We were almost there, thank the Lord. Recalling the map that Little Lloyd had shown me, I knew we'd be entering from the south side and would make a stop at Harold's Full-Service Esso Station for our final card drawing. Then we'd have to motor through Abbotsville, down Main Street, and out onto the Delmont Highway for about eight more miles to Red's Stop, Shop and Eat.

Maybe, just maybe, we would make it in time.

As we got closer to Abbotsville, traffic began to pick up, which would only get worse since it was Saturday evening, when everybody came to town. I wish somebody would tell me what kind of pleasure people take in cruising up and down Main Street, but I knew the high-schoolers would be out, cars would be stacked up out into the street by the drive-ins, and pedestrians would take their time ambling from one sidewalk to another. At the thought of the impediments to come, I just about lost all heart.

But not Mr. Pickens, for he began weaving in and out between slow-moving cars, passing on the left when he could, and on the right when he couldn't. Then he turned so fast and so sharply into Harold's Full-Service Esso that the edge of his foot pedal scraped against the pavement, scaring me to death. Mr. Pickens skidded us to a stop between the gas pumps and the door of the station, and let the motor idle.

He lifted his visor as I turned loose of him and straightened up. "You doing all right?" And without waiting for an answer, blew his horn and called out, "Harold, get your sorry self out here!"

Lord, I'd forgotten what we'd have to put up with in Harold, the slowest human under the sun. The only reason he was still in business was because his was the last station in town where you could have your gas pumped and your windshield cleaned without getting out of the car. He said he didn't believe in self-service, but it took him half an hour to tell you why. I'd never lingered to hear it all. The only customers he had left were old ladies who didn't know how to pump their own, and didn't want to learn.

Harold came strolling out the door, dressed in his usual grease-covered coveralls, his hair hanging down over his glasses and a welcoming smile on his face. He was just as pleasant and helpful as he could be, if you could put up with him.

"Where's the deck, man?" Mr. Pickens said, both of us

taking note of Harold's empty hands. "Give us a card, so we can get out of here."

Harold stopped, looked us over, and finally drawled, "Thought there wouldn't be any more of you. Everybody else's been and gone."

"Yeah," Mr. Pickens said. "That's why we're in a hurry. How 'bout that deck of cards?"

Harold lifted a hand, nodded his head, and finally turned to go back inside. "Got 'em under the cash register."

"Oh, me, Mr. Pickens," I said, having opened my helmet for a little air. "He's so slow I can hardly stand it."

"Hold on. He's coming."

Anxious to see him moving, I leaned down to peer through the station's window. My heart thumped as I saw the large clock hung up on the wall. Almost twenty of five, and even as I watched, the big hand ticked off another minute. Harold had barely rounded the counter. It was all I could do to hold myself in check.

Finally he ambled out to us, smiling as he held out the deck but, as I reached for a card, he pulled back. "Better shuffle 'em."

He awkwardly shuffled the cards, while my hand was left hanging in midair. "Hurry up, Harold," I urged, wondering why in the world the Poker Run's organizers had made his station one of our stops. I intended to lodge a protest, if I ever got back to Red's.

"Here you go," Harold said in his unhurried way. He tried to fan the deck out, but the cards were all bunched together.

I reached for a card again, but he pulled them back. "Whoops," he said. "Better fix 'em better'n that."

"Just give me a card, Harold, any card," I said, so agitated by this time that I could've snatched the whole deck from him. Watching him as he continued to fumble around just about sent me over the edge. "If you don't let me have a card right now, Harold Cox, I'm coming off this thing and thrashing you to within an inch of your life!"

"It's all right," he said, not at all offended by my threat. "I got it this time. Here you go." He fanned the deck with a flourish. And dropped every last one of them.

It was all I could do not to shriek in despair, and even Mr. Pickens had had enough. He revved the motor and rocked the cycle on its brakes, then leaned down and picked up a card from the ground.

"The three of spades, Miss Julia," he said and dropped it. "Get him to initial your scorecard, and let's get out of here."

I'd already surreptiously recovered my card from my secret hiding place, so I grabbed Harold's arm and in no uncertain terms said, "Sign here."

"Sure thing. Just let me get a pencil." And unbelievably, he turned to go back into the station.

Mr. Pickens nearly came off the cycle reaching for him. He snagged Harold's coveralls and dragged him beside us. "Use this," he ordered, and stuck a ballpoint pen from somewhere in his jacket into Harold's hand. With his tongue stuck out, Harold laboriously wrote in the three of spades and his full name. I snatched the scorecard from him and, in my anxiety, stuck it back in my brassiere without giving a thought to the public exposure.

Mr. Pickens put one foot on a pedal and prepared to take us out of there, for which I was so thankful I could've cried.

"About eight more miles," he said, lowering his visor.

"Hallelujah," I said, and lowered mine, getting myself ready to run the gauntlet on Main Street.

Before he could lift his other foot from the ground and

give us the gas, another roaring motorcycle pulled in and braked in front of us, stopping us cold. A hot streak of the most irate kind swept through me as soon as I saw the black cycle with orange stripes. Another delay! And by somebody who ought to've been minding her own business.

Tammi pushed up her visor and smiled in a flirtatious way at Mr. Pickens. Then she flicked her head toward me and said, "Why don't you get a real woman to ride with, J. D.?"

It came to me like a flash: *She thinks I'm Hazel Marie!*

Before Mr. Pickens could say a word, I flipped up my visor and snapped, "I'll have you know he's already *got* a real woman. And I'll tell you another thing, young lady—if you're looking for trouble, you've just about found it. Now get that thing out of our way!"

Her mouth had dropped open at the sight of me, and it stayed that way. As Mr. Pickens backed us away from her machine, she was too stunned to make a move to stop us.

Mr. Pickens revved the motor and headed toward the street. And we almost made it.

Mr. Pickens slammed on the brakes, almost catapulting me over his shoulders. We skidded to within a hair's breadth of a sheriff's squad car that had barreled to a stop directly in front of us, tires screeching and siren whomping.

"Go around him, Mr. Pickens!" I yelled. "I'll pay the ticket!"

I didn't know what we'd done to deserve a traffic stop, but I didn't aim to find out. I was a law-abiding woman, as anybody could tell you, and I wasn't all that eager to engage in a high-speed chase, but this deputy was going to have his hands full if he thought he was going to stop us tonight.

The window of the squad car slid down, and Deputy Coleman Bates yelled over the rumbling of Mr. Pickens's motorcycle, "I know about the deadline, so come on! You've got an escort!"

"Coleman!" I cried. "What're you doing here? Where's Binkie?"

"False alarm!" he yelled back. "She's home eating ice cream."

And off he took, heading down Main Street, blue light bar flashing and siren screaming. Mr. Pickens stepped on the gas, getting us up to speed before we even hit the street. We bounced over railroad tracks and went tearing off after Coleman. Mr. Pickens hunched over the handlebars—for the aerodynamics, don't you know—and I hunched over him, my coattails flapping like Zorro's cape. Coleman's siren cleared out the block in front of us, then two deputies on official sheriff's motorcycles and wearing knee-high shiny boots, came peeling out of a side street, lights and sirens going, and tucked themselves on each side of Coleman's patrol car.

Lord, it was a spectacle of thrilling proportions! Lines of cars separated before us, pulling over left and right; people on the sidewalks stopped and stared; buildings flashed by before my eyes; stoplights, streetlights, and shop lights whizzed by, and I was clamped onto Mr. Pickens like my life depended on it. Which it did.

One after the other of the motorcycle deputies pulled ahead of Coleman to hold cross traffic at the intersections so we could fly down the street without stopping. Then they'd catch up and pass us to provide the leading escort. Before I caught my breath good, we were beyond the traffic lights and on the Delmont highway, leaning into the curves and screaming down the straightaways.

I squeezed Mr. Pickens's chest until I felt him grunt. I

was so proud of him and our civic-minded sheriff's department, I didn't know what to do. And I was downright thankful that only Hazel Marie and I knew I was out in public in a pair of pants that were unzipped, unbuttoned, and about to slide off.

Chapter 35

There were no street lights on the Delmont Highway, but it wasn't as dark as the mountainous and tree-lined roads we'd been on. There were houses, for one thing, most with lights on, and more traffic on the highway, which didn't bother us because they got out of our way. And who wouldn't, with all those sirens going full blast.

I glanced up at the sky, washed with a pinkish tint from the sun that was already below the horizon. Clouds were piled up again in the west, but for now, the rain was holding off.

But all I could think of was the ticking of the clock. What if we got to Red's at two minutes after? Or one minute after? I knew Thurlow Jones and his idea of a great joke. He wouldn't cut me a bit of slack, and a near-miss on my part would only add to his fun. It made me ill, just thinking about it.

I wanted to look at my watch, but knew it was too dark to see it and I was too scared to turn loose of Mr. Pickens to even try. So I held my breath, hoping I could hold up time, too.

We leaned into a long, sweeping curve and, as we were

coming out of it, I saw lights glowing against the low-lying clouds. Mr. Pickens yelled something but the wind snatched it away. I knew what he was saying, though. We'd made it. We were coming up to Red's, where the parking lot was blazing with pole lights and strings of lights strung around on everything that was standing.

I could see more parked motorcycles, the chrome on them glinting in the lights, than I'd ever seen in my life. They were lined up along the front of the restaurant, parked at the side, stuck between cars, pickups, trailers, vans, and two flatbed trucks. And people! My word, half the town must've come out to welcome in the riders. And we were the last of them.

We began to slow down to make the turn into the lot and, with all the sirens and flashing lights our motorcade was exhibiting, swarms of people who'd come in from the Run stopped what they were doing and stared at us. There were dancers out in the sidelot, men standing around motorcycles, men and women going in and out of the restaurant and clustering around the vendor booths—they all stopped and stared, bunching up together to see who was coming in with a police escort. I felt like a visiting dignitary.

We bumped into the packed gravel lot as the sirens died down to a whine. Mr. Pickens slowed his machine and headed toward the door of the building.

I banged my hand on his shoulder. "Find Thurlow!" I yelled. "Run him down, if you have to!"

I wouldn't've put it past the old goat to hide in the crowd until it was past five. I swept the crowd, looking for him, and saw Mrs. Causey, Sister Flora, and Mr. Wills waving and jumping up and down. The Reverend Mister Abernathy stood beside them, welcoming us with a broad smile. It looked as if word had gotten out about the importance of my timely arrival.

I glanced around, looking for Pastor Ledbetter, but he was nowhere to be seen. He was probably sulled up in his study, justifying himself for his principled stand, while Emma Sue was out spreading her wings.

And, Lord, there was Lillian, right in front, and standing beside her was Thurlow Jones. Mr. Pickens saw them, too, for he braked to a stop so that I was eye-to-eye with them.

I snatched off my helmet, giving not one thought to the flattened state of my hair, and demanded, "What time is it?"

Mr. Pickens cut off his motor, looked at his chronograph watch, and said, "Four minutes to five!"

Lillian said, "I got two minutes till, but I'm fast."

Thurlow Jones pulled out a pocket watch, studied it with great seriousness, and announced loud and clear, "Three after, railroad time."

The people who'd crowded around us protested with a loud "No-o-o." But I didn't need any encouragement.

I came flying off that motorcycle, one hand clutching my downward-creeping pants and the other reaching for that no-good, lying, bandy-legged little pest.

He turned to dodge into the crowd, but Lillian had him by the coattail and she dragged him back.

I got right up in his face and said, "You look me in the eye and tell me it's after five!"

"Well," he said, grinning and looking somewhat abashed. Or maybe snagged and caught. "Maybe that's why trains don't run on time."

"The check, then," I demanded, holding out my hand.

"Oh, I'll get it to you tomorrow. That be all right?"

It was all I could do not to pound him into the ground.

The sorry thing was enjoying this! Teasing me, putting me off, dragging the whole thing out, and me in dire peril of losing Willow Lane and my home—to say nothing of my trousers and my temper.

"Thurlow," I said, a dangerous tone, which he undoubtedly recognized, vibrating in my voice. He stepped back a pace, but Lillian jerked him to a standstill. "Thurlow, I'll have you know, I've been through rain, fog, and mud; I've been crammed into a sidecar and plopped on a seat not big enough to sneeze at; I've been followed and pursued by unknown personages, almost run off the road, and sabotaged on top of that—which *you* may have to answer for. I've been unclothed and redressed so that I'm not fit to be seen in public, yet I've ridden miles through the wilderness, restrained myself from injuring a red-headed woman and from tearing up Harold Cox's Esso station, and raced down Main Street, breaking every traffic law in the book, and I have gotten here absolutely *on time!*" My voice had reached epic dimensions by this time, and I had the full attention of the audience and Thurlow Jones. "So," I said, shaking my finger in his face, "do you think I'm going to wait till tomorrow to get that check? Think again!"

He grinned, reached in his pocket, and pulled out a folded check. "Don't get in an uproar. I'm just foolin' with you."

I took it and examined every inch. It would be just like him to have failed to sign it. But no, it seemed to be in order, and I cannot tell you what a burden was lifted from my soul.

But just to make sure, I narrowed my eyes at him and said, "Don't you even think of stopping payment on this."

And he had the nerve to be offended. "What do you take me for? I'm a man of my word, and that check's as good as gold."

"It better be," I said, somewhat mollified. "Or I'll be after you like you won't believe."

Then he edged up to me and said, "That wouldn't be a bad thing at all. Why don't you invite me over next week?"

My eyes rolled so far back in my head, I didn't think they'd ever come back down. If he thought I would sit at a table with him after his recent bout of self-inflicted organ damage, he would have to think again. I turned my back on him so fast that I felt another slippage in the leather department. I whispered to Lillian, "I'm about to lose these britches. Where's the ladies' room?"

She took my arm and pushed us through the crowd and into the restaurant. People were still gathered around the windows, where they'd watched our entrance and the ensuing confrontation; a few were sitting at tables, intent on getting service, and Willie Nelson was singing "On the Road Again" on the jukebox. An infelicitous selection, if you ask me.

Lillian cleared our way into the restaurant, heading for the ladies' room. "Comin' through," she called. "Got us a 'mergency."

I should say we did. I just couldn't get a grip on Hazel Marie's pants, and I feared they'd soon be around my ankles. But people were pouring back inside, so we were stopped time and again for congratulations on an outstanding run.

Mary Alice McKinnon ran up and whispered, "We need to get together and tally up the proceeds from the Run. I think we're close, Miss Julia, but I'm still counting what came in from the riders and from Mr. Jones."

"Find us a quiet spot," I said, "if there is one. I'll help as soon as I visit the ladies' room."

She nodded and backed away as more people pushed between us. They wanted to hear about every little thing—

Sam's sabotaged cycle, who'd done it, how fast we'd gone, and on and on. Questions, backpats, handshakes came at me from all sides, while all I wanted to do was get behind a closed door and adjust those pants.

Through a momentary gap in the crowd, I caught sight of the man in the Burberry raincoat. He was sitting at a table in the far corner, his raincoat draped over a chair so that the signature plaid was in plain sight. He gave me a nod and a quick smile, which I neither understood nor returned. I will tell you what's a fact: I was bone-tired of being followed around by strangers, either on motorcycles or off. And as the crowd surged around Lillian and me again, it came to me that the fat boys and Tammi hadn't been the only strangers dogging our tracks that afternoon.

Just as we got to the ladies' room door, LuAnne threw her arms around me and cried, "Julia! I've been worried sick about you. What happened? Oh, I'm so thrilled that you got Thurlow's check. Tell me all about it."

"LuAnne," I said, "unhand me. I've got business to tend to, then I'll talk to you." Then I saw the brown bottle in her hand. "Are you drinking *beer?* Is that *beer?*"

LuAnne was a Presbyterian of the near-fundamental persuasion, and I could not believe that she'd taken to drink, as she so evidently had.

She flapped her hand at me. "Oh, Julia, don't be so judgmental. It's non-alcoholic beer, and not a thing wrong with it."

Well, look who was calling who judgmental, but I didn't call her on it.

"Listen, Julia," she whispered, beer fumes emanating from her breath, even if they were non-alcoholic. "I can't wait to tell you about Big Bill, and what a time we had."

Lillian grabbed my arm and pulled me away. "Sorry, Miz

Conover, but Miss Julia got to go to the bathroom." And she pushed me through the door into a ladies' room with considerably more space than the last one I'd been in.

As soon as the door closed behind us and I had looked under the stalls to be sure we were alone, I let my coat fall open. The mangled remnants of Hazel Marie's leather trousers were bunched up far below my hipbones. "Lillian, would you just look at what I've been subjected to?"

Lillian gaped at the sight. "Law, Miss Julia, I never thought I ever see you in a pair of britches."

"Well, if you'll notice, you're not seeing me in them now, because they're not half on."

We began laughing then, and I almost lost what was still hanging by a few threads.

Then, suddenly aware that some biker chicks might come in to use the facilities, I got myself under control. "Where's Hazel Marie, Lillian? We have to change clothes. Although," I said, looking again at the mutilated condition of her leather pants. "I don't think she'll want these back. Where is she, anyway?"

"None of 'em be back yet. Mr. Red, he send a flatbed to pick up that motorsickle of Mr. Sam's, an' some more folk went to bring everybody back."

"Then there's no telling when they'll get here." I flopped down on a bent folding chair that was a convenience of the facilities and prepared to endure my half-dressed state a while longer.

"It don't matter. Miss Hazel Marie call me right when you and Mr. Pickens leave that place, and she tell me to bring you both somethin' to put on." She reached for a Winn-Dixie bag on the counter. "I got 'em right here in this paper sack."

I jumped up, almost losing what I was holding onto.

"Bless her thoughtful heart! Oh, Lillian, this is all turning out all right. We've got Thurlow's money and all those sponsorships, which will surely be enough. And I'll give it to Clarence Gibbs Monday morning, which means you're going to have a house on Willow Lane and I'm going to keep the one I have. You don't know about that, but I'll fill you in later. And furthermore, I've got my own clothes again."

"She call Coleman, too," Lillian said, smiling so that her gold tooth gleamed in the flourescent light. "She tell him to get you here on time, an' he evermore did, 'long with Mr. Pickens, who ever'body here say a motorsickle-ridin' fool."

I started laughing, a mixture of elation, for having saved mine and Lillian's bacon, and relief, for having survived that arduous journey without a scratch. I threw my arms around her and hugged her. "I love you, Lillian. And I love Hazel Marie and Little Lloyd and Coleman and Mr. Pickens and Sam. But you, most of all." I gave her another squeeze. "Now help me out of these tacky things."

Chapter 36

It made a world of difference to be back in a button-down-the-front dress and cardigan, as well as to replace Hazel Marie's droopy tights with a pair of hose. After a good bit of work with what Norma had called helmet hair, I was as close to my normal self as I could get with what I had to work with in Red's ladies' room.

Just as Lillian and I went back out to the main room of the restaurant, Sam, Hazel Marie, and Little Lloyd came in the front door. We hurried over to them, past groups of bikers and others who'd come to see the end of the Poker Run. A jukebox was playing and, off in a side room, there was the click of pool balls, and never-ending calls to the bartenders. I ignored it all, edging my way toward the door amid more congratulations as I passed.

When I finally got to the ones I most wanted to see, I called out over the uproar, "Thank goodness you're all back safe and sound."

"And you, too," Sam said, giving me a big smile and rubbing his hand along my arm. "We've already heard how Pickens got you here with only a minute or two to spare. Congratulations, Julia, you did it."

"Oh, Miss Julia," Hazel Marie cried, throwing her arms around me. She still had on my dress with her biker boots and her leather jacket, making an unlikely combination. "You don't know how worried we were. There we were, stuck out there with Sam's broken Harley, not knowing where you were or whether you got here on time or what. Oh," she went on, "here's your pocketbook. I haven't let it out of my sight."

"Thank you, Hazel Marie," I said. "I feel lost without it. Lillian has a change of clothes for you in the ladies' room, which I expect you'll be glad to get into."

"What happened, Miss Julia?" Little Lloyd asked, pulling at my sleeve. "Was it fun? Did you like riding with J. D.?"

The answer to his last question was *Not especially,* but I said, "Let's just say I'm glad I did it, but you won't catch me doing it again. As for riding with Mr. Pickens, he got us here on time and in one piece, so I am thankful to him."

I believed in giving credit where credit is due, and Mr. Pickens deserved to be commended for his efforts on my behalf, as well as for not smearing us all over the highway. Coleman deserved praise, as well, and Little Lloyd's eyes got even bigger when he heard about our escort.

Mr. Pickens pushed his way through the crowd and pulled Hazel Marie close. "Hey, honey. Glad you're back." He ruffled Little Lloyd's hair, then said, "Anybody hungry? That barbeque's waiting for us."

"Let's go eat," Sam said. "They've got it set up under a tent outside. Come on, Julia, you need feeding."

"You run on, Sam," I said, looking around for Mary Alice. I caught sight of her waving over the crowd. "I'll join you in a few minutes, but right now I have to help Mary Alice go over the figures."

Pushing and sidling through the crowd, I made my way to

Mary Alice, who was waiting for me next to the bar, the busiest and most raucous area in the place.

"Back here, Miss Julia," Mary Alice said. "Red's letting us use his office. I've got everything ready to tally up."

We walked through a narrow hall, past the men's and ladies' rooms, meeting one bleary-eyed biker coming out of the former. When Mary Alice closed the door of the office behind us, there was a considerable lessening of noise, I'm happy to say. Counting money is a serious business, and we needed no distractions. The tiny space held a desk, stacked with invoices, order sheets, and a hubcap filled with stale cigarette stubs. A large executive chair loomed behind the desk, looking as old as the hills, and boxes of who-knew-what were stacked around the room. Posters, calendars, and notices covered the walls, and I'm not even going to mention the scantily clad models shown on most of them. Some of their poses were absolutely scandalous, and I was surprised they could get away with putting something like that on public view.

"Where are we, Mary Alice?" I asked, as she sat behind the desk and I drew one of the straight chairs closer to her.

She opened the ledger and the folder that she'd brought with her. Then she set a small calculator next to the ledger. "Let's see, now," she began. "Red had all the registration money counted by the time I got back. It's here in this sack." She pulled out a bank bag from her tote bag, and held it up. "We had sixty-five riders, paying twenty-five dollars each. So that makes sixteen-hundred and twenty-five dollars."

She entered that into the ledger, as my shoulders slumped. That amount wasn't going to get us far.

"Okay," she went on. "Let's start at the top. We have that first fifty thousand from Mr. Jones."

"Yes, and here's the second check," I said, handing her the one I'd nearly broken my neck to get. "That makes one hundred thousand."

She put the check in the bank bag and added the amount to her ledger. "I've already deposited, let me see, sixty thousand that Mr. Sam collected from various people around town—businessmen and the like."

"One hundred and sixty thousand," I said, trying to keep a running account in my head. "Plus the registration money. That's, um, one hundred sixty-one thousand and what?"

"Six hundred twenty-five," she said, even before the calculator confirmed it. "Now, let's count up the sponsorships for the lady riders, at a thousand dollars a pop." She giggled at the thought. "Mrs. Ledbetter has eleven thousand, if you can believe. A lot of people wanted to see her ride. Mrs. Conover has three thousand, and Mrs. Stroud pulled in three. The garden club went all out for her. Norma Cantrell has two thousand, and you brought in six, not counting Mr. Jones's big checks, of course. Hazel Marie has four thousand, and I brought in three." She giggled again. "My boyfriend donated most of that. He's so sweet. Then, a Mrs. Hoffman—I don't know her—brought in two thousand, which I heard her husband paid after daring her to ride. Then three others from the church got a thousand apiece, making three thousand. Look at this, Miss Julia," she said, turning the ledger for me to see. "The Harleys for Heaven brought in a cool six thousand. Those Baptists really support what they believe in." She pushed the hair out of her eyes, and banged away at the calculator. I'd given up trying to keep count in my head by this time.

"The Young People's group at church donated fifty-five dollars from their car wash and leaf raking," she went on. "Then various others gave a total of twenty-four hundred and eighty dollars, and the folks who live on Willow Lane and Reverend Abernathy's church came up with eleven hundred and thirty-five dollars. And that's it." She raised her head and looked at me. "Now, for the grand total." Clearing her calculator and putting it to work again, she started adding up the sums. Then she sat back and blew out her breath. "Well, I get a grand total of two hundred eight thousand, two hundred ninety-five dollars in all. Wow, this is wonderful. We only have forty-one thousand, seven hundred and five dollars to go. But the home tour is still to come, so maybe we can make it."

"I doubt the home tour will bring in more than a couple of thousand," I said, thinking that even if it proved more lucrative than that, I didn't have the time to wait for it. My house was on the line. "Add another forty thousand to the grand total."

Mary Alice frowned. "Where does that come from?"

"I am swearing you to secrecy, Mary Alice," I said. "Thurlow Jones promised an additional ten thousand dollars for every woman over fifty who'd participate in the Poker Run. None of them know about that stipulation, and I wouldn't announce their names for anything in the world. I'm not even going to tell you who they are, but I figure there're at least four who qualify, with a few years to spare, and I intend to get another check from Thurlow tonight."

Mary Alice started laughing so hard she could hardly do her sums. "I bet I could guess who they are," she said. Then, seeing my face, she added, "But I won't."

When she got back to business and added everything up, she said, "Okay, the final tally is two hundred forty-eight thousand, two hundred and ninety-five. Surely the home tour will bring in the last seventeen hundred and five dollars."

"I can't wait for that," I said, pulling out my checkbook

and writing a check for the last amount. "Count it up again, Mary Alice, and let's be sure."

She did, then said, "Okay, we've got it, all except that forty thousand you said Mr. Jones would give."

"I'll go get it right now," I said, standing and preparing myself to approach Thurlow again. "Now, Mary Alice, you guard that money with your life over the weekend. Then get it in the bank the minute it opens Monday morning." I turned to leave, then thought of something else. "Oh, one more thing. Why don't you find the Reverend Abernathy and ask him to announce the final tally tonight? A good many Willow Lane folks're here, so there's no reason to keep them in the dark any longer."

She agreed, and I left, intent on tracking down Thurlow and getting the whole money-raising campaign wrapped up. Walking out into the restaurant, I found a number of men and women still at the bar, and all the tables filled with people eating barbeque. Not seeing anybody I knew, I walked out into the parking lot and was drawn, shivering in the damp night air, to the large open space on the side by the sound of a live band. There was a misty fog in the air that formed haloes around the pole lights. Long tables had been set up, and lines of people were going down each side, filling plates. I saw Little Lloyd and Sam in one line, and I started toward them.

Before I'd made more than a few steps, Thurlow Jones stepped out from a row of parked motorcycles. I couldn't help but jump back a little, not wanting to be too close in case he had a sudden relapse.

"Well, Mrs. Julia Springer," he said. "Off that motorcycle and not a bit worse for it."

"You're just the man I'm looking for, Thurlow."

Even though we stood half in the shadows, I saw him

throw back his shoulders and preen a little. "I figured you'd come around," he said. "Most women do."

"I'm not most women, as you ought to know by now," I told him. "And I've come around to get another check from you."

"Good Lord, woman! Haven't you gotten enough from me? I'm about bled dry, to say nothing of being weak as water from drinking outta that spring. I tell you, I never had such a run of bad luck as I got from that stuff." He cackled at the remembrance of his heretofore unknown condition of unparalleled growth, then he went on. " 'Course, I thought I'd hit the jackpot at first, but it turned sour on me. Now, if I could just figure out the right dosage, it'd be a boon to mankind."

I had no desire whatsoever to listen to the intimate details of his mysterious malady, and was mortally offended that he wanted to share them with me.

"I heard about your indisposition," I said, trying to sound sympathetic while moving away from the specific subject. "But that should teach you not to go putting everything you see in your mouth. You ought to see what it did to Lillian's snowball bush. Still, you've done us all a good turn. Clarence Gibbs was intending to fob that water off on an unsuspecting public, and what happened to you—I don't need any details—has to give him pause. Even if the correct dosage could be figured out, there wouldn't be many men who'd want to serve as guinea pigs. Who knows? The wrong dose could spur the opposite reaction and put them out of commission on a permanent basis."

"Hush your mouth, woman!" Thurlow reared back. "Don't even think such a thing. Because I'm tellin' you right now that I am one hundred percent back to normal. 'Course, I was always better'n normal to begin with."

"I am not interested in whether you're normal or abnormal. And you have a nerve speaking of such things to me, even though I don't know what you're talking about. Now, Thurlow, the way I see it, you owe us another forty thousand dollars."

"What? How you figure?"

"You remember," I reminded him, "and don't tell me you don't because you thought it up, yourself. You said you'd donate ten thousand dollars for each quality woman over the age of fifty who'd ride in the Poker Run. You saw them— Mrs. Ledbetter, Mrs. Conover, Mrs. Stroud, and Norma Cantrell. Count them, that's four, and I'm letting you off easy—there're a few others who're right on the verge, and may even be over it."

"How do I know they're all over fifty?" He leaned over and leered at me. "You, Julia, look about twenty-five to me."

"Quit acting the fool, Thurlow," I snapped. "I don't have time to put up with your carrying on. You made this deal, so live up to it. Write the check."

He grinned. "You've made me a poor man this night."

"Uh-huh, I believe that."

He wrote out the check and I turned it toward the light to be sure he hadn't shorted us. "Thank you, Thurlow. You have a big heart, and nobody's going to forget what you've done. Now," I went on, "I'm going to suggest that you take some of that money you have squirreled away and fix up that house of yours. Get the yard cleaned up and reattach the shutters. It's an eyesore to the whole community."

I happened to glance over his shoulder and saw something that drew my attention fast. Two hulking figures were tinkering with a motorcycle parked further down the row. One was sitting in the driver's seat, while the other was checking a tire. Even in the shadowy light, there was no mistaking the two fat boys who'd almost run us off the road.

"You'll have to excuse me, Thurlow," I said. "I have a little more business to take care of."

I marched myself over to the men and stood next to the motorcycle, my hands on my hips. "Far be it from me," I said, "to accuse anyone who just might be innocent, but I want to know if you two gentlemen had anything to do with putting a certain Harley machine out of commission at a certain convenience store a few miles from here."

The two huge individuals looked at each other, and I took a good look at them. Lord, they were big, sloppy even, with large necks and huge chests. And hairy! They must've never come close to a razor or a pair of scissors. I'd've never had the nerve to accost them if a couple of hundred other people hadn't been within a call or two. Still, I didn't think they ought to get away with what they'd done to Sam's motorcycle.

"Well, ma'am," the hairiest one said in the softest, squeakiest voice I'd ever heard. It has always amazed me that the bigger the man, the higher his voice. Something to do with hormones, I expect. "We sure do hate to hear that a fine Harley get messed up, but when money gets tight, well, some people might be in a bind. You know how it is."

Indeed, I did. Just look at what I'd done to raise some. But a line had to be drawn somewhere.

"That's a poor excuse, if you ask me," I said. "I ought to turn you in to the sheriff who, I have no doubt, would put you both under the jail. Why, besides vehicular vandalism, you tried to run us off the road. I almost had a heart attack, and you ought to be ashamed of yourselves."

"Well," one of them said, as they both hung their heads at being caught out. I declare, it just went to show how bullies will back down if you stand up to them.

"Tell you what, ma'am," the other one said. "We just was talkin' about it, and we feel real bad about fiddlin' with that

Road King. An' we was just cuttin' up on the road. We wouldn't of hurt you none. Say, why don't we come over and fix your bike? We're good mechanics, and we'll make it up to you."

"Well, that is certainly nice of you, but it's not my machine," I said, taken aback by how agreeable they were, as well as by their assumption that I would own such a vehicle. "I'll pass the word along to the owner. Now, I have no intention of carrying this any further, since crippling that motorcycle didn't affect the outcome. But I want to know who thought up that stunt."

They stood there, shifting from one foot to the other, looking like boys who'd been caught doing what they shouldn't have been doing. Which, indeed, they had been.

"I don't know as we oughtta . . ." one started to say.

"It don't matter," the other one said, shrugging. "It's no skin off our backs to tell her, 'specially since he shorted us on the payment. Ma'am, he didn't give his name, just offered a coupla hundred to anybody who'd take that Harley outta the race, which I ain't sayin' we did or we didn't. He was real stoop-shouldered, though."

I knew it. I just knew it. I gritted my teeth at the thought of Clarence Gibbs and his unfair business practices. "Gentlemen," I said, "I appreciate your forthrightness, and I hope this will teach you not to engage in any more vandalism on this or any other Poker Run. You won't get off so easy the next time, not if I have anything to say about it."

The vengeful feelings I'd had toward them began to shift over to the real culprit, so I left them in peace. After all, they'd been as nice as they could be, just misguided.

As I looked for Sam and Little Lloyd in the rib-eating crowd, the band suddenly went silent. The revelers all turned toward the bandstand where a man I assumed to be Red, himself, whistled into the microphone and told everybody to quiet down.

"Listen up, folks," he said. "The first order of business is to announce the winner of the Poker Run. We had a lot of good hands, but a royal spade flush takes the pot. And the winner is . . ." He raised his hand, as the drummer beat the fire out of his drum. "Mrs. Emma Sue Ledbetter! Come on up here, Emma Sue, you pretty little thing, you!"

Even from where we were standing, I could see how red her face turned when her name was called out. But she quickly recovered and seemed thrilled to death at her good fortune. She ran up onto the bandstand as the crowd clapped and yelled. I thought to myself that it might be the first time in her life that Emma Sue had received so much attention, and it pleased me to see it. After a great deal of carrying on, which Emma Sue seemed to enjoy, Red presented her with the prize. It was a white T-shirt, plain enough from the back, but downright garish with the Harley eagle across the front.

"Lord, Sam," I whispered to him. "What have we done? She may see this as some sort of sign and take up gambling from now on."

Sam laughed. "Larry Ledbetter's going to have a fit, but he may have to buy her a Harley to go with it."

Red took our attention again, as he quieted the crowd for the next item on the agenda. "Hold on, folks, the highlight of the Poker Run is comin' up. I want to introduce the Reverend Morris Abernathy. He has an announcement to make, so let's give him a good ole bikers' welcome." As the slightly inebriated crowd stomped and yelled, he stepped aside and motioned to the slight figure who stood behind him. "It's all yours, Rev."

I stood between Sam and Little Lloyd, crossing my fingers

that the Reverend wouldn't be intimidated by that sea of strange, hairy, and mostly white faces turned up to him. But a preacher is accustomed to addressing all kinds, and he stepped up to that microphone like he was born to it. I'm not going to repeat the message of gratitude and thanksgiving he gave, but he was interrupted several times with applause, whistles, yells, and shouts. When he began to thank the Lord for all of us who'd worked so hard, I thought my heart would swell up and explode. I saw Lillian and her friend Mrs. Causey, lean against each other, crying and laughing together.

Little Lloyd jumped up and down, yelling and clapping with the best of them. "We did it! We did it! Miss Lillian's going to get her house back."

"Cross your fingers, Little Lloyd," I said. "We still have to make it official with Mr. Gibbs."

Sam put his arm around my shoulders and said, "Aren't you glad now that you rode with me?"

"Now that it's over, yes, I am. But, Sam, I'd be in ever so much better shape if I'd ridden the whole way with you. Mr. Pickens took years off my life."

His arm tightened around me. "You can go the rest of the way with me, Julia. They say that happy people live longer, so we might even pick up a few years along the way."

I nodded, not knowing what to say to him, especially since I wasn't exactly sure what he was saying to me.

~ Chapter 37

Well, there's not much more to tell, which is just as well as it's never pleasant or edifying to have your ill-advised choices opened up for public viewing. Still, everything I did was for the good of others, and it all worked out in the long run. Even though I did have to endure a prolonged state of apprehension for dealing with the likes of Clarence Gibbs, who everybody knew looked after number one, first and foremost. Getting in bed with him, as we businesspeople are wont to say, was an unwise choice, to say the least.

Another dicey decision I'd made was agreeing to get as many "quality ladies," as Thurlow called us, as I could to participate in the Poker Run. If my friends had known they were asked mainly because they met the age requirement, my name would've been stricken from any number of invitation lists.

Still, it worked out, in spite of Thurlow's having the nerve to ask Emma Sue, Helen, and LuAnne right to their faces if they were over fifty; I almost had to shake them to get them to admit to it. Not a one of them would ever see sixty again. Well, maybe fifty-eight.

And agreeing to make that run on a motorcycle? Have you

ever heard of anything so untypical of a mature and cautious woman? Even though I came through unmarked and un-scathed, my reputation as commentator on all things correct and proper suffered damage from which it still hasn't recovered. Take the Sunday morning after the Poker Run, while I was still reveling in my triumph, when LuAnne showed up for services in a pair of trousers. When I indicated to her that they were hardly appropriate for formal church services, she'd just gaped at me. Then she said, "You don't have a whole lot of room to talk, Julia, considering what you showed up in at Red's yesterday."

And you wouldn't believe the whispers, rumors, and flat-out gossip that have been bouncing around town about me and Thurlow Jones. Ever since the amount of his checks became common knowledge, people have wondered aloud at what I'd been willing to do to get it. It wasn't enough that I'd risked my neck on two motorcycles, with all the near-misses attendant on each one. Oh, no, there must've been something more going on between us. Why else would he hand over that much money?

I declare, people always have to assign some ulterior motive to every good deed. Believe me, I had not sold Thurlow Jones one thing but, come to think of it, maybe it was a compliment of sorts that people had no trouble believing that my attentions were worth that amount of money.

So, see, it wasn't all fun and games, regardless of how Mr. Pickens viewed it, and, yes, I suffered some repercussions from my decision to help others. And if I benefited from it, as did Lillian and her neighbors, who among you would hold it against me?

After the high point of claiming Thurlow's checks and of getting into my own clothing that Saturday night, I existed in a state of agitated turmoil until Monday morning rolled around, when I could finally conclude my business with Clarence Gibbs. I was at Binkie's office thirty minutes early to make sure that Mary Alice had deposited the funds in the bank. Then I had to suffer an untold amount of anxiety waiting for Binkie to show up. All I could think of was that she might be lying in at the hospital, and wouldn't be able to come to work.

"If that's the case," I told Mary Alice McKinnon, as I paced the floor in Binkie's reception area, "I'll just drag Mr. Gibbs up to the delivery floor, and Binkie can arrange my deliverance from him, as well as her own." I stopped short, coming up against another scary thought. "And where *is* Mr. Gibbs, anyway? What if he doesn't come, Mary Alice? What if neither of them gets here? I declare, I'm so nervous, I'm about to jump out of my skin."

But then Binkie waddled in, looking tired and over-burdened. And who wouldn't in that condition? As far as I was concerned, that baby could make its appearance just as soon as Binkie completed my transaction.

"Binkie, honey," I said, immediately concerned for her well-being. "Get in your office and rest yourself. You don't look well at all, which isn't a nice thing to say, I know. But I'm worried about you."

"Thanks, Miss Julia," she said, taking off her coat and going into her office. Mary Alice bustled around with files and folders, ready to help her get set up for the business at hand. "I'm not feeling so well, either. But I want to get this sale closed for you as soon as we can. Is Clarence here yet?"

And in he walked. Or rather, stormed. Clarence Gibbs

was not in a good mood, and he made no effort to hide his unhappy state.

"You sure that check will clear?" he asked, as he sat hunched over in a client's chair in front of Binkie's desk. The bags under his eyes were darker than usual, indicating to me that I'd not been the only one to have a few restless nights.

"Absolutely sure," I snapped. "You can call the bank if you need peace of mind. But I tell you right now, Mr. Gibbs, I am not in the habit of bouncing checks, and I resent your implication."

"Bid'ness is bid'ness," he said, so mad that he could hardly bring himself to look at me.

"Exactly. And if you can't stand the heat, stay out of the kitchen."

Binkie suppressed a smile as she pushed the forms in front of us for our signatures. He scrawled his name, each time breathing out between his teeth to make sure we knew how much he hated doing it.

Throughout the signing and notarizing and passing of money, he was not in the least gracious about relinquishing any and all claims to my house or about selling me, as the treasurer of the Willow Lane Fund, the Willow Lane property.

But the way I looked at it, he'd gambled on the chance of getting both, and he lost both. That's just the way the cards fell and, if I'd had a mind to question him on the subject of those fat boys, who I was convinced he'd hired, something more than cards might've fallen.

Even though I couldn't prove a thing, he should've counted himself fortunate to walk out unhindered and unharmed, with a check for two hundred and fifty thousand dollars in hand. He had nothing at all to complain about, but of course he didn't see it that way.

When our business reached its conclusion to my satisfaction, if not his, I thought to try to lift his spirits. "Mr. Gibbs," I said, as he prepared to leave. "You should thank your lucky stars that things have worked out this way. What if you'd put an untold amount of money into that water-bottling scheme of yours, and every man in the country came down or blew up or was otherwise incapacitated with the affliction that hit Thurlow Jones? Why, just think of the lawsuits you'd be embroiled in. You should be grateful that we came along and saved you from such a fate."

But he couldn't see it that way, and wouldn't even shake my hand. I decided I'd never do business with him again.

"Miss Julia," Binkie said as soon as Clarence Gibbs took his grudging self off, "would you mind running me over to the hospital? I'm not feeling so good."

"My land, Binkie!" I looked at her, seeing the strain around her eyes and the way she held her hands around herself, bending over every now and then. "Is it time? This is not another false alarm, is it? Oh, my goodness. Mary Alice, call Coleman! Tell him we need another escort."

I was scrambling around to get our coats and help Binkie out of her chair. "And the doctor. Call him, too," I called as Mary Alice, looking as scared as I felt, hurried to the phone. "Oh, Binkie, honey, where're your keys? I walked over here, so I don't have my car. Oh, I hope I can drive your car. Mary Alice, we need some help in here." Binkie couldn't straighten up. I put my arm around her as she shuffled down the hall, all bent over with the pangs of imminent birth.

"Oh, Lord," I moaned, thinking how ill-prepared I was to face the facts of life in such a graphic manner. I'd lived this long without becoming intimately acquainted with the details of giving birth, and I didn't want my ignorance rectified in an attorney's reception area. "Hold on, Binkie. We'll get there. Just whatever you do, please, please, don't have this baby on me."

⌐

She didn't. Her little girl was born some eight hours after we got to the hospital. Typical first baby, which of course I'd known all along. I'd made myself comfortable in the waiting room, but Coleman saw his baby daughter come into the world. They were gracious enough to invite me in to view the proceedings, but I declined. Better that they have the moment to themselves, don't you know.

It's been some days now since the birth, and they still haven't agreed on a name for that child. Well, Coleman would agree to anything Binkie wanted—that's the kind of man he is—but it's Binkie who can't make up her mind. She had even considered Colleen or Colleena, after Coleman you see, but Hazel Marie said those names reminded her of a country-western song, and I reminded Binkie that a child had to live with its mother's choice all its life.

Binkie swore up and down that if it'd been a boy she would've named it Harley, in honor of the Poker Run. I didn't believe her for a minute, but you never know with her.

Little Lloyd was deeply disappointed at first that it wasn't a boy. For some reason, he'd gotten into his head that they would've named a boy after him. They didn't disabuse him of the notion, for which I was grateful. But to tell the truth, there were a gracious plenty Wesley Lloyds already around. One dead and buried, of course, and the other, my heart's delight. I didn't need any more of them.

Little Lloyd was still thrilled over my exploits on those

motorcycles, especially on Mr. Pickens's, and he couldn't stop talking about it. The idea of our riding through the darkening day, racing against time and being escorted by Abbotsville's finest to turn up just in time to claim the prize and save Willow Lane became the stuff of song for him. He wandered around the house for days reciting "The Midnight Ride of Paul Revere," except he kept changing it to "The Twilight Ride of Miss Julia," which, to my ear, lost something in the translation. But then, I'd been putting up with Sam's painful attempts at poetic utterances, so maybe I was tone deaf by that time.

❧

While a group of volunteers made plans to refurbish many of the houses on Willow Lane, Lillian and I entertained ourselves by discussing the remodeling of her house, drawing and redrawing floor plans. But it took me forever to get her to that point. At first she wouldn't have anything to do with it, saying she couldn't afford to remodel anything. I had to sit her down and explain in no uncertain terms that I had purchased her house from the Willow Lane Fund, and I could do anything I wanted with it. And since she was too proud and high-minded to accept a gift, my plan was to rent it to her at the same rate she'd been paying Clarence Gibbs.

"But Lillian," I went on, being as reasonable and businesslike as I knew how, "the thing is, I want to fix it to your specifications. I've never lived in a rental house, so I don't know what needs to go in one. One of these days you may decide to move, and I'll have to lease it to somebody else. I have to make it rentable, don't you see?"

"Yessum, I see what you sayin'. An' one of these days, I might pass over, an' that house be for rent again without me movin'."

"Exactly. Now, tell me what ought to go in the kitchen."

In that way, I was able to find out what she wanted in a place to live. Then I added a few conveniences on my own. I didn't tell her about those, nor did I tell her that the house would be hers free and clear on the day that I do my own passing over. I just regret that I won't be around to see how surprised she'll be.

⤙

Well, Hazel Marie and Mr. Pickens—I just don't know what I'm going to do with those two. Hazel Marie is more and more like a daughter to me but, even so, I am well aware of my limitations as far as expressing opinions or offering advice are concerned. So far, she and Little Lloyd remain with me in my house, although Mr. Pickens is a frequent and well-received visitor. I enjoy him, myself, if only he'd curb that tendency to tease people beyond endurance.

It was only a day or so ago that he'd sidled up to me and whispered, "Miss Julia, I want to thank you from the bottom of my heart."

"Why, whatever for, Mr. Pickens?"

"For getting Tammi off my back for good. She's dropped me like a hot potato and, as I guess you've noticed, Hazel Marie is a happier woman for it."

"Yes," I said. "I have noticed that you two seem to be on much better terms here lately. I'm glad to see it, and I hope that you'll not jeopardize anything again." I frowned then, wondering what he was getting at, since I could never tell what was on his mind. "But you can thank Hazel Marie's sweet nature for overlooking the machinations of such a determined former wife. I had nothing to do with it."

"Yeah, you did." He grinned that devilish grin and put his arm around my shoulders. He leaned in close and said,

"When you lifted your visor down at Harold's Esso, and Tammi saw the kind of woman I was consorting with, she knew in a minute that she was outclassed. I think she's gone into hiding."

"Oh, Mr. Pickens, you are so bad about teasing people."

"Just you, Miss Julia," he said, laughing so that his black eyes sparkled, "just you."

➤

There's no telling what will happen between him and Hazel Marie. She says she's not anxious to move back in with him, although he wants her to and tells her so every chance he gets. But she tells him that she's waiting to see if any more discarded wives show up on the horizon. It gets away with him something awful, but I'm glad to see that she can hold her own with him. Lord knows, that's what he needs.

ᴄ*Chapter 38*

And the man in the Burberry raincoat? I declare, I'd been so leery of him, avoiding him and refusing to speak to him and doing everything I could to keep my distance. I'd thought, well, there's no telling *what* I thought, but I'd wanted nothing to do with him, fearing an additional pile of problems. As it turned out, all he was doing was waiting to see who would end up with the Willow Lane property.

I'd come home from the hospital that Monday, absolutely spent with exhaustion after waiting for Binkie's baby to arrive, and there he was, sitting in my living room.

He stood as I walked in, offered his hand, and said, "Mrs. Springer, Jack Nolan's the name. I hope you don't mind that your housekeeper let me wait for you here. I told her it was important, even urgent, that I speak with you."

Well, I did mind, and I was surprised that Lillian hadn't sent him packing. Still, he was well-mannered enough, and I had to admit by this time my curiosity had gotten the best of me so I was anxious to hear him out.

"Have a seat, Mr. Nolan," I said, right sharply. "And explain what it is that you want from me. But before you go any further, you should know that I have personal friends in the Abbot County Sheriff's Department, and they won't take kindly to anyone who gives me any aggravation."

He sat somewhat near the edge of my Duncan Phyfe sofa and smiled. Then he handed me a business card. "I represent the Tarheel Fertilizer Company, and our research department is interested in that spring on the Willow Lake property. I take it that you're the owner of record now?"

"Why, no, I'm not the owner of record. I am on the Committee to Save Willow Lane, and the treasurer of the fund. As such, I have no authority to discuss that property with you. And even if I were, it's not for sale."

It just flew all over me that everybody and his brother, it seemed like, were all of a sudden wanting that property. It had set there going to wrack and ruin all these years, and nobody cared. And now, just look.

"Hear me out, Mrs. Springer," Mr. Nolan said, looking ever so earnest. "We're not interested in the property itself, just the water from the spring."

"Why in the world would you want that, Mr. Nolan? You may not be aware of its pernicious qualities."

He hunched forward on the sofa and began to tell me more than I ever wanted to know about fertilizer. "It's like this, Mrs. Springer: we've been experimenting to improve our root-growth products. We already have a dandy fertilizer on the market. Well, that's what it's called, Dandy-Gro, and when we heard about that spring, well, I must say it was cause for rejoicing at Tarheel headquarters."

"Just how did you hear about it? The first victim has barely gotten out of the hospital."

"I stay in touch with a lot of local growers and farm supply stores, so I've been hearing rumors about that spring for a long time. To tell you the truth, I didn't give them much credit, but after what happened to Mr. Jones, well, let's say it's got our attention now."

I certainly didn't intend to discuss Thurlow Jones's mishap with a perfect stranger, or with anybody else for that matter. But after witnessing the unseasonable spurt of growth in Lillian's snowball bush, I thought to myself that the water could be of benefit to the farming community.

"You realize, don't you," I began, "that the water has to be handled carefully. Why, Mr. Nolan, if you overused it, you might have corn and, well, snowball bushes growing like kudzu, just taking over the cities. You couldn't make it available over the counter, so to speak."

"No intention of doing that. Our research department would figure out the right proportions and mix it with our Dandy-Gro Root Enhancement. It could change the way we farm."

"I don't doubt that for a minute," I said, a number of startling visions springing to mind.

"So, Mrs. Springer," he went on, "all we want to do is hook up a pipe, run it through the woods back there, and locate a holding tank where it'd be out of sight. Our trucks would draw it off as we need it, and we'd pay the owners by the gallon."

I looked up at the ceiling, considering. "How much?"

"That, I don't know. Your people would have to talk with my people but, believe me, Mrs. Springer, if that water'll do what we think it will, you've got a gold mine back there."

"All the water would be in a closed system?"

"Yes, that's what we'd want. But of course, if you wanted a trickle left for local use, we'd work with you on that."

"Oh, no, Mr. Nolan. After what I've seen and heard about that water, I wouldn't want a drop of it for local use. Why, there's likely be a stampede for it as it is now, and our hospital's not equipped to handle medical emergencies on such a scale.

"With that understood," I said, standing to indicate that the interview was over, "I'll talk to the Willow Lane Committee right away, and let you know something as soon as we decide."

Mr. Nolan stood and shook my hand. "I think you'll find us a good company to do business with."

"One other thing, Mr. Nolan," I said as we walked toward the door. "Did Clarence Gibbs know about your interest?"

"Oh, yes. Since he was the owner, I began to feel him out as soon as I got to town. We were willing to buy the whole parcel just to get the water, but he kept putting me off. It was only later that I learned he'd tied everything up, hoping to get your house, too. I had to wait, just like he did, to see if you came up with the purchase price in time."

He gave me a knowing look, seeming to appreciate how I'd managed that. Then he shook his head. "I don't think he could decide between selling to us or sinking a lot of money into a bottling plant. But if he'd put that water on the market, even diluted, well, it's a good thing you saved him from the consequences."

I held the door for him and said, "Clarence Gibbs would be a better man if a few consequences came his way. But don't get me started on that. I'll be in touch, Mr. Nolan; don't leave town until you hear from us."

~

Sam came over last night and had dinner with Little Lloyd and me. Hazel Marie and Mr. Pickens were out somewhere, no telling where. I didn't know and I didn't ask.

After we'd eaten, Lillian and Little Lloyd went upstairs to

watch television, while Sam and I sat in the living room, watching the fire in the fireplace. I was feeling very warm and satisfied with the way things had turned out at the meeting of the Committee to Save Willow Lane. What it came down to was that we were going to have our cake and eat it, too—the Willow Lane residents would reoccupy the houses again, while enjoying the benefits of selling water to the Tarheel Fertilizer Company. And maybe we all would benefit from a new and improved root enhancer when it hit the market, although I would be unlikely to use it. Oh, and we decided to protect the cemetery with a wrought-iron fence, creating a small parklike setting with a historic marker to honor the dead.

But to my dismay, the Tarheel folks, in an environmental-protection frenzy, went ahead and left a trickle in the spring, saying it would serve as a natural water feature for the area. Thurlow Jones, however, insisted on the erection of a warning sign that he, himself, worded:

!DANGER!
DIRE CONSEQUENCES RESULT
FROM INGESTING THIS WATER!

I had given him credit for being concerned about his fellow men until I heard him say that the sign was to remind himself not to tamper with the water again. He said that every now and then he was tempted to try small doses to see what it would take to get the ideal response.

And I was sorely tempted to call him over to the house later that week so he could see the consequences of fooling with that water. I'd just finished my toilette when Lillian banged into the kitchen, shrieking her head off.

"*Miss Julia! Miss Julia!*" she screamed. "You got to see it. Come quick!"

All of us, Hazel Marie and Little Lloyd included, dropped what we were doing and flew down the stairs.

"What is it?" I called, fearing the worst.

As Lillian led us outside and around to the back of the garage, Hazel Marie gasped, "Don't tell us it's still growing!"

"It'll be a jungle!" Little Lloyd yelled.

Well, not quite. The once-exuberant snowball bush had used up all its strength. There it lay, dried up and yellowed, in tendrils on the ground, not even a shadow of its former self.

"It done withered on the vine," Lillian said.

"Oh, the poor thing," Hazel Marie said.

"The poor thing, nothing," I said. "Poor Thurlow, if he gets a rebound like this."

We looked at each other and started laughing, while I hoped that Little Lloyd wouldn't know what tickled us so.

"Well," I was finally able to say, "I guess the honorable thing would be to tell the fertilizer company about this."

"I wouldn't, Miss Julia," Hazel Marie said. "They're going to do their own research, so they'll find out soon enough. Besides, for all we know, Thurlow may not've had the same reaction. I don't guess you'd want to ask him, would you?"

She guessed right, so I threw up my hands and said, "We'll let the buyer beware, then."

After all that excitement, I began to feel complacent about the upcoming home tour and flower show. It had lost some of its steam for me, since we no longer needed the revenue from it. Income, however, is always welcome. It was all I could do, though, to put up with LuAnne's new enthusiasm for fund-raising. She announced to me that she had found her calling, even though she had not given one thought to what she'd be raising money for, much less to the toll it takes on the ones doing the raising. Her latest idea was to have another Poker Run and flower show in the spring, of all things. I was quick to inform her that I didn't know of a cause in the world that would induce me to get on a motorcycle again.

"But, see, Julia," she'd said, her hands fluttering around. "You wouldn't have to ride, although I don't know why you wouldn't want to. You could enter the flower show, though, because I'm thinking we could have categories like Burnout Pit and use smoke tree branches, or Motorcycle Mania and use helmets or biker boots or oil cans for containers. Or—I know—maybe have one called H.O.G. Heaven and use Birds of Paradise in the arrangements. That would really be something, wouldn't it?"

"Really something," I agreed, but refrained from saying what that something would be. "And who or what would you be raising money for? I'll tell you this, LuAnne, I expect there's not a soul in Abbotsville who'd be willing to shell out another cent. We've asked about all we can ask of them."

"You really know how to put a damper on somebody else's ideas, Julia," she said. "I just know that a combination Poker Run and Flower Show would be a big draw, and those bikers would have an opportunity to put a little refinement in their lives. Big Bill Beasley, for one, would love it."

I couldn't believe it. "LuAnne, the last thing in this world that Big Bill Beasley or any other of those bikers would love is a display of flower arrangements. That's the most unlikely thing I've ever heard of."

She got mad at me then, and went home, but not before telling me that I wasn't the only one who could do whatever she pleased. "Emma Sue and I are thinking of going into business," she said, lifting her head in pride. "If not fund-raising, then maybe bridal-consulting or catering or some thing. Pastor Ledbetter said she couldn't do it, but she's going to, anyway. And I want you to know that we were going to ask you to come in with us as a silent partner. But, since you couldn't stay silent if your life depended on it, we'll just get our financial backing somewhere else."

I let her have the last word, since that proved I could hold my tongue when I wanted to. Then I went into the kitchen and had a cup of coffee with Lillian, the one person I could count on not to aggravate me beyond endurance.

❧

In spite of the fact that things had worked out to my satisfaction, there was still a nagging concern on my conscience. Sitting there on the sofa with Sam, I decided that this quiet evening was a good time to free myself of it.

"Sam," I said, after a few deep breaths to get my nerve up, "I hope you won't hold it against me, but I have a confession to make."

Although we'd started out with a decorous distance between us on the sofa, somehow we'd both edged toward the middle. So I felt him stiffen when I announced my intention to admit a wrongdoing.

"Is it about Thurlow?" he asked.

"Thurlow!" I did some stiffening of my own. "Why would I have anything to confess about him?"

"I don't know, Julia. He just seems mighty taken with you."

"Well, I am certainly not taken with him. The idea! Why, Sam, that old man's crazy! He hardly comes to my shoulder, and he's careless with money." I stopped, wondering if that last charge should be counted against him. Thurlow had put the Willow Lane Fund over the top, for which he deserved proper appreciation. But that didn't mean I had to admire his profligacy. "Besides, he's not clean."

"Well, preserve us from uncleanliness," Sam said, laughing. "So if it's not Thurlow, what could you have to confess?"

I turned my head as a wave of shame swept over me. I couldn't bring myself to admit that I'd doubted his sanity, that I'd feared he'd been on a downhill slide into a mental fog, and that I'd watched him like a hawk for any sign of the senility that I'd convinced myself he was suffering from.

"On second thought," I said, thinking that I shouldn't disturb the serenity of the evening. "Maybe another time would be better."

Sam slipped his arm around my shoulders, letting it lay along the back of the sofa. "This is as good a time as any, Julia, because I have a confession to make to you. I confess that I've been remiss in not making my intentions clear. So I'm going to remedy that right now. Julia Springer, I confess that I think you are the bravest and most loyal woman I know. Even though you're prone to go off half-cocked on occasion, you absolutely delight me. What it comes down to, Julia, is this: I want you to stay away from Thurlow Jones and stick close to me. My heart can't take any more distress than you've already put it through."

My own heart about stopped at that moment, as I mentally thanked Thurlow for being good for something more than doling out money. Then I took Sam's hand and leaned my head against his chest, unable to stop the smile that spread across my face. If I had ever had one doubt about the state of his mental health, it had just been put to rest.

"Now," he said, squeezing my hand. "I'm ready to hear your confession."

"Well," I said, deciding that some confessions are better

left unmade. What Sam didn't know wouldn't hurt him. "I don't want to hurt your feelings, Sam, but that poetry you've been sending me is just, well . . ."

"Beautiful?"

"Yes," I said, looking up at him. The old saying that beauty lies in the eye of the beholder came to mind and, as no other eye would ever see his poetic efforts, I spoke the unvarnished truth. "Yes, it's beautiful to me."

➤

Viking is proud to bring readers
another Miss Julia adventure,

Miss Julia
Meets Her Match

coming in April 2004

The following is from the latest
rollicking installment that answers
the most burning question of all:
Will the feisty Miss Julia meet
her own match in love?

{ Chapter 1 }

"Where y'all gonna live?" Lillian asked, as she beat three eggs, one after the other, into a bowl of cake batter. "If you thinkin' 'bout tyin' the knot, somebody gonna be movin'."

"I'm not studying a move." I was at the kitchen table, folding towels taken from the dryer. The window rattled from a gust of late April wind, and I glanced outside to see more rain clouds moving across the sky.

"Huh. You better be studyin' on it, Miss Julia. 'Cause either Mr. Sam be movin' in here or you be movin' in there."

"That's too far down the road to worry about," I said, not wanting to worry about it either down the road or at the moment. "And, see, Lillian, that's part of the problem. Tying the knot. I don't know that I want to be tied to anybody, even Sam, who's as fine a man as I've ever known. But that's what happens when you marry. I've had a taste of doing things my way, you know, since Mr. Springer passed." I smoothed out a hand towel, smelling the packaged fresh air aroma rising from it. "Even if that freedom came too late in life to be of much use. Lillian, do you realize that I was married for almost forty-five years, and never had a moment's peace? Always fearful of what would set him off, what would displease him, what I was

I

doing wrong, and on and on. Now, I don't have to answer to anybody, and I'm not at all sure I want to give that up."

"Mr. Sam, he seem like he pretty easy to get along with," Lillian commented as she greased three cake pans, then sprinkled flour in them. "I doubt he pull on that knot too much. 'Sides, he tied up, too. Least, the man s'posed to be."

"Yes, and isn't that the trouble?" I pushed aside the hand towels, folded, stacked, and ready for the linen closet. "Everybody expects a wife to toe the line, but a husband? I tell you, Lillian, the only change marriage makes in a man's life is he gets his food cooked and his laundry done."

"I don't know as I'd go that far," she said, as she poured the batter into the cake pans, then shook each pan so the layers would bake evenly. "'Course, I jus' look at other folkses' marriage, not mine. 'Cause you hit the nail on the head when it come to mine."

"Oh, Lillian," I said, just done in by all the decisions that were piling up, waiting for me to get to them. Well, actually only one decision, but from that all the others would flow. "I don't know that I want to marry anyone again, much less have to decide where to live when, *if*, I do." I rested my head on my hand. "It's more than I want to deal with."

I lifted my head then, as more thoughts on the subject jumped up in my mind. "You know, it used to be that where a couple lived was never a question. The man decided, and that was it. The woman was expected to pull up stakes, leave her family and friends and everything else and go wherever he said. And be happy about it, too." I bit my lip, remembering my own wretched experience. "I don't think it was ever even discussed when Wesley Lloyd proposed to me and, Lord knows, it didn't occur to me to question whatever he said. I took it for granted that I'd leave my home and move into his. Not that I wanted to stay home, but still."

"I think that what the Bible tell a woman to do," Lillian

said. She opened the oven door and arranged the pans on a rack, the heat making her brown arms glisten with perspiration.

"Well, that's where you're wrong, because it's the other way around," I said. "It says a *husband* should leave his father and mother and cleave unto his wife." She and I looked at each other, as we both recalled that while I'd done my share of cleaving to Wesley Lloyd, he'd done a good bit of his to somebody else.

But turning my mind back to the current problem, since Wesley Lloyd was dead and gone, I'd been up one side and down the other over it, and I still couldn't decide. Hazel Marie'd said she knew exactly what I ought to do, but her mind was filled with one romantic notion after another, so I wasn't a bit surprised by where she stood. Then she'd gotten serious and said, "Miss Julia, all you have to do is decide what *you* want, then just do it."

Well, of course that was the crux of the matter. I didn't know what I wanted—whether to marry again and run the risk of another betrayal or to stay a single widow and run my life the way I wanted to. I don't mind saying it—I had thoroughly enjoyed doing just that the past few years since laying Wesley Lloyd in his grave, especially since I had free rein of half of his sizeable estate, Little Lloyd being the beneficiary of the other half.

Actually, I'd hardly ever made a decision based purely on my own wants. There'd always been responsibilites and obligations to other people that came into play and, as I am of a generous nature, I usually bowed to whatever somebody else wanted.

So, ever since Sam had come up with the idea of us marrying, I'd been keeping myself busy, trying not to think about it in hopes that I wouldn't have to give him a final answer. I didn't want to lose him, but I wasn't sure I wanted him full-time, either. The fact of the matter was, I was about half mad that he hadn't left things as they were. But, no, he had to bring up something that put my life in turmoil.

Well, Lord knows, he'd hinted around about it long enough, but when he finally got serious the actual thought of being his wife, with all that that entailed, made my heart leap inside my chest. But I'd answered with my head, and my head said, "Don't rock the boat." Still, he'd kept on and on at me, telling me I'm not getting off the hook, and that he's a patient man and sooner or later I'm going to give in and make him a happy man. And to tell the truth, the upshot of it all put me on edge so bad I could hardly stand it. I've prided myself on being a fairly decisive woman, but the agitation and indecision I'd been under made me ready to bite somebody's head off.

The one thing that did tempt me, though, was Sam's ability to make me laugh, which I did whenever he started rattling off his many admirable qualities. I don't think Wesley Lloyd made me laugh even once during all the years of our dour marriage. He made me frown a lot, cry on too many occasions, and nurse a sorrowful heart all the time.

Lord, I never thought I'd even consider such a thing as marrying again. Once you've done it and suffered from it, you're not all that anxious to get back into a similar situation. Of course, Sam was not Wesley Lloyd Springer, not by a long shot. I'd gone into marriage with Wesley Lloyd without an inkling that such a respected pillar of the church and the community could've ever done what he did do—which was to enter into more than a decade of dalliance with Hazel Marie Puckett, produce a son and heir, and leave me to clean up the mess he left and end up with both mistress and son living under my roof. And if you think that's a strange arrangement, you wouldn't be the only one. But by this time I'd come too far to let what other people think bother me. Lillian says I'll have stars in my crown for doing it, and I don't doubt it, even though it hasn't been as hard as I'd feared or as one might think.

Still and all, I'm stuck with the conviction that men, as a general rule, can't be trusted as far as you can throw them. And I speak from painful experience.

I raised my head as I heard Hazel Marie's car pull in the driveway and, in a few minutes, she came through the back door, shrugging out of her raincoat. It was a wonder to me how much better she looked the older she got. Not that she was all that old, forty-something being an enviable age from my vantage point, but I'm talking about comparisions to what she looked like before she had the wherewithal to purchase suitable clothes and have her hair professionally done. Which was what she'd been doing that morning.

I smiled at her as she stuck her umbrella in the stand. "Your hair looks very nice, Hazel Marie." And it did, the highlighted streaks of blonde on blonde shone in the overhead kitchen lights. "Velma is finally learning how to do it right."

Hazel Marie pulled out a chair at the table and immediately began to fold towels, since I'd fallen down on the job. "Miss Julia, you'll never believe what I heard at the beauty parlor."

"There's no telling. What?"

"Well, oh, I'm sorry, Lillian," she said. "I didn't even speak to you, which just shows how stunned I am. I'm so full of the latest gossip that I can't think of anything else."

Lillian laughed, her gold tooth flashing. "Gossip do that to you sometime. 'Specially if it real good gossip."

"Well, this is as good as it gets." Hazel Marie took a deep breath, trying to calm herself before imparting her news. "Miss Julia, guess who's having an affair."

"I don't have any idea and, Hazel Marie, if you heard it at Velma's, you ought to consider the source."

"Oh, I do, but everybody's talking about it. I mean, out loud and everything. This wasn't something whispered and speculated about. It was told as a fact, because she's been seen coming out of the Mountaintop Motel."

"Well, my word," I said, drawn into the story in spite of my natural aversion to gossip, having suffered considerable anguish myself from wagging tongues. "Who?"

Hazel Marie leaned across the table, smiling with the assurance that she was going to shock me good. "Miss High and Mighty, Norma Cantrell, herself."

"No!" I reared back in my chair, suitably shocked. Norma Cantrell was our Presbyterian pastor's secretary, and she ran his office like a third world dictator. I'd never had much use for her, but the pastor thought she hung the moon. "That can't be true." Then I thought about it, rubbing my fingers across my mouth. "Are you sure?"

"As sure as I can be. It was Mildred Allen who saw her at the Mountaintop."

"Well, I say." That iced the cake for me, until I thought of something else. "And what was Mildred Allen doing there?"

"Collecting for some fund or another," Hazel Marie said. "She had to go twice. They kept putting her off and still didn't donate a thing. That's a pretty ratty motel, from what I hear. A perfect getaway place if you don't want people to know what you're doing or who you're doing it with. Of course, Norma didn't expect anybody she knew to be there. Velma said that Mildred said she didn't think Norma saw her because she hid behind a laurel bush when Norma came out of one of the rooms. And not once, but both times Mildred was there." Hazel Marie stopped and thought about it. "I expect it was a pretty big laurel bush, considering Mildred's size. But, anyway, Norma thinks it's still a secret."

"Well, now, Hazel Marie, there could be a perfectly innocent explanation, you know."

"Like what?"

"I don't know. Maybe she has a sick friend."

"At a place like that?"

"It does sound suspicious, and I'll admit I'm not all that

surprised. Norma's always struck me as having more going on underneath than she lets on."

"Yes," Hazel Marie said, "but it's hard to imagine that she'd get involved in a seedy affair since she's so particular about everything."

"Norma's been divorced almost all her life," I told her, as Lillian came to the table with cups and the coffee pot. She liked a little spate of gossip as well as the next person. "The way I heard it, she married right out of high school, but hardly a year later, her husband ran off with their next-door neighbor. Norma's been living off sympathy ever since. People think her heart was broken and that she'll never recover, but this just goes to show, doesn't it? So who is she supposed to be seeing at the Mountaintop?"

Hazel Marie smiled. "You'll never guess."

"Just tell me, Hazel Marie," I said. "I can't imagine who'd even be interested in her. Her husband certainly wasn't."

"Well, nobody knows for sure, but the Honorable Clifford Beebee was mentioned. Can you believe that?"

"My word," I said again, mumbling it this time as I tried to absorb this turn of events. "If this gets out, Clifford Beebee's political career is over in this town. To say nothing of his marriage, because I don't believe Gladys'll put up with it."

"Sound like to me it already got out," Lillian said, as she stirred sugar into her coffee. "But that man been mayor so long, he pro'bly think he b'long there."

"You're right about that, Lillian," I agreed. "Nobody's been willing to run against him for ever so long, so he probably thinks he can get away with anything."

"Well, not this time," Hazel Marie said. "Because I heard that Bill Denby's going to go up against him in the primary this spring. You know him, don't you? He's the service manager at the Chevrolet dealership. Somebody said his campaign slogan's going to be 'Fix It and Run It,' which is what he says the town needs, just like a car. Mayor Beebee just might get taken down a notch or two, considering how high-handed he is."

"I should say, high-handed. Why, it's gotten so that none of the commissioners dares do anything without his say-so. At least, that's what I hear. I'm not all that politically minded, myself. But what I want to know is why the mayor's name is being linked to Norma's? Did Mildred see him, too?"

"No, but she saw his car," Hazel Marie said, her eyes dancing with the image that produced. "You know that big ole thing he drives? You can't miss it, and everybody knows it. It was parked right outside the room, and Velma said that Mildred said that she waited as long as she could after Norma left to see if he'd come out of the room, too. But she had to go to the bathroom real bad and couldn't wait any longer.

"But," Hazel Marie went on, a smile playing around her mouth. "You haven't heard it all yet."

"I don't think I can stand much more. What else are they saying under the hair dryers?"

She put her hand on my arm and said, "Now, I'm not sure I believe this, but here goes. When Velma was combing me out, she whispered that there's talk going around about *Emma Sue Ledbetter*."

"*What!* With the mayor?" I was stunned, having no idea that the mayor was man enough for two women plus his wife.

"No, no," Hazel Marie said, patting my arm. "I've changed subjects."

"Well," I said with some relief that our preacher's wife was not linked with another man. "Thank goodness."

I knew that Emma Sue would no more make herself a topic of this kind of gossip than she would fly. Although, as I thought about it, she had been trying out her wings a little here lately.

"Besides," Hazel Marie went on, "Norma's got the mayor all

tied up. At least, I guess she has. A few other names were mentioned in connection with hers, so nobody knows for sure who all she's catting around with. But what I wanted to tell you is that Velma said that Emma Sue made an appointment to have a complete makeover. And I'm talking hair color, makeup, everything."

"No!" I scrunched up a bath towel in my hands, unable to believe what I was hearing. "Hazel Marie, that is more unbelievable than Norma Cantrell traipsing around in a motel room. Are you sure?"

"Velma showed me her appointment book because I couldn't believe it myself. And there it was, Emma Sue Ledbetter, Thursday at seven P.M. Velma's doing her a favor by taking her after hours, so nobody'll be there with her."

"Pour me some more coffee, Lillian," I said, holding out my cup, more shaken with this item than I'd been to hear about the preacher's secretary. The preacher's wife, on the other hand, was known far and wide for her outspoken views on the value of a woman's natural beauty. Which to me meant the way you look when you first get up in the morning, and as far as I was concerned, every woman in the world needed a little help.

"Why?" I asked. "Why would Emma Sue suddenly want to make herself over? Why, Hazel Marie, you remember when she criticized you for wearing eye shadow? And I've heard her say many a time that since there'll be no Avon or Mary Kay products in heaven, women ought to get themselves prepared to do without down here. And she can get downright vicious on the subject of lipstick." I stopped and smoothed out the towel. "Wonder what's come over her?"

"Velma thinks Emma Sue may be having an affair, herself," Hazel Marie said, which nearly shocked me out of my chair.

"The preacher's wife! Hazel Marie, what a thing to say. No, not Emma Sue Ledbetter, no way in the world would she do such a thing."

"Well, all I know is that when a woman's thinking about it, the first thing she does is buy new underwear. And getting a new look may be along the same line."

Lillian started laughing then. "Law me, I never heard the like."

"One thing's for sure, though," Hazel Marie said, "if she starts using makeup, she's going to have to do something about all that crying she does. Her face'll be a mess if she starts overflowing. Can you imagine?"

"I certainly can," I said, recalling Emma Sue's tendency to cloud up and cry whenever she got her feelings hurt, which seemed to be about all the time. "Well, Hazel Marie, I don't know what's going on in this town, but we'd do well not to repeat any of this." I thought about it for a few minutes, then went on. "Of course, I'll have to tell Sam, and I know you'll tell Mr. Pickens, but that's all. Lillian, you won't tell anybody, will you?"

"No'm, I'm right bad to listen, but I don't do much passin' on." She got up and checked the cakes in the oven, then came back to the table. "Sound like to me, though, that they a awful lot of people not real happy with what they got an' they out lookin' for what they like a whole lot better."

Coming from Viking in April 2004

**The latest rollicking installment of this wildly popular
Southern comedy-of-manners raises the burning question:
Will the beloved steel magnolia meet
her own match in love?**

Miss Julia Meets Her Match

In *Miss Julia Meets Her Match* Julia's long-time beau, Sam Murdoch, wants to tie the knot. But Miss Julia isn't about to give up her independence so easily. For the moment, too, there are so many other matters that require her attention. Such as Dwayne Dooley's plan to build the Walk Where Jesus Walked Christian Theme Park, a re-creation of the Holy Land complete with actors, sound effects, and trailer hookups. Meanwhile, the whole town is buzzing with rumors. The preacher's secretary was spotted leaving a sleazy motel with the mayor's car parked nearby. Even Miss Julia's own home is not immune to shock waves—the arrival of Latisha, housekeeper Lillian's five-year-old pistol of a great-granddaughter, shakes up Miss Julia's household like a bunch of Fourth of July firecrackers.   *ISBN 0-670-03293-X*

For Other Miss Julia novels, Look for the

**Miss Julia is a proper widow—a lady of a certain age with a
determined commitment to correct behavior and right living,
which she'll tell you about in a minute since she has the
sharpest tongue south of the Mason-Dixon Line.**

Miss Julia Throws a Wedding

In *Miss Julia Throws a Wedding,* we find Miss Julia feeling a little wistful when Hazel Marie, once her late husband's paramour and now her best friend, prepares to move out and live in sin with that marriage-shy Mr. Pickens. Suddenly, to Miss Julia's delight, a wedding is in the offing: Handsome Deputy Coleman Bates and attorney Binkie Enloe announce their plans to run down to the courthouse and tie the knot. But Miss Julia insists they have a real wedding ceremony and vows to make it happen. When a missing preacher, a crowd of uninvited guests, and a queasy bride threaten the happy event, Miss Julia is there to restore order, confirming her undying motto: if you want something done right, you have to do it yourself!   *ISBN 0-14-200271-2*

Miss Julia Takes Over

When Miss Julia burst on the scene in her fictional debut, *Miss Julia Speaks Her Mind*, this proper lady of a certain age found her orderly world turned upside down when Hazel Marie Puckett appeared with her nine-year-old son, Little Lloyd, who looked disturbingly similar to Miss Julia's late husband. Now, in *Miss Julia Takes Over*, Miss Julia must tackle another disruption when Hazel Marie doesn't return from a dinner date with a fund-raiser who, in Miss Julia's opinion, wears his shorts too tight. She and Little Lloyd help search for Hazel Marie, running into adventures ranging from a most indelicate display of fisticuffs to a high-speed car chase on the track of a NASCAR Speedway, all the while standing strong . . . because if Miss Julia doesn't take care of things, who will?   *ISBN 0-14-200089-2*